Praise for *L*

"Jeff and I spent years working together at *20/20,* and his no... tures the essence of storytelling and the art of the interview. The plotline is ripped straight from the headlines, and the book is sharp and fast-paced, a page turner that will hold your attention right down to the chilling climax."

—Barbara Walters, Host of ABC's *The View, 20/20, ABC Evening News, ABC News, and* NBC's *Today Show*

"Ethan Benson is a new kind of hero, cast in the role of crime-fighting sleuth. Sensitive and insecure, dogged and determined, sharp-witted and loving, he refuses to take no for an answer as he strives to uncover the truth. A broadcast journalist who's built his reputation on hard-hitting investigative reports, he struggles in the changing world of television news, where substance has been replaced by screaming cable news pundits and corporate masters."

—Al Roker, Host and Weatherman of NBC's *Today Show*

"Jeff Diamond has translated his 25 years as one of television's leading investigative reporters into a twisting and turning murder mystery that will keep you riveted. You won't be able to put it down. Diamond captures the nuances of TV production as he draws on the real world of TV news crime reporting. *Live to Air* is the perfect read for anyone who enjoys fast-paced and very realistic storytelling out of a real network newsroom."

—Av Westin, Vice President,
ABC News Creative Development;
Executive Producer, *20/20*
Executive Producer, *ABC World News Tonight*;

LIVE TO AIR

AN ETHAN BENSON THRILLER

JEFFREY L. DIAMOND

RIVER GROVE
BOOKS

Published by River Grove Books
Austin, TX
www.rivergrovebooks.com

Distributed by River Grove Books

For ordering information or special discounts for bulk purchases, please contact River Grove Books at PO Box 91869, Austin, TX 78709, 512.891.6100.

Design and composition by Greenleaf Book Group and Debbie Berne
Cover design by Greenleaf Book Group and Debbie Berne
Cover images: © istockphoto: spxChrome, Zeffss1

Publisher's Cataloging Publication Data is available.

ISBN: 978-1-63299-031-0

First Edition

Other Edition(s):
eBook ISBN: 978-1-63299-032-7

PROLOGUE

THREE BLACK LINCOLN NAVIGATORS slowly made their way down Eighth Avenue in Park Slope, Brooklyn. It was two o'clock on a clear and cold Monday morning in the middle of March, the temperature hovering around twenty degrees, the air crisp and still. A layer of ice crystals shimmered as the full moon rose in the north sky, casting eerie, ghostlike shadows that danced up and down well-kept brownstones sitting along narrow, tree-lined streets. A dog began barking, interrupting the deathly silence, as the caravan of cars waited for a traffic light on the corner of Flatbush Avenue, then headed to the Brooklyn Bridge and Manhattan.

Four burly men sat shivering in each car, bundled up against the cold, wearing old leather coats and gloves and dark woolen hats pulled down over their ears. Fully loaded Beretta 9mm handguns bulged in shoulder holsters under their arms, and Uzi submachine guns rested silently at their feet, carefully hidden under piles of dirty clothes and tattered blankets. Their leader, a small, well-dressed man named Nikolai Stanislov, was sitting in the backseat of the lead car. He was wearing a long camel hair coat, a gray pinstripe suit, white shirt, and yellow tie. A thick, jagged scar ran down the side of his face from just below his left eye to the corner of his mouth, an ugly disfigurement he proudly considered a badge of honor earned in a knife fight when he was growing up in a Brooklyn ghetto everyone called Little Russia.

The caravan continued driving, inching along the empty roads, then veered left onto Tillary Street and up the ramp to the bridge. Nikolai puffed on a Cuban cigar, choking the car with thick, arid smoke. Sitting next to him was a tough-looking twenty-year-old, small and compact in build, with jet-black hair and a scowl on his face. Violent and hotheaded, Pavel Feodor had done his first stint in juvenile detention when he was twelve after nearly beating a schoolmate to death. In and out of trouble ever since, he'd been arrested for armed robbery, breaking and entering, auto theft, and drug dealing, making him one of the most notorious young hoods in the city.

As the Lincolns crawled onto the FDR Drive, the two men sat in silence, the gang leader puffing away on his cigar, the young man peering blankly at the wall of skyscrapers looming above him, his right hand jammed into his pocket, slowly caressing his Beretta, feeling the touch of the cold steel.

"Relax, Pavel, you're gonna wear a hole in your coat," Nikolai said. "This job will be over soon, and then you can go back home to your warm bed with a little extra cash for that little slut—that *gopnitsa* you call your woman."

Pavel didn't respond. He just looked out the window and fingered his handgun, the gang leader now worrying he'd made a mistake bringing him along for the ride. As the caravan reached the tip of Manhattan, he took one last drag on his cigar and flipped it out the window. "Talk to me, Pavel. What's eating you?"

"I don't like Mexicans. I don't trust them. What if they try to rip us off?"

Nikolai touched his scar, feeling the jagged surface of the skin. "That's my problem, not yours," he said, anger burning in his voice. "I've dealt with this cartel many times. I know them. How they act. How they think." He tapped his forehead. "So you do your job, and I'll do mine. Am I making myself clear?"

Pavel nodded, never changing his expression, his eyes fixed on a homeless man sleeping under a box in a doorway.

Nikolai leaned forward, the biting cold seeping into the car through the partially opened window, sending a chill up his spine. "Don't make me sorry, Pavel. I stuck my neck out for you with the *Pakhan*." His face became hard. "He wanted me to get rid of you. Said you were too wild. Too unpredictable. So don't disappoint me tonight. You know what I'll do to you if you do something stupid. It won't be pretty."

He smiled and patted Pavel on the cheek.

Still there was no reaction.

The caravan inched along, reaching Battery Park on the tip of Manhattan and heading up West Street, past the new World Trade Center and the 9/11 Memorial, before making a left onto a dimly lighted side street called Tenth Avenue in the heart of the Meatpacking District. The neighborhood was dilapidated; piles of garbage spilled out of trash cans and rats scurried under parked cars, avoiding traps placed every few feet on the sidewalks.

Nikolai whispered into the driver's ear, a thug with bushy eyebrows and a scraggly red goatee. "Cut the lights and make the next right. That's Little West Twelfth. Then drive down to the end of the block." They picked their way around potholes and a broken-down car or two, past a boarded-up brick building and an old-man bar, and into a narrow alley leading to a secluded parking lot hidden behind a warehouse belonging to a wholesale meat distributor.

"Everybody out," Nikolai said, checking the chamber of his Beretta.

The car doors flew open, and the heavily armed men spilled out into the darkness. After checking to make sure there was nobody watching from the windows of the surrounding tenements, Nikolai walked to the back of his Lincoln, unlocked the liftgate, and pulled out two duffel bags. Then he faced his men. "Yuri, take three guys and guard the alley. Anatoly, you take everybody else and fan out around the parking lot. Make sure your guns are drawn and in plain sight. I want them to know we mean business. And for God's sake, everybody stay calm. No shooting. Unless I say so." He spun around and pointed at Pavel. "You. Stay with me."

Picking up the duffel bags, he walked up a short flight of stairs, pulled out a set of keys, and unlocked a door on a loading dock in the back of the warehouse. He placed the two duffel bags on the ground, turned, and peered around the parking lot.

Everybody was in position.

Now all they had to do was wait for the Mexicans.

They didn't have to wait long.

Two Cadillac Escalades pulled into the alley and stopped, six Mexicans climbing out toting high-powered handguns and Walther HK MP5 assault rifles. Their leader, a short, round man with a pencil-thin mustache, motioned to his men to wait by the cars and strutted over to the loading dock, showing no fear. He was holding a .357 Magnum as he approached Nikolai, who was standing in the doorway—Pavel right behind him—his Beretta drawn and aimed at the Mexican's head.

"Marco, my friend, glad you could make it," Nikolai said, a touch of sarcasm in his voice.

"Good evening, señor. It's nice to be here, to do business with you again. It's very cold tonight, too cold for me and my men. Let's not waste time. Do you have the money?"

Nikolai pointed to the two duffel bags sitting on the platform. "It's all right here. One million in cash. In unmarked hundred-dollar bills. Just as we agreed. Do you want to count it?"

"No, that's not necessary. I trust you. We've done business before. Just open the bags so I can see the greenbacks."

Nikolai unzipped the two duffel bags.

The Mexican looked in. The cash was stacked and bound in ten-thousand-dollar packets.

"Where's the heroin?" Nikolai said as his eyes darted to his men.

The Mexican slowly turned and opened the back of the lead Cadillac. There—stacked in four large suitcases—was two hundred pounds of pure, uncut heroin, neatly packaged in gallon-size Ziploc bags. "Here's your heroin. Just as we promised. A bargain for a million dollars." He pulled out a bag from one of the suitcases and dangled it in the air.

Nikolai stared at the white powder, then studied the Mexican's face, looking for telltale signs something was wrong. "I wanna test it before I make the buy. I've been burned in the past," he said suspiciously.

"Señor, you don't trust me? I trust you. I no count your money. You told me it was all there, and I believe you. I'm telling you the heroin is pure, the best money can buy." There was outrage in the Mexican's voice. He looked like a man whose honor had been scorned.

Seconds ticked by. It felt like hours.

Then Nikolai nodded to a man standing in the shadows. "That's my chemist, Marco. Give him the bag."

The Mexican never took his eyes off Nikolai as he tossed the package onto the ground. The chemist knelt and pulled a small test tube out of his pocket—cutting a small hole in the plastic bag and dropping a pinch of heroin into a clear liquid. After shaking it for a moment, he stared at the test tube. "This stuff is high quality, Nikolai. Just like the man says, it's close to 100 percent pure."

"See, my friend, we don't lie," Marco said, a smirk on his face. "The cartel likes doing business with you. We wouldn't cheat you."

There was another long pause, Nikolai still uncertain. Something didn't feel right. The tone in the Mexican's voice too confident, too spurious, like he was hiding something. He turned to his chemist. "Take a bag from the bottom of a suitcase. Test it. I wanna make sure."

"No. I can't let him do that, Nikolai. Nobody touches the heroin until you give me the money."

"No money. Until we test a bag from the bottom. A bag we pick. What's the problem, Marco? Are you trying to cheat us?"

The Mexican's face hardened. He gestured to his men to close the liftgate, then made his way back to the lead Escalade, his .357 Magnum drawn and aimed at Nikolai. "No deal, señor. We trusted you when you said you had the cash. Now you don't trust us when we say the heroin is the best money can buy. This is no way to conduct business. There is no honor."

Silence, as Marco opened the passenger door and started to climb in.

Nikolai walked to the edge of the loading dock and stopped, ordering his men to hold their fire. Nobody moved. Then Pavel, hovering in the background, all but forgotten in the heat of the moment, suddenly began to scream, hatred filling his eyes. "You fucking wetbacks. You're all the same." As he raised his gun, Nikolai lunged forward, trying to grab his arm, knowing his young protégé had snapped.

"Damn it, Pavel. Don't shoot. The deal's a bust. You're gonna bring the cops down on us."

But Nikolai was a second too late.

Pavel pulled the trigger, and a bullet ripped through Marco's shoulder.

Pandemonium broke out, the other Mexicans surrounding their leader and opening fire with their automatic weapons, spraying bullets around the parking lot, the sound echoing like blasts from a cannon. Two of Nikolai's men went down, hit in the chest, arms twitching and feet kicking spasmodically. As they lay dying, blood poured from their mangled bodies and pooled in large circles on the pavement.

Nikolai ducked behind one of the Navigators, cursing at Pavel as he emptied his Beretta into a Mexican, blowing off most of his head, his brains splattering on the loading dock and up against the wall of the warehouse.

Holding his bloody arm, Marco stumbled into the backseat of his Escalade, his men continuing to hose the parking lot—*rat, tat, tat*—trying to protect him. Then they climbed into the two Cadillacs, gunned the engines, and roared onto the street, Pavel racing after them like a madman, squeezing off one shot after another. A Mexican leaned out the window and fired his Walther, ripping a stream of bullets through Pavel's leg, sending him crashing to the ground, his head smashing on the pavement, his eyes rolling into the back of his head.

Then silence.

Nikolai slowly stood and peered at the carnage. Two of his men were dead, and Pavel was lying in a heap, unconscious—blood gushing from his leg, spilling in torrents all around him. Lights clicked on in the surrounding buildings, and people leaned out their windows and screamed. Nikolai picked up the duffel bags and raced to his Navigator, dropping the cash in the back and slamming the door. "Don't stand like idiots," he said, bellowing at his men. "The cops are gonna be here soon."

"What about the dead guys?" the chemist said, pointing at the bodies littering the ground. "We can't just leave them."

Nikolai walked over and kicked Pavel. "I don't care about this little shit. He's bleeding like a pig and ain't gonna make it." He kicked him again. "This is all his fault, the crazy motherfucker. I should never have brought him. Leave him for the cops. They can't link him to us."

"What about everybody else?"

"I don't give a shit about the Mexican, but take our guys. The *Pakhan* won't like it if we leave them."

Two minutes later, they tore out of the alley, one car after the other. When they reached the corner of Little West Twelfth and Washington Street, they pulled to a sudden stop. Sprawled on the sidewalk was another body—a pretty young woman lying on her back, twisted and broken. Nikolai rolled down his window and cursed. "Goddamn it, the bitch must've been hit in the crossfire. This is a problem. A big problem." He lit a cigar and motioned to his driver. "Get us the fuck outta here."

Then the caravan pulled through the intersection and weaved along the empty streets as police sirens wailed in the distance. Soon they crossed the Brooklyn Bridge and left Manhattan, vanishing into the dark night.

CHAPTER 1

IT WAS OPPRESSIVELY HOT, the air thick and sticky, a late-July thunderstorm rumbling in from the west. Flashes of lightning streaked through Ethan's bedroom, followed by loud claps of thunder and heavy raindrops. He lay quietly, watching the light show and listening to the cacophony of sound. Drenched in sweat, he looked at the clock. It was four o'clock. After carefully pulling back the covers, he slipped out of bed. Standing naked, he stared at his wife, Sarah, and watched her shallow breathing, marveling at how she could sleep so soundly with all the noise filling the room. He kissed her on the nape of her neck, pulled on a red T-shirt and a pair of blue jeans, tiptoed across the floor, and gently closed the door.

Ethan Benson was a tall, handsome man standing a little over six foot three, with blue eyes and curly black hair that he wore short and neatly trimmed. A touch of gray showed at his temples, and a handful of age wrinkles circled his eyes. Sometimes brash and sometimes stubborn, he was outspoken and at times even arrogant, but his warm and charismatic personality was endearing, often stopping a conversation dead in its tracks when he entered a room.

Yawning, he walked down the center hallway, cautious not to make the loose floorboards creak, and opened the door to his son's bedroom. Luke was fast asleep, his yellow Labrador retriever, Holly, standing guard next to the bed, her tail thumping rhythmically on the floor. He smiled, brushed a lock of hair from the little boy's forehead, then carefully backed out of the room. As he made his way to the kitchen, he felt restless, unsettled, his mind cycling through the same nagging questions that had kept him awake all night. *What's wrong with me?* he thought, worried. *Is it my job? Is it my marriage? Is it something else in my life? Why can't I sleep?*

Frustrated, he made a pot of coffee and continued to his study, flipping on the lights and casting the room in a warm glow. Newspapers and magazines were strewn about his desk, documents stacked in huge piles on the tables, and a half dozen large ashtrays overflowing with cigarettes. Plopping down in a worn leather chair, he grabbed a bottle of Motrin for the pounding in his head and tried to remember how much scotch he'd consumed before going to bed. Was it three glasses? Was it four? Was it more? Christ, he had to get his drinking under control.

Rubbing the bridge of his nose, he decided to check the headlines. An award-winning producer on *The Weekly Reporter*—a television newsmagazine on the nation's number one network, the Global Broadcasting System—Ethan was the consummate news junkie, never wanting to miss a big story or feel out of touch. He turned on his computer and began to read: The price of oil had climbed two dollars on the British Mercantile Exchange, threatening to drive up gasoline prices at the pump, Congress had proposed new cuts in military spending to balance the budget, and a Palestinian terrorist had blown himself to smithereens in a crowded marketplace in Jerusalem, killing twenty-seven and injuring a score more.

They were all breaking news.

All important.

All his kinds of projects.

He sighed, knowing the show would never program any of these stories, now only interested in rapes and murders and high-profile sex scams—tabloid topics he abhorred to the bottom of his heart. What had happened to real journalism? To real reporting? To his thirst to discover the truth? Was that why he was hitting the bottle so hard?

He poured another cup of coffee and clicked on his messages.

A dozen emails had landed in his inbox. Most were unimportant, clutter from midlevel management, but as he scrolled through the list, he noticed a message from his boss, Paul Lang, the executive producer of *The Weekly Reporter*. How had he missed that one? It was flagged urgent, response requested, and had been sitting in his mailbox since early the night before. Ethan took a long drag on his cigarette, angry at himself. He should have checked and answered before going to bed. He opened the message and read:

Ethan, where are you? The senior producers and I haven't heard from you in weeks. Not since your last story aired. I can't run my show when my staff is AWOL. I'd like you in my office tomorrow morning at 10:00 a.m. sharp. I have a high-profile story I need you to produce. Let me know if you can make the meeting. And be there on time.

Ethan read the message a second time. It was just like Paul to question his productivity. Ethan had been cranking out one blockbuster story after another, and there was nobody on the staff any faster. *Am I in trouble? Should I shoot him a quick email and tell him I'll be there?* he thought, scratching his head. *He can't possibly be awake, not at this hour. I'll wait and call him when I get to the office.*

He clicked off his computer and walked back to the bedroom, but decided he might wake up Sarah if he climbed into bed, so he slipped on a pair of loafers, picked up Holly's leash, and headed out for some fresh air.

. . . . .

The rain had stopped falling and the sky was brightening in a kaleidoscope of colors as he climbed off the elevator and made his way through the lobby. Ethan lived on the Upper East Side of Manhattan and had spent all of his forty-four years in the same apartment on the corner of Ninety-First Street and Madison Avenue. Feeling invigorated, he waved good morning to Winston the doorman and headed out to the street. Rays of sunshine were peeking through the clouds, and pools of water sat shimmering on the sidewalk. His neighborhood felt warm and inviting, and Ethan began whistling, his headache disappearing as he strolled down Fifth Avenue and into Central Park.

Then his cell phone rang.

He fumbled in his coat pocket and pulled out his iPhone. "Shit, it's Paul," he whispered to himself, his mood darkening once again. "I should've returned that damn email." After taking a deep breath, he answered, "Hello?"

"Hi, Ethan, hold on for Paul." It was Monica, Paul's number

one assistant. God, they were already in the office. He waited for what seemed like an eternity before Paul barked into the receiver.

"Where the hell are you?" There was no "Good morning. How are you? What are you doing awake at this hour?"

Ethan responded calmly, hiding the disdain in his voice. "Hi, Paul. It's pretty early for a telephone call, don't you think? I'm walking my dog, then heading back to my apartment and into the office. Should be there in about an hour."

"I sent you a message last night. Did you get it? I haven't heard a word from you. Nothing."

"I just saw it. So what's up?"

"You know what's up. I told you I've got a big story for you. Why didn't you answer my email?"

Ethan hesitated, trying to control his temper. "Because I didn't read it until just a little while ago and thought it could wait."

"What do you mean you thought it could wait?" Paul was now yelling. "This is important. I need to know if you're available for an assignment."

"Well, you've found me, and I'm definitely available. So what's the story?"

"It's the Pavel Feodor case. It's been front page in all the newspapers. The guy was just convicted. First-degree murder."

Ethan recalled seeing the headlines but had no memory of the details.

Paul droned on. "It's a crash, and I want you to jump on it right away. You're not doing anything at the moment, are you?"

"I'm in between stories," Ethan said sharply, not backing down. "I was on the air just a couple of weeks ago, and I've been pitching ideas ever since. But I don't do crime stories, Paul. You know that. Isn't there somebody else who could produce this story?"

"There's nobody else," Paul said indignantly.

Ethan hesitated, realizing there was no way to avoid the assignment. "So what's so special about this murder?"

"I'm too busy to give you specifics. I'll fill you in when I see you at the meeting, and so help me God, don't be late."

He hung up the phone.

Ethan lit another cigarette and took a deep drag. "Why are all conversations with that guy the same—short, sweet, and full of sarcasm? He's a real piece of work," he said to himself. "No wonder I can't sleep at night." He stroked Holly between the ears and started back to his apartment, his mind spinning as he tried to remember anything he might have read about the Pavel Feodor case.

But there wasn't much.

In fact, there was nothing.

. . . . .

Sarah was standing in the foyer getting ready for work as he pushed through the door and put Holly's leash on a table. She was dressed in a dark-gray suit, a satin shirt matching her slate-blue eyes, and open-toed high-heel shoes. A touch of makeup accented her silky smooth skin, and her long blonde hair, freshly washed and smelling of jasmine, sparkled as it flowed over her shoulders and down her back. Ethan's heart skipped a beat. She hadn't aged a day in ten years and was just as beautiful as the first day they'd met. He leaned over and kissed her tenderly on both cheeks. "Hey, babe, you're off to work early this morning."

"I've got a ton of paperwork piled on my desk and a dozen impatient lawyers clamoring for my time." She looked in the mirror, smoothing her eye shadow, then peered at his reflection in the glass. "You look pale, Ethan. Do you have another headache?" she said cautiously.

"No. Had one when I got up, but it's gone now."

"Did you drink too much last night?"

"Not too much."

"How much?"

"Come on. Not now, Sarah," he said ruefully.

She continued staring at his visage. "So why the long face, Ethan?"

"I just got off the phone with Paul."

"At seven thirty in the morning?"

Ethan slumped into a chair, suddenly weary from his sleepless night. "Yeah. He was pissed as usual and chewed me out for not answering an email."

"Why'd he do that?"

"Because he says he can never find me and wants me to produce some story about some big-time murder. A guy named Pavel Feodor."

"You don't do crime stories, Ethan. That's not your thing."

"I know. I know. And I know nothing about this case. Do you?" he said, hoping she'd learned something about the murder at the Manhattan District Attorney's office, where she worked as a legal assistant.

"Pavel Feodor has been hot gossip for months," she said, surprised. "But I didn't work on the trial, so I don't know much more than what was whispered in the hallways." She blotted her lipstick on a tissue. "Tell you what. I'll ask around and see what I can find out."

"That would be great," he said, rubbing the bridge of his nose, the pounding in his head starting to flare up again.

"You really do look awful, Ethan," she said stonily. "What's goin' on?"

"Nothing, babe. I'm just tired."

"I've heard that before. Will you be home for dinner tonight?"

she said as their six-year-old raced into the foyer wearing his camp uniform and holding his baseball glove.

"Dad, there's a Yankee game on TV tonight. Want to watch it with me?"

"Sure, Luke, sounds like fun."

"Ethan, don't make promises you can't keep," she said icily as she peered at her face in the mirror one last time.

"I'll do the best I can, Sarah. You know that."

"That's what you say now, but something always comes up and you forget about us. Let's go, Luke. I don't want to be late for the bus." She smiled, blew him a kiss, and walked out the door.

Ethan stood motionless, listening to Sarah's high heels clicking on the floor as she made her way to the elevator, angry at himself for always putting work ahead of family. Then he lit another cigarette and headed to his study, sitting down at his desk and rebooting his computer. After running his fingers through his hair, he punched in Pavel Feodor's name and pulled up a year's worth of newspaper and magazine stories.

It was time to get ready for his meeting.

CHAPTER 2

THE GLOBAL BROADCASTING SYSTEM was headquartered on West Fifty-Seventh Street between Broadway and Eighth Avenue. It was a huge structure, Gothic in style, built in the 1920s by a big oil conglomerate. GBS had bought the building in the late 1960s and converted it into a television network. The complex housed every division of the corporation—radio, Internet, sports, entertainment, and news—each occupying several floors. Staffed twenty-four hours a day, the broadcast center was a beehive of activity, pumping out programming, filling the airwaves.

Ethan hopped off the bus and looked at his watch. It was just after nine. Plenty of time before his meeting with Paul. He hustled down the block and pushed his way through a revolving door and into a cavernous lobby with a marble floor, potted plants, and an oversized seating area. The receptionist was sitting behind a large desk, sporting a cheerful smile and talking to a large group of noisy tourists waiting to be escorted to a taping of one of the many talk shows on the daytime schedule.

Ethan searched for his ID card, swiped it through an electric eye, and passed through a turnstile. Hustling down to the elevator bank, he squeezed onto a crowded car and rode up to the tenth floor, then made his way through a maze of hallways, stopping to say hello to a handful of producers before unlocking his office on the far side of the building.

The room was big and bright with beautiful views of Central Park and the New York City skyline. Facing the door was a large oak desk sandwiched between two file cabinets stuffed with documents, video disks, and DVDs. A reclining chair sat in the corner under a floor lamp, and a large leather sofa covered with scripts and newspapers was pushed up against the wall. Sitting proudly on a credenza under the window was an Emmy Award for an investigative report Ethan had produced on political corruption in Washington—a story the show would no longer program—a relic from the past.

Ethan sat down at his desk and opened the file folder of Pavel Feodor articles he'd downloaded in his study. As he leafed through the pages, a short, heavyset woman with mousy blonde hair and sparkling green eyes handed him a Grande Mocha from the Starbucks across the street before plopping down and making herself comfortable on the couch. Mindy Herman was an associate producer, and at twenty-five, one of the best journalists on the show. She specialized in stories about big-city crime and urban blight and knew her way around New York City's halls of justice like a predator searching for prey.

"Hey, what's shaking, Ethan?"

"I'm about to take a meeting with Paul," he said, sipping his Grande Mocha.

"That sounds like fun, I guess. What's he want?"

"To assign me a new story. Some murder involving a guy named Pavel Feodor. Know anything about it?"

"Of course," she said, her eyes flashing. "You haven't been following the case?"

"Just the headlines. Not much more."

"Jeez, Ethan, the network's been all over the story for months. Don't you watch our programming?"

"Yeah, almost every day," he said. "I just haven't focused on Pavel Feodor."

"So you're going to meet Paul and don't know anything about this guy or the murder he committed."

"That's the gist of it," Ethan said, waving his folder. "I've skimmed through a couple of these articles but don't have a real good feel for the crime. Can you give me a quick summary of what happened?"

Mindy got up and moved to a swivel chair in front of his desk. She began attacking the mess around his computer, straightening documents and putting a handful of paper clips back in their box. She was almost as obsessive as Ethan—one of the big reasons they loved working together. "Come on, stop fussing. I don't have a lot of time. Tell me about Feodor," Ethan said impatiently.

"You really don't know anything about him, do you?"

"Just bits and pieces. So who the hell is he?"

"A real piece of work," she said. "Busted dozens of times as a kid. Was in and out of juvenile detention."

"For violent crimes?"

"He was arrested once for attempted murder but got off. And since his juvy record is sealed, only the police and the DA know for sure about that part of his life. But the tabloids make him out a real monster."

Ethan pulled out his iPad and started taking notes. "So what's this case about?"

"There was a gun battle in the middle of the night about a year and a half ago in the Meatpacking District. No eyewitnesses. The police say a small-time gang was trying to buy heroin from one of the Mexican cartels, but the deal went south. Feodor was one of the shooters. The cops found lots of bullet casings. So they know he wasn't the only thug firing away."

"Hold on a second," Ethan said, grabbing a newspaper clipping out of the folder. "I read about the drug deal. Here it is. Says the shootout took place at some wholesale meat distributer, a place called Fernelli's Beef and Poultry."

"Yeah, in the parking lot behind the building."

Ethan continued skimming through the article. "Who got killed?"

"A Mexican was shot dead. They found his body, but not much of his head. It was blown off. Sounds gross." She wrinkled her nose. "The cops think some of the other shooters were wounded, but they didn't find any other bodies and couldn't ID the blood in any of their databases. So they aren't sure who they are."

"So it's a heroin deal and a shootout," Ethan said, still unclear why Paul was so interested in the story. "Where does Feodor fit into all this?"

"The cops found him at the crime scene—lying in an alley leading from the parking lot to the street. At first they thought he was dead like the Mexican. He was barely breathing and bleeding like a pig, his leg torn to shreds. I think he was in a coma for a couple of days, at least that's what I seem to remember reading. Oh, yeah, and he was holding a Beretta."

"I read about the Beretta." Ethan flipped through another article until he found what he was looking for. "The police say it's the murder weapon."

"Yeah. Feodor's gun killed the girl."

"What girl? I don't remember seeing anything about a girl."

"God, Ethan, how many of those articles did you read?"

"I told you. I only had time to skim through a couple of them. So who's the girl?"

"Somebody who happened to be in the wrong place at the wrong time," she said, leaning back in her chair and putting her hands behind her head, a sheepish grin on her face. "And you have no idea who the girl is?"

"Nope."

"And you're about to go into a meeting with the big boss."

"Yup. That's why I need you to tell me what happened. So I don't look like an idiot when I'm sitting across from Paul and any of his team of misfits who happen to be at the meeting."

They both laughed.

"Okay. Okay," Mindy said, pausing and staring at Ethan, once again serious. "The dead girl is none other than Cynthia Jameson—the nineteen-year-old daughter of New York's deputy mayor, and this, my dear, is the reason why this is the biggest crime story of the year."

Ethan sat quietly, wondering how he'd missed what had certainly been front page news for months. Shit. He was definitely losing his edge. He peered at the folder, then slid it across his desk. "Since you're the expert on Pavel Feodor, tell me which of these articles I should read before I go into the meeting."

Mindy picked up the file. "This *Vanity Fair* story has good background on Feodor, and this *Time* magazine article is good on the trial." She continued shuffling through the documents. "Here, found it. This one's the best. It's from *The New York Times Magazine*. Ran a couple of Sundays ago. If you read this one first, you'll be in good shape."

Ethan looked at the story and then at his watch. Nine thirty. "It's long, but I have plenty of time," he said, placing the article on top of the pile. "Now I need you to go. I wanna show Paul I'm still one of his best producers and know more about Pavel Feodor than anybody else in that damn meeting."

"There's just one more thing, Ethan," she said, heading to the door. "I don't have much on my plate. Just two projects, both in editing, and my producers are almost finished. See if you can get me assigned as your associate producer."

"I'll talk to the management and bring you on board," he said, already beginning to read.

"Great. Let me know how it goes," she said, waving good-bye.

Ethan watched her hurry down the hall, then gazed out his picture window at the sun peeking over the top of a luxury apartment building on Fifth Avenue. Now he understood why Paul was so eager to assign him the story—guns, gangs, drugs, and politics—not his cup of tea, but perfect for the new reality of the show.

He turned around and buried himself in the *Times* article.

CHAPTER 3

A HALF HOUR LATER, ETHAN climbed off the elevator and walked into a small waiting room on the eleventh floor. A receptionist named Jennifer was talking to a friend on the telephone and texting on her iPhone. She looked up at Ethan, said she had to go, and hung up. "Good morning, Ethan. Who are you here to see?"

"Paul. I have a ten o'clock meeting. Is he in his office?"

Jennifer pulled up Lang's schedule on her computer. "He knows you're coming. Says so right here. But he's running late. I think he's still in a production meeting with his senior staff. I'll buzz you through and you can check with Monica. She'll let you know how he's doing and when he'll be ready to see you." She hit a button under her desk and unlocked the door.

Ethan said thanks and walked onto the floor.

The first thing he noticed was the silence—no televisions blaring, no telephones ringing, no small groups of people huddled together and talking. All the doors along the long, carpeted hallway leading to Paul's suite of offices were closed. Most of the staff—the bookkeepers, budget officers, personnel managers, and tech support—worked banker's hours, routinely coming in late and going home early.

But on Paul's end of the floor, it was a different story.

Secretaries shuttled trays of coffee and bagels in and out of his meeting, production associates sorted through scripts, and desk assistants logged camera dailies on screening machines. Huddled in a conference room facing the Empire State Building, Paul and his inner circle were working on the broadcast schedule. Ethan could hear them arguing through a partially opened door as they debated the mix of stories and what order to stack the segments. It was business as usual—the senior management making their pitch, sucking up to the boss, trying to score points.

It was a game Ethan hated.

A game he refused to play.

He continued walking and heard his name shouted from down the hall. It was Monica, and she was so flustered she could hardly get the words out. "Ethan, you're late. I've been looking all over for you. Paul's having a coronary."

Ethan checked the time. It was just after ten o'clock. "Take a deep breath, Monica. Jennifer told me Paul's running behind schedule. So I'm not really late, am I?"

"No, not really," Monica said, beginning to relax. "But you know how he gets. He's just being Paul the control freak. He's giving everybody a hard time, including me."

"That's what I thought," Ethan said softly. "Let's go and let him know I'm here. Then maybe he'll stop raising hell and yelling at everybody." He smiled and fell in behind her as she scurried down a shiny red hallway covered with pictures of Paul posing proudly with Presidents Clinton, Bush, and Obama; with George Clooney, Nicole Kidman, and Jack Nicholson; and with dozens of other masters of the universe. "Goddamn," Ethan muttered under his breath as he stared at the wall of fame, "there really is no limit to the man's ego."

Lang was still screaming when they reached the conference room. "Wish me luck, Monica," Ethan whispered, straightening his tie and pushing his way in, the room suddenly growing quiet as he sat down in an empty chair at the end of a long mahogany table. Paul was standing, arms crossed, like a commander flanked by his most trusted advisers—Joyce Cox and Lenny Franklin, his senior producers, and Dirk Fulton, his senior story editor. A short man with long silver-gray hair pulled back in a ponytail, Paul was dressed in an expensive Ralph Lauren suit, a custom-made blue oxford shirt, a silk Hermes tie, gold wire-rim glasses, and his trademark diamond stud earring. He wasn't particularly good looking, but wasn't bad looking either—except when he got angry. Then he became downright ugly. "Where the fuck have you been?" he said, contempt in his voice. "We called all over the building and couldn't find you."

"I was just down the hall," Ethan said a little too casually. "I didn't think I was late."

"You're always late and shirking your responsibilities."

"Well, I'm here now," Ethan said, trying but failing to diffuse the tension in the room. "So let's not waste any more of your precious time. Tell me about Pavel Feodor."

Paul pounded the table, his face reddening. "Watch your mouth. The only reason you're sitting here is because you're not working on anything and I need somebody with your production skills to produce this story. A lot of people around the company are watching, and I'm hoping you're up to the task."

Ethan sat quietly, wondering if Paul was under some kind of pressure from somebody higher up in the corporation. That would explain the terse email, the early morning telephone call, and all the histrionics he was now experiencing. "Look, Paul, don't dress me down in front of everybody," Ethan said calmly. "We can talk about my work habits later if you'd like. Let's talk about the murder. That's why we're here, right?"

There was an awkward pause, everybody waiting for Paul to react as he slowly sat down and began tapping his fingers on the table. "Fair enough, Ethan. You and I will meet about your work habits—or your lack thereof—in private as soon as we're finished in here. Now tell me what you know about Pavel Feodor."

"I know more about this story than you think," Ethan said, opening his briefcase and pulling out his newspaper and magazine clippings. "I know who he is. Who the victim is. And what happened the night of the murder. I also know he confessed to the cops but never told anybody, not even his attorney, how or why he killed Cynthia Jameson. Now, I find that pretty interesting, don't you?" He waited, and when he didn't get a response, plowed on. "And according to the research I've read, the jury convicted Feodor entirely on circumstantial evidence and his videotaped confession. So are we all 100 percent sure the police and the prosecutor got it right?"

Paul started doodling on a yellow pad as he always did when he was thinking, then turned to Dirk Fulton. "He's got a point there. Fill him in on what you've got going, Dirk."

Fulton cleared his throat. "I've been working on this story about a month, Ethan, with one of my best researchers, David Livingston." Fulton nodded at David, who was sitting just behind him. "He's got good sources in law enforcement—both here and in Washington—and has already met with the NYPD and the district attorney's office. One of the prosecutors shipped him the court docket, so we have a full record of the police investigation and the trial."

"When can I get a copy?" Ethan said, turning to David.

"Later today, but I gotta warn you, it's huge. Tens of thousands of pages."

"Ship it to my apartment. It's quiet there, and I'll get through it much faster if I organize it at home."

"David's also trying to schedule an interview with Nancy McGregor, the ADA in charge of the case," Fulton said without missing a beat.

"She's critical to our story," Paul said, interrupting. "You need to follow up. She's a priority booking."

"I won't let the ball drop," Ethan said, a little too sharply.

"Don't. Make sure you land her," Paul said, pushing back even harder.

"Okay, the two of you, enough. You're making me feel like a ping-pong ball," Dirk said, glancing back at his researcher. "David's also been networking with the deputy mayor's office and his wife. What's her name?"

"Sandy," David said.

"Has she been helpful?" Ethan said, pulling out his iPad and beginning a new page of notes. "Has she told you anything about Cynthia beyond what's been printed in the newspapers?"

"Not really," David said reluctantly. "She and the deputy mayor have been waiting for us to assign a producer before opening up about their daughter."

"Well, now I'm on board," Ethan said sincerely. "Can you set up a meeting?"

"As soon as I get back to my office."

"Good. And how about family photos and home videos?"

"Working on it," David said. "The deputy mayor's press secretary, Sylvia Rosenberg, has promised me copies. Hopefully we'll get them soon."

"And the Jamesons will sit down for an on-camera interview?"

Ethan said, wondering if David had already broached the subject and booked a shooting date with the press secretary.

"Yes."

"When?"

"We need to pick a day."

"Where?"

"We can do the interview at their apartment," David said confidently. "They live on Fifth Avenue, somewhere in the eighties."

"And what about visuals? Can we shoot B-roll at their apartment?" Ethan said, knitting his brow as he typed away on his iPad.

"It all depends on the kids," David said, flipping through his notes in a spiral notebook. "Oh, here it is. Sandy told me her two younger kids are still pretty freaked out by the murder, and she's not sure she wants to expose them to our cameras. So we're gonna have to play it by ear and see how they're doing. We can definitely shoot the interview in their apartment, but maybe no pictures."

"Okay. We'll work that out when I meet them," Ethan said, pausing to finish a list of the story elements they'd been discussing. "And what about her friends? Cynthia was a student at Columbia University, right? Will they talk to us?"

"Can't this wait until later?" Paul said, interrupting again. "Let's move this along. I'm running late for another meeting."

Ethan turned off his iPad and put his research back into his briefcase, then turned to the executive producer. "I just have a couple more questions, Paul. Then we'll be done. I'm assuming Pavel Feodor is the centerpiece of the story. Has he agreed to an on-camera interview?"

Paul removed his glasses and began cleaning them with a handkerchief. "What do you take me for, Ethan, a fool? Of course Feodor's agreed to an interview. I would never program a story like this without the main character. Wouldn't get much of a rating doing a write-around. Everybody and his brother has done that. We're the only news organization with an interview. Feodor is our exclusive."

"And is Feodor ready to talk about what happened that night? Or is he just playing games with us?" Ethan said, hoping to find out if there were any guidelines for the interview.

"His attorney has assured me over and over again that his client wants to come clean and tell us his side of the story. The guy's name is Frankie O'Malley. He's a public defender. Talk to him. He'll tell you the same thing."

"That's the first call I'll make," Ethan said as he began thinking about the difficulties of shooting a prison interview. "And where do we stand with Rikers Island? That's where they're holding him, right? Do we have permission to bring in our cameras?"

"I've been working on that for weeks," Paul said quietly.

"And when will you know?" Ethan said, seeing the worry on Paul's face.

"When the powers that be are ready to make the decision," Paul shot back. "Hopefully soon."

"Maybe I should pick up the negotiations from here," Ethan said. "Might be more productive if I coordinate the logistics with Rikers Island."

"No," Paul said sharply. "The negotiations are delicate. And I'm too far into it to remove myself from the mix. You might screw things up."

"Come on, Paul, you know me better than that," Ethan said levelly. "I've booked dozens of sensitive interviews for you, and there's never been a problem."

"I don't care how good you are, Ethan. I said I'd handle the negotiations. That's my decision, and it's final."

Ethan stared around the room looking for support, but when nobody came forward, decided not to press the point any further—at least for the moment. "Okay, we'll do it your way, Paul," he said, pushing his chair away from the table. "Who's the point person on my story, Lenny or Joyce?"

"Lenny," Paul said. "I've asked Joyce to help him with his other projects. He's got plenty of time to work with you. Check in with him every day and let him know what you're doing. He'll keep me posted."

"No problem," Ethan said, nodding to Lenny. "And while we're talking about staffing, I'd like Mindy Herman as my number two."

Paul turned to his senior producers. "What's Herman doing? Does she have time to work with Ethan?"

Joyce Cox scanned through a computer printout listing all the current assignments. "She's got a couple of stories on her plate, but they're winding down. She can handle a new project."

"Done. She's yours," Paul said, "and so is David. Any other questions?"

"Just one," Ethan said. "Who's the correspondent?"

An uneasy silence filled the room.

"I've been waiting for you to ask that question," Paul said, starting to doodle again on his yellow pad. Then he looked up at Ethan. "This is the biggest story we'll program all year. ABC, NBC, and CBS have been circling for weeks, trying to steal the Feodor interview out from under us. So far I've managed to fend them off. My bosses at the network have also promised a ton of on-air promotion. That should help us get a huge rating, and you know how important that is to the show."

"Okay, Paul, I get it. This story's important. Who are you assigning?"

"I want to give it to an anchor. I've talked to Peter Sampson. He's agreed to clear his schedule and take on the story."

Ethan didn't know how to react. He'd worked with Sampson in the past, and it was common knowledge on the show that they didn't see eye to eye. "With all due respect, I don't think that's a good idea. Peter never does this kind of story. He usually sticks to big entertainment interviews and celebrity profiles where there's little prep work, a day or two of shooting, and maybe a week or two of writing and editing. This story is much more complicated and is going to take up way too much of his time. What about Julie Piedmont? She's our coanchor and has an excellent Q rating. She's a much better choice than Peter, don't you think?"

"Be careful, Ethan. You're out of line here," Paul said glaringly. "I know you guys have a history, but Peter Sampson has been anchoring this show since the day we went on the air. He's the face of *The Weekly Reporter*. I want him to do this story. Not Julie Piedmont. She won't get us as big a rating."

"Well, I disagree," Ethan said.

"I don't care what you think," Paul said, banging on the table. "I've made my decision and have already briefed him. Peter's the talent. Make the best of it." He picked up his yellow pad. "We're done here," he said, pointing at Ethan. "I want to talk to you now—in my office."

Ethan took a deep, calming breath, then followed Paul out of the conference room and past Monica who looked up from her computer. "Is there anything I can get you guys? Coffee, tea, maybe water?"

"Nothing," Paul said, waving her off. "And close the door. We need privacy." He wheeled around and faced Ethan. "Take a seat."

Ethan dropped into a chair across from Paul's desk as the executive producer paced over to a picture window and peered out at Rockefeller Center in the distance. "Ethan, Ethan, Ethan," he said. "What am I gonna do with you? You've been working on my show for a long time, and for the most part, you've done an excellent job. But the past few months, well, I don't know what to make of you. You're not the same person I once knew and respected.

You've become lazy and unreliable and pigheaded. What do you have to say for yourself?"

"I don't think I've changed," Ethan said defensively. "I still deliver more hard-hitting and high-rated stories than anyone else on your staff. You shouldn't be angry with my work habits. You should embrace them as a model for all your producers."

Paul cut him off. "Don't be smug with me, Ethan. I don't tolerate this kind of behavior from any of my other producers. How dare you talk to me like this. How dare you ignore my emails. How dare you come to my meetings late. Don't you want to work for me anymore?" He let the last question hang in the air as he walked over to his desk and sat down, never taking his eyes off Ethan.

"Of course I want to work for you, Paul. I'll do a good job on this story, and you know it."

"But I'm not sure I trust you anymore. Your behavior is inexcusable."

"Are you threatening me, Paul?" Ethan said, the hair on the back of his neck bristling.

"Yes. I'm putting you on notice. I don't like the way you're doing your job, and I'm not sure I want you on my show anymore." He leaned across his desk and peered into Ethan's eyes, pausing a moment before continuing. "And if you step out of line one more time, I'll pull you off the Feodor story and send you off packing. This is your last chance, Ethan."

"Okay, Paul," Ethan said, trying to keep his voice from shaking. "I'll play the good soldier and deliver you a blockbuster story." He leaned back in his chair. "And on top of that, I'm gonna win another Emmy Award for this project and place it next to the one I've already won for your show."

"You're a conceited bastard, Ethan, and I'm tired of it," Paul said, his voice cold and threatening. "But deep down I still think you can produce something I'll be proud of, and that's the only reason you're still working for me. So make the most of it. Your ass is on the line."

"Are we finished?" Ethan said.

"Not quite." Paul shuffled a stack of papers on his desk. "I know you don't like Peter Sampson, and I know he doesn't like you. I had to spend a lot of time convincing him to let me assign you to this story. So make an appointment and go see him. He's waiting to hear from you. Now I think we're finished."

He pointed to the door.

Ethan grabbed his briefcase and tucked his iPad under his arm, then slowly walked out, past Monica who'd listened to the conversation through the closed door and was now ready and willing to repeat each and every word in vivid detail to anybody who asked.

Making his way down the long red hallway, he never once looked at Paul's smiling face peering out from the dozens of photos. Lang had rattled his confidence and rattled it good.

He had a lot to prove to his boss.

And a lot to prove to himself.

CHAPTER 4

"HEY DAD, YOU GONNA WATCH THE game with me?" Luke said, excitement on his face as Ethan walked into the living room and sat down on the couch next to Sarah. "The Yanks are ahead four to two in the eighth. Teixeira's hit two home runs, and in one more inning, they're gonna beat the Red Sox." He pounded his fist into his baseball glove.

"Think their relief pitching will hold, little man? There's no more Mariano Rivera," Ethan said, grinning from ear to ear.

"You betcha. So far, the new guys have been great. If they bring in Andrew Miller, or what's his name, Dad? Oh, yeah, Dellin Betances, the game's in the bag."

"Okay, Luke, the inning's over," Sarah said. "Time for bed. That's our deal."

"Come on, Mom, I'm not tired yet. Lemme watch 'til the end."

"Luke, it's already way past your bedtime. Listen to your mother. Tomorrow's a camp day, and you have to get up early."

"Not fair, Dad."

"A deal's a deal. Let's go. I'll tuck you in."

Luke ran over to Sarah, who was reading a John Grisham novel, *Sycamore Row*, and gave her a hug and kiss. "Good night, Mom. I love you."

"I love you, too. Now off to bed."

Luke picked up his Yankee hat and ran out of the room, Holly right behind him, like two peas in a pod.

"I'll be right back, hon. I wanna make sure he climbs into bed and turns off the lights." Ethan slowly walked down to Luke's bedroom and waited as his son brushed his teeth. He'd been closeted all afternoon in his study, memories of his meeting with Paul clouding his judgment as he started organizing a copy of the court docket David had dutifully shipped to his apartment. He'd already spent hours staring at the documents, smoking one cigarette after another, unable to concentrate on a story he loathed. Somehow he had to put aside his principles and apply the same skills he'd honed over the years to a subject he had no interest in pursuing. It was going to take all his strength, all his resolve, and it wasn't going to be easy. After hours of soul searching, he'd decided to take a short break and spend time with his family.

"Come on, Luke, what's taking so long?" he said, knowing he had to get back to work in the salt mines.

"Be there in a minute, Dad." Luke flushed the toilet, then scooted across the room and hopped into bed, rearranging his stuffed animals before fluffing the pillows and climbing under the covers.

"Great game, huh, Luke?" Ethan said, smiling at his son.

"Yeah, Dad. Do you really think they'll win?"

"It's a sure thing, Lukie. They still have that old Yankee magic."

Luke paused a split second. "But how will I know? I'm gonna be asleep when the game's over."

"Don't worry. I'll leave you a note on your bedside table. It'll be there first thing in the morning when you wake up."

"You won't forget?"

"Cross my heart." He kissed his little boy on the end of his nose and turned off the lights. "Good night, Luke. I love you."

"Love you, too, Dad."

Ethan sighed. His son was growing so fast, and he was missing so much. With feelings of melancholy, he made his way back to the living room. Sarah had turned off the game and was lying on her back, reading.

"Is the book any good?"

"It's like all of Grisham's novels," she said. "Lots of character development at the beginning, intrigue in the middle, and then gangbusters at the end. I've got about fifty pages to go. It's hard to put down."

Ethan sat beside her, placing her feet in his lap. "How was your day, babe?"

"Busy. I'm working a new case—an insider trading scandal at one of the big brokerage houses on Wall Street."

"Which one?"

"Wouldn't you like to know," she said, a mischievous grin on her face. "Can't talk about it until the DA goes public. Then I'll give you the inside scoop. Are you making any progress with the documents?" she said, putting Grisham down on her lap.

Ethan leaned back on the sofa and closed his eyes. "Not much. I have no interest in this story. It seems like such a waste of time. There are so many other important projects I should be doing. But Paul doesn't care about real stories, about real journalism anymore. All he cares about is the ratings."

"How was Paul in the meeting this morning?" she said, studying the deep anguish on his face.

"Difficult," Ethan said, reaching for a cigarette. "He's assigned Peter Sampson to my project."

There was a momentary pause as Sarah sat up on the couch.

"Ethan, you and Sampson don't work well together. He makes your life miserable. Is there any way you can change the assignment?"

"I tried, but Paul wouldn't budge," Ethan said, exhaling a thick cloud of smoke through his nose. "I'm just going to have to suck it up and make it work."

"When are you meeting with him?"

"I don't know. Maybe next week. Peter's too busy to see me until then."

"He's always too busy to see you."

"That's the name of the game with him," Ethan said, stubbing out his cigarette in an ashtray and reaching for another, then deciding to hold off and putting down the pack. "Sarah, did you find out anything about my story today? You said you'd do some sleuthing at the office for me, remember?"

"I didn't come up with much. The district attorney's working on the sentencing, and all the planning is taking place behind closed doors, so nobody knows what's really going on—only that something big is about to happen."

"That doesn't help much," he said, disappointed. "Anything else?"

"Not really. But I did bump into Nancy McGregor this afternoon."

"She's the lead prosecutor on the case. We've been trying to book an interview with her."

"I know," Sarah said, her eyes sparkling mischievously.

"How'd you find out?" Ethan said eagerly.

"Come on, Ethan, how do you think? She told me your office has been trying to reach her for days."

"And what else did she say?"

"That she was looking forward to meeting you."

"That's a relief," Ethan said, relaxing. "Think she'll do an

38

on-camera interview with Sampson? Paul's desperate to make her part of the story."

"I don't know. You're going to have to ask her that question yourself when you sit down with her."

Ethan made a mental note to email David and remind him to call Nancy McGregor again first thing in the morning. "Did she pump you for information about me?" Ethan said curiously.

"Of course."

"What did she wanna know?"

"The usual stuff. Are you honest? A good journalist? Will you do a balanced story? The same questions everybody asks."

"And what did you tell her?"

"That you were a jerk," she said with a devilish smile. "All kidding aside, Ethan, I told her you were the best producer in the business. A seasoned professional. Somebody she could trust."

"My biggest fan," he said, tickling her foot. "Is that it, babe? Is there anything else I should know about?"

"Just that she's curious about what you'll say in your story and what questions you'll ask if she agrees to sit down for an interview. I told her I had no idea and that she could talk to you about that kind of stuff when she meets you."

"Perfect," he said, glancing at the clock sitting on the table. "Mindy's coming over in a little while to help me wade through the court docket."

"Mindy's working with you on the story?"

"Yup," he said, smiling. "That was my only victory this morning with Paul."

"Well, that's a big one," she said. "You guys make a good team. Maybe she can find some way to help you get into the story. Just because it's a murder doesn't mean it isn't important." She picked up her book, then looked back at Ethan. "And please, Ethan, don't drink too much tonight. I don't want to smell scotch on your breath when you come to bed."

"What do you mean?" Ethan said, growing defensive.

"I mean just that. I don't want you drinking any more tonight. You've already had a few at that bar, McGlades. You stopped there on your way home. Didn't you?"

"How'd you know that?"

"Come on, Ethan. You stop there on your way home almost every day. It's pretty obvious, hon."

"But I only had one or two."

"Yeah, but you also had one or two in your study while you were working."

"You've been counting my drinks?" he said, astonished.

"Of course, Ethan, I'm worried about you. You've been drinking way too much the past couple of months. You gotta get it under control. It's becoming a problem."

"I can handle it," he said as the doorbell rang. "Please, don't worry, babe. I'm okay, really."

But he avoided Sarah's eyes as he hurried out of the room—pushing the truth to the back of his mind.

. . . . .

Mindy was waiting patiently, toting a large shoulder bag, when he opened the front door. After giving her a quick hug, he led her through the apartment, Sarah looking up from her book and saying hello when they stopped at the living room. After spending a minute or two catching up—Ethan bouncing nervously from one foot to the next—he interrupted their conversation, blew Sarah a quick kiss, and led Mindy down to his study.

The room was an unholy disaster.

File folders were piled haphazardly on his desk, boxes

randomly scattered about the floor, and loose documents covered every inch of counter space. "Jeez, Ethan, what a mess. Have you made any progress at all going through this stuff?" She randomly picked up a folder and started skimming through the contents.

"Not much," he said as he flipped on his desk lamp and grabbed two bottles of water from the wet bar.

"Where do you want to start?" she said, dropping her shoulder bag on the floor and pulling out a yellow pad to take notes.

"Maybe with the police reports. I found them in the bottom of a box before I put Luke to bed. They're buried somewhere on my desk." He sat down and rummaged through a stack of paperwork. "Here they are. Who was the lead detective on the case? Do you remember, Mindy?" he said, placing a half dozen file folders on the floor to clear a space in front of him.

Mindy opened a page of research in a loose-leaf notebook and ran her finger down a list of possible interview subjects she'd put together before heading to Ethan's apartment. "A guy named Edward Jenkins. Do you have his report?"

Ethan fanned through the documents. "Here it is. It's dated March 24—the day after the murder." He grabbed a yellow marker from the top drawer, began highlighting a passage on the second page, and then read it out loud:

The victim, Cynthia Jameson, was found lying face up on the sidewalk on the corner of Little West Twelfth and Washington Street in the Meatpacking District. She was approximately twenty feet from the entrance to the Standard Grill—a high-end steak house that caters to a wealthy clientele. Detectives are canvassing the area looking for eyewitnesses. So far we haven't located anybody who saw the shooting.

```
A high-caliber bullet appears to have entered
her chest near her heart and exited through
her upper back. There was blood on her coat
and blouse and a large pool around her body.
Her eyes were wide open, her tongue hanging out
of her mouth, and deep scratches on her cheeks
and neck. Lab techs at the crime scene believe
she was awake and struggling to breathe as she
bled out, and that death occurred several min-
utes after she was gunned down.
```

Ethan read the passage a second time, fixating on the grisly details, then scanned through a stack of newspaper stories. "The descriptions of the body match almost word for word to Jenkins's police report," he said, looking up at Mindy. "Do you remember reading anything about what she was doing in the Meatpacking District that night?"

"Just a little," Mindy said, rifling through her shoulder bag for her copy of the *New York Times Magazine* article. "It says right here she was out partying with friends and was apparently minding her own business when she walked straight into the bullet."

"Was she alone when she left the Standard Grill?" Ethan said.

"The police aren't sure. Nobody seems to know if she was with somebody else who didn't come forward after they found the body."

"Don't you think it's strange the police never pinned that down? Might've shed some light on the chain of events leading up to the murder."

"Maybe," Mindy said, sipping her water. "But the jury didn't have a problem not knowing. They convicted Feodor in less than an hour."

Ethan nodded and jotted himself a note to find out exactly

what Cynthia was doing just before she was shot, then continued thumbing through Jenkins's police report, searching for any tidbits he might've missed. When he got to the bottom of the third page, he highlighted another passage. "Listen to this, Mindy. It describes where Jenkins found Feodor":

```
The perpetrator was lying on his side about
fifty feet from the entrance to the parking
lot behind Fernelli's Beef and Poultry. There
was blood everywhere—splattered on a chain-
link fence and flowing down the alley. When I
first approached him I thought he was dead like
the Mexican we found near the loading dock.
His face was pasty, and he didn't appear to be
breathing. But when I leaned over and placed
my finger on his neck, I felt a faint pulse and
radioed for an ambulance. That's when I noticed
he was holding a Beretta 9mm handgun in his
right hand. I bagged it and gave it to a CSI
for testing and immediately began focusing on
Feodor as my prime suspect.
```

"This seems strange, Mindy," Ethan said, dropping Jenkins's report on his desk. "Why did Jenkins finger Feodor at this stage of the investigation? Why'd he rule out everybody else involved in the shootout? There doesn't seem to be enough evidence to move Feodor to the top of the list, does there?"

"It does seem strange now that you mention it," Mindy said, picking up the document and rereading the passage. "What do the other cops say?"

Ethan grabbed the other police reports and cross-checked them against Jenkins's. He was astonished to discover that each and every detective had come to the same conclusion—targeting Pavel Feodor as the killer—almost from the moment they found him in the parking lot. "I don't know, Mindy, how could they all be so certain he did it? Something seems off here."

"Does seem premature," she said, perplexed. "Do you want me to track down Jenkins, see if he'll talk to us?"

Ethan lit a cigarette and blew a smoke ring. "Yeah. Ask him if he'll meet us in the Meatpacking District. I wanna take a look at the crime scene—see where he found Feodor and how far he was from Cynthia's body. Maybe Jenkins can show us what he thinks happened that night."

"I'll reach out to him."

"Good, and do it first thing in the morning." He stubbed out his cigarette and yawned, stretching his arms way over his head. "Look, Mindy, it's late. Let's call it a night and pick up first thing tomorrow." He walked over to the wet bar, grabbed a half-empty bottle of Black Label, and poured a finger of scotch. "Want one?" he said, holding out the bottle.

"I'll take a pass," she said, tilting her head questioningly. "It's a bit late to start drinking, don't you think?"

"Maybe. But I'm too wired to sleep."

"Shouldn't you lay off the booze tonight? I didn't mention it this morning, but you were clearly hungover before you met with Paul."

Ethan sipped his scotch. "Yeah, I was, but I'm a big boy, Mindy. I know what I'm doing."

"Suit yourself," she said, hoisting her bag onto her shoulder. "I know you don't wanna hear this from me, but you drink too much, Ethan, and I don't think you know it." She hovered a moment, concern on her face, then turned and left.

Ethan stood frozen in place, staring at the empty room before draining his glass and wiping his mouth.

First Sarah.

Now Mindy.

Was his drinking that obvious?

Deep down in his gut he knew that it was.

Grabbing his iPhone, he checked the score of the Yankee game. They'd lost five to four—a trio of relief pitchers, including Betances and Miller, blowing the save in the bottom of the ninth. Where in God's name was Mariano Rivera? He jotted down the score on a sheet of paper and left it on Luke's bedside table. After straightening the covers and kissing his son, he walked back to his study and poured another scotch.

He wasn't ready for bed or ready to face Sarah.

So he settled in at his desk with a stack of documents for another long night.

CHAPTER 5

ETHAN RODE THE ELEVATOR DOWN to the lobby and hurried out of the building. It was just after eight, and he was scheduled to meet Detective Jenkins at the crime scene in less than an hour. Mindy was pacing back and forth when he got to the corner of Fifth Avenue, holding two cups of coffee. "Ethan, you're late. It took me all day yesterday to set up this survey. Jenkins doesn't have a lot of time, and I don't want to keep him waiting. We gotta get going."

She handed him a coffee.

Ethan smiled sheepishly. "Sorry, I was up most of the night going through documents and slept through my alarm clock. We'll make it." He hailed a taxi and they climbed in. "We're headed to the intersection of Little West Twelfth and Washington Street in the Meatpacking District," he said, gulping his coffee and scalding his mouth. "Any idea how long it'll take us to get there?" The cabby didn't answer. He just hit the meter, gunned the engine, and took off down Fifth Avenue.

"I guess he's not talking," Mindy said as the car pulled into heavy traffic.

"Guess not," Ethan said, opening his briefcase and pulling out a file folder. "Take a look at this and let me know what you think. He handed her a copy of the autopsy report. It was dated March 26 and signed by the deputy coroner—a pathologist named Leonard Toakling.

"I see you're making your way through the court docket," Mindy said, scanning the five pages.

"That's all I've been doing—organizing the damn paperwork. It's driving Sarah and Luke crazy. It's driving me crazy too," he said, a thin smile spreading across his face. "At least I'm getting into the story. I didn't think that was possible. Look, read the last page. I've underlined the key paragraph."

Mindy flipped through the document and read the passage:

The victim was murdered by a single gunshot wound to her upper torso. It entered her body just above her heart and exited the lumbar region of her upper back, shattering her L4 vertebra. No bullet or bullet fragments were found in her body. From the size of the entry wound and the damage at the exit wound, I've determined the murder weapon was a handgun, either a Glock 30 or a Beretta 9 mm. The bullet severed the victim's aorta, stopping the flow of oxygenated blood from her heart to her other organs. The damage caused massive bleeding as noted in the police reports. Death occurred within minutes as her organs shut down. The time of death was approximately 3:30 a.m. The type of death was a homicide.

"So the deputy coroner's findings confirm she was killed by the gunshot," Mindy said, handing the document back to Ethan.

"Just like Jenkins wrote in his report."

"Have you confirmed the bullet came from Feodor's gun? He was holding a Beretta when they found him."

"Not yet. I've looked through just about everything the DA's office sent us, but I can't find the ballistics report."

"That's strange," Mindy said, puzzled. "You'd think they'd give us that piece of information. It's pretty basic to their case. Maybe it was an oversight?"

"Maybe," Ethan said suspiciously. "I'll ask Jenkins if he's got a copy. We need to make sure the bullet that killed Cynthia came from Feodor's gun. Then we'll have the last bit of proof that he actually murdered her."

It was taking the cabbie a long time to go downtown. Traffic was crawling on Fifth Avenue, and Ethan was beginning to lose patience. "Is there a faster way to get there?" The cabbie didn't respond. He just stepped on the gas, made a quick turn onto Fifty-Seventh Street, and headed to the West Side Highway. There was even more traffic going crosstown.

"Shit. We're not gonna make it," Mindy said, worried.

"Jenkins'll wait for us. He wants to meet us as much as we want to meet him. This is his big chance to go on national television."

"You're damn right he does," she said, smiling, then scanning a to-do list she'd prepared for the cab ride. "When are we talking to Sampson?"

"Late tomorrow afternoon. His assistant emailed me this morning and confirmed we're in his schedule at four o'clock. You need to make sure David knows about the meeting."

"And have you contacted Feodor's attorney yet?"

"Late yesterday. I'm meeting with him at five o'clock."

"Do you want me to go with you?"

"No. I need you back at the office pushing the story forward. Ride David and make sure he gets me in to see Nancy McGregor. I'm worried we're not in her schedule. I've got a whole list of questions I wanna ask her and need to lock in her interview." The taxi stopped for a red light at the corner of West and Horatio streets. "This is close enough," Ethan said, reaching for his wallet. "Let's get out and walk the neighborhood." He paid the fare and watched as the cabbie screeched away from the sidewalk. "That was the weirdest cab ride. That guy never uttered a single word."

"Nope. Not a one," Mindy said jokingly. "Not the friendliest of blokes. Now which way do we go, Ethan?"

He punched Fernelli's Beef and Poultry into his iPhone and pulled up a Google map of the Meatpacking District. "It's right there, and we're over here." He showed Mindy the route they had to take. "Only a couple of blocks uptown and one block east." They started walking, passing a wholesale meatpacking company where sides of beef were sitting outside an old broken-down warehouse. Clouds of flies hovered over the carcasses as men dressed in bloody aprons stood about shooting the breeze. At the corner of Little West Twelfth, they headed up the block, passing more dead animals standing unattended in crates, waiting to be butchered and packaged. The smell in the hot morning sun was stifling. Fernelli's was sitting derelict at the end of the block, no longer in business, the doors padlocked, the windows boarded up, the front gate hanging from its hinges.

Detective Edward Jenkins was waiting by the front door smoking a cigarette. A big man with broad shoulders and a narrow waistline, his thick black hair was neatly trimmed and parted on the side. He was dressed in a tailored black suit, white shirt, and gray tie. Except for the bulge under his arm where he holstered his handgun, he looked more like a Park Avenue attorney than a New York City cop.

Ethan disliked him immediately.

"Sorry we're late," he said casually. "We got stuck in the rush hour traffic."

"Not a problem," Jenkins said, grinning. "It's always a mess at this hour. Makes you want to move out to the suburbs where life's a little slower and there's far less crime."

Ethan ignored the detective's feeble attempt at humor.

"So this is where the gun battle took place," he said pointing at Fernelli's. "It's pretty spooky down here. What's it like in the middle of the night?"

"Even creepier," Jenkins said. "The perfect place for a drug deal. This neighborhood is one of the last locations in Manhattan where animals are butchered for the retail meat market. So the powers that be at City Hall let things slide because there are no high-end companies complaining about their tax dollars. They don't fix the potholes. They don't collect the garbage. And they let the rats run wild. But if you walk a couple of blocks in any direction, you're gonna find a whole different world. Lots of la-di-da boutiques and specialty stores and high-class restaurants. At night, the streets are teeming with the rich and famous hopping from one club to the next."

"That's what Cynthia Jameson was doing the night she was murdered. She was clubbing, right?" Mindy said.

"Yup. She was partying with friends and ended up just around the corner at the Standard Grill. Want me to show you where we found her?"

"In a minute," Ethan said, trying to get his bearings. "But first, I'd like to see where the gun battle took place."

"Follow me. I'll give you the cook's tour." Jenkins pushed open the broken gate and headed down the narrow alley bordered by Fernelli's on one side and a tenement on the other. "The parking lot's in the back," he said. "You can't see it from the street."

"So it's private," Ethan said, looking up and down the alley.

"Totally. It's tucked away out of sight from prying eyes, the perfect place for a drug deal. That's why the gang picked it. They thought they could grab the heroin, pay off the dealer, and make their getaway. A quick, simple, and foolproof plan. But something went horribly wrong, and as you know, all hell broke loose."

"Detective, who owns this parking lot?"

"It took us awhile to figure that out. There were a lot of shell companies protecting the identity of the real owner. We finally traced it to a big international food conglomerate."

"Which one?"

"I don't remember," Jenkins said, averting his eyes. "We didn't think it was important. So we didn't pursue the lead and just passed the information on to the Feds. I guess I could get you the name if you think it's important. I must have it in a file somewhere."

"No big deal. I'll call if I can't figure it out myself," Ethan said, wondering why the detective didn't think there might be some connection between Fernelli's and the gang involved in the shoot-out. He filed that thought in the back of his mind and pushed on. "Can you show us where you found all the blood?" Ethan said, walking to the middle of the parking lot.

"Mostly over there," Jenkins said, making his way to a chain-link fence and pointing at the ground. "There were two big pools right here and more splattered over there on the side of this building." He touched a section of bricks. "But we didn't find any bodies; not here."

"And you're sure all the blood came from just two guys? I think that's what I read in your police report," Mindy said inquisitively.

"The lab techs are positive. All the blood came from two guys."

"And you don't know who they are, do you?" Ethan said bluntly.

"Nope," Jenkins said. "We couldn't match the DNA in any of our databases."

"But you did find one body," Mindy said. "The Mexican."

"He was on the other side of the parking lot near the loading dock," Jenkins said, walking over to a spot fifty feet away. "He was lying here with most of his head blown off. Probably got shot by somebody at pretty close range. That's what the CSIs thought after they finished all their measurements."

"And you don't know who he is?" Ethan said.

"He wasn't ID'd either. We just know he was Mexican, probably from one of the cartels."

"So a total of three guys were either wounded or killed in the gun battle," Mindy said, sweeping her arms around the parking lot.

"Yup. That's what I wrote in my report. And, of course, the fourth guy was Pavel Feodor."

"And where'd you find him?" Mindy said.

"He was in the alley, near the street." Jenkins walked another fifty feet and stopped. "He was lying right about here, covered in blood and barely breathing. In fact, when I first found him I thought he was dead."

"And you think that's why he was left behind?" Ethan said, beginning to feel that Jenkins's account of the crime scene sounded a little too rehearsed.

"Nobody's really sure, but the prosecutor believes the other gang members didn't think he'd last long enough to talk. They must've been pretty damn surprised when they heard on the news he was alive and kicking," Jenkins said, chuckling.

"But Feodor never told you who he was with that night, did he?" Mindy said. "At least that's what I read in the newspapers."

"Nope. Just said he was part of some random group of thugs he met at a bar right before the drug deal went down, and that they opened fire when the Mexicans tried to cheat them. He's a tough little guy. Closed like a book when he doesn't wanna talk."

"Okay, I've got the lay of the land," Ethan said, trying to decide how to shoot a reenactment of the gun battle so the audience would think they were a fly on the wall actually watching it. "Now show us where you found Cynthia Jameson's body."

"Over this way," Jenkins said, heading out of the alley and up to Washington Street. "She was lying right here on her back not too far from the front door of the restaurant," Jenkins said, pointing up the block.

Kneeling, Ethan looked at the Standard Grill and then back at Fernelli's. "The bullet must have ricocheted back and forth against a couple of these buildings before it hit her. There isn't a straight line of sight between here and where you found Feodor."

"That's what the CSIs believe. You can see bullet holes in the bricks if you look closely." Jenkins pointed at a building across the street from the restaurant. "The slug that killed Cynthia was embedded over there next to the specialty food store. It was pretty mangled when we found it, but it definitely came from his gun. There was just enough left to make a match."

Ethan took one last look up and down the block, then turned to the detective. "You know, I've searched through the court record but can't seem to find the ballistics report. I really need a copy for my files. It's a key piece of evidence, and the GBS attorneys are gonna want to see it when they review my story for accuracy. Do you have a copy by any chance?"

Jenkins hesitated, his eyes blinking spasmodically. "Well, I must have it somewhere, but I can't give it to you without checking first with Nancy McGregor. I'm under explicit orders not to release any documents to the press without her approval."

"Well, we've got calls into the DA's office, and I guess we can wait a couple more days until we get in to meet her," Ethan said as he studied the detective's face. "I was just hoping you could cut through some of the red tape and get it to me quickly."

"It would be better if you went through Nancy," Jenkins said, still blinking.

"Not a problem," Ethan said, shaking the detective's hand. "I've just got one more question. Would you be willing to come back down here and take us through all this again when I have my cameras?"

"Sure," Jenkins said, more composed. "I'll have to run it through my public affairs people, but I can't imagine they'll object. Let's plan on it."

"Excellent," Ethan said, turning to Mindy. "Did I miss anything?"

"Not that I can think of."

"Good. We'll be in touch," Ethan said.

They said their good-byes, then hiked the three blocks to Fourteenth Street and hailed a taxi. "So what did you think of Jenkins?" Mindy said, raising an eyebrow.

"He was lying," Ethan said icily.

"About what?"

"The ballistics report."

"Why'd you think that?"

"Because he started blinking furiously when I asked him for the document."

"That doesn't prove anything."

"Maybe not, but I wouldn't bet against me. He's hiding something," Ethan said, a distant look on his face. "Nothing he showed us this morning adds up—the gun battle in the back of that parking lot, the location of Cynthia's body a block away, Feodor lying in the alley. Doesn't it seem like a stretch that a bullet fired from Pavel's gun somehow found its way into Cynthia's body?"

"Come on, Ethan. A jury listened to all the evidence and convicted him. I'm sure he killed her."

"I know. But something doesn't feel right," he said, perplexed.

"Ethan, I've seen that look on your face before. What are you thinking?"

"I don't know," he said, pulling out a cigarette. "We need that ballistics report. I think it's important."

"I'll have David call his contact at the DA's office when I get back to the Broadcast Center. See if he can get them to send it right away. Where are you heading now?"

"Home," he said. "I want to double-check a couple of documents before I go see the public defender."

"Getting all your ducks in a row?"

"That's the name of the game."

"Sure you don't want me to go with you?"

"No. I got this covered. We'll talk later."

After dropping Mindy off at the office, he taxied to his apartment on the East Side. He had four hours until his meeting with Frankie O'Malley.

Just enough time to get ready.

CHAPTER 6

ETHAN DROPPED HIS BLUE BLAZER on the couch and sat down at his desk. The Venetian blinds in his study were half open, and bright sunlight filled the room, casting geometric patterns across the furniture and bookshelves. After checking his email and finding no messages from Paul, he flipped through a stack of folders until he found a packet of crime scene photos buried on the bottom of the pile. He lit a cigarette and carefully read the cover page listing all the pictures the DA's office had sent him in the court docket. There were eighteen in total, taken by a police photographer and carefully labeled as "Exhibit 21."

He inhaled a deep drag of smoke, walked over to an empty table, and lined up the photos in three neat rows. The first was a series of tight shots of uniformed police officers drawing circles around pools of reddish-brown blood smeared on the pavement, and crime scene investigators scraping samples to analyze in the lab. There were a handful of medium shots of the surrounding buildings—the bricks covered in more blood splatter and highlighted with more chalk. Ethan closed his eyes, trying to remember exactly what he'd seen, the photos clearly matching what Detective Jenkins had painstakingly pointed out in the parking lot. He opened a page of notes in his iPad and quickly typed several questions for the detective's interview.

Then he grabbed a half dozen images of Pavel Feodor lying unconscious in the alley—Jenkins standing or kneeling in every shot, examining the gunman, pointing at evidence. Feodor was curled on his side, a blue woolen hat askew on his head, his leather jacket bunched up around his waist. Blood had sprayed in a wide arc around his body, covering his legs and groin. In one shot, Ethan could clearly identify Feodor's face and see a handgun, presumably the Beretta that killed Cynthia, clutched in his right hand. He remembered reading in the newspapers that Nancy McGregor had used these photos to place Feodor at the crime scene and show the jury he was holding the murder weapon.

Ethan dropped the pictures on the table and scooped up the final batch, carefully looking at each one. Three wide shots showed Cynthia's lifeless body, the Standard Grill in the background, and dozens of cops and lab techs hovering in the foreground. Ethan could see her arms and legs sticking straight out, but little else—a clean shot of the corpse blocked by all the activity going on around her. Walking back to his desk, he rummaged through a drawer and pulled out a magnifying glass. After angling a floor lamp to throw more light on the photos, he moved the magnifier back and forth but soon gave up. The images became too fuzzy. "Damn, why can't I see any blood?" he said to himself, frustrated.

He lit another cigarette and punched a number into his iPhone. "Hey, Mindy, it's me."

"What's up?"

"Has David called the DA's office yet?"

"He's just about to."

"I have another request. I've been poring over the crime scene photos. Most of them are pretty good, but there are only a couple of Cynthia, and I can't see any blood. Tell David to ask them for close-ups of her body."

"Why is the blood so important, Ethan? We know Feodor shot her in the chest. It's in the autopsy and in all the police reports."

"I know, but I wanna see what she looks like."

"Does this have anything to do with the missing ballistics report?" Mindy said, wondering out loud.

"Maybe," Ethan said, the wheels in his head spinning.

"More proof for our attorneys?"

"No. More proof for me."

"So you do have doubts about the case."

"Yeah. I guess I do," Ethan said. "Have David talk to his contact and tell him not to send up any red flags that we have questions about the murder."

"I'll make sure he's careful."

"Good. Let's talk after my meeting with O'Malley." He hung up the phone and looked at his watch. Shit. Almost two o'clock. No time for lunch.

He walked over to a another stack of file folders sitting on a chair and rifled through them until he found what he was looking for—a thick document bound by a rubber band—the transcript of Pavel Feodor's confession. It was dated March 29, six days after the murder, and stamped with the official logo of the Sixth Precinct in Lower Manhattan. The names of two cops were clearly printed on the top of the first page—Officer Randy Tempko and Detective Edward Jenkins. So Jenkins was one of the cops who interrogated Feodor. That made sense. He was the lead detective and knew more about the murder than anybody.

He pulled off the rubber band, sat back down at his desk, and flipped to the second page. Written on the bottom was a notation by the transcriber saying the confession had been videotaped. Ethan didn't remember seeing a video in the court docket. Any videos for that matter. He picked up his iPad and added it to the list of things he needed to track down.

Then he began to read.

The first fifty pages were pretty straightforward, the interrogation handled mostly by Tempko, who asked a lot of background questions establishing where Feodor had grown up, where he lived, and about his history in and out of juvenile detention. The officer had done his homework and seemed to know everything about Feodor's long criminal past. As he continued reading, he noticed that big sections of the transcript were blacked out. Somebody had redacted his copy of the document. But who and why? He wrote himself another reminder to request a clean copy.

At the top of page 69, he finally found what he was looking for—Pavel Feodor's account of the shootout and the murder:

TEMPKO: I just want to make sure I've got your story straight. You were in the parking lot behind Fernelli's in the Meatpacking District. You were with a bunch of guys you'd met earlier that night. Where did you say you met them?

FEODOR: We've been going over this for hours. Are you guys stupid or something? I told you I met them in a bar. I have no idea who they are. We were drinking.

TEMPKO: How many drinks did you have?

FEODOR: I can't remember. I was drunk.

TEMPKO: Funny, there was no alcohol in your blood when they found you. I don't believe you were drinking or in a bar that night.

FEODOR: Believe what you want; that's my story.

TEMPKO: Fuck off, you little asshole! You're a liar! We know you weren't at a bar. Who were you really with? I'm tired of your stinking bullshit.

FEODOR: I'm not talking anymore. This guy's out of control. And besides, I'm hungry. I haven't had any food or water since this morning. And my leg hurts. I need a break.

JENKINS: No break, Pavel, but you can have some water. Randy, go get him a bottle. (Transcriber's note: There's a brief pause as Officer Tempko leaves the room.) Sorry about that. My partner sometimes gets a little hotheaded. So let's pick up where we left off. You were in a bar where you met these guys, some random guys you didn't know.

FEODOR: You got it.

JENKINS: What happened next?

FEODOR: Man, I've told you over and over again. I'm sick of this. They told me they were going to buy some junk from some wetbacks they knew. They asked me if I wanted in on the deal. I said yes. It sounded like easy money. So we left the bar and went to Fernelli's and waited for the Mexicans to arrive. That's it. That's how I ended up in the parking lot. End of story.

JENKINS: What happened when the Mexicans got there? (Transcriber's note: There's another pause as Detective Tempko walks back into the room and hands Feodor a bottle of water.)

FEODOR: I'm not answering any more questions

if that guy stays in here. He's crazy.

JENKINS: Calm down, Pavel. Just talk to me. Forget about my partner. You and I have an understanding. I'm just trying to help you. I'll ask the questions. What happened next?

FEODOR: Man, I've told you. The Mexicans tried to cheat us and somebody started shooting and all hell broke loose.

JENKINS: Did you fire your gun?

FEODOR: Yeah, I fired it. Everybody did. I got one of the Mexicans in the arm, and then I ran after their cars and emptied my gun, but I didn't hit nobody else.

JENKINS: Did you see Cynthia Jameson on the corner?

FEODOR: No. I didn't see no girl.

JENKINS: Did you kill her?

FEODOR: No. How could I shoot her if I didn't see her?

JENKINS: Come on, Pavel, you're not telling me the truth. We found you lying in the alley. You were holding a Beretta. We found the bullet that killed Cynthia. It came from your gun. You killed her. Tell me what happened.

FEODOR: (Transcriber's note: There's a pause as Feodor takes a sip of water.) I don't remember what happened. I may have seen her, but I don't remember shooting her.

JENKINS: So you admit seeing her?

FEODOR: Maybe. I think so, but it's all pretty fuzzy.

Ethan paused and reread the passage. Could Feodor have been close enough to the street to see Cynthia? Ethan didn't think so. He'd been way back in the alley when he was shot, and the buildings were in the way. So why did Feodor say he'd seen the girl? Was he telling the truth or just trying to get the cops to stop harassing him? Ethan added the questions to the list on his iPad and picked up the transcript, puzzled. The document was missing page 71. Where was it? Was it somehow omitted when the district attorney's office made his copy? Did somebody pull it out on purpose? He checked his watch. No time to make another call and find out—not until later. He had to finish up and leave for O'Malley's. So he continued reading until he got to the top of page 75. Then he found the critical passage:

JENKINS: Did you murder Cynthia Jameson?

FEODOR: I don't remember.

JENKINS: Come on, Pavel, we know you did it. Tell us the truth! (Transcriber's note: Both officers stand up and start pounding on the table.)

FEODOR: Fuck off. I don't remember.

JENKINS: You're lying!

TEMPKO: Tell us! Did you murder Cynthia Jameson! Confess!

FEODOR: Well, maybe I . . .

TEMPKO: . . . Killed her! You did it, Pavel! Admit it! You murdered Cynthia Jameson!

FEODOR: Maybe, maybe I shot her. I'm getting mixed up.

JENKINS: You murdered her!

TEMPKO: In cold blood!

FEODOR: Yeah, I must've done it. I must've murdered her. I did it! It had to be me.

There it was, the confession—Pavel Feodor admitting to firing his handgun and murdering the girl. He opened a thick notebook and flipped through his research until he found a Post-it marking a *New York Daily News* article written the day the confession was played in court. The text in the newspaper matched word for word. His transcript appeared to be accurate—or was it? There was that missing page and those redactions. Were they important? And if so, why?

He had to get a clean copy.

He just had to.

Ethan checked the time. It was almost four o'clock. He had to go. Placing the confession in his briefcase along with Jenkins's police report and the crime scene photos, he headed to the street where he hailed a taxi and began the thirty-minute trip to the public defender's office.

CHAPTER 7

ETHAN HOPPED OUT OF THE CAB on the corner of Broadway and Fulton Street and gazed around the intersection. The neighborhood was one of the oldest in the city, the buildings packed together like sardines, some quaint but ramshackle, some ready for the wrecking ball. Hordes of people paraded like a marching band—couples pushing babies in strollers, upwardly mobile executives heading home from work, and young college kids scurrying in and out of cheap restaurants and dive bars. After getting his bearings, Ethan hiked down Broadway until he got to number 57, a small nineteenth-century office building that was under renovation. Pallets of bricks and bags of concrete were stacked on the sidewalk, and new windows were lined up on wooden pallets near the front door. He hurried past a work crew building a scaffold and climbed a rickety staircase to the fourth floor.

The offices of Frankie O'Malley, attorney-at-law, were at the end of a short hallway facing the back of the building. Ethan pushed his way into the waiting room and was greeted by a platinum-blonde receptionist who was showing a lot of cleavage and typing away on a computer.

"Mr. Benson?" she said.

"Yes, that's me." Ethan smiled on the inside at her heavy makeup, puffed-up hair, and long, fake fingernails, thinking she was straight out of central casting for a cheap Hollywood crime thriller. "I have a four o'clock appointment with Mr. O'Malley," he said cheerfully.

"He's expecting you. Go right on in." She batted her baby-blue eyes and went back to her typing.

Ethan noted the fresh paint, thick carpeting, and new furniture as he walked through an inner door and into the attorney's office, where he was stunned by the opulence. There was a fifty-inch digital television and a state-of-the-art sound system, original artwork, fancy wall sconces, crown moldings, and a custom-made picture window with sweeping views of Lower Manhattan. It looked like the office of a Fortune 500 executive, not the humble abode of a public defender. Where had all the money come from?

Frankie O'Malley was reading a legal brief and immediately got up to greet him. "Mr. Benson, so pleased to meet you." He shook hands vigorously. "Come, let's sit by the window where we can gaze at the wonderful view of the city." He waved Ethan over to a soft leather couch in a formal seating area. "I wanna thank you for dropping by this afternoon," he said. "My client, Mr. Feodor, wants to know your take on his case before he agrees to tell you on camera what really happened the night Cynthia Jameson was murdered. I'm sure you understand he has to be careful before doing the interview."

Ethan stared at the attorney. Was there a hidden agenda in the meeting? Was he here to pass some kind of test? He decided to choose his words carefully. "Well, I know you've been talking to my boss, Paul Lang, and I'm sure he's been filling you in on the direction of our story."

"Paul and I have had several conversations. But he's the executive producer and you're the producer. I know how it works in television. This is going to be your story and not his. So I want to hear your vision of the segment, then I'll discuss it with Pavel before I take you out to Rikers Island so he can meet you in person."

"So the interview isn't locked in stone?" Ethan said cautiously.

"No. Pavel's 99 percent sure he wants to do it, but you need to convince me and then him of your intentions before we sign off."

Ethan shifted in his chair. This wasn't his understanding. Nor Paul's. He was going to have to sell himself and the show all over again. "I understand Mr. Feodor's concerns," Ethan said diplomatically. "But I can assure you I'm gonna produce a fair and balanced story."

"Good. That's what I wanted to hear," O'Malley said, flicking a piece of lint from his thousand-dollar Paul Stuart sports coat. "So tell me, what's your take on his case?"

"It's pretty straightforward. My story's gonna follow what's been reported in the newspapers and magazines. I'm gonna give some background on Mr. Feodor—who he is, where he came from, how he got to this moment in his life, how he feels about killing Cynthia Jameson—and then I'm gonna describe the murder, his arrest, and what happened during the trial. That's about it, Mr. O'Malley. Unless I dig up some new angle on the case."

"Ah, that's what I was hoping you'd say, Mr. Benson, that you were looking for something new that's never been reported. My client may have confessed to the police, but he says the cops and the prosecutor don't know everything that happened the night of the murder. So far he hasn't told anybody the names of the people he was with. He hasn't even told me, but he keeps hinting he's now ready to reveal who was behind the drug deal."

"Are you saying he's been lying about who was involved in the shootout that night?" Ethan said, trying to decide where the public defender was heading with all this. "I just read the transcript of his confession, and by the way, I'm missing a page. Page 71. Have you seen it?"

"Of course," O'Malley said, "and everything else the prosecution redacted."

"Anything important?" Ethan said, hoping O'Malley would shed some light on the sections that were omitted.

"No. Just a lot of gobbledygook. A lot of crosstalk and loud banging. The prosecution removed page 71 and the other meaningless sections to make it easier for the jury. It's quite clear why they did it when you read the full transcript and screen the entire video."

"I don't have the video. The DA's office didn't send it to me. Can you give me a copy? I'd like to check the redacted pages myself."

"I'm afraid not, Mr. Benson. The tape isn't here anymore. This is just a small office, and I carry a big caseload. So I shipped it and most of the evidence from Pavel's case off to storage. It'll be much easier and faster if you ask Nancy McGregor. I'm sure it's just an oversight. She'll give it to you."

But Ethan wasn't so sure about this.

Or that O'Malley was telling him the truth.

"Okay, I hope to meet McGregor in the next week or so," he said, deciding not to push the issue any further. "I'll ask her when I see her."

"That would be best," O'Malley said, straightening a stack of magazines sitting on a side table. "May I ask you, Mr. Benson, what did you think of Pavel's confession?"

"Well, for one, he definitely admitted to shooting and killing Cynthia Jameson."

"Yes, indeed, he did."

"And he definitely said the shootout started after the Mexicans tried to sell them some bad heroin, but he was adamant that he didn't know the names of the other gang members and that he just went along for the ride to make some extra money."

"That's what he told the police, but now he's telling me he has names and wants to tell your show who they are and what really happened the night poor Cynthia was murdered."

Ethan paused and leaned back in his seat. "You know, Mr. O'Malley, I don't really get it. Why's he changing his story now? If he'd come clean during the trial, he might have avoided a first-degree murder conviction."

"Good point, but I can't answer that. I pleaded with Pavel to tell me the truth and to tell the jury, but he's a peculiar young man. Kinda marches to his own drummer."

"But why does he want to talk now?" Ethan said, still questioning Feodor's motive. "I still don't understand."

"Because," O'Malley said.

"Because of what?"

"Because he's afraid he's going to be executed. The sentencing hearing is coming up in a few weeks, and Nancy McGregor in the district attorney's office is pushing hard to convince the governor to make an exception of my client because of the heinous nature of his crime and allow the judge to sentence him to death. The state of New York hasn't executed anybody for over half a century. And Pavel doesn't want to be the first. He may be tough on the outside, but he's really a coward on the inside."

"But do you think that's gonna happen?" Ethan said, remembering that Sarah had told him the district attorney was working on the sentencing behind closed doors. Maybe that's why there was so much secrecy and why she couldn't find out anything about the discussions.

"It's hard to tell," O'Malley said. "There's a big law and order movement in New York that wants to bring back the death penalty—not only for this case. And there's a good chance the governor will bow to the pressure. That's what Pavel's afraid of."

"So he's hoping to buy himself a deal by coming forward and giving us some new information about the murder," Ethan said.

"That's exactly right," O'Malley said.

"And you agree this is a good strategy?"

"Yes, I do," O'Malley said. "It can't hurt. It can only help him."

Ethan peered at the public defender skeptically. "Do you think there's any chance Pavel will recant his confession when he does our interview and say he didn't kill Cynthia Jameson?"

O'Malley squirmed in his seat. "I can't answer that, Ethan. He won't tell me."

"And how do we know he's going to tell us the truth?"

"I can't answer that, either, and I'm his attorney. But he says he'll only talk to *The Weekly Reporter*, and only if he thinks you're going to help him."

"Why did he pick us, Mr. O'Malley?"

"Because I told him your news show has the highest rating on television, and he wants to reach as many people as possible. That's the answer, Ethan, pure and simple."

"Well, I can assure you I'm gonna get a lot of airtime and do the best job I can to tell his story—fair and square."

"I know that, Mr. Benson. I already trust you just from the brief time we've spent together this afternoon." O'Malley stood, adjusted his Brooklyn Law School diploma hanging on the wall, then sat back down. "Do you have any more questions? I have another meeting with a new client in a few minutes."

"Just a couple," Ethan said, pulling the crime scene photos from his briefcase and handing them to O'Malley. "The district attorney's office sent me these pictures of Cynthia Jameson's body, but there are only three of them. I can't see anything but her arms and legs. Did they send you any others?"

O'Malley thumbed through the photos, then handed them back to Ethan. "I have a more complete set, and some of the images are quite horrifying. Cynthia was really disfigured by the bullet from Pavel's gun. It blew a big hole in her chest, splattering blood over everything. I'm sure you don't have those pictures, Mr. Benson, because the DA's office doesn't want you airing them in deference to her family."

"I would never do that," Ethan said honestly. "Do you still have copies?"

"Of course," O'Malley said.

"Can I get them from you?" Ethan said hopefully.

"Frankly, I don't want you seeing them either. They might influence the questions you ask during your interview. And I can't take even the smallest risk you might show Pavel one of those horrid pictures while your cameras are rolling. Can you imagine how that would affect public opinion, Mr. Benson?"

"Well, I didn't think it would hurt to ask."

"It was a logical request, Mr. Benson. You're a good reporter." He glanced at his watch again. "You really must go. It's time for my next meeting. So when do you want to shoot my interview, Mr. Benson?"

"In a couple of weeks. We'll pick a date that works for the both of us as soon as I set my shooting schedule."

"I'm looking forward to it," O'Malley said. "And I'll talk to Pavel and figure out when we can go see him at Rikers Island." They stood and shook hands. "Call me if you have any questions."

As Ethan headed out the door, he felt uneasy. There was something unsettling about Frankie O'Malley. He was too slick. Too polished. Too slimy. Like a snake in the grass. So he decided, then and there, to ask Mindy to run a complete background check on the public defender.

. . . . .

O'Malley stood in the waiting room, listening, until he could no longer hear Ethan's footsteps echoing down the staircase, then turned to his receptionist. "Cancel my next meeting and hold my calls, Grace. I don't want to be interrupted." Anxious, he walked back into his office, locked the door, and punched a number into his cell phone.

"Nikolai, it's me."

"Has he left yet?"

"Just now."

"What's he like, Frankie?"

"He's going to be a problem," O'Malley said, flustered.

"What do you mean?" Nikolai said coldly.

The public defender sat down in an armchair facing the big picture window. Sunlight was shining off the glass tower of the new World Trade Center, the building shimmering in a rainbow of yellows and golds and reds. "He's smart, and he's asking lots of questions. He wants to know about the missing page in the confession and asked me for the video. He's also snooping around for more photos of Cynthia's body at the crime scene."

"Does he know what really happened?"

"I don't think so, but he's meticulously going through the evidence and digging into the case."

"And what about Pavel? Do we need to worry about him as well, Frankie?"

"I'm not sure, Nikolai. I don't know how much longer I can control him."

"Maybe we need to pay him more money. Will that keep him quiet?"

"I don't think he cares about money anymore. He doesn't want to die and thinks if he talks to the press and tells them the truth about that night, it'll save his ass." There was a moment of strained silence; the only sound coming through the phone was Nikolai's heavy breathing.

"Look, Frankie, I've taken good care of you since you took the case, and so far, you've done a real good job for me. So go see Pavel and make sure he holds up his end of the bargain. I don't want him talking to the press about us."

"I'll see what I can do."

There was another long pause and more heavy breathing.

"Good, Frankie. We have an understanding. Don't force me to bring this up with the *Pakhan*. He won't be happy. Keep me in the loop."

The connection clicked off.

Frankie sat motionless, staring at a bank of fluffy white clouds hanging over the skyline. Damn. How was he going to convince Pavel not to talk? He couldn't let that happen, and if he did, well, he didn't want to find out what the *Pakhan* would do to him.

He shuddered at the thought.

CHAPTER 8

PETER SAMPSON'S OFFICE WAS tucked away on the southeast corner of the eleventh floor, two doors down from Paul Lang. It had floor-to-ceiling windows, European wallpaper, and expensive oriental rugs complementing the antique furnishings purchased from the best showrooms in the city—a fifteen-thousand-dollar gold-leaf desk, a twenty-thousand-dollar Louis XIV end table, and a thirty-thousand-dollar hand-gilt English armoire filled with dozens of designer suits the anchorman wore when hosting the show. The corporation had spared no expense to keep Sampson happy, his office the most lavish and decadent in the building.

When Ethan walked through the door, Sampson was sitting at his desk dictating letters to his secretary, a stunning young Latina named Consuela Santana who'd been hired more for her beauty than her brains—like most of the assistants, bookers, and researchers who made up his staff. He acknowledged Ethan with a wave of his hand and pointed to a plush red satin couch where he wanted him to sit. Without uttering a word, he continued tweaking his schedule—accepting a lunch date with Katie Couric, declining a dinner invitation with Senator Chuck Schumer, and postponing a meeting with Julie Piedmont, his coanchor, who he never made time for. He rattled on for five minutes, then asked Consuela to bring him a cup of coffee.

"Ah, I see you've brought your team—Mindy Herman and David Livingston. Would you guys like coffee?" he said, turning to Ethan.

"No, thanks. We're all coffeed out," Ethan said quietly.

"Then maybe a bottle of water?"

"No. We're good," Mindy said cordially.

"Fine. Fine. Just one cup, Consuela, in the English china." He scooted his chair over to his computer. "I just need a few more minutes to go through my email." Ethan shot Mindy and David a quick glance, then stared at the anchorman's pink shirt and red suspenders and the bald spot on the top of his head.

After five minutes of silence, Consuela glided back into the room and placed the coffee on his desk. "Is there anything else you need at the moment?"

"No," he said, typing away, never blinking an eye.

Ethan cleared his throat, hoping to catch his attention. "Peter, are you almost ready for us?"

"Almost there. Just let me finish my email."

Ethan leaned back, trying not to scream. Another five minutes. Then Sampson turned and sipped his coffee. "I don't have a lot of time," he said, checking his Rolex. "I'm going to an important cocktail party tonight and have to leave for my apartment in half an hour to change into a tux. We need to make this quick."

"Okay, but we have a lot of ground to cover," Ethan said imploringly.

"Please stop," Sampson said, cutting him off. "I haven't forgotten your style. You start every meeting this way. Then you proceed to bombard me with unnecessary information I don't need to know. It's one of the many reasons you and I don't get along, and the main reason I objected when Paul told me you were the producer on this project."

Ethan hesitated, knowing he had to be careful. The anchorman and the executive producer were like brothers, almost legendary on New York's high-flying social circuit. They lunched together, partied together, and were in and out of each other's offices a dozen times a day. Ethan knew that every word he said to Sampson would be repeated verbatim to Paul, and the last thing he could afford was for his boss to pick up any negative vibes about his attitude. That would only exacerbate the delicate truce that now existed between the two of them.

"Look, Peter, we haven't worked together for a long time," Ethan said deferentially. "Let's try not to get off on the wrong foot. I just want to bring you up to speed on our story, tell you who I've been talking to and who I think we need to interview. It shouldn't take too long, but it's important."

"Good," Sampson said, "that's more like it. Short and to the point. I've been talking to Paul, and he's been filling me in. So I have a pretty good idea of the game plan." He stared from Ethan to Mindy to David and then back to Ethan. "So Paul said you were getting the court docket. Do you have the documents?"

"Yes, and I've been plowing my way through them."

"Anything I should know about?"

"Nothing yet," Ethan said, deciding it was way too early to tell Peter he was missing some key evidence.

"Let's move on then," Sampson said, thrusting out his chin and straightening his tie. "And what about the prosecutor, Nancy McGregor. Is she booked for an interview?"

"Tell Peter," Ethan said, nodding to his researcher.

"She just agreed in principle," David said, squirming in his seat. "I've set up a meeting for tomorrow afternoon to go over the story and answer her questions. We'll try to get her to commit to a shooting date when we see her."

"And the public defender, Frankie O'Malley?"

"Ethan met with him yesterday," Mindy said, jumping into the conversation. "He wants to do an interview. We just need to tell him when."

"Ah, the illustrious Ms. Herman," Sampson said with a touch of sarcasm. "I see you're earning your keep just like Mr. Livingston and my good friend Mr. Benson here." He put his feet up on the desk. "And what about the centerpiece to our story? Do we have an update on the Pavel Feodor interview?"

"Paul thinks we're getting close," Ethan said thoughtfully. "But so far, no decision on whether we can bring cameras into Rikers Island. Hopefully we'll know soon."

"Very good, Ethan. Paul just told me the exact same thing. I just wanted to make sure you were in the loop. You've passed my test with flying colors. All of you have." Sampson grinned, then glanced back at his email. "And the deputy mayor? When are we doing his interview?"

"We're not sure," Ethan said regretfully. "David's been trying to book a meeting with him, but so far we've had no luck with his press secretary. Do you happen to know Bernard Jameson, Peter?"

"I've met him a couple of times at social functions. His family owns the First Mercantile Trust Company—a big investment fund with controlling interest in dozens of steel, insurance, pharmaceutical, and energy companies. The guy's worth more than a billion dollars. I've been hearing rumors that he's planning to use his vast wealth to run for mayor next year."

"I've been reading the same thing in the gossip columns," Ethan said. "But I thought the murder had forced him to back-burner that decision."

"Ah, that's what you'd think, but he's a shrewd politician," Sampson said, finishing his coffee. "I'm sure he's gonna use the publicity surrounding his daughter's murder to tap into the sympathy vote, and when the timing's right, he's gonna cast his name into the hat. Mark my words, Ethan, he's gonna run." Sampson paused a moment, then put down his cup. "Maybe if I call Bernard I can cut through some of the red tape and get you in to see him."

"Think you can reach him?" David said, furrowing his brow.

"Mr. Livingston, I'm the anchorman of this show. He'll take my call." He yelled for Consuela. "Get the deputy mayor on the phone."

"Right away, sir." A minute later, she poked her head into the room. "The deputy mayor's on line one."

Sampson looked over at Ethan. "Sit there. All of you. He may have a question I can't answer." He cleared his throat. "Mr. Deputy Mayor, how nice to talk to you." There was brief silence. "Yes. I'm doing the story about your daughter." More silence. "Yes. Yes. I'm doing the interview with you and your wife."

Ethan watched the anchorman, impressed with his charm.

"As a matter of fact, I'm sitting here with my producer. His name is Ethan Benson, and he's really quite good once you get to know him," Sampson said. "No. No. You haven't met him yet, and that's why I'm calling. I was hoping to set up a time when he could come by and meet you and Sandy." Sampson placed his hand over the mouthpiece and whispered to Ethan. "He's checking his schedule but thinks he may be free first thing tomorrow morning. Does that work for you?"

Ethan nodded. "All I've got tomorrow is McGregor. Everything else can wait."

"That works for my producer," Sampson said when Jameson came back on the line. "Shall I have him call your press secretary to work out the details? Good. I'll make sure they talk." There was a short pause. "Yes, I know this has been terribly difficult for you and your family. I'm sorry for your loss." Another pause. "Yes, I'm looking forward to seeing you too, Deputy Mayor. Thank you for your time."

He hung up the phone.

"Now that wasn't too difficult, was it?" Sampson said as he reached for his suit jacket. "Well, I'm out of time and must go."

"Have we missed anything?" Ethan said imploringly as he glanced at Mindy and David.

"We need to go over the production schedule," Mindy said helpfully.

"Ah, you're full of surprises, Ms. Herman," Sampson said, a gleam in his eye. "You just reminded me of one last thing we need to talk about before I head off to my cocktail party. I can't do any shooting until after Labor Day. I start vacation next week and will be out at my weekend house in East Hampton for the rest of the summer. I'm open to doing an occasional meeting, but you'll have to drive out to me. I won't be back in the city until after the holiday."

"But Paul's thinking of running our story in the middle of September," Ethan said, dumbstruck. "When will we schedule the field work? How will we get ready for the interviews? Where will we write and edit the story if you're not here?"

"Those are your problems, not mine," Sampson said, pushing his chair away from his desk. "You figure out some way to get me ready for production and then let me know how you plan to do it."

Ethan stared at Sampson, furious, knowing he was fighting a losing battle. "Okay, Peter, I'll talk to Consuela and schedule a trip out to East Hampton when you're not too busy. That way we can at least keep the story moving forward."

"Good. Glad we've cleared that up." Then Sampson buttoned his suit jacket and hurried out the door—stopping briefly to check in with Consuela—before vanishing down the long red hallway and onto an elevator.

"Jeez, that was much worse than I expected," Mindy said, aggravated.

"Yeah, Peter's pretty pompous and self-centered," Ethan said soberly. "But I gotta give him credit, he knows much more about this story than I thought. We should be okay if we keep him in the loop and don't let him get to us."

"But how are we gonna make the airdate if he won't work until after the holiday?"

"I'll figure it out," Ethan said, sounding more confident than he felt. "Look, I'm goin' to McGlades for a quick drink before heading home. You guys wanna join me?"

"I'll take a pass," Mindy said.

"Me too," David said. "I need to call the deputy mayor's press secretary and make a plan for our meeting."

"So I guess I'm drinking by myself," Ethan said, disappointed. "See you in the morning." Then he hopped on an elevator and rode down to the lobby, crossed Fifty-Seventh Street, and headed straight to the bar for one quick pop to take off the edge.

That's all he needed.

Or so he thought.

CHAPTER 9

ETHAN LAY SPRAWLED ON A loveseat, his feet propped on a well-worn ottoman, staring at Sarah still snuggled under the covers sound asleep. Closing his eyes, he rubbed his temple, his nerves frayed, his head pounding like a bass drum. His quick drink at McGlades had turned into a marathon, one shot of scotch after another, until he'd staggered home three sheets to the wind, well after Sarah had turned in for the night. Standing, he headed to the bathroom, flipped on the lights, and looked at his reflection in the mirror. His face was drawn, his eyes bloodshot. After popping a couple of Motrin, he brushed his teeth and climbed into the shower.

Feeling better, he toweled off and slowly got dressed.

Sarah began to stir, and he sat down beside her, stroking her hair, gently kissing the nape of her neck. She purred softly. "What time is it, Ethan?" she said, rolling over on her side.

"Almost eight. I gotta leave in a couple of minutes. Mindy and David are meeting me in the lobby. We're scheduled to preinterview the deputy mayor and his wife in about an hour."

"What time did you get home last night?" she said, rubbing the sleep from her eyes. "I didn't hear you come in."

"Sometime after midnight."

"Were you working at the office?"

Ethan hesitated—too ashamed to tell her the truth. "Yeah. I was blocking out story elements and putting together the production budget." He hated lying but knew she'd be furious if she found out he'd spent the night getting drunk at a bar. He quickly changed the subject, hoping she wouldn't smell the alcohol on his breath or see the anguish in his eyes. "What's your day look like, babe?"

Sarah yawned—still not fully awake. "I'm dropping Luke off at Brad's apartment before I go to the office. His mom's taking the boys to Jones Beach, and the four of us are planning to have dinner when they get back. I'm assuming you're working late and can't join us?"

"Probably not. I'm making progress on my story but keep finding things that don't add up. Something's off, but I don't know what it is."

"Well, I'm sure you'll figure it out," she said, pouting. She draped her arms around his neck and flashed a seductive smile. "Got time for a quickie? Would be nice before you disappear again."

He kissed the end of her nose. "I only wish. Maybe when I get home tonight."

"You're no fun." She punched him playfully, then suddenly grew serious. "Ethan, I got a call from Nancy McGregor. She said she wants to have lunch today and catch up, but she sounded kinda funny on the telephone. Have you had your meeting with her yet?"

"No. I'm scheduled to see her this afternoon."

"What do you think she wants?" Sarah said, sitting up. "Do you think she's gonna ask me about your story again?"

"I hope not," he said, alarmed. "We still haven't locked in a date for her interview, and we've been asking her office for some evidence we can't find in all those documents she sent over, but I can't imagine that's a problem." He shifted uneasily on the bed, his instincts screaming. "Sarah, please be careful about what you tell her. I have no reason to suspect she's gonna bail on us, but don't say anything that might come back and haunt me."

"Come on, Ethan, you know me better than that," she said, smiling. "I promise not to give away any of your trade secrets." She crossed her heart. "Besides, Nancy's a friend, and I'm sure all she wants to hear about is Luke and what I've been doing all summer. Can't be more than that."

"Just be careful," he said, still worried McGregor had some ulterior motive. He reached for his pack of Marlboros and lit a cigarette. "Time to go. I gotta be at the deputy mayor's in half an hour," he said, leaning over and kissing her one last time.

"And Ethan, come straight home tonight."

"I will, babe."

"No McGlades?"

"No McGlades."

"Promise?"

"I promise I won't stop for a quick drink," he said, feeling guiltier about lying to her.

"Now go say good-bye to Luke," she said, burrowing under the covers.

Ethan grabbed his briefcase and headed to the kitchen where Luke was munching a bowl of cold cereal and watching cartoons. "Hey, little man, I hear you're going to the beach with Brad today. Listen to his mom and be careful in the waves."

"I will, Dad," he said, putting a spoonful of Honey Nut Cheerios into his mouth.

"And make sure Mom walks Holly before you leave. You won't forget, will you?"

"No way. Are you coming home early tonight?"

Ethan looked into his innocent eyes. "I don't know, Luke. I hope so."

"You gotta work, right? That's what Mom always says, but I thought I'd ask anyway." He went back to watching television. "Bye, Dad."

"Bye-bye, Luke," Ethan said, hovering a moment in the doorway, wishing he could spend more time with his son and more time with his wife. Life was just too damn short.

. . . . .

A butler was waiting as Ethan stepped off the elevator and into a lavish foyer leading into Bernard Jameson's multimillion-dollar penthouse on Fifth Avenue. He was wearing a formal black waistcoat, gray flannel pants, perfectly polished black shoes, a starched white shirt, and a fire-engine-red bowtie. Sneering, he introduced himself as Wendell and escorted Ethan down to a parlor bigger than his own living room before dashing out the door in search of the deputy mayor and his wife.

Jameson's press secretary was sitting at a formal seating area, frantically scribbling notes on an iPad. She immediately stood and walked over to greet him. "Ah, Mr. Benson, I'm Sylvia Rosenberg. I see you've met Wendell. He intimidates a lot of people, and so does this apartment," she said, jabbering away without taking a breath. "The Jamesons are megarich and have no problem flaunting it. I'm sure you've read about them in all the best magazines, especially since their daughter's murder," she continued, wheeling around to face Mindy, who was standing right behind Ethan. "And who is this, may I ask?"

"My associate producer, Mindy Herman," Ethan said.

"Pleasure to meet you," the press secretary said, shaking hands. "And I need no introduction to your researcher. David and I have already spent gobs of time together working on your story. Nice to see you again, Mr. Livingston."

Ethan listened, trying to be polite, as Rosenberg droned on about Jameson's vast business empire and extensive portfolio of real estate holdings. Mercifully, her monologue was cut short by the sound of footsteps bouncing off the marble floors as Bernard and Sandy Jameson slowly made their way into the parlor. The deputy mayor's arm was draped around his wife's waist—providing moral support—as she held a lace handkerchief to wipe away tears welling up in her eyes.

"You must be the producer that Peter Sampson told me about yesterday," Jameson said, staring warmly at Ethan. "As you can see, Sandy's had a tough morning. Your visit has brought up a lot of memories, some good, some not so good. She'll be better in a little while."

"I'm sorry for your loss, Mrs. Jameson," Ethan said, trying to find something comforting to say. "I can't imagine what you and your family are going through."

"Thank you, Mr. Benson." She patted her eyes with the handkerchief. "I'm still trying to cope with Cynthia's murder. She was such a wonderful daughter. I miss her all the time." She slumped into an overstuffed Victorian couch, disappearing into the cushions.

Ethan introduced Mindy and David, and they sat down around an antique coffee table, Wendell the butler asking if anybody wanted tea or coffee.

"Just bring a full service for everybody and make sure to serve some fruit and those wonderful pastries we bought this morning," Mrs. Jameson said, sniffling.

The deputy mayor gently squeezed her hand. "I'm not sure where to begin, Mr. Benson. I was hoping we could talk about Cynthia and what this senseless murder has done to our family and to all the citizens of this great city."

Ethan thought he sounded more like a politician than a father, his words measured, his tone insincere. Maybe he was already running for mayor. "Mr. Jameson, why don't you describe your daughter to me?"

The deputy mayor took a deep breath. "Cynthia was my pride and joy, bright and inquisitive, strong and sensitive. She was a sophomore at Columbia University—an honor student studying political science. She wanted to follow in my footsteps and go into public service after graduation." He paused, looking off into the distance. "I still can't believe she's been taken from us in such a senseless way. It's tragic. Just tragic."

Ethan waited patiently, and when he realized the deputy mayor had nothing more to say, turned to his wife. "What can you tell me about your daughter, Mrs. Jameson?"

"She was a beautiful young woman, and we were close. Very close. We went to the theater and to the opera. We attended parties and benefits and ate at all the best restaurants. And we traveled around the world together—just the two of us—to Europe, Asia, and South America. Oh, I still can't believe she's gone." Her eyes became red and puffy as tears flowed down her cheeks.

"Now, now, dear," Jameson said soothingly. "I know this is difficult for you."

She stared into her husband's eyes pleadingly, then back at Ethan. "You have to understand, Mr. Benson, we had no secrets with Cynthia. She always confided in us. Both of us. And she loved her little sister and brother, Susan and Ned, more than you can imagine. She did everything with them. It's such a loss for all of us." Her voice trailed off as she sank deeper into the sofa.

"Mrs. Jameson, would you like a moment before we go on?" Ethan said, handing her a box of tissues from the coffee table.

"No. No. I'm okay. Really." She blew her nose.

"Then maybe you can show us your family photos," Ethan said, trying to move the meeting forward. "We need to paint a visual picture of your daughter, and Ms. Rosenberg has told David we could take the photos back to our office when we leave today."

"How many will you need?" the deputy mayor said.

"As many as you'll share with us," Ethan said. "We're planning to run a very long story, and the only way for our audience to fully understand how difficult this has been for you and your family is to see Cynthia during the happier times in her life."

"Do you want pictures of Susan and Ned, too?" Sandy said.

"We need all of you—a full set of portraits of your family— of Cynthia growing up, going to school, playing with her brother and sister. Pictures that show Cynthia and your family during special occasions that are meaningful to you."

"And you want them today?" Sandy said, sounding surprised.

"That would be very helpful," Ethan said resolutely. "We'll make copies and get them back to you as soon as we can."

"I don't see any problem with giving them the photos, Bernard, do you?" she said, turning to her husband, waiting for a reaction.

"No. You can take whatever you want, Mr. Benson."

"We'd also like some of your home videos," David said. "The same kinds of moments."

"That won't be a problem either," the deputy mayor said quietly.

Wendell walked back into the parlor holding a silver tray with the refreshments. He placed it on the table next to a single red tulip sitting in a small crystal vase.

"Please serve everybody," Sandy said, composing herself. "Then go into the library and bring back a good selection of photo albums and home movies. You know which ones are my favorites."

"Yes, Mrs. Jameson, right away." He poured coffee and tea and paraded out of the room.

"Thank you," Ethan said, turning to the deputy mayor. "I have another question for you, Mr. Jameson. Why was Cynthia in the Meatpacking District the night she was murdered? I've read accounts in the newspapers and recently asked Edward Jenkins, the lead detective on the case, about it. But as her father, maybe you can fill me in on what she was doing down there." Ethan paused, reading the pained expression on the deputy mayor's face. "I know this isn't easy, but I've walked around that neighborhood. Some of the streets are pretty sketchy."

"We keep asking ourselves that question," Jameson said quietly, his voice quavering as he struggled with his emotions. "She was dating a nice young man at the time—a student named Jacob Lutz who she met in one of her classes at Columbia. We liked Jacob very much. He was from a good family, a wealthy family— his father's in textiles, if I remember correctly. Anyway, Cynthia went down to the Meatpacking District that night with a group of friends to celebrate the end of midterm exams, and then she met Jacob for a late dinner at the Standard Grill. It's a popular steakhouse with the young crowd."

"Did she go there often with Jacob?" Ethan said as he tried to reconcile the deputy mayor's account of the evening with what he'd read in the research.

"I'm not really sure," the deputy mayor said. "All I know is they were there that night, and that Jacob left the restaurant without my daughter at about one in the morning to get some sleep. He wants to be a lawyer and had an early meeting with his college adviser the next day. He told us he kissed Cynthia goodnight, left her sitting alone at the bar, and headed back to his apartment in Morningside Heights. When we called and told him she'd been murdered, he was devastated."

Ethan pulled on his lower lip reflectively. "What did Cynthia do for the two hours she was alone? Do you have any idea? The police say she wasn't murdered until sometime around three a.m."

"It gets a bit fuzzy at this point. The bartender remembers her talking to a few people, maybe having a drink or two, and then leaving by herself just before the gunshots. He says he thought it was a car backfiring and that he didn't realize what had happened until he heard the police sirens." The deputy mayor's voice trailed off, hot anger spreading across his face. "Cynthia was in the wrong place at the wrong time and paid for it with her life. That madman Pavel Feodor shot her down like a dog. Murdered her for no good reason." He paused and took a deep breath. "Mr. Benson, this is very difficult for me and my wife. Do you have any more questions? I'm not sure we can talk about my daughter any longer."

"Nothing else that can't wait," Ethan said consolingly. "We can stop if you'd like. You've been very generous with your time."

"Thank you, but I do have one last question before you leave, Mr. Benson."

"Please, call me Ethan."

"Okay, Ethan. I've been hearing from the district attorney's office that you're planning to interview Pavel Feodor."

"Yes. We're working on the logistics and ground rules."

"So let me ask you. Why in God's name do you want to put that piece of scum on television? My wife and I find it very disturbing that you're planning to give him any airtime at all. We just don't understand what the world gains from listening to someone who's so blatantly evil."

Ethan sensed he was treading in delicate waters and didn't want to upset the deputy mayor or his wife or give them any reason to back out of the interview. "I think it's important journalistically," he said, choosing his words carefully. "Pavel Feodor reached out to us through his attorney and says he has new information about what really happened that night, and to me, it's important for our viewers to hear what he has to say. I know he's been found guilty and is about to be sentenced, but he didn't take the stand during his trial and has never talked publicly about the murder. Maybe he's finally ready to open up and bare his soul." He looked from the deputy mayor to his wife. "And I promise you we won't just ask him softball questions or give him an opportunity to make excuses. We'll be tough on him. I'll make sure of that."

"Fair enough," the deputy mayor said cordially. "I can't say I agree with you, but I understand your reasoning."

"Is there anything else you'd like to talk about?" Ethan said.

"No. That was the one thing my wife and I were most worried about."

"Anything else we need to go over, Mindy?"

"Just one more thing," Mindy said, turning to Sylvia Rosenberg. "We were hoping to say hello to Ned and Susan while we were here today. Have you had a chance to discuss this with the deputy mayor and his wife?"

"We've been talking about it all morning," Rosenberg said. "What do you think, Mrs. Jameson? Are the kids up for it?"

"No, not today," Sandy said, sighing. "Susan's still having a tough time getting over Cynthia's death, and Ned has withdrawn into a shell and won't tell us what he's thinking or feeling. My husband and I are more worried about him than our daughter." She grabbed the deputy mayor's hand for support. "We'll make a decision when you come back with your cameras. Maybe then you can meet them."

"I understand," Ethan said as they all stood up. "Thanks for your time this morning. You've been very helpful. I have a much better sense of how you're doing and how to plan the questions for your interview."

"And thank you, Ethan," the deputy mayor said, once again sounding like a politician. "Please say hello to Peter Sampson for me. It was very kind of him to call yesterday. We're both looking forward to seeing him at the interview." Jameson smiled broadly, then spun around to his press secretary. "Sylvia, give Mr. Benson a quick tour of the apartment and help him pick a shooting location. Make sure to show him the great room. That might be perfect for his cameras. And Ethan, don't forget Wendell is gathering the family photos and home videos. Take whatever you want."

Then the deputy mayor walked out of the parlor, his arm resting on his wife's shoulder as he led her through the apartment and up a majestic staircase to the living quarters. Ethan thought they looked broken, unable to move beyond the tragedy that had irrevocably changed their lives, and tried putting himself in their place, wondering how he'd feel if he somehow lost Luke in a random act of violence. Trembling ever so slightly, he followed the press secretary down a long hallway and into the great room.

CHAPTER 10

TWO HOURS LATER, ETHAN WAS sitting in a yellow cab on the FDR Drive, heading to his meeting with Nancy McGregor at the Manhattan District Attorney's office. The traffic was at a standstill, a car having flipped over at Forty-Second Street, its front end smashed like an accordion, its tires shredded like confetti. Nobody had been seriously injured—the passengers stood about surveying the damage as police cars and tow trucks slowly inched their way through the sea of humanity crawling along the highway. "Who's meeting us when we get to the DA's office?" Ethan said, craning his neck as they approached the scene of the accident.

"My contact, Nelson Brown," David said, checking the time. "He works with McGregor and is in charge of all the evidence in the case."

"Is he the guy you've been calling about the crime scene photos and the ballistics report?"

"He's the guy."

"And so far, no luck?"

"No luck."

"I'll make sure to ask McGregor," Ethan said, making a mental note not to forget. "Where we linking with this guy?"

"In front of the building. He wants to escort us up to Homicide on the ninth floor and personally introduce us to the ADA."

The taxi snaked its way through the chaos, exiting at Fourteenth Street, then weaved through a series of side streets until it reached One Hogan Place and the entrance to the building. Ethan climbed out, paid the twenty dollars on the meter, and gave the driver a handsome tip for making good time. "Do you see Nelson Brown?" he said, gesturing to David.

"He's coming down the steps," David said, pointing to a portly man dressed in a rumpled blue suit, white shirt, and yellow tie who was racing toward them, a grin on his face.

"You must be Ethan Benson," Brown said, thrusting out his hand.

"Yes. And this is my associate producer, Mindy Herman. And of course, you know David."

"Indeed, I do," he said, pushing his eyeglasses up his nose. "Nancy told me to bring you up through the freight entrance. That's where you'll bring your equipment when you do her interview. Follow me. It's not too far." He led them around the massive sixteen-story structure, occupying an entire city block and housing more than five hundred attorneys, to a loading dock in the back of the building. Above the massive double doors, emblazoned on a bronze plaque, were the words: "Justice is the firm and continuous desire to render to each man the due process of the law." Ethan wondered if the same principle had been applied to Pavel Feodor. After meeting the lead detective and the public defender, he was having his doubts. Maybe the case would look different after he sat down with McGregor.

Maybe.

Brown flashed his ID, and a security guard waved them into the building. They hustled down a winding corridor with no doors and windows until they reached a bank of elevators.

"This is perfect," Ethan said, gesturing back down the hallway. "There are no stairs, and it's just a short run from the loading dock."

"Will there be a lot of equipment and a big crew, besides you guys?" Brown said, ringing for an elevator.

"Not too big," Ethan said. "Two cameramen, two soundmen, a grip to help with the equipment, maybe a lighting director, my anchorman, Peter Sampson, and of course, the cameras, audio decks, and lighting gear."

"Sounds big to me. You'll need a large space to do the interview," Nelson said, rubbing his chin. "Nancy's office won't work. It's too small and cluttered. But there's a good-sized law library just down the hall from her. Rows of red and green books, cherry paneling, and beautiful tan leather chairs."

"That might work," Ethan said.

"I'll show you after the meeting," Brown said as an elevator opened and they stepped in. "Nancy's in Suite 903. She's cleared the rest of her day for you. Time to go on up and meet her."

· · · · ·

The ADA was sitting at a long table in a conference room two doors down from her office surrounded by piles of papers and dozens of exhibits from the case. There was a bank of telephones, a fax machine, and a brand-new Xerox churning out documents. She stood up and walked over to Ethan, shaking his hand with a firm grip. "I'm Nancy McGregor, and welcome to our war room."

"I'm Ethan Benson, and this is my production team." He introduced Mindy and David. "Thanks for meeting with us this afternoon."

"It's all part of my job," she said, flashing a toothy smile. "You know, I had lunch with Sarah today, but I bet she already told you that. We talked about you and your family and what you've been doing all summer, but she was very protective about your story. I couldn't get one word out of her. Not one." She shook her finger and rolled her eyes. "Maybe I'll have more luck with you."

Ethan grinned.

McGregor was younger than he'd expected, not a day over thirty. She was petite, maybe five foot two and a hundred pounds, with long, silky-black hair pulled back in a ponytail and emerald green eyes that sparkled when she talked. She was dressed in a light-blue business suit, a cream-colored silk shirt, and beige high-heel shoes. "Shall we get started?" She motioned to the table, and they all took seats. "So Ethan, what do you plan to ask me in the interview?"

Ethan studied her countenance before answering. She seemed pleasant enough, at least on the surface, but her voice had a slight edge to it, direct and no-nonsense, like a seasoned courtroom litigator. "I can't give you the questions," he said. "That's against company policy. But I put together a list of bullet points that'll give you a pretty good idea of the topics I hope to cover."

He slid the document across the table.

McGregor put on her reading glasses, glanced at the two pages, then looked up at Ethan. "This seems pretty straightforward to me. The topics are all about what happened the night of the murder, the police investigation, and the trial. I sent you the case documents. So I'm sure your interview will be based on the evidence. What about Cynthia and her parents? Are you going to ask me about them?"

"Bullet points sixteen and seventeen," Ethan said, gesturing to the memo.

"Yes. Of course. Must've missed them," McGregor said, removing her glasses. "I hope you ask lots of questions about the Jamesons. Cynthia was a lovely girl, so sweet and innocent, and they're such a tight-knit family." Her voice trailed off as if she were feeling their pain. "They've suffered so much since her murder, and your story, if it's handled the right way, might ease some of their anguish. Have you met the deputy mayor and his wife yet?"

"We spent the morning with them," Mindy said, speaking for the first time. "They were very broken up about the murder, but nonetheless, very gracious."

McGregor smiled, shifting her eyes from Mindy to Ethan. "I knew you'd like them. They're very outgoing—warm and loving—in spite of everything they've been through. What about the kids. Did you get to meet Ned and Susan?"

"Not this morning," Ethan said. "We're hoping to include them in our story, but we'll have to see how they're doing when we go back to shoot the interview."

"I hope you have better luck than I did," McGregor said reflectively. "I only met them once or twice and couldn't convince either Bernard or Sandy to let me put them on the stand. The trial was just too big a media circus. In the end it didn't matter. The evidence against Feodor was so overwhelming; I got my conviction without needing their testimony." She paused, straightening a stack of papers on the table before abruptly changing the subject. "So Ethan, have you gotten through all the documents I sent you? Do you have everything you need?"

"I've read most of the docket and think we're in pretty good shape, but we are missing a few things."

"I can't imagine what," McGregor said. "I had Nelson send you everything I thought was important."

Ethan hesitated a moment, trying to read the stony expression on her face. "Well, first off," he said, "I don't seem to have the ballistics report. I need a copy to show my audience how you tied the bullet that killed Cynthia to Feodor's gun."

"We didn't send you the ballistics report? Must be an oversight," McGregor said impetuously as she turned to Brown. "Get them a copy right away, Nelson. Anything else, Ethan?"

"I don't have all of Pavel's confession," he said, grabbing his copy from his briefcase and showing it to the ADA. "I've gone through the transcript very carefully. Your detectives did a great job, but big sections have been blacked out, and there's a page missing—page 71. Any way I can get a clean copy?"

McGregor shot Brown another quick glance, then turned back to Ethan. "We sent you the same copy we entered into evidence. All we did was clean up references to crosstalk and extraneous sounds to make the transcript easier to follow. I explained that in court, and the judge signed off without a problem."

"That's what Frankie O'Malley told me when I met him the other day, but I'd like to read an unedited version, if that's possible," Ethan said in his most persuasive voice.

"I don't see any harm in giving them a clean copy, do you?" McGregor said, shifting her eyes back to Nelson Brown. "We gave one to O'Malley. Send it along with the ballistics report."

"And what about the videotape? Can I get a copy of that, too?"

McGregor hesitated, nervously tearing at the corner of a file folder she was holding. "I can't release that to you, Ethan. I didn't enter the raw video into evidence and never showed it to the jury. So it's not part of the public record. But I sent you the short clip I played in court. You should have a copy of that."

"Do we have it?" Ethan said, peering at David.

"No. I haven't found it."

"Another oversight," she said, waving her hand. "Send that over as well, Nelson."

"But why can't you give me the full confession?" Ethan said, turning back to the ADA. "The public defender told me it was okay with him if you gave me a copy. Is there any reason to keep it from the public now that Feodor's been convicted?"

McGregor stared at Ethan suspiciously. "Maybe not. I'll have to discuss it with my staff. Get back to us in a couple of days, and I'll let you know what we decide," McGregor said as her iPhone pinged. "It's the district attorney." She paused and read the email. "He wants to meet right away about the sentencing. So I'm afraid I've got to go. Any more questions?"

"Only one," Ethan said levelly, "and it happens to be about the sentencing."

"Shoot," McGregor said as she began stuffing documents into a folder.

"Frankie O'Malley told me that the district attorney has been talking to the governor about reinstating the death penalty for the Feodor case and that you've been pushing very hard to make that happen." Ethan paused and watched as the ADA's lower lip began to quiver. "Is that what you're about to discuss with him?"

McGregor tensed. "I'm not going down that road," she said frostily. "That's for the district attorney and the governor and maybe the state legislature to decide, not me. But if you want my opinion, I think Pavel Feodor is the worst kind of predator. He murdered that poor girl in cold blood and shows no remorse. None whatsoever. There's no doubt in my mind that spending the rest of his life behind bars is too good for him. He needs to be put to death for his crime—pure and simple. That's what I believe. And that's what I hope happens."

Ethan paused, stunned by the hatred in the ADA's eyes. Why

had her mood suddenly shifted so dramatically? Why had she become so vehement? Was he missing something? "You know, I've read the police reports and a good portion of the trial transcript," he said, "and I know Pavel Feodor has a long rap sheet of violence, but that doesn't make his case any different from all the other murders that take place in this city. Why do you want to execute him? Is it because the victim is the deputy mayor's daughter?"

"Of course not," McGregor said, still agitated. "If you look at the crime scene photos of Cynthia's angelic face, at her lifeless body, at the torrents of blood soaking her clothes and covering her skin, then you'd understand my reaction and why I believe he deserves the ultimate punishment."

"But I don't have those pictures," Ethan said softly, trying to diffuse the tension growing in the room. "All you sent me were wide shots. Maybe if I could see some close-ups of her body, some images that show what Pavel Feodor actually did to her, I'd understand why you feel so strongly that he deserves to be put to death."

"Not gonna happen," McGregor said firmly. "I've sent you all the images I'm willing to release. I don't want the public—or the deputy mayor's kids for that matter—seeing the more graphic pictures of Cynthia. I won't take that risk, and neither will the deputy mayor."

Ethan stared at the anger in McGregor's face and decided to back off. She wasn't going to change her mind. She wasn't going to give him the crime scene photos with all the blood—just as Frankie O'Malley had warned him. "I understand," he said reassuringly. "I'll go with the pictures I have to describe the murder and use documents to explain your position on the death penalty. And I'll do it tastefully to protect the deputy mayor's family. You can trust me, Ms. McGregor. I'll make it work."

"Good," she said, her iPhone buzzing back to life. "It's the district attorney again. I can't keep him waiting any longer. It was a pleasure meeting you, Ethan. Let me know when you're coming back with Peter Sampson, and I'll work you into my schedule. I'm more than happy to sit down and do the interview with him. I think your story is important, and I want to be part of it." She smiled and shook everybody's hand. "If you need anything else, anything at all, don't hesitate to call."

. . . . .

Ethan accompanied Nelson Brown to the law library with its rows of books and fancy furniture, told him the room was perfect for the interview, then rode the elevator down to the lobby where David and Mindy were waiting.

"That went well," Mindy said, a little too loudly. "But she sure got flustered when you asked her about the death penalty. Why'd you put her on the defensive like that?"

"Not here. Too many people. Somebody from her office might overhear us." Walking out of the building, they headed west on Hogan Place until they reached the No. 4 subway. "You're right, I was a bit too hard on McGregor at the end of the meeting, but I had to find out just how willing she is to continue helping us with our story."

"But she promised to give us almost everything we're missing," Mindy said quizzically.

"True," Ethan said knowingly. "But I think she's finished cooperating with us—except for the interview."

"Why? Do you think she's hiding something?" she said, tilting her head.

"Maybe."

"What could she be hiding?"

"I don't know yet. But we need to find out."

"Jeez, Ethan, you said the same thing after we met with

Jenkins," Mindy said, connecting the dots. "Think they're working together—trying to cover up something?"

"That would sure throw a monkey wrench into our story, wouldn't it?" Ethan said, intrigued.

"So how do we prove any of this?" she said warily.

"First, when you get back to the office, check in with your sources at the NYPD and see if there's anything going on between McGregor and Jenkins beyond the case. Then ride Nelson Brown and make sure he sends us the documents McGregor just promised us. Let's see if they cooperate."

"And what do you want me to do, Ethan?" David said eagerly.

"I want you to start digging into Fernelli's Beef and Poultry, find out if there's a connection between the company and the murder, and if Jenkins or maybe McGregor swept it under the rug."

"And what're you gonna do, Ethan?" Mindy said as they climbed into a taxi.

"I'm gonna take the night off and spend some quality time with my family. I need to get away from our story and relax. Maybe then something inspirational will pop into my head and I'll figure out what we're missing here."

CHAPTER 11

ETHAN SCOOTED DOWN THE red hallway and up to Monica's desk feeling rested and motivated after spending a leisurely evening at home with Sarah and Luke. He hadn't been tempted to hide in his study or lose himself in the court docket, not even for a moment, and had somehow withstood his craving for a glass of scotch that had pounded every square inch of his body from the second he'd walked into his apartment. Maybe Sarah was right. Maybe it was time to stay away from the bottle. Time to stay sober.

"Is Paul free for a minute?" he said, peeking into the executive producer's office through the half-open door.

Monica didn't look up from a crossword puzzle. "He's busy. He's going over the fall programming with Lenny."

"Well, I need to see him about the Feodor story."

"Can it wait? His morning's all booked up. I can schedule you in sometime this afternoon," she said, continuing to work on the puzzle.

"I need to see him right away," he said, smiling as he pushed his way past her desk and into Paul's office.

Lang was sitting at a table near the window reading a script, his expression tense, his body rigid, as his senior producer stood at a large metal board moving story ideas around in the schedule. Ethan pulled up a chair and waited patiently, watching Paul cross out sentences, trim sound bites, and slash airtime with the precision of a master architect wielding a red pencil to the blueprint of a carefully designed floor plan. "We need to talk," he said, interrupting the heavy silence.

"Indeed, we do," Paul said frostily as he neatly placed the script on the table. "What's happening with your story? You were supposed to brief Lenny every day on your progress, but he hasn't seen you in quite some time. Why is that, Ethan?"

"I've been busy," Ethan said calmly, "slugging my way through the court documents and preinterviewing characters. I've already met with the lead detective, the prosecutor, the public defender, and the deputy mayor, and they've all agreed to go on camera. Mindy's working on a schedule, and we hope to begin the field production soon."

"Does Peter know?" Lenny said as he pulled up a chair next to Ethan.

"I've been updating him on a regular basis," Ethan said, turning to Paul. "I'm planning to meet him in East Hampton later in the week and go over everything."

"How do you plan to convince him to shoot with you?" Paul said stonily. "He doesn't want to interrupt his vacation."

"Haven't figured that out yet, but I'll twist his arm somehow," Ethan said confidently.

"You better," Paul said, glancing back at the script. "I'm still planning to run your story in September." He crossed out another line of narration. "Is there anything else I should know about?"

"I've found some inconsistencies in the police investigation and am missing a couple of key documents," Ethan said earnestly.

"But I'm not sure it means anything, so at the moment, I'm still planning to produce the same story we've been talking about."

"Good. I knew you could do it if you put your mind to it," Paul said sarcastically. "Now I have an update for you on the Feodor interview. The district attorney and the warden have both approved my request to bring cameras into Rikers Island." He glanced smugly at Ethan. "So you see, I took care of it—just as I said I would at our first meeting. All you need to do is lock in a shooting date."

"Well, I hate to burst your bubble, Paul," Ethan said, unruffled. "But we still have a problem that could scuttle the interview."

"What problem?" Paul said as he doodled nervously on the script. "I thought I just solved our last problem."

"Not quite. When I met the public defender, Frankie O'Malley, he said in no uncertain terms that the interview isn't a slam dunk, that Pavel Feodor wants a face-to-face meeting with me at Rikers Island before he fully commits. And if he likes me and the direction I'm taking the story, then and only then will he do the interview with us."

"Are you telling me we might lose Pavel Feodor? Maybe to another network?" Paul said, alarmed.

"No. I'm not saying that, Paul," Ethan said, trying to put a positive spin on the problem. "I'm just saying that I have to figure out a way to make sure he doesn't back out at the last minute."

"How're you gonna do that?" Lenny said, concerned.

"I'm gonna use a little charm and grace and tell him honestly what I hope to report about the murder and his case."

"And what if that doesn't work?" Paul said.

"Then I may need to throw him a bone," Ethan said cleverly. "What are you willing to offer him, Paul, to sweeten the deal?"

Paul tapped his fingers on the table, then looked up at Ethan. "I don't wanna lose this interview. It's way too important for the show. Tell Feodor we'll give him a big block of airtime—the entire hour of programming—and that we'll make his story a special edition of *The Weekly Reporter*."

"That should work," Ethan said, pleased.

"When are you meeting him?"

"This afternoon. That's why I barged in here unannounced. I needed new marching orders before heading out to Rikers."

Paul cracked a wry smile. "So now everything's riding on your shoulders, just like you wanted, Ethan. So don't fuck things up. Convince that little bastard to do the interview. The show's depending on you, and, I'm afraid, so am I."

. . . . .

Ethan sat next to Frankie O'Malley in his Porsche Carrera as it cruised through a warren of side streets in Astoria, Queens, searching for the Francis R. Buono Memorial Bridge that connected civilization to the Rikers Island jail complex. "If you don't know where you're going," O'Malley said hauntingly, "there's absolutely no way to find this stinking place. It's as if the city wants to hide the refuse of society where they can lock the door and throw away the key."

"That hardly applies to your client," Ethan said, checking the directions on Google Maps. "Everybody knows who he is and what he did, and everybody's waiting to see how the court's gonna punish him. He's undoubtedly the most infamous killer in the country."

"And that's one of the reasons you're meeting him today," the public defender said. "We're hoping that once you talk to him, you'll walk away with a different take on his crime so you can help us change his public image. Just wait and you'll see. He's not the monster the press and the prosecutor have made him out to be."

Ethan smiled, remembering Feodor's long rap sheet of violence. "Take a left at the next corner," he said. "The bridge is just up ahead."

O'Malley turned and approached the first security checkpoint. A large sign hung across the road warning the public it was entering the largest house of detention in the nation. Ethan stared at the ten buildings looming in the distance, dark and ominous, that housed more than fourteen thousand inmates on an island in the East River surrounded by a fifteen-foot-high chain-link fence topped with razor wire.

It looked like the set of a horror movie.

The last place Ethan wanted to go.

After being waved through by a police officer, they pulled onto the three-lane bridge behind a line of cars and inched their way to the main gate and a second security checkpoint where a tall, heavyset corrections officer sporting the body of a weightlifter walked up and peered into the driver's-side window. "Identification, please."

O'Malley showed him their driver's licenses, and the officer ran down their names on a computer printout. Then he circled the car, never taking his eyes off either one of them. "The warden's waiting for you at the Visitor's Center," he said when he got back to O'Malley. "Drive through the gate and follow the road until you get to the red brick building on the right with all the windows."

Five minutes later, they pushed through a revolving door and into a noisy vestibule jammed with dozens of people waiting to be admitted to the cellblocks. They were greeted by a painfully thin Hispanic woman with long, curly brown hair and a short, squat man who was balder than a cue ball. "Frankie, good to see you again. And you must be Ethan Benson," the bald man said. "I'm Jose Morales, the warden here at Rikers Island, and this is Gloria Jimenez, my chief of public affairs."

"It's a pleasure," Ethan said enthusiastically. "I'm glad you had time to see me today."

"Oh, more than happy to oblige you," Morales said, vigorously shaking Ethan's hand. "Let's go sit for a few minutes and chat about the dos and don'ts at the prison. Then I'll send you down to the North Infirmary Command Building with Ms. Jimenez so you can meet Pavel Feodor."

. . . . .

Pavel was sprawled on a dirty mattress in an eight-by-ten-foot cell, his eyes fixed on the peeling paint as he desperately tried to block out the screaming bouncing around the cinderblock walls of his cellblock. It was a loud, horrific wailing, followed by brutal moaning, and then chilling silence. Standing, he paced around his cell, wondering who'd been beaten and which gang was sending a message and to whom. He'd been imprisoned like a caged animal in the North Infirmary Command Building since his arrest—first in the hospital wing where addicts, psych patients, and victims of the daily violence were taken and pieced back together, and then on H Block, where sex perverts, rapists, and notorious killers waited for trial and then to be sentenced.

Daylight was filtering into his cell through a small window below the ceiling as he peered into a mirror. His face was drawn and gaunt, his once-powerful physique frail and razor thin. *What's happenin' to me?* he thought despondently. *I'm wastin' away. Slowly disappearin'. Soon I'll be nothin'.* He slipped into an orange prison jumpsuit and looked at his watch. *I got less than an hour until my meeting with that producer from the television show. Should I cancel? Should I go through with it? Should I bail out of the interview?* Torn with self-doubt, he worried he was signing his own death warrant at the hands of some unknown assassin if he talked to the press. *Maybe I should wait and see what happens?* he thought, continuing to pace around his cell. *Maybe the judge will decide not to fry my sorry ass? Maybe he'll just give me a long prison sentence? Maybe I'm worryin' for no good reason? Shit. What the fuck should I do?*

Lunch was sitting on a dirty tray—two pieces of burned toast, a thin, watery soup, a mystery meat, and cold coffee. The food was inedible, but he was hungry and needed to keep up his strength. So he picked up a piece of toast and realized for the first time in his miserable life that after spending a year and a half in this hellhole he was scared—really scared. *Christ, they're gonna do it. They're gonna execute me and send me straight to hell. I know it, and I can't let that happen. Can't. Can't. Can't.* Growing more agitated, he hurled the toast against the wall, sat back down on his bed, and waited.

He didn't wait long.

Three heavily armed prison guards pushed through the security door and onto H Block, rapping their nightsticks on the bars as they slowly made their way down the long corridor and over to his cell. One of the officers, a small, slightly built man named Jimmy Benito, pointed his nightstick at Pavel's head and grinned a toothless grin. "Well, well, well, look at what we have here. Our most infamous inmate—our pint-sized punk—who murdered that sweet, tasty little girl just for the fun of it."

"Fuck off, Benito. I'm not up for your bullshit today. Just cuff me and take me down to the visitors' room. I don't wanna be late for my meeting."

Benito raked his nightstick back and forth across the bars, the yelling and screaming on the cellblock suddenly grinding to a halt as the other inmates waited to see what would happen next.

"Oh, we're the tough guy today," he said unmercifully. "Maybe you won't act like such a big shot when they dust off the needle and shoot you full of poison."

Pavel stared into the guard's face, wondering if he was about to be beaten. Then he cautiously backed away as Jimmy Benito unlocked the door, walked into his cell, and jammed the nightstick up against his throat.

Nobody moved.

Nobody said a word.

Then Benito viciously kicked the tray of food—the coffee splashing the walls, the mystery meat rolling under the bed, the soup splattering the floor. "Whoops, guess I got a bit careless, Pavel," he said with a snigger. "You'll have to clean up the mess when you get back. Now turn around and put your fucking hands behind your back. You know the drill."

Pavel faced the wall, not moving a muscle, as Benito slapped on a set of manacles, chaining his hands and feet. "Okay, shithead, let's go. We don't want to keep your television producer waiting." Grabbing his collar, he shoved Pavel out of the cell—tripping the locking mechanism and sliding the door shut. "Now you listen up real good, you little fuck face. As the commanding officer here on H Block, I'm gonna start paying special attention to you now that the big boys are ready to draw and quarter you. Then, hopefully, I'll get to watch when they strap you onto that cold gurney, slip that needle into your skinny little arm, and put your stinking ass to death. Won't that be fun?" he said as he clubbed Pavel across his back with his nightstick.

Pavel winced in pain.

"I get it, Mr. Prison Guard. You're planning to take real good care of me, just like that guy they brought into the infirmary. Was it you or one of your goons who beat the living shit out of him?"

"I only wish," Benito said gleefully. "The guy was shanked in a knife fight by a couple of drug dealers who said he was a snitch. The doctors tried to put him back together, but they just couldn't stop all that blood gushing out of the gash that severed off half his face. Man, did my heart a world of good to see his life force drain out of his body and onto the floor."

"The guy's dead, isn't he?" Pavel said, knowing the truth.

Benito smiled. "Yeah, he bled out. That's one less asshole we have to worry about. Maybe next time it'll be you."

. . . . .

Ethan was sitting at a table in the visiting room between Frankie O'Malley and Gloria Jimenez when Pavel Feodor was dragged through the security door, his chains wound so tightly around his body he could barely put one foot in front of the next. They all stood as the prison guards pushed him into a chair bolted to the floor, secured a leather harness around his waist, and locked his hands and feet into steel restraints. "Jimmy, I want you to stay here in case our good friend decides to try something stupid," Jimenez said, motioning for the other two officers to step out of the room. Then she turned and faced Feodor. "But that's not gonna happen, is it, Pavel?"

Feodor glared back at her.

"I didn't think so," she said, smirking as she addressed Ethan. "This is unusual for us here at Rikers. We rarely let the press meet our inmates, and never in private. So you're gonna have to live with the security and the extra ears listening to your conversation. You have an hour. I suggest you get started."

Ethan nodded and stared at Feodor, unable to read the blank expression on his face. He hesitated, then carefully backed into his first question. "Thanks for seeing me today, Pavel. Your attorney says you want to hear about my story, so where would you like me to begin?"

"I got nothin' specific to ask you, Mr. Producer. Just want to listen to you talk." He smiled truculently and turned to O'Malley. "Light me a cigarette, Frankie. I'm bound so tight by these restraints, I can't even scratch my ass." O'Malley placed a Camel in his mouth and struck it with a match. "Now go ahead, Mr. Benson, talk to me," Pavel said, inhaling a drag of smoke.

"All right," Ethan said cautiously. "I'm producing a story about you, about Cynthia Jameson, and about the murder. It'll include a lot of pictures of the crime scene, a lot of hard news coverage of the investigation and trial, and several interviews with key people involved in your case."

"Are you interviewing my attorney?"

"Yes," Ethan said steadily.

"What about that prosecutor bitch, Nancy McGregor? Are you interviewing her as well?"

"She's a big part of my story."

"And the deputy mayor?"

"The deputy mayor and his wife, too. I can't leave them out. My audience is gonna want to know how they're feeling, how they're getting on with their lives now that you've murdered their daughter." Ethan abruptly stopped, seeing the disdain on Pavel's face. Was he getting angry? Was he losing him? Was he about to check out of the interview?

"Go on, Mr. Benson. I wanna hear more. Why do you wanna interview me? That's my biggest question."

Ethan didn't hesitate. "Because I'm a reporter, Pavel, and I tell all sides of a story, including yours. I want to hear about the heroin deal and the shootout and why you murdered Cynthia Jameson. And I want to hear it from you and not just from other people who think they know what happened." He paused, letting his words sink in. "And because, Pavel, this is your one and only chance to set the record straight."

Feodor glanced at his attorney and then back at Ethan. "You're pretty sure of yourself, aren't you, Mr. Benson? But how do I know you're gonna give me a fair shake? How do I know I can trust you?"

"Well, I can't tell you exactly what I'm gonna say, because I don't know all the facts yet. I'm still doing research and talking to a lot of people," Ethan said with conviction. "But I can promise you, I don't have an agenda or any preconceived notions, and am only looking for the truth. And the only way I can do that is if I hear from you. That's why I need your interview."

Feodor took another long drag on his cigarette. "Frankie, take the butt out of my mouth and light me another one." He turned his attention back to Ethan. "That doesn't answer my question, Mr. Benson. I don't give a shit what you say in your story. I only care what you say about me. How do I know you won't be like all those other fucking reporters who've been writing one lie after another about me? How can I be sure you won't say I'm some kind of sociopath—some kind of crazed killer— and make things worse?"

Ethan hesitated again, trying to decide how to proceed, then rolled the dice. "Look, I can't guarantee you what I'm gonna discover as I keep digging into your case, but I can promise you I'll be fair and accurate and balanced, and the best way to ensure that is for you to sit down with Peter Sampson. My boss thinks it's so important, he's willing to give you the full hour of programming."

"He'll commit the entire show to me and my interview?"

"That's what he told me this morning."

Feodor turned to his attorney. "What do you think, Frankie? Should I trust this guy?"

"I'm not so sure, Pavel." He glared stonily at Ethan. "I need a written contract guaranteeing that you'll give my client all that airtime and that you won't smear his name. That you'll report exactly what he says and not edit anything in his interview. Are you willing to put that down on paper, Mr. Benson?"

"I can't make those kinds of promises," Ethan said honestly. "You know that, Frankie."

"Well, then I can't agree to your interview. Either accept our ground rules or we're pulling out."

Ethan stared at the public defender, then pushed back his chair and stood up. "Guess I'm finished here," he said coldly. "Thanks for your time. There's nothing more to discuss."

"Hold on. Don't be so hasty," Feodor said haltingly. "I'm not sure I agree with my attorney. I like you, Benson. I think you have balls." He shifted his eyes to O'Malley. "Frankie, I'm runnin' the show here. Not you. So shut the fuck up and don't say another word." He gazed back at Ethan. "I'm gonna do your interview, Mr. Benson. I think you're gonna cut me a fair shake. So when do you wanna bring in your cameras?"

"Do you have a date in mind, Gloria?" Ethan said, relieved.

"The warden and I have discussed it," she said. "Next Friday at eleven o'clock. That gives us ten days to beef up security and get the jail ready for your crew. Does that give you enough time, Mr. Benson?"

"Won't be a problem for me, and what about you, Frankie?"

"If it's okay with Pavel, I guess it's okay with me," he said apprehensively.

"So we're all set," Ethan said, already worrying about how he was going to break the news to Peter Sampson.

"Then I think we're done here," Jimenez said, motioning to

Jimmy Benito, who was standing in the back of the room listening to every word. "Get the other guards and take Pavel back to his cell."

. . . . .

Frankie O'Malley climbed into his Porsche, grabbed his cell phone, and punched in a number. "Nikolai, it's me."

"Where are you?"

"I'm still at Rikers Island—in my car in the visitors' parking lot."

"Are you alone?"

"Yeah. Benson's still inside meeting with the warden and that bitch, Gloria Jimenez, from the press office."

"What happened with Feodor?"

"Pavel liked Benson and agreed to do the interview. He's gonna talk to Peter Sampson."

"That's not good, Frankie. You couldn't stop it?"

There was a long pause as the public defender lit a cigarette, his hands shaking uncontrollably. "I tried, Nikolai, really, but Pavel won't listen to me anymore."

"The *Pakhan*'s gonna be pissed when I tell him. What have you found out about Benson?"

"Only that's he's real good at what he does. Nothing else. So what are you gonna do, Nikolai?"

"I'm not sure yet. I need to know more about Benson."

"And what do you want me to do?" Frankie said nervously.

"Come up with a plan."

"What kind of plan?"

"Isn't that obvious, Frankie? Mull it over a little while and then get back to me."

The connection went dead.

Frankie dropped his cell phone on the passenger seat and

tossed his cigarette out the window. A single bead of sweat collected on his forehead, then slowly dripped down his cheek and onto his shirt. *What the fuck was Nikolai suggesting? What does he want me to do?* There was only one thing he could think of, and that, to Frankie O'Malley, was unimaginable.

He turned on the air conditioning and waited for Ethan.

Then he fumbled for another cigarette and began to panic.

CHAPTER 12

IT WAS AFTER ELEVEN WHEN Ethan opened the front door. His apartment was dark and oppressively quiet as he walked from one room to the next turning on the lights. Luke was asleep in his bedroom, Holly lying on the floor, thumping her tail like a pendulum. He reached down, stroked her head, and whispered, "Good girl, Holly. Good girl. Don't wake little Luke." Then he straightened the covers and quietly backed out of the room, glancing at his son one last time before searching for Sarah. He found her sitting on the couch in his study, surrounded by documents, a small lamp casting a narrow beam of light on her face. Her eyes were red and bleary, and he knew she'd been crying.

"Ethan, where have you been? I tried calling, but you didn't answer. I've been worried sick."

"I'm sorry, babe. I was at Rikers Island all afternoon meeting with Pavel Feodor. Then I had to go back to the office and brief Paul and Lenny. Tell them I'd ironed out the last details of the interview. You know what it's like. I couldn't get out of there."

"But I left you a half dozen messages. Why didn't you call me back?"

"Guess I lost track of time," Ethan said, feeling ashamed. He'd listened to her voice mails and knew she wanted to talk. Why hadn't he called her back? Had he been too busy? Too preoccupied with his story? Or was he worried she wanted to check on him and see if he was out drinking?

Sarah searched his face imploringly. "I just got off the phone with Mindy."

"You talked to Mindy?"

"Yeah," anger creeping into her voice. "She said you'd left the office hours ago. At dinnertime. Where'd you go, Ethan?"

He looked down at the floor.

"Did you go to McGlades?"

He heaved a deep sigh. "Yes. I stopped in for a couple of drinks. It was a long day."

"I don't care about your long day. Tell me. Are you drunk?"

"Maybe a little."

"Well, that's just great," she said furiously. "You promised me you wouldn't go back there, then you break your word and get drunk at that terrible place. Why'd you lie to me? I'm your wife, Ethan."

Ethan didn't know what to say. He just knew it was time for the truth.

"I'm sorry I didn't call, and I'm sorry about my drinking." He fumbled for a cigarette. "It's hard to explain, but I haven't been myself lately. I try putting on a front so everybody thinks I'm still this hotshot producer who slays dragons and gets to the truth, but I don't have the same confidence anymore. When I meet with Paul, he yells and screams and barks orders at me. It never used to bother me, but now I get sarcastic and combative and sometimes say things I shouldn't."

"Are you in trouble at the office?" she said worriedly.

"Maybe," he said, disheartened. "Paul put me on notice when I started the Feodor story."

"Was he serious?"

"I think so. He told me if I didn't get my act together, he'd fire me."

Sarah sat quietly, tucking her feet under her body, waiting for him to go on.

"His threat is one of the reasons I've been working so hard. I wanna prove to him I'm still the best producer on his staff. And I wanna prove to myself I can still do it."

"And that's why you're drinking so much?"

"One of the reasons. It helps me relax. It helps me forget. And it helps me sleep. I can't sleep anymore without the scotch."

Sarah leaned forward. "Ethan, why haven't you told me any of this? Why'd you hide it from me? I don't understand."

"I don't know, babe." He wiped a tear dripping down her cheek. "I guess I'm trying to figure it out myself, and I know there's no reason to feel the way I do, but I'm scared on the inside." He paused and looked into her eyes. "Sarah, sweetheart, I know I've been shutting you out and making excuses and not always telling you the truth. And I know I've been wrapped up in my own world and not spending enough time with you." He paused and kissed her hand. "It's a problem, and I have to change."

"Your drinking isn't our only problem," she said, overwhelmed. "We need to talk about Luke. He's hurting too. You don't spend enough time with him either, and he misses you terribly."

"But I was here last night."

"That's one night. That's not enough."

"What do you mean?"

"Tonight, when you didn't come home, he kept saying, 'I wish Dad didn't work all the time. I wish he was here with me.' Then he moped around the apartment until I put him to bed."

"Is he okay?"

"Of course he's okay. He's six and forgets things quickly. But I'm worried about the long-term effects your erratic behavior is going to have on him."

"And how about you?" Ethan said, feeling like a failure as a father and a husband. "Can you forgive me for my bad behavior?"

"I don't know, Ethan," Sarah said, searching his face. "I can't live like this anymore—waiting for you to call, waiting for you to come home, not knowing if you're out drinking at that bar. It makes me so angry."

"I'm sorry, Sarah."

"You keep saying that, and you should be. It's not fair to me, and it's not fair to Luke. He thinks you're mad at him. That he's done something wrong. He doesn't understand what going on."

"I'll talk to him. Tell him I'm planning to spend a lot more time with him."

"You'll have to do more than that. You'll have to show him you really mean it." More tears welled up in her eyes.

"Sarah, can you forgive me for today?" Ethan said, trying to read the emotions flooding her face.

"I don't know. I'm so confused. You're not the same man I fell in love with."

"Do you still love me?" he said, his heart sinking.

"I still love you. But it's getting harder. I hate your drinking."

"I know. I know. I'm gonna stop."

"You keep saying that, but I don't know if I believe you."

"I'll see somebody who can help me," he said desperately. "Maybe a shrink."

"I've already found somebody, Ethan," she said coolly, getting up and walking over to his desk. "Guess you didn't find his business card buried in all this mess. I left it here a couple of days ago." She handed him the card and sat back down.

Ethan stared at the psychiatrist's name, Dr. Fred Schwartz, a specialist in drug addiction and alcohol abuse.

"He's one of the best," Sarah said, "and I've already talked to him. He's waiting for you to call."

Ethan put the card in his shirt pocket and put his arm around her. "I'll make an appointment to see him. Very soon. I promise."

"I want to believe you, Ethan. Please don't disappoint me, and please don't disappoint Luke." She gazed into his eyes, then placed her head on his shoulder.

Ethan ran his fingers through her hair and caressed her neck, kissing her cheeks and her eyelids and her lips. He held her tenderly, trying to cast down the wall that had grown between them, knowing he had to get his life back on track, and knowing there wasn't much time before it was too late. "Sarah, I love you. With all my heart. I don't want to lose you."

"I don't want to lose you either, Ethan. Promise me you'll change."

"I promise, Sarah. I'll work hard and find some way to stop drinking." Then, as he was about to kiss her again, his iPhone rang, breaking the moment, pushing them apart. He looked at the screen and sighed. "I need to take this," he said, walking over to his desk.

"Who is it?" Sarah said, searching his face.

"It's Mindy," he said as he answered the phone. "Hey, I'm with Sarah. Hang on a second." He put down his iPhone and walked back to the couch. "I didn't mean to hurt you, babe, really, I didn't."

"I know that, Ethan," she said, touching his cheek. "Now talk to Mindy, but come to bed soon." Ethan gazed after her longingly as she walked out of his study—her silky blonde hair flowing down her back, her lithe body peeking through her nightgown. Then he remembered Mindy. "Sorry you had to wait."

"Jeez, Ethan, I heard you and Sarah. Hope I wasn't interrupting anything."

"No. No. We were just trying to clear the air, but we're done. So it's okay to talk now. What do you have for me, Mindy?"

"I just got off the phone with David. He tried calling but couldn't get through to you. So he called me instead."

"What did he want?" Ethan said, sitting down at his desk.

"He's been digging into the financial records of Fernelli's Beef and Poultry."

Ethan pulled out his iPad and began taking notes. "Who owns it?"

"A company called Zurich Foods," she said. "It's a big international conglomerate based in Europe with several holdings here in the states. One of them is Fernelli's."

"Anything else?" he said, typing away furiously.

"It's a public company. So he was able to download their earnings reports and tax filings. There didn't seem to be anything irregular, so he called a source at the SEC who said the company is perfectly above board."

"So how does Zurich Foods fit into our story?"

"He's not sure yet. But he found a contact here in New York who may be able to help us."

"Who is it?" Ethan said, his mind racing as he reached for a pack of Marlboros and pulled out a cigarette.

"A private investigator named Lloyd Howard. The guy says he's got information on Fernelli's that'll turn our story upside down."

"What information?"

"Howard wouldn't tell David on the telephone. He wants to meet you in person."

"When?"

"Tomorrow afternoon at four o'clock in Brooklyn. Just you and David. And he wants to be paid."

"How much?" Ethan said, already worrying about the extra cost to his production budget.

"Five thousand dollars up front and in cash."

"That's a shitload of money. Paul's gonna have a coronary."

"I know. But David says the guy comes highly recommended by his sources. He may be more than just a good lead for us."

Ethan paused before making the decision. "Let's do it. I wanna talk to this guy. You'll have to hustle in the morning to push the paperwork through the system and get the cash. Put him on the books as a consultant."

"I'll get the signatures," she said, "but you have to get Paul to approve it."

"I'll take care of Paul," Ethan said directly. "Call David back and tell him to set up the meeting. Make sure he gets Howard to agree to some extra work for the five thousand dollars, and put it into the contract. That'll make it easier for Paul to swallow."

"What time are you heading to the office in the morning?"

"I'm not," Ethan said, looking around the room at the stacks of file folders. "I'm gonna work from home and finish going through the rest of the court docket."

"Will you have time to pick up the money?"

"No. David'll have to bring it with him."

"Okay. I'll take care of everything on this end and email you an address as soon as we know where Howard wants to meet."

"You're the best, Mindy. Talk to you tomorrow."

Ethan clicked off the phone, his mind a jumble of thoughts. What in God's name could this guy know about Fernelli's Beef and Poultry that would blow his story wide open? Was it evidence Detective Jenkins or Nancy McGregor had buried during the investigation? Was it something else? He stared at a bottle of Black Label sitting on his desk, desperately wanting a drink. Then he remembered his promise to Sarah.

Flipping off the lights, he padded to the bedroom, climbed out of his clothes, and slipped into bed. Sarah was lying on her side, still awake, waiting for him. He snuggled up close, wrapping his arms and legs around her, their bodies becoming one.

Slowly his eyes grew heavy, his breathing rhythmic. And he drifted off to sleep.

CHAPTER 13

ETHAN SPLASHED THROUGH A wave of puddles dotting the sidewalk as he made his way through the raindrops to a hole-in-the-wall restaurant called Dexter's Diner on Metropolitan Avenue in Williamsburg, Brooklyn. A cold front had ripped through the city, bringing heavy rain and wind and dropping the temperature nearly twenty degrees. He pushed through the front door, shaking off his raincoat, and walked to the back of the room, past a dozen empty tables covered in dirty dishes and leftover food. There was nobody around to clean up the mess as he slipped into a red vinyl booth, pulled out his iPad, and waited. Fifteen minutes later, the front door swung open, and David, soaked to the bone, shuffled in. After scanning the empty restaurant, he found Ethan and sat down. "Sorry I'm late," he said guardedly as he looked around at the filth.

"No problem," Ethan said. "But why are we here? This place is a dump."

"Because this is where Lloyd Howard wanted to meet. It must be part of his turf."

Ethan frowned. "Well, I wish he could've picked someplace a little cleaner. Do you want coffee while we wait?"

"That would be great."

Ethan waved for a waitress—a Goth teenager dressed in black with black eyeliner, black lipstick, and black polish on her fingers and toes—and ordered a pot of coffee and two cups.

"So how'd you find this guy?" Ethan said as he peeked at a menu.

"I know you talked to Mindy last night," David said, "but the short of it is my source at the SEC knew this group supervisor at the DEA and gave me his number. So I called, and he told me that he'd been watching Fernelli's for years, that he didn't have anything solid, but that Lloyd Howard—the PI we're about to meet—was one of his informants."

"And that's how you found Howard?"

"Yup."

"And he can be trusted?"

"My DEA source says he's not only trustworthy but knows more about the illegal drug trade in New York than most of his on-the-ground agents."

The Goth waitress came back with the coffee and placed two cups on the table. Ethan's was dirty. So was David's. He rolled his eyes, then said curiously, "So who is this guy, Lloyd Howard?"

David grinned and pulled out a thick folder stuffed with documents. "I ran a computer check on him and found out he's a former New York City detective who was once assigned to narcotics out of the Ninetieth Precinct here in Brooklyn. He spent years working undercover—infiltrating street gangs. Remember the Jose Sanchez bust a couple of years ago?"

Ethan racked his brain but had no memory of the story. "Okay. We're not playing *Jeopardy*. Tell me about Sanchez."

"He was the boss of a big-time drug operation in Bushwick.

He sold heroin, cocaine, and methamphetamines. His pushers would hang out around schools and sell dope to the kids. The community was in an uproar, pressuring the cops to do something about the problem. But Sanchez eluded the authorities for years. Then he was finally busted. It made headlines in the *New York Post*, the *Daily News*, and all the other tabloids."

"How's Lloyd Howard connected to Sanchez?" Ethan said, flipping through the articles.

"He was the cop who brought him down. He spent six months undercover as a member of Sanchez's gang before the NYPD set up a sting, sent in the cavalry, and made the arrest."

"So he was a narc," Ethan said, still wondering how Howard could help with their story. "Why'd he leave the force?"

"He told me he'd come too close to being made too many times. Thought his luck was running out and didn't want to end up in the East River. So he quit and became a private investigator. He says it's the smartest decision he's ever made. Makes twice the money, takes half the risks."

"I still don't understand what this guy brings to the table."

"He says he's got information on Feodor and would be willing to share it with us if the money's right."

"Did you bring the cash?" Ethan said.

"I picked it up from Mindy before I left," David said. "The five thousand dollars is in my briefcase, along with the paperwork Howard needs to sign to become a GBS News consultant."

"I hope this guy's worth it. I had a bitch of a time getting Paul to agree to the cash. He said it creates all kinds of problems with the IRS, as well as with the network brass who watch every penny we spend. Did we write a clause into the contract stating Howard would do extra work for all that money? I told Paul that's part of the deal."

"It's on the second page. Lemme show you."

As David reached for his briefcase, a tall, gangly man with a thick black beard walked up to the table. He was trim and muscular and was wearing torn blue jeans, cowboy boots, and a worn-out leather vest. "Are either one of you David Livingston?" he said, his eyes darting back and forth.

"I'm David, and this is my producer, Ethan Benson. You must be Lloyd Howard."

"That's me." He pushed into the booth next to David and ordered a cup of coffee.

"Would you like some lunch?" Ethan said.

"I ate already." He turned to David. "Do you have my money?"

"It's right here." He pulled out an envelope and handed it to the PI.

Howard counted the fifty crisp one-hundred-dollar bills and slipped them into a zippered compartment of a shoulder bag he was holding.

"I also have an employment contract you need to sign for our business office," David said eagerly.

Howard put on a pair of drugstore reading glasses, carefully scanned the paperwork, then signed and dated the bottom line on the last page. "I guess I'm now an employee of *The Weekly Reporter.* Never done anything like this before." He looked at Ethan. "So where do you wanna begin?"

"You tell me. What do you know about the Feodor murder that'll help me with my story?"

"Just that almost everything you've read is a lie."

"What do you mean?" Ethan said, bewildered.

"First off, Fernelli's Beef and Poultry isn't your run-of-the-mill wholesale meat distributor. It's a front for the Russian Mob."

"I thought it was owned by Zurich Foods," Ethan said, astonished. "The SEC told us they had nothing on them."

"They don't. But Fernelli's is managed by a guy named Nikolai

Stanislov, a part-time lawyer out of Brighton Beach and full-time underboss in the Kolkov crime family."

"That's a pretty damning allegation," Ethan said skeptically. "How do you know that's true?"

"I've been tracking this guy and his ties to organized crime for years," Howard said. "He works for Alexey Kolkov—the *Pakhan*, the syndicate boss who controls most of the heroin, cocaine, crack, crystal meth, grass, and hashish that flows in and out of Brooklyn. Kolkov moves millions of dollars of illicit drugs through a vast business network each month and has no competition. His goons strong-arm anyone who tries to move in on his territory. And he's ruthless. The cops find bodies stuffed in garbage cans, floating in the Gowanus Canal, and dumped in abandoned buildings all the time."

Ethan motioned to the Goth waitress to bring another pot of coffee. "How'd you find out about Kolkov?"

"I heard about him when I worked undercover. Many of the pushers were part of his organization, and it was common knowledge on the street that the drugs came from him."

"Did you ever meet him or any of his lieutenants?" Ethan said.

"I never got far enough up the food chain," Howard said casually. "The closest I ever came to the brain trust was when we busted Jose Sanchez." He glanced at David. "Did you tell Ethan about Sanchez?"

"Just told him," David said.

Howard continued. "We confiscated about five million dollars of heroin and a half million in cash. We arrested Sanchez and most of his gang. They're all serving long jail sentences."

"And what was Sanchez's link to the Russians?" Ethan said, still trying to figure out where this was heading.

"Sanchez bought all his drugs from Nikolai Stanislov," Howard said. "He was the point person."

"And how do you know that?"

"Once again, from the pushers. They all knew Stanislov was the go-to guy and that he worked for Kolkov," Howard said, pausing and sipping his coffee. "And they were all terrified of him too. Said, just like Kolkov, he'd kill his own mother if she got in the way of a deal."

"Why didn't you bust Stanislov or Kolkov when you took down Sanchez?" Ethan said thoughtfully.

"We didn't have enough proof. The Russians don't leave loose ends. So we passed all our information on to the Feds, and the DEA has been watching Stanislov and Kolkov ever since. But they can't make a case either. So Alexey Kolkov still has a monopoly on the illegal drug trade in Brooklyn, and Nikolai Stanislov is still his top deal maker."

"Are you sure?" Ethan said.

"Positive," Howard said. "I may not be a cop anymore, but I still have my sources."

Ethan thought a moment, trying to process all the information Howard had just told him. "So how does Pavel Feodor fit into this?"

"Feodor worked for the Russians. Rumor on the streets is that Stanislov was in charge of the drug deal the night Cynthia Jameson was murdered, brought Feodor along as part of his crew, and that they all were involved in the shootout."

"And you're 100 percent sure of this?" Ethan said, flabbergasted.

"Absolutely," Howard said. "I heard it from several people I trust."

"And your sources say the Russian Mob was behind the heroin deal with the Mexican cartel?"

"Yup."

"And that Pavel Feodor was part of the crew and one of the shooters?"

"Yup."

"I've read the transcript of his confession," Ethan said, still skeptical. "Feodor never once mentioned Nikolai Stanislov or Alexey Kolkov or the Russians. So are you saying he was lying during the police interrogation?"

Howard pulled on his beard and grinned. "That's one way you can look at it, but I have my own theory. The Russian Mob has a long reach, and if Pavel Feodor had ratted on them, he'd probably be dead already. So I'd say he's been trying to save his own skin."

Ethan processed everything he'd just learned, but still didn't see how the Russians' involvement changed anything about Cynthia's murder. He needed to flush out the lead. "Can you put me in touch with any of the people who told you about this?" he said. "I've got a bunch of questions I'd like to ask them."

"Lemme see what I can do, but remember, my sources are street people. They aren't your model citizens."

"Are they reliable?" David said, jumping into the conversation.

"All of them are informants for the police."

"And have they told the police any of this?" David said.

"All of it," Howard said without hesitating.

"So why didn't the cops run with it?" Ethan said.

"That's a good question. I have no idea."

Ethan motioned for a check, wondering if Detective Jenkins knew about the Russians and if he was sitting on the connection. But why would he do that? It didn't make any sense. Or did it? "How fast can you set up a meeting, Lloyd? I'd like to talk to your sources as soon as possible."

"I'll work on it."

"And are you willing to go on camera and tell all this to my anchorman, Peter Sampson?" Ethan said, realizing Howard had new evidence never reported in the press.

"I don't know, Ethan. That'll blow my cover. I could end up a marked man."

"What if we shoot you in shadow and distort your voice?" Ethan said, hoping to ease Howard's fears. "Then we'd hide your identity."

Howard paused, stroking his beard again. "That might work, but I still need to mull it over."

"Fair enough," Ethan said. "Let me know what you decide."

. . . . .

A hard-looking man in a black Lincoln Navigator watched as Lloyd Howard hurried down the street and Ethan and some guy he'd never seen before hailed a taxi in front of the diner. He lit a cigarette and punched a number into his cell phone. "Nikolai, it's me, Anatoly," the man said with a heavy Russian accent. "I follow Benson to restaurant in Williamsburg. Like you tell me. He in there a long time meeting two guys. One I don't know. The other that private investigator, Lloyd Howard."

"Shit. What the fuck was Howard doing there?" Nikolai said. "Are you sure it was him?"

"Positive. I'd know scumbag anywhere."

"Do you think he told them about us?" Nikolai said.

"Maybe," Anatoly said, watching Ethan and David getting soaked to the bone. "I no hear—how you say in English—too much as they stand on corner making good-byes. All that noise. The rain—*tap, tap, tap, tap*—pounding on roof of car. How much does wiseass PI know about us?"

"Plenty," Stanislov said, a smidgen of fear in his voice. "All about me and Feodor."

"Nikolai, not my business to make decision, but Benson just got into taxi with new guy. Want me to follow? Maybe make disappear?"

"Not yet. Alexey needs to make that decision. You need to tell him everything you just told me. He's gonna want to know about Howard and Benson. It complicates things. So come right back."

The connection went dead.

Anatoly stubbed out his cigarette and jammed his foot on the accelerator, pulling away from the curb and cutting off traffic as he sped off to Brighton Beach to meet with Nikolai and the *Pakhan*. Then he smiled and kissed his handgun. *Fun and games*, he thought. *All part of day's work.*

CHAPTER 14

NIKOLAI STANISLOV PACED around his office, back and forth, then exploded in a fit of rage, raking an arm across his desk, knocking everything to the floor. "Fuck. Fuck. Fuck. That fucking Benson doesn't stop. He's gonna figure it out. About me. About Pavel. About what happened that night. I can't let that happen. Can't. Can't. Can't!" He nervously ran his finger over his scar, then pounded his fist on the wall. "I gotta stop him," he said, screaming to the empty room. "And I gotta stop Pavel. I can't let him talk, not to *The Weekly Reporter*, not to anyone." He began laughing hysterically, then grabbed his briefcase and headed for the door.

As he pushed out onto the sidewalk, a subway train rumbled by on an elevated track, screeching to a halt in the station. A wave of Russian immigrants piled out, like a swarm of bees leaving their hive, and flooded the street. Nikolai peered into their faces, one by one, making sure he hadn't been recognized, then made his way past a row of ethnic food stores. He bought a bunch of grapes from a street peddler and popped one into his mouth as he crossed

Brighton Beach Avenue at the Saint Petersburg Bookstore, looked over his shoulder one last time, then ducked into a seedy bar and grill called Sasha's Café.

The restaurant was almost empty, a handful of gangbangers drinking at the bar, a few old men playing poker at a rickety table near the window. Nikolai ordered a shot of vodka and made his way to the back of the room. Sitting alone in front of a computer was the *Pakhan*, Alexey Kolkov. Stanislov sat down across from him and downed his drink, then snapped his fingers and ordered another. "Anatoly should be here any minute, Alexey. We need to talk about Pavel."

The *Pakhan* turned off his computer, looked up, and said in nearly perfect English, "So, Nikolai, what's so important it can't wait? I'm a busy man, and you know how I hate being interrupted when I'm going through the financials." A bear of a man with a short, thick neck, big hands, and stubby fingers, Alexey Kolkov was wearing a white open-collared knit shirt, neatly pressed gray slacks, and expensive Bally loafers. There were tufts of brown hair sprouting on his chest, gold chains hanging around his neck, and a big diamond ring on his pinky finger. He was fifty-five and a business tycoon who owned a string of legitimate companies in construction, waste management, and trucking, where he laundered the profits from his gambling, prostitution, and drug operations. He was rich, powerful, and despotic—an underworld oligarch— somebody to be avoided at all costs.

Another train rumbled by on the elevated tracks, the sound deafening, the vibrations sending shock waves through the restaurant. Kolkov sipped his vodka and waited for the train to pull out of the station, then peered contemptuously at Stanislov. "Nikolai, Nikolai, my friend, how long have we known each other?"

"A long time, Alexey."

"And how long have you been my number two? Ten years? Twelve years? Maybe more?"

"Since we closed the deal with Zurich Foods and took over the management of Fernelli's," Nikolai said, averting his eyes.

Kolkov took a long drag on a Cuban Cohiba and blew a thick stream of smoke out his nose. He peered around the restaurant. "All of you, out," he shouted, flicking an ash on the floor. "I want to talk to Nikolai alone." Everybody stood up and left, except for his bodyguard.

"Petrov, bring me more Stolichnaya. And bring it now." The bartender, with a white dish towel draped over his arm, quickly poured two drinks and placed the bottle on the table. "To your health, Nikolai, drink up. *Na zdorovie.*"

They drained their glasses.

Alexey poured himself another drink, then stared at Nikolai, unwavering. "Is Pavel going to be a problem? Is he going to do the interview with Peter Sampson?"

"Yes, Alexey. Next week," Nikolai said pensively.

"And you've tried to stop him?"

"Yes, Alexey."

"And you've been working with that public defender friend of yours, the guy you bribed?"

"I've been leaning on Frankie O'Malley."

"And what does he say? Can he stop Pavel?" Kolkov said, never taking his eyes off his underboss.

"No, but he's been trying."

"And more money's not gonna work, is it?" Kolkov said dryly.

"Pavel has no use for money anymore now that he's been convicted. We can't buy him off. O'Malley says he wants to cut a deal with the district attorney and thinks the interview is his ticket to get talk of the death penalty taken off the table."

The *Pakhan* glared at Stanislov piercingly. "Drink up, Nikolai, you're gonna need sustenance to soften our conversation." Kolkov poured him another Stolichnaya. "And what about our mole at Rikers Island? Is he watching Pavel?"

"Every day." Kolkov downed the shot.

"Can the mole do anything to stop him?"

"I don't know, Alexey. Maybe," Nikolai said, his lower lip trembling.

"Find out," Kolkov said, vexed. "You should have put a bullet in Pavel's head in that fucking parking lot. What were you thinking? You just left him there."

"I thought he was dead. We all thought he was dead. We had no idea the doctors would bring him back to life."

"But they did. And he's about to talk. Now you have to clean up your mess!" Kolkov pounded the table. "And what about this television producer you told me about, Ethan Benson? Is he gonna be a problem too? Who else has he been talking to besides Pavel?" Kolkov said, picking a piece of tobacco off his tongue.

Before Nikolai could answer, the front door opened and Anatoly Gennadi pushed into the bar. He motioned to the bartender to bring him a glass, then made his way to the back of the room and sat down next to Nikolai.

Anatoly Gennadi was a hit man, violent and ill tempered, standing six foot four and weighing two hundred and fifty pounds, with broad shoulders and bulging muscles. He was wearing a neatly pressed blue blazer, a yellow button-down shirt, black jeans, and perfectly polished black shoes. Packed in a shoulder holster under his left arm was his weapon of death—a fully loaded Ruger .357 Magnum.

"Anatoly knows more about Benson than I do," Nikolai said, turning to the hit man. "Tell the *Pakhan* everything you just told me on the telephone."

Anatoly poured a glass of vodka. "I follow Benson for a couple of days. Tail him to Meatpacking District where he meet detective showing him Fernelli's. I follow to O'Malley's office and to Rikers Island where he visit Pavel. Then this afternoon, he goes to Williamsburg and meets with private investigator, Lloyd Howard."

Kolkov turned to Nikolai. "Is that the guy who can link you to Feodor?"

"That's the guy, Alexey."

"So this producer, Ethan Benson, probably knows about us," the *Pakhan* said, frustration spilling across his face. "He's definitely gonna be a problem." He spun around and faced the hit man. "Do you know where Benson lives?"

"I already watch apartment. He's got little kid and pretty wife. How Americans say it? A real piece a ass—long blonde hair, nice boobs. Every day he goes work, goes bar, gets drunk, goes home, walks pretty yellow dog, goes bed."

"So you know his routine?" Kolkov said, smiling.

"I got it down, just like Nikolai tells me," Gennadi said.

"And he hasn't seen you, Anatoly, has he?"

"*Nyet*, Mr. Kolkov. I not give self away. I careful, but the guy's got big smarts. He figure out pretty soon he being followed."

"Nikolai, when did you say Feodor's doing the interview?" Kolkov said, no longer smiling, now cold and calculating.

"The end of next week," Nikolai said.

The *Pakhan* poured another vodka. "Anatoly, I want you on Benson like a blanket, twenty-four hours a day. Use as many men as you need. I want to know everything he does and everybody he sees. Crank up the heat a little. Let him see you."

"I take good care of Benson, Mr. Kolkov. You no worry."

"And check in with Nikolai. Use a burner, a new one every day, and make sure to destroy the old one. I don't want your calls traced."

"I use new phone. Watch Benson. Go right now." Anatoly stood, toasted the *Pakhan*, then left the bar.

Alexey turned to Nikolai, rolling his Cohiba in his fingers. "Nikolai, during all our years together, I've never doubted you. But you misjudged Pavel, badly. You should have gotten rid of him long before that heroin deal. He was too wild. Too unpredictable. And I told you that. If he links us to the murder, it'll bring the Feds down on us—all of us, including me. So while Anatoly is watching Benson, I want you to see the mole. Tell him to crank up the heat on Feodor."

"I'll set up a meeting right away."

"Good," Alexey said. "We're running out of time."

"Don't worry, Alexey, the guy's not gonna talk," Nikolai said reassuringly.

"He better not, and if he does, well, you probably have a good idea of what I'll do to you."

Nikolai stared at the *Pakhan*, sweating profusely, downed his drink, and without saying a word, stood and made his way out of the restaurant, knowing he was treading on thin ice. When he reached Brighton Beach Avenue, he stopped and lit a cigarette, cursing his bad luck. Then he looked up into the sky, droplets of rain splashing his face.

He needed a plan. A good plan. A way to stop Pavel.

CHAPTER 15

ETHAN SAT HUNCHED OVER HIS desk in front of a cold mug
of coffee and an untouched plate of bacon and eggs as he finished
putting documents into a loose-leaf notebook he planned to give
Peter Sampson when he trekked out to East Hampton later in
the day. He'd been working since four a.m., unable to sleep, writing a briefing memo, three pages of questions, and a preliminary
production schedule for his interview with Pavel Feodor. After
adding them to the front of the notebook, he got up to make a
fresh pot of coffee when his cell phone rang. He stared in disbe-
lief. *Who could be calling at this hour?* he thought, scratching the
back of his head. But when he checked the LCD screen on his
iPhone, there was no name and no telephone number.

The call had been blocked.

"This is Ethan Benson." He heard a long pause and heavy
breathing. "Hello, is anybody there?"

More silence.

Then a woman cleared her throat. "You don't know me,

Mr. Benson. My name is Edith Templeton. I work in the district attorney's office for Ms. McGregor."

Ethan hesitated, wondering why she was calling in the middle of the night. "How'd you get my cell phone number, Ms. Templeton? It's unlisted."

"It wasn't very difficult. I have access to lots of information."

Ethan sipped his cold coffee and lit another cigarette. "So how can I help you, Ms. Templeton?"

"It's me that wants to help you, Mr. Benson," she said, whispering into the telephone. "I have evidence from the Feodor case. Evidence you want from Ms. McGregor that she's never gonna give you."

"What evidence?" Ethan said, suddenly alert.

"You have to guarantee me you won't tell anybody you got it from me," she said. "If they find out, I'll lose my job."

"If who finds out?"

"I can't tell you that, Mr. Benson. But put two and two together and promise me you won't tell anybody you talked to me."

"That won't be a problem," he said reassuringly. "I'm a journalist. I protect my sources."

"I'm still not sure I can trust you, Mr. Benson," she said with a sense of urgency in her voice. "Maybe I should hang up?"

"Don't do that, Ms. Templeton," Ethan said, backpedaling. "You'll be my confidential source. I won't discuss our conversation with anybody. I give you my word." More heavy breathing. Ethan waited on pins and needles, praying this whistleblower would believe him.

"I have a package I want to give you, Mr. Benson."

"What is it?"

"I can't tell you on the telephone."

"Why not?"

"Somebody might be listening."

Ethan covered his mouthpiece, exhaling deeply, trying to temper his growing excitement. "When can you give it to me?"

"You can have it right away."

"Do you want to meet somewhere?"

"No," she said, suddenly raising her voice. "Too risky. If somebody sees us together, it'll be the end of me."

"Okay. Okay," he said apprehensively. "Tell me what you wanna do."

"I'm gonna drop off the package with your doorman. Give me five minutes, then go down to the lobby and get it." She paused momentarily. "We've been talking too long. I need to go."

"Hold on a second. Are you sure you don't want to meet?"

"No."

"Is there a number where I can reach you?"

"No. It's better if I call you, and please, please, don't call me at the office."

"I won't, Ms. Templeton. I give you my word."

"Wait five minutes, then get the package."

She hung up.

Ethan double-checked his iPhone, hoping Ms. Templeton's number would show up on one of his apps. But there was no way to trace the call. No way to reach out to her except at the DA's office—and that was certainly out of the question. As he watched the minutes tick by, he wondered why this woman—this perfect stranger—was willing to help him, and who in the district attorney's office she was possibly afraid of. Was it Nelson Brown? Nancy McGregor? Maybe somebody else?

Another mystery to solve.

He lit a Marlboro, counted to a hundred, then headed for the door.

. . . . .

It was still dark, the sun hovering just below the horizon, when Ethan flipped on the lights in his office, threw his briefcase onto the couch, and sat down at his desk. Grabbing a scissors, he cut the string binding the package he'd picked up from the doorman and stared at the cardboard box before lifting the top and pulling out a manila envelope marked "Pavel Feodor Confession Video." He turned it over in his hands, then reached for a second envelope labeled "Crime Scene Footage." *Interesting*, he thought. *I don't remember seeing a reference to a crime scene video in the research.* As he continued rifling through the box, searching for something else, Mindy walked through the door. "What the hell are you doing here?" he said. "It's a bit early to be at work."

"I couldn't sleep. Got too much shit to do to get ready for Sampson. What's that, Ethan?" She pointed to the box and the discarded brown paper sitting on his desk.

"A care package that was left for me in the lobby of my building."

"New evidence from the Feodor case?"

"Looks like it."

"Who gave it to you?"

"A source."

"Who, Ethan?"

"Come on, Mindy, you know I can't tell you that. All I can say is somebody called me in the middle of the night, told me she had evidence I needed to see, then dropped the package off with my doorman."

"So your source is a woman?" Mindy said, trying to wrangle a name out of him.

Ethan smiled. "No way, Mindy. I'm not spilling the beans, no matter how hard you try."

"Okay, okay," she said, "but you can't fault me for asking." She scooted around his desk and looked over his shoulder. "So what did she give you?"

"Two videos."

"What are they?"

"I'm not sure yet," Ethan said, picking up the envelopes. "This one appears to be the clip of the confession that Nancy McGregor played for the jury. David never got a copy from her, did he?"

"Nope. We've been wondering if she'd ever get around to sending it," Mindy said, a cynical smile twisting her mouth. "And what's in the other envelope?"

"It appears to be footage of the crime scene. We haven't found that anywhere, have we?"

"Hell no," Mindy said. "Didn't even know it existed. I thought the only images were still pictures."

"That's what I thought too," Ethan said. "Shall we go take a look?"

Mindy looked at her watch. "It's a bit early. Lemme call the overnight tape room coordinator, see if there's anybody available." She picked up the telephone and made the call. "We've got Room 903. Joel Zimmerman's just locking a segment for this week's show. He's waiting for us."

. . . . .

They made their way down to the editing floor, passing a dozen empty Avid rooms before reaching Room 903. Joel Zimmerman was sitting in front of a bank of monitors, typing a set of commands into a keyboard and creating a new file for their story. "Hey, guys, what the hell are you doing here so early?" he said. "I thought the only fools working at this hour were people like me stuck on the dead man's shift. So what do you wanna screen?"

"We're working the Pavel Feodor murder," Ethan said, "and a source just slipped us these two videos." He handed Joel the DVDs.

"Which one first?"

"Let's screen Pavel Feodor's confession."

Joel pulled the disk from its plastic sleeve and dropped it into a playback machine. The first frame popped into the preview monitor.

"How long is it?" Ethan said.

"Forty-seven seconds," Joel said.

"So it's probably the clip McGregor played in court," Mindy said, disappointed. "I was hoping it was the raw video."

"Fat chance. Let's take a look," Ethan said.

Joel punched another command into his keyboard and the clip began rolling. It was a grainy wide-angle shot recorded on an old video camera mounted in the upper left hand corner of the interrogation room. You could barely make out the features of Feodor's face. "Can you clean up the picture?" Ethan said, staring at the monitor. "Zoom in a little tighter."

"I'll try," Joel said, "but the image is gonna fall apart."

"Try anyway."

Joel adjusted the video and blew up the shot.

"You're right," Ethan said. "Still can't see his lips moving." He rubbed his eyes, frustrated. "Play the whole thing, Joel."

They all watched as Pavel Feodor admitted to shooting the Mexican, chasing the cars through the alley, and murdering Cynthia Jameson. Ethan peered at the video, trying to read the expression on Feodor's face, but the image was just too distorted, and he couldn't tell if he was telling the truth or confessing under duress. "Has the sound been edited?" he said, wondering if anything had been taken out of context.

"There's no way to know unless we compare it to the original," Joel said. "Do we have a copy?"

"The DA's office won't give it to us," Ethan said harshly. "The prosecutor claims it's too graphic, too explosive, and the trial judge agreed with her. So nobody's seen the raw video. Nobody except Feodor's attorney." He turned to Mindy. "Does our clip match what McGregor played in court?"

"Word for word—at least according to this *New York Post* article." She handed him the story.

"So it's the same clip she showed the jury," Ethan said, scanning the verbatim. "And for argument's sake, let's say it matches the redacted confession they sent us in the court docket. But what if it's been changed or doctored in some way? We need to get our hands on the raw video, Mindy, and a clean version of the transcript. I wanna make sure the clip isn't a fake."

"That's gonna be tough," Mindy said, matter-of-factly. "As far as we know, nobody has a clean copy of the videotape other than O'Malley, and he won't give it to us either."

"Well, I need it," Ethan said. "Tell David to call Nelson Brown and bug him. McGregor promised to send us an unedited transcript. If she steps up to the plate and releases it, then at least we can use that to check the clip."

"David's been trying, but Brown's giving him the runaround— just like he is with everything else we're missing."

"I don't care. Tell him to call again."

"Okay. Okay. But I can't promise you anything."

"Don't argue with me. Just do it." He closed his eyes, trying to calm down. "Sorry, Mindy, I didn't mean to snap at you." He took a series of deep breaths. "Okay, I'm better now. Let's screen the other DVD." He smiled and handed the disk to Joel. "Is there sound?"

Joel checked his audio mixer. "Yup, there's sound."

"Play it."

For the next ten minutes, they watched a frighteningly surreal video of the crime scene investigation. Detectives were racing in and out of the shots, hovering over Pavel Feodor and examining Cynthia Jameson's lifeless body as lab technicians dressed in white suits and masks pored over the carnage, collecting evidence. "Stop it for a second, Joel," Ethan said fervently. "Can you zoom in a little tighter? I can't really see what they're doing."

Joel blew up the image, but the picture—like the confession—was too grainy and slowly dissolved into nothing but a blur.

"Why don't the police buy new cameras?" Ethan said, frustrated. "The city can't be that broke. Pull the image back until it clears."

Joel zoomed back and froze the frame.

"Can you see any blood on her body?" Ethan said, facing Mindy.

"Can't tell. There are too many people in the way and the angle's all wrong. Maybe there'll be a better shot later in the video?"

"That'll be the day," Ethan said, disappointed. "Roll it again, Joel."

The editor hit play, and the camera panned wildly around the parking lot capturing more pandemonium as the NYPD continued to work the crime scene. As a detective was stringing police tape around a pool of blood smeared in a grotesque pattern at the base of a chain-link fence, Ethan sat bolt upright in his seat. "Did you hear what that cop just said?"

"I heard it," Mindy said. "And I'm not sure I believe it. Rack the tape back thirty seconds, Joel, and play it again."

Ethan sat motionless, mesmerized, as the camera panned left to right, then pulled back and settled on a wide shot of a detective dressed in an expensive wool overcoat talking to a group of cops standing around Cynthia Jameson's lifeless body. "Is that who I think it is, Mindy?"

"Yeah. It's Detective Jenkins."

"And did he really just say that?"

"Yeah. He just told everybody he's been ordered to review all the police reports. Jeez, Ethan, why would he say that?"

"I don't know, Mindy."

"Do you think he changed anything?"

"That wouldn't surprise me. I told you I don't trust that guy," Ethan said, wondering if someone might've ordered Jenkins to sanitize the evidence. But why would anybody do that? Was somebody trying to frame Feodor? "Look, this videotape changes everything. It's our first real proof that the police may have tampered with the evidence. Mindy, I want you to transcribe the video. I want to read everything else Jenkins says and bring it with us to East Hampton. Joel, can you burn me a copy of the video so I can show Peter?"

"Not a problem."

"How long will it take?"

"Not long. It only runs an hour."

"So we have time to screen the rest of it?"

"Absolutely."

"Okay, let's see if the cops are hiding anything else." Ethan put his feet up on a chair and watched the rest of the crime scene video Ms. Templeton had just slipped him. It was a real game-changer for his story. A real smoking gun.

CHAPTER 16

THE TRAFFIC WAS LIGHT AS they turned onto Montauk Highway and headed down the narrow two-lane road to East Hampton. They'd left the office at eleven, planning three hours for the drive to Peter Sampson's sprawling estate on Lily Pond Lane in one of the most exclusive communities in the country. Ethan had insisted Peter carve out most of the afternoon to prep for the interview and go over the story. The anchorman had grumbled, saying he was too busy, but Ethan had held his ground, and after much moaning, Sampson had cleared his schedule. Now Ethan prayed he hadn't forgotten and wouldn't be faced with an army of houseguests.

That would be typical of Peter.

He lit a Marlboro and stared out the window. Puffy white clouds were dancing across the sky, dappled sunshine casting a myriad of patterns over the crystal-clear waters of Shinnecock Bay. "How much longer until we get there?" Ethan said as Mindy passed an old pickup truck chugging along at a snail's pace.

"Maybe half an hour. Did you tell Paul about the crime scene video?"

"I had a long conversation with him before we left. Told him what Jenkins said."

"And?"

"He was blown away," Ethan said candidly. "Authorized me to keep digging, to use Howard and not worry about money. Said he'd approve any additional costs beyond the five thousand dollars. Have you asked Lloyd to tap his sources in the NYPD and do a background check on Jenkins?"

"Just before we left. He suspects there's been a cover-up too, but like us, can't figure out why."

"Maybe it's Feodor's connection to the Russians?" Ethan said, stubbing out his cigarette in the ashtray. "Maybe they're behind the cover-up and are paying off Jenkins? That's what they do, right? They bribe the police."

"Come on, Ethan, we haven't nailed down that the Russians even know Feodor. That's just a theory at the moment."

"Howard's junkie sources should help us prove that," Ethan said, searching for landmarks as they approached East Hampton.

"Has Howard set up a meeting?" Mindy said.

"Tonight at midnight. He's gonna email me a location in Brooklyn as soon as he figures it out." Ethan grabbed his iPad and checked the directions. "It's not much farther. Make a right at the next corner. That should be Ocean Avenue."

They turned and drove down a beautiful, tree-lined street. There were huge mansions, one after another, with expensive cars, manicured lawns, swimming pools, and tennis courts. They stopped at a traffic light, then made a sharp right onto Lily Pond Lane, just missing an upper-crust family out for a ride on their top-of-the-line bicycles. Here the homes were bigger and even more opulent, the picture of unbridled wealth, a paradise for the rich and famous.

"So this is where Peter Sampson spends his free time," Mindy said, taking it all in.

"His house is just on the left," Ethan said. "Number sixty. It's right on the ocean."

Mindy pulled into the driveway and up to a security gate, picking up a phone mounted on a freshly painted white fence-post. She pushed a button and listened as the last few bars of the William Tell Overture announced their arrival. "Hello, who may I say is calling?" a woman said in a high-pitched voice with a Spanish accent.

"It's Mindy Herman. I'm here with Ethan Benson. Mr. Sampson's expecting us for a meeting."

"Come right on in," the woman said without hesitation. "It's me, Consuela."

"I didn't know you were out here with Peter," Mindy said, surprised.

"One of the perks of the job," Consuela said. "Get to spend a lot of time at the beach."

They drove up a gray pebble driveway to a ten-bedroom, eleven-bath, European-style compound set back on a large land-scaped ridge. The main house had an air of elegance with white stucco walls and a terra-cotta roof, the wood trim framing the big bay windows painted aquamarine blue, the front door a titian red. A wide porch appointed with overstuffed chairs and wrought-iron tables wrapped around the first floor, and big clay pots filled with blue hydrangeas and pink and yellow rose bushes added a myriad of colors to the manicured façade.

Ethan opened the car door and climbed out. "It looks like a movie set, doesn't it? And the inside's decorated just like his office—expensive antique furniture, Persian rugs, and original artwork everywhere you go. There's even a screening room with state-of-the-art equipment in the basement. He gave me the grand tour the last time I was here."

Consuela was waiting for them when they reached the front door and ushered them into the house. "Where's Peter?" Mindy said, staring at an original Picasso hanging over a Louis XIV side table in the foyer.

"Mr. Sampson's sitting out back by the pool," Consuela said. "He's reading *The New York Times*. Would you like an iced tea or some lemonade?"

"Iced tea would be great," they both said, almost at the same time.

Consuela led them down a long hallway and out a sliding glass door to a flagstone patio—a cool breeze blowing off the ocean, the sound of the waves rolling up on the beach. Sampson was lying on a lounge chair sipping a glass of iced coffee. He was dressed in a white polo shirt, white shorts, and white sneakers, a pink cotton sweater draped over his shoulders, the arms carefully folded across his chest. Ethan thought he looked more like a tennis pro relaxing before a championship match than the most famous anchorman on television.

"Ethan, so good to see you," Sampson said, smiling. "And you too, Mindy. Glad you could both make it. It's a beautiful day, so I thought we'd work out here by the pool. We'll get much more done in the sunshine." Sampson waved them over to a glass table with three director's chairs positioned in front of a computer and a large monitor. "Ah, here comes Consuela with your iced teas." He handed her his empty glass. "I'd like a fresh coffee with a little milk and sugar. You know how I like it."

"Right away, Mr. Sampson," she said, setting down the two iced teas and disappearing into the house.

Ethan looked up at Sampson, all business. "Our interview with Pavel Feodor is next Friday, so I've brought you some research to read and a couple of videos to screen. It's gonna take us a couple of hours to go through everything. So we better get started."

Sampson chuckled. "Somehow I knew you were going to say that. Never out of character, are you, Ethan." He adjusted the sleeves of his sweater. "So what goodies are you giving me while I'm here at the beach soaking up the sun? Are you going to ruin the rest of my vacation?"

"Sorry, I know it's a lot, but it's important." He handed Sampson a big research notebook. It was almost three inches thick. "Take a quick look, then I'll walk you through it."

"What is this? A copy of the Encyclopedia Britannica?" Sampson said as he thumbed through the first few pages. "I thought this was a straightforward interview with a murderer." He dropped the notebook on the table with a thud. "Why do I need to read all this?"

"Because the story's changing."

"What do you mean it's changing?" Peter said quizzically. "Pavel Feodor's been convicted and is about to be sentenced. That's the story, isn't it?"

Ethan looked at Mindy, then back at Sampson. "That's what we first thought, but I want you to screen something. It'll help explain why you need to read all these documents." He reached into his briefcase for a disk and loaded the crime scene video into the laptop, the first frame popping onto the screen. "The police shot this the night of the murder," Ethan said, tapping the monitor. "As far as we know, nobody, except for a handful of cops and maybe the prosecutor, even knows it exists."

"Where'd you get it?" Sampson said as Consuela came back with his iced coffee, then scooted over to the pool to soak up some sun.

"From a source," Ethan said.

"A source you trust?" Sampson said, sipping his coffee.

"Yes."

"And where'd your source get it?"

"The district attorney's office," Ethan said with no hesitation.

"Are you sure?"

"Positive."

"And you have no doubt it's real?"

"I have to second source it, but, yes, it's real, Peter. It's been carefully hidden away by somebody in that office. Nobody in the press has seen it. This is our exclusive."

Sampson stroked his chin, then said, "Okay, what do you want to show me?"

Ethan fast-forwarded until a wide shot of a group of CSI sifting through evidence filled the screen.

"What should I be looking for?" Sampson said, staring at the video.

"Just watch," Ethan said, transfixed. "The camera's panning and locking on a shot of a guy crouching on the ground wearing a fancy overcoat. That's Edward Jenkins—the lead detective. He's talking to the lab techs, and see, he's about to write something on a notepad." Ethan froze the video. "It's not a great shot, but I had Joel Zimmerman play with the image in his Avid room, and when you adjust the pixels, move it around, and blow it up, you can just make out what he's writing. It says, 'No blood on the body.' I have the enhanced version of the shot on another disk Joel made for you."

"Leave it with me. I'll screen it later," Peter said impatiently. "So this detective says there's no blood on Cynthia Jameson's body, and he's the lead detective on the case?"

"Yup. But when Mindy and I met him last week in the

Meatpacking District, he straight out lied to us. Said that Cynthia Jameson was covered in blood—like a soldier butchered in a battle."

"What did he write in his police report?" Sampson said, staring at the monitor, the image of the detective writing on his notepad still frozen on the screen.

"It's in your research book," Mindy said, "along with the rest of the police reports. And they all say the same thing—that the bullet that killed Cynthia Jameson left her a bloody mess. That's what the prosecutor said in court. And that's what's been reported in the press."

Peter picked up the research book and skimmed through the documents. "So why did Jenkins change his story?" Sampson said. "And why did the other cops all say the same thing?"

Ethan smiled. "I'll show you why." He fast-forwarded the tape a few minutes, then played the video. "There's Jenkins again talking on his cell phone. It's just a short conversation, and he's whispering, so we can't make out what he's saying, but keep watching." He pointed at the screen. "See, he puts the phone into his pocket, then walks to the middle of the parking lot. Now, listen carefully. This we can hear loud and clear." Ethan cranked up the volume:

"Okay, everybody, this is important. I just got off the phone with the captain. This is a high-profile case. The victim is the deputy mayor's daughter, Cynthia Jameson, and the press is going to be all over the murder. So somebody with a much higher pay grade than me is ordering us to send all our paperwork up the ladder for a formal review. I've been told to collect all your crime scene reports as soon as they're finished and pass them upstairs, then I'll get them back and personally put them into the case file. Am I clear on the protocol for this investigation? Nothing, and I mean nothing, is to be placed into evidence until it goes through me and I get approval from the powers

that be. Then, and only then, will I put your paperwork into the evidence locker. Everybody got that?"

"Stop the video," Sampson said, sipping his iced coffee. "This certainly puts a twist in our story, Ethan. What does it mean?"

"Well, I can't prove anything yet," Ethan said, popping the disk out of the computer. "I need to get my hands on some close-up shots of Cynthia's body and confirm there really was no blood. And so far, nobody will give them to me. But it sure seems like the cops were taking orders from somebody to doctor the crime scene evidence and maybe pin the murder on Pavel Feodor."

"But who would order such a thing?"

"I don't know," Ethan said scornfully, "but I'm sure as hell gonna find out."

Sampson looked up at the sun disappearing behind a dark cloud, then took off his sunglasses. "Have you told Paul?"

Ethan nodded. "I screened the tape with him before we left."

"And what does he think?"

"He told me to make sure the crime scene video is real and to find the missing pictures of Cynthia's body. I'm already working on it."

Sampson stared at the empty screen. "Can you leave the disk with me? I want to watch it again when I have more time. This video is gonna be toxic when we air it."

"The disk is yours," Ethan said, dropping it on the table. "We've got other copies at the office."

"And where's the disk of the shot your editor cleaned up for me? I want to screen that one too," Sampson said, "so I can see exactly what Detective Jenkins wrote on his notepad."

Ethan fished it out of his briefcase, along with a copy of Feodor's confession. "You should look at this, too. It's the clip of the confession Nancy McGregor showed the jury. It'll give you a good sense of Pavel's speech patterns and how he carries himself when he's talking. Should be helpful before you do the interview."

"Good. I was hoping you'd found that," Peter said, grabbing the disks and his research book. "Now I'm afraid you'll have to excuse me. Billy Joel's coming over for a game of tennis and a late afternoon swim." He started to get up, but sat back down. "Is there anything else in this research book that's important, besides the police reports?"

"The entire book's important," Ethan said, exasperated. "Read my memo and the interview questions first. Then go through the newspaper articles and the additional documents. The book is your bible. It'll give you all the background you need before you sit down with Feodor."

"What about all the arrangements for my trip to Rikers Island?" Sampson said, turning to Mindy.

"There's a preliminary schedule in your notebook as well, right after the interview questions," Mindy said. "I'll email Consuela updates and a final itinerary the day before the shoot."

"Anything else we need to go over, Ethan?" Sampson said, checking his watch. "I'm really out of time."

"Just the airdate," Ethan said, waiting for an explosion.

"What about the airdate?"

"Paul moved us up in the schedule after he screened the crime scene video this morning. He wants to run our story to kick off the new season."

"When's that?"

"The Thursday after Labor Day," Ethan said.

"Not gonna happen. I'm not back from vacation until right after the holiday. I already told you that. Get Paul to change it."

"I'll see what I can do," Ethan said, knowing Paul would never change his mind. "But if I can't get him to push us deeper into the schedule, I'll figure out some way to get everything done."

"You do that, Ethan, but I'm not gonna do anything—and I mean anything—beyond the interview with Feodor. No additional homework. No additional traveling. And no additional shooting. I'm on vacation and don't forget it. Now please excuse me, but you really must go."

Ethan didn't say another word until they were back on the highway and heading to New York. "Well, that went much better than I expected."

"Jeez, Ethan, how can you say that?" Mindy said incredulously. "Peter's refusing to lift a finger for our story except for the Feodor interview."

"I'll get him to change his mind," Ethan said confidently. "He's really just a pussycat—all bluster and no bite. Besides, our meeting was a smashing success. We got through everything on our checklist. We screened the crime scene video, we gave him the confession video and the research notebook, and he seems to be into the story. If he does the reading and the prep work, we should be good to go."

"That's a big if, Ethan, don't you think?"

"Yeah. But you gotta have faith," Ethan said, snapping his fingers. Then he leaned back in his seat and closed his eyes. *Man, Peter Sampson's a real piece of work*, he thought, smiling to himself. *But, you know, he's smart and perceptive and powerful. Maybe Paul's right. Maybe Peter is the best choice for this story.*

CHAPTER 17

DAVID LIVINGSTON WAS STANDING on the corner when Ethan arrived at the entrance to the Fourteenth Street Union Square subway station. Their meeting with Lloyd Howard and his junkie informants was going off as planned at a coffee shop in Coney Island called Rocco's—Ethan hoping to second-source Feodor's connection to the Russian Mob and learn what role the syndicate played in Cynthia Jameson's murder. They hopped onto the Q Line for the forty-five-minute ride and sat down in the last car. "Did you bring the Panasonic DV cam?" Ethan said, turning to his researcher who was rummaging through a heavy shoulder bag.

"It's in here," David said as he pulled out the instruction manual for the digital camera.

"Which one is it?"

"The small two-chip."

"Do you know how to use it?"

"I've shot with it a couple of times," he said as he leafed through the first few pages of the booklet. "It's got a wide-angle lens and works great in available light. I just need to white balance the colors and make sure the computer is set up properly."

"Did Howard tell you how many junkies are coming?" Ethan said, suddenly worried they were heading off on a wild goose chase.

"He's not sure," David said, adjusting the autofocus on the back of the camera. "He's been talking to four or five of his informants who routinely work with the police, and who he says are reliable."

"Will they all be there?"

"Probably not. They're addicts, Ethan. He's hoping two or three will show up and be straight enough to carry on a conversation."

"Well, if they give us permission, I'll want you to roll the camera. Who knows, maybe they'll say something about the murder we'll use in the story." Ethan pulled out his iPad and reread the notes from his first meeting with the private investigator. "Did Lloyd give you background on any of his sources?"

"Only on one," David said. "A guy named Leonid Karloff—a street pusher busted in an undercover sting operation a couple of years ago."

"Don't tell me. A sting Lloyd Howard helped set up."

"Yup, you got it. Howard told me Karloff's arrest made all the newspapers. So I looked him up on LexisNexis and found a bunch of stories about him. Give me a second. I'll send you the best one from my iPhone."

Ethan waited for the article to land in his mailbox, opened the message, and started to read. It was two columns in the *New York Post*, dated two months before the beginning of Feodor's trial. About halfway down, Leonid Karloff's name popped into the body of the story. "This is interesting. It says right here that Karloff is a small-time hood the Feds have been watching for quite some time, and that he's a known associate of Nikolai Stanislov.

That's the guy in the Russian Mob Howard told us about." Ethan kept on reading, hoping the article would somehow link Karloff to any drug deals in the Meatpacking District. But there was nothing.

"Does Karloff know Feodor?" Ethan said, clicking off his iPad.

"Howard says he does."

"What's his connection?" Ethan said.

"Karloff's going to tell us tonight," David said. "Lloyd thought it would be best if we heard it directly from him."

"Do you think we can trust this guy?"

"I don't know, Ethan. We just have to wait and see how stoned he is when we meet him. Then we can make a decision if we can use him as a source or include him in our story."

Ethan shrugged his shoulders and absentmindedly looked out the window as the train rumbled along, passing small two-story commercial buildings and squalid single-family homes sandwiched between great mounds of garbage. After fifteen minutes, they pulled to a stop at Coney Island–Stillwell Avenue and got off the train, hurrying down a crumbling flight of stairs and onto the street, the subway roaring out of the station and down the El, headed to the next stop. "How far is the coffee shop from here?" Ethan said, peering up and down the block.

"Not too far. Rocco's is right on the boardwalk." They started walking, the streets mostly deserted, the stores mostly boarded up and out of business. Abandoned cars, furniture, and old refrigerators littered the sidewalks and pockmarked the alleyways. "This whole neighborhood is fucking creepy," David said, disgusted.

"What did you expect?" Ethan said. "We're in the perfect home away from home for Brooklyn's junkie population. I'm sure that's why we're meeting here and not on Park Avenue." They continued walking, past a Nathan's Famous Hot Dogs, a Subway Sandwich Shop, and a 7-Eleven where two addicts in ragged clothes were sleeping in the filth. When they got to the corner of West Nineteenth Avenue, they stopped and searched for the coffee shop. "There it is," Ethan said, "on the next corner." They hurried across the street and pushed their way through a grimy glass door and into the restaurant. Ethan choked on the smell of heavy grease—a short-order cook slinging home fries on a dirty grill behind a cluttered serving counter.

He stopped and looked around the restaurant.

Lloyd was sitting in the back with two men slumped over the table, shoveling food in their mouths. They were both white, in their early twenties, and on first glance, relatively clean and well-dressed for heroin addicts.

"David, go talk to the cook and ask him if it's okay for us to shoot pictures in his restaurant. Tell him who we are and show him the camera."

"Sure thing, Ethan."

Ethan walked over to the table and sat down next to Howard. The two men looked up but didn't say a word. "How's it going, Lloyd? Who are your friends?"

"The guy on my right who forgot to wash his face is Simon. Just Simon. No last name. He's not gonna talk too much. I think he just came for the sausage and eggs. The other guy across the table is Leonid Karloff."

"David told me about him," Ethan said. "Do they know who I am?"

"They know," Lloyd said.

"And that I work for *The Weekly Reporter*?"

"We've been talking about your show ever since we got here."

Ethan turned to David who flashed him a thumbs-up about shooting the interview as he worked on the camera settings. Then he faced the two junkies. "Would you guys like to tell me a little about yourselves before we get started?"

Simon kept eating.

But Leonid put his fork down. There were deep circles under his eyes, and his skin was pallid, his long brown hair unkempt, his expression sad, almost despondent. "You know, I used to live in a nice apartment in a good neighborhood. I had a wife and kids and a job—kinda like a normal person—but now that's all gone. I just can't kick the smack. It's got me hooked by the balls." He picked up his fork and pushed the eggs around on his plate, his gaze vacant.

"You wanna tell me anything?" Ethan said, peering at Simon. He waited patiently, but the junkie continued staring into the distance, ghostlike.

"Simon's pretty stoned," Howard said. "He shot up just before we got here, but Leonid's coming down off his high. So he's pretty together and definitely wants to tell you what he knows. We discussed your camera, and they're both okay with you recording whatever they say—at least at the moment."

"Are you gonna pay me for my information?" Leonid said, picking at a piece of sausage stuck in his teeth, his hand trembling. "I need to score bad. My fix is wearin' off."

"I can't pay you," Ethan said apologetically. "We don't work that way. I can buy your breakfast, maybe a little food for later, but that's it."

Leonid scratched the two-day growth on his chin and looked at the private investigator. "I told you that's how the press works," Howard said. "They don't pay like the cops. But I take good care of you, don't I? And if you want that to continue, I suggest you answer Mr. Benson's questions."

Leonid nodded. "Okay. I got it. No money."

Ethan waved over to David. "Go ahead and start rolling. Concentrate on Leonid—the guy on Howard's left. He's gonna do most of the talking. Give me a series of tight shots. Lots of cutaways of their faces and hands and the food so we can put together a sequence in the editing room."

David began making a sweeping wide shot of the room, then knelt down on the floor and began shooting insert shots around the table. When he finished, he focused the lens on Karloff and motioned that he was ready to record the interview.

Ethan asked his first question.

"How do you know Pavel Feodor?"

"Shit, man, I've known him since I was kid," Leonid said. "He lived down the street from me in Brighton Beach, and we went to school together until he was busted and went off to juvy."

"Were you friends?"

"You could say that."

"And what was he like?"

"He was a fucking wild man. He liked to beat up on everybody. The whole neighborhood was scared of him. I was too." Leonid took a bite of toast, a sprinkle of crumbs falling on his shirt.

Ethan locked eyes with David. "Are you getting this?"

His researcher nodded and zoomed into Leonid's face. His lips looked dry and cracked, his brow was sweating.

"Are you still friends with Pavel?" Ethan said, trying to keep the conversation moving as Leonid began to nod out.

The junkie looked up. "I ain't seen him in almost two years. He's in jail, remember? You think I'm dumb or somethin'?"

"No. No. You're right," Ethan said, realizing he had to be more circumspect with his questions. "When was the last time you saw him?"

"Right before I got hooked on the heroin. When we first started doing small jobs for the Kolkov crime syndicate."

"When was that?" Ethan said.

"A couple of months before the deputy mayor's daughter got

herself murdered," Leonid said, his nose running as his withdrawal symptoms began spiraling out of control.

"And were you still part of the Mob when Cynthia Jameson was murdered?"

"No, man, they'd kicked me out by then. I was already hooked, and they didn't trust me anymore. Does anybody have a tissue?"

Ethan pulled a package of Kleenex from his pocket, handed it to Karloff, and asked his next question. "And what about Pavel, was he still working for Kolkov?"

Leonid peered over at the private investigator.

"Go ahead and answer Mr. Benson's question. Tell him what you told me," Howard said, urging him on.

"Yeah, he still worked for the number two guy, Nikolai Stanislov. The guy with that big scar running down his face."

Ethan held his breath, hoping he was about to hit pay dirt. "And was Stanislov involved in the heroin deal that night in the Meatpacking District?"

"That was his deal with the Mexicans," Leonid said. "Everybody knows that. We all thought some really good shit was about to hit the street."

"Was Feodor with him?" Ethan said.

"Fuck yes. And so was a whole bunch of other guys."

"And did Feodor fire the weapon that killed the deputy mayor's daughter?"

"How should I fucking know that? I wasn't there that night. But that's what everybody says—including the cops."

Ethan turned to David. "I hope you're recording this."

"I got it."

"Are you still tight on his face? I wanna see his expression."

"I'm tight. You can see every pore on his skin."

Ethan turned back to Karloff. "Do the cops know about Feodor and Stanislov?"

"Sure as shit. I told the cops Nikolai Stanislov was at the shootout and that Pavel was with him."

"Are you sure that's what you told the police?" Ethan said, pressing the point.

"Yeah. That's what I told that detective, Edward Jenkins."

"The lead detective on the Feodor case?"

"That's the guy."

Simon looked up from his plate, saliva running down his chin. "And I told him the same thing. Stanislov and Feodor were both there that night the girl got killed. Lots of junkies gave Jenkins that information." Simon's eyes fogged over, and he looked back down at his plate.

Ethan paused. So Edward Jenkins knew about the Russians. Did he know before he interrogated Feodor? Did he pass it up the chain of command? Did he tell Nancy McGregor? The cover-up was deepening. "And both of you have no doubts the Russian Mob was involved in that drug deal?" Ethan said, wanting to make sure it was clear on the videotape.

"Why would we make up a story like that?" Leonid said. "Stanislov works for Alexey Kolkov who controls the illegal drug trade in Brooklyn. And I'm positive it was the Mob that tried to pull off that heroin deal the night of the murder. They always used Fernelli's to do business. Always. And still do." He started to spasm, his entire body beginning to twitch. "Are we almost done? I gotta get a fix."

"One more question," Ethan said. "Are you 100 percent sure you told all of this to Detective Jenkins? This is important, Leonid."

"I told that cop everything I just told you. And he paid me good money for the information. Are you sure you can't pay me something? Just a little?" He gestured with his fingers, his thumb and forefinger an inch apart.

"I can't give you any money to feed your drug habit," Ethan said softly. "I can't do it, Leonid."

"Okay, okay. I just thought I'd ask one more time."

"Is there anything else you want to tell me?" Ethan said beseechingly.

Leonid shook his head no.

So did Simon.

Ethan turned to David. "Are we good? Anything else you need to shoot? Any more cutaways?"

"No, I've got everything we need."

"Then I think we're done," Ethan said, facing the two junkies. "Thanks, guys, I have no more questions."

Leonid fidgeted with his shirt collar, then stood up, nodded good-bye, and headed for the door, Simon stumbling along right behind him. David continued rolling, shooting a wide shot of the two addicts crossing the street and disappearing around the corner. Then he spot-checked the images in the camera's LCD screen and sat down at the table.

"How'd they look through the lens?" Ethan said, anticipating the worst.

"Like junkies," David said.

"Can we use the interview? I'm worried they won't seem believable on camera."

"Simon won't work. He's way too blown out," David said without hesitating. "But Karloff should be okay as long as you ID him as an addict and a paid informant for the cops. I'm pretty sure the audience will buy his story."

"So now we have a second source linking Pavel Feodor to the Russians and telling us that Detective Jenkins knew all about it." Ethan turned to Howard. "Have you found out anything about Jenkins from your sources at the NYPD?"

"Just that he's a tough son-of-a-bitch and on the take. Nobody's given me any proof, but that's what I'm hearing from my friends on the force."

"So he could've taken money under the table to corrupt the chain of evidence on the Feodor case," Ethan said thoughtfully.

"That's very possible," Lloyd said.

"Now we just have to figure out if and who he was working for. Look, Lloyd, have you decided to do the interview with Sampson? I need you on camera. I'm not sure the suits at GBS are gonna let me rely just on Karloff."

"I'll do it as long as you shoot me in shadow and don't reveal my identity—just as you suggested."

"Deal," Ethan said, relieved. "One more question before we go. Do you have any idea how to find this guy, Nikolai Stanislov?"

Howard smiled. "He's got a law office in Brighton Beach under the El when he's not cracking heads for his Mob boss."

"Can you take me there? I'd love to get a look at him."

"Just pick a day."

"Sometime next week. I'll let you know when." Ethan pushed his chair away from the table and stood up. "Let's get the hell out of here. I'm beat." Then he pulled a fifty-dollar bill out of his wallet and handed it to the cook. "I'd be in your debt forever if you don't tell anybody we were here tonight."

The cook nodded and pocketed the money, then continued moving grease around on the grill as they walked out of the restaurant.

"How're you guys getting home?" Howard said.

"We're taking the subway," Ethan said.

Howard looked at him as if he were cross-eyed. "The trains only run every hour at this time of the night. Come on, I'm parked around the corner. I'll drive you back to Manhattan."

CHAPTER 18

NIKOLAI STANISLOV SAT IN his Lincoln Navigator under a large oak tree. The temperature was hovering in the mid-90s, the heat scorching, the sun blinding. Massive thunderheads darkened the western sky, sending lightning bolts across the horizon and peals of thunder through the thick, humid air. Nikolai couldn't wait for the rain. He hated the summer and longed for the cool, dry temperatures of the fall. Maybe the storm would bring some relief. He wiped his brow with a handkerchief and stared at his cell phone, dreading the call he was about to make. Then he punched in the *Pakhan*'s private number. "Alexey, it's me."

"Are you calling from a secure telephone?"

"I'm using a burner. I'll get rid of it as soon as we hang up."

"What's happening with Benson? Is Anatoly following him?"

"He's got men tailing him around the clock."

"Does he know we're watching?"

"Not yet. Anatoly's waiting for the right moment to scare the shit out of him."

"What's Benson been doing?"

Nikolai opened the window and lit a cigarette. He'd forego the air conditioning for a hit of nicotine. "Nothing unusual. Going to work. Going home. Drinking his scotch. Fucking his wife. The normal stuff."

"Cut the crap, Nikolai. This isn't a joke." Alexey's voice boomed through the telephone. "Who's Benson been talking to? Who's he been seeing? That's all I want to know."

"Just his anchorman, Peter Sampson, and the team of people he's working with. Nobody else we need to worry about." He thought about telling the *Pakhan* that the hit man had lost him for over six hours after he got on the subway the night before, but decided there was nothing anybody could do about it now. Better to keep his mouth shut.

"And what about Pavel?"

"Our mole stops by and sees him every day. Harasses him just for good measure."

"When are you meeting the mole?"

"In about an hour," Nikolai said, nervously flicking an ash off the cuff of his white shirt.

"Good," Alexey said aggressively. "I want you to call me as soon as you're done, and Nikolai, I'm hearing disturbing news from Jenkins and some of the other cops on our payroll at the Sixth Precinct. Ethan Benson is asking lots of questions. Jenkins thinks he can link us to Fernelli's and that Sampson is going to say in their story we were involved in Cynthia Jameson's murder."

Nikolai took a long drag on his cigarette, too stunned to speak.

"Are you listening, Nikolai?"

"Yes, Alexey."

"Good. So don't fuck with me. The last thing I want is for that television show to find out from Pavel that the rumors they're hearing are true. Do you understand?"

"I'll talk to the mole," Stanislov said, the threat ringing home loud and clear. "We'll stop the interview."

"Good, Nikolai. You know what I want the mole to do." An uneasy silence. "Offer him enough money and make it worth his while."

"You're sure that's what you want, Alexey?"

"Are you questioning my decision? You should know me better than that. Just do it, Nikolai."

The *Pakhan* cut the connection.

Nikolai clenched the burner, his face red with anger, then suddenly wheeled around and smashed the phone into the car door, cutting his hand on a sliver of plastic. A trickle of blood dripped down his fingers as he looked up at his bodyguard in the front seat. "Yuri, I need a new phone."

Yuri pulled a burner out of the glove compartment and tossed it to him.

"Now drive me to the boardwalk," Nikolai said, checking the time. "I wanna pick up a sandwich and a beer at Ttankov's Grill and eat my lunch on a bench across from the restaurant. That's where I told that little asshole to find me." He looked out the window and up at the sky. It was getting darker, the clouds creeping closer. Maybe the rain would hold off a bit longer—just until he finished his meeting with the mole.

· · · · ·

A half hour passed before he spotted the prison guard slowly making his way down the boardwalk. Jimmy Benito was late. He was always late. And Nikolai was tired of always waiting for him. Maybe it was time to find somebody new on the inside at Rikers Island. Somebody more reliable. After glancing around to make sure they were alone, he motioned for the prison guard to come over.

The mole was dressed in worn blue jeans, a torn work shirt, an old wrinkled blazer, and cheap sneakers. He was carrying a brown paper bag with a bottle of Irish whiskey, and after taking a long pull, approached Nikolai, wobbling from side to side, before plopping down on the bench.

"Jimmy, are you drunk?" Nikolai said, repulsed.

"No. I just have a pleasant buzz," he replied, his voice heavy as he slurred his words. "It's my day off. I'm allowed to have a good time."

"Change of plans. I don't want to talk to you out here. You're making a spectacle of yourself. Let's go into Ttankov's. There's a room in the back where we can meet in private."

They got up and walked over to the restaurant, Yuri trailing, hovering just out of sight. When they reached the reservations desk, Nikolai handed the maitre d' a hundred-dollar bill, and they were escorted through a side door, down a long corridor, and into a small, windowless room with a single table.

"Sit, Jimmy," Nikolai said, pointing to a chair facing the back of the room.

The prison guard finished his whiskey and dropped the bottle on the table, knocking over a wine glass. Turning to the maitre d', he said, "Bring me a can of Bud."

"No more drinking," Nikolai said fiercely. "Get him some food and a black coffee. I need to sober him up so he understands what I'm about to tell him."

The maitre d' picked up the empty bottle and scurried out of the room, closing the door as he left.

"Okay, Jimmy, fill me in. What's going on with Pavel?"

"Nothin's changed. I stop and see him every day. Give him his three meals, harass him like I always do—waving my nightstick, threatening to beat him—but he ain't scared of me. He's a tough little shit."

The maitre d' put a sandwich and a cup of coffee on the table, then walked back out as quickly as he'd walked in.

"Drink it, Jimmy. It'll help you think straight."

Benito took a long gulp, burning his mouth.

"Who's Pavel been seeing?" Nikolai said, trying to cut through the cobwebs.

"Nobody, really. He spends most of his time lying on his bed, smoking one cigarette after another, doin' nothing." Benito's eyes fluttered. "The warden won't let him out of his cell. Says it's too dangerous for him to mingle with the other inmates, especially the blacks. They all hate him. He calls them niggers and curses them. He wouldn't last more than five minutes in the general population. He'd end up on a slab in the morgue."

Nikolai listened quietly, but Benito wasn't telling him anything he didn't already know. "How's his mood, Jimmy?"

"The guy seems okay to me. He's lost some weight, and he's not sleeping so good. But he ain't acting any different. He's still the same old asshole. Hey, do you think I could get a beer now?"

"No. Finish your coffee and eat your sandwich. I told you. No more booze." Nikolai lit a cigarette, never taking his eyes off the prison guard's face. "Look, you've been doing a good job watching Pavel. Really. You've earned every penny I'm paying you. But things have changed, and I need you to take care of a problem for the *Pakhan*. He doesn't want Pavel doing the interview with *The Weekly Reporter*."

The mole didn't react. He took a bite of his sandwich.

Nikolai slapped him across the face, trying to shock him back to life. "What are you hearing about the interview?" Nikolai said angrily.

Benito dropped his sandwich and rubbed his cheek. "Nothin'.

I already told you everything I know about that producer who was in to see him the other day with Frankie. I know the *Pakhan*'s worried about what Pavel's gonna say, but there's nothin' I can do about that television show. I can't stop the interview."

"But I think you can, Jimmy."

"How? The warden's approved it. He's picked a location on H Block. He's puttin' up extra security cameras all along the route Pavel's gonna take when we walk him from his cell to the interview room. And he's handpicked a crack team of prison guards to make sure it all goes off smoothly. The place is gonna be locked down as tight as a drum. What do you want me to do about it?"

"I want you to silence Feodor."

"What?"

"I want you to kill him."

Benito licked his lips. "That's not part of our deal, Mr. Stanislov. You're paying me to snoop on him, not kill him. I've never murdered anybody before." Benito's hands began shaking as he reached for a cigarette.

"You don't have a choice, Jimmy. The *Pakhan* wants him dead, and we both agree you're our best option. O'Malley's too stupid to stop him and has no way to get in there and kill him, so you have to come up with a plan and take him out."

Benito gulped his coffee. "I can't do it, Mr. Stanislov. I can't. There's no possible way. Please. You gotta find somebody else."

"There is nobody else," Nikolai said, pounding his fist on the table. "Yuri, I need you in here, now." The door swung open and the bodyguard slipped into the room, sitting down next to the mole. "Say hello to Mr. Benito." The big man smiled and unbuttoned his coat, exposing his Beretta 9mm handgun. "So, Jimmy, how are you gonna take care of our problem? Any ideas?"

"I don't know, Mr. Stanislov. I need time to think. Shit, it ain't gonna be easy."

"You don't have a lot of time," Nikolai said, his eyes boring into the prison guard. "The interview's next week. So you gotta get rid of him in the next couple of days."

"And what's in it for me? I'm taking all the risk here. If something goes wrong, it ain't you goin' down. It's me."

"How does fifty thousand dollars sound to you?"

Benito stared at Nikolai, his jaw dropping, his mouth agape.

"That's a lot of money, Jimmy."

"I don't know, Mr. Stanislov. You're asking me to kill somebody who's been front page news. I think it's worth a lot more than fifty grand. I think it's worth at least a hundred."

Nikolai leaned across the table. "Well, I can go back to the *Pakhan* and tell him you want more money, but he thinks fifty thousand dollars is more than fair. He's not gonna be happy if I tell him you thought his offer wasn't generous enough. What do you think he's gonna say, Jimmy? Do you think he's gonna be pissed?"

Benito glanced at Yuri and then back at Nikolai. Both men were staring at him, waiting. "Okay, okay, I'll do it for the fifty. But I need a couple of days to come up with a plan." He looked down at his cup of coffee. "I could really use a beer. Just one. I'm a little shaky on the inside. This was kinda unexpected."

"Yuri, go get Jimmy a beer," Nikolai said, sucking on a cigarette. "You need to call and let me know how you're gonna do it, once you figure it out. Mr. Kolkov wants to make sure it's done the right way. He doesn't tolerate mistakes."

Benito nodded as Yuri walked back into the room and placed a can of Bud on the table. Jimmy drained it all at once. "When do I get my money?"

Stanislov shoved an envelope across the table. "Here's twenty-five thousand. You get the rest when Pavel's dead."

Jimmy stuffed the envelope into his breast pocket. "I need to go," he said, trying to stand and collapsing back into his chair, light-headed from the beer and the whiskey.

"Now, now, Jimmy. Get a grip on yourself. I just made you a rich man. You should be happy." Nikolai turned to his bodyguard. "Give him a hand, Yuri. He's a bit shaky on his feet. Walk him back to his car and make sure he gets off without a problem." He faced Benito. "Always a pleasure doing business with you," he said, sticking out his hand. Then, without warning, he punched him in the pit of the stomach with the force of a jackhammer.

Benito collapsed to the floor, doubled up in pain.

Stanislov leaned over and whispered into his ear. "Listen to me, Jimmy. And listen to me real good. The *Pakhan* wants Feodor dead and he wants you to take care of it, and the sooner the better." Then he gently patted Benito on the face and said to Yuri, "Get him the hell outta my sight. He's a worthless piece of shit."

The bodyguard yanked Benito off the floor and pushed him out the door.

Nikolai sat back down and flipped open the new burner. Then he punched in Kolkov's telephone number. "Alexey, it's done. I just gave the mole the money. He's gonna take care of our friend." He waited for a response but only heard a loud click as the *Pakhan* hung up the phone without saying a word.

Cursing, Nikolai pulled a fresh handkerchief from his coat pocket, mopped the sweat from his brow, and stormed out of the restaurant, knocking over the maitre d' as he walked into a downpour.

It had finally started to rain.

Maybe now there'd be some relief from the heat.

CHAPTER 19

IT WAS SEVEN A.M., AND THE RAIN had finally stopped, leaving a dewy mist hanging over the city. Ethan was walking Holly down Fifth Avenue, trying to clear his head as she pulled him from one tree to the next. He thought about letting her run free in Central Park, but was too tired to chase her across the grassy meadows or through the wooded forests. Ignoring a sour taste in his mouth, he lit a cigarette and worried about his story. He had less than a week until his interview with Feodor, and he still hadn't buttoned up the loose ends. His meeting with the heroin addicts had linked Pavel to the Russians, but he was still missing the key evidence he needed to prove the existence of a cover-up or reveal a conspiracy.

Questions. Questions. Questions.

And no time to nail down the answers.

Frustrated, he tossed his cigarette into the gutter and continued walking, trying to decide what to do next. He stopped to let Holly do her business at the base of a tree, then crossed the transverse at Eighty-Fourth Street and sat down on the steps in front of the Metropolitan Museum of Art. Out of the corner of his eye, he noticed a late-model black Lincoln Navigator as it slowly cruised by and pulled to a stop.

He stared at the car.

Had he seen it before?

Curious, he stood and slowly headed toward the Lincoln, noticing two big men sitting in the front, watching him intently. He kept walking, another block, pretending to ignore them, a cold sweat soaking his shirt, then peered back at the Lincoln. One of the men had climbed out the car and was now leaning against the hood. The other was still sitting in the driver's seat, his beady eyes fixed and piercing.

Who were they?

Why were they watching him?

He pulled out his iPhone and dialed Mindy.

"Jeez, Ethan, it's a bit early to be calling, don't you think?" she said.

"Sorry, but something weird's going on. There are two guys tailing me."

"What do you mean?"

"Just what I said. I'm being followed down Fifth Avenue by two guys in a fucking black Lincoln Navigator."

"Have you seen them before?"

"Yeah. I'm pretty sure this isn't the first time I've seen them," he said, agitated. "I'm almost positive that car's been parked outside my building the past couple of nights. Somebody's keeping tabs on me."

"Think you're in danger?"

"How the hell should I know?" he said, raising his voice. "Hold on a sec. One of the guys—a really big guy—just got back into the car." He lowered his cell phone to his side as the Lincoln burst across the street, slowed to a crawl as it approached him—the two men leering menacingly—and then disappeared around the corner.

He stood motionless, paralyzed with fear.

"Ethan, what's going on? You still there?"

He lifted his iPhone. "I'm here, Mindy. They just left." He took a deep breath. "I think somebody's sending me a message, and I think I know who it is."

"Who, Ethan?" she said, mystified.

"It's gotta be Alexey Kolkov."

"Why do you think it's the Russian Mob?"

"Who else could it be? They must've found out I talked to Lloyd or to the junkies or to God knows who else."

"I don't know, Ethan, maybe you're imagining it?"

"I'm not," he said, shouting again. "Two guys are coming after me. I just saw them with my own two eyes."

"Calm down, Ethan. What do you want me to do?"

"Call David. Tell him to reach out to his contacts in Washington and ask them if the Russians ever drive black Lincoln Navigators."

"Should I call Lloyd too? He's been tracking Kolkov for years. Maybe he knows?"

"Good idea," Ethan said, beginning to worry about Sarah and Luke. "I gotta go home, make sure my family's okay, then I'm gonna head to the office. Meet me there in an hour."

. . . . .

Anatoly Gennadi was standing in plain sight when Ethan reached the corner of Ninety-First Street. He followed him down the block yelling obscenities, and hovered until Ethan hastily disappeared into the lobby of his building. Then he made his way to

Madison Avenue and hauled himself into the passenger seat of the Lincoln. "Mischa, watch front of building while I make call to Nikolai. Ethan's been busy boy this morning." He pulled out a burner and dialed Stanislov's number.

It rang twice before Nikolai picked up, still groggy with sleep. "Who the fuck is this?"

"It's me, Anatoly. I tail Ethan Benson. I thought you'd want to know what big producer does so early in morning."

Stanislov sat up in bed, fully awake. "Fill me in."

"He left apartment at seven. We follow down Fifth Avenue. Walks dog. Dog takes piss. Dog takes shit. He smoke cigarettes, reads iPhone, then sits on steps at museum. Same as always in morning."

"Did he meet with anybody?" Nikolai said disdainfully.

"*Nyet*," Anatoly said.

"Did you confront him like the *Pakhan* told you to?"

"*Da*. I make sure I was in face, not once, two times. I yell, curse at him. He saw me."

"Did you scare him?"

Anatoly's expression turned dark. "He big-time scared, Nikolai. He call somebody after I get out of car first time. Never take eyes off me. Has long face. Screams on telephone."

"Good. Soon he'll put two and two together and figure out who we are, then, maybe, he'll back off his fucking story."

"What you want me to do now?" Anatoly said, relishing the possibilities.

"Keep following him," Nikolai said. "I want him to know we're watching his every move. Is he back in his apartment?"

"*Da*."

"What do you think he's doing?"

"Shivering in boots. Ha, ha, ha. Worrying what I do next."

"You're a bundle of laughs, Anatoly. Call me when he's on the move again. I want to know where he goes."

· · · · ·

Stanislov put down his burner, clenching his fist in a ball, trying to control his temper. *That fucking Benson*, he thought, irritably. *I gotta get rid of him. And I gotta do it soon. But how? How? How?* Then he looked down at the hooker sleeping next to him and shook her violently.

Her eyes blinked open. "Where am I?" she said, confused.

"You're in my damn bed, bitch. I want you outta here in five minutes. I got things to do." He pulled a five-hundred-dollar bill out of his wallet, folded it into a neat little square, and tossed it at her. Then, without warning, he exploded, brutally kicking her, sending her crashing to the floor, her head hitting the hardwood with a loud thump. Screaming, she grabbed her clothes and dashed out of the room.

Stanislov grinned like a Cheshire cat, then stalked her into the hallway, enjoying her unbridled fear as she stuffed the money into her purse and made her way through his house, naked and confused. Pulling open the front door, she stopped and yelled, "You motherfucking asshole. I'm gonna call the cops, you scumbag."

"Don't talk back to me, cunt. I'll teach you respect." He lunged, pummeling her with his fists, splitting her lower lip and breaking her nose. Blood poured down her face and onto her breasts. Then he picked her up like a ragdoll and hurled her against the wall where she hung suspended in midair for an instant before slowly sliding to the floor. Dazed, she spit out a tooth, climbed to her hands and knees, and crawled out the door.

Laughing hysterically, Nikolai grabbed her clothes and tossed them after her, watching as she picked them up, stumbled to her feet, and ran down the block.

After slamming the door, he lit a cigarette and thought about Benson. Maybe it was time to rough him up a bit. Maybe it was time to give him a good beating. Maybe then he'd get the message—just like the hooker—and stop working on his story.

He picked up the phone and called the *Pakhan*.

. . . . .

Ethan double-bolted the front door, dropped Holly's leash onto the floor, and made his way to his study. He poured himself a big tumbler of scotch and stared at the rich, brown liquid as Sarah padded into the room, barefoot, a horrified look on her face. "Ethan, you're not going to drink that, are you? It's eight o'clock in the morning for Christ's sake."

"I've been thinking about it, but you're right, it's probably a bad idea." He placed the glass on his desk. "Can't have alcohol on my breath when I go see the boss," he said a little too flippantly.

"That's not funny, Ethan. Don't joke about your drinking. You promised me you'd take your problem seriously. Here, I brought you some coffee." She handed him a mug. "Where'd you go with Holly? You were gone for an hour. I was starting to get worried."

"I had to get out of the apartment," he said cautiously. "I was up most of the night and needed some fresh air. Come sit with me for a minute before Luke wakes up. We need to talk." He grabbed her hand and led her over to the couch. "Sarah, have you seen a black Lincoln Navigator parked anywhere on the street the past couple of days?"

She sat forward, surprised. "I don't think so."

"Are you sure?"

She thought a moment. "I honestly don't remember, Ethan. Maybe? I never pay much attention to who's parked outside our building. Why? What's going on?"

Ethan calmed his voice, hoping to temper what he was about to tell her. "I was just followed down Fifth Avenue by a black Lincoln Navigator."

"What?"

"There were two big guys in the front seat. One of them got out and stood there watching me. Then he tailed me down our block yelling and screaming like a wild man. He seemed to know where we lived."

"Who are they, Ethan?"

He paused, debating what to say. "I'm not sure, babe, but I'm gonna find out."

"Are they after you?"

He didn't answer.

"Talk to me, Ethan. Am I in danger? Is Luke?"

"Maybe." He climbed off the couch and paced around the room.

"Are they still out there?" she said, frightened.

"I don't know," he said, walking to the window and peering down at the street. "Yup, I can see them. They're double-parked on the far side of Madison Avenue about a third the way up the block toward Park."

Sarah pulled her knees up to her chin and wrapped her arms around her legs. "Why are they after you, Ethan? What did you do?"

"I didn't do anything," Ethan said defensively as he sat back down. "But, you know, when I was out with Lloyd Howard the other night, I talked to a couple of junkies who knew Pavel Feodor and connected him to the Russian Mob. Maybe they found out about me."

Sarah's hands began shaking. "The Russian Mob's involved in the murder and is keeping tabs on you because of your story?"

"Maybe," he said, lighting a cigarette.

"Why didn't you tell me, Ethan? Why am I just hearing this for the first time?"

"Because until this morning, I didn't think we were in danger," he said, raising his voice. "Besides, I just spotted those two thugs and don't really know who they are. I just told you that."

"Why are you yelling?" Sarah said. "I'm scared. Really scared, Ethan. I don't think Lukey and I can stay here until you figure things out."

"I don't think you can either," Ethan said, trying to control his own fear. "Call your office and tell them you're sick. Then pack up some stuff and go to your sister's in Ohio. You'll be safe there until this blows over."

"And what about you?"

"I can't leave, Sarah, you know that. I gotta finish my story and find out why those guys are after me."

"You're not going to do something stupid, are you, Ethan?"

"I'll be careful," he said comfortingly. "Now go pack. I want you outta here and on a plane right away."

She got up without saying another word and hurried out of the room.

Ethan walked over to his desk and stared at the scotch, then picked up the tumbler and swilled it down all at once. Feeling better, he headed down the hall to help Sarah get ready to leave.

CHAPTER 20

AN HOUR LATER, ETHAN PUT Sarah and Luke into a
Minuteman Taxi, handed the driver their suitcases, and quickly
looked up and down the block. At first he didn't see the Lincoln
Navigator and thought that sending his family off to Ohio was
foolhardy, a hasty reaction to a moment of stress. But then he
found it hiding behind a delivery truck, sitting like a sentinel,
the same two men in the front seat, watching. He motioned
to Sarah to roll down the window. "It's still on the corner near
Madison Avenue."

"Where? I don't see it?"

"Behind the FedEx truck."

She looked out the back window and spotted the Lincoln.
"What do we do now, Ethan?" she said pleadingly.

"Stick to the plan. Take Luke and head to the airport. I'll wait
here until you're out of sight and make sure they don't follow you."

"And what if they do?"

"I'll call, and we'll figure something out." He leaned into

the taxi and kissed her, then turned to Luke. "Take care of your mommy, little man."

"And what about you, Daddy? Those are bad men. Who's gonna take care of you?" Luke said, his little face looking up, bewildered.

"I'll be fine, Lukey. Don't worry." He rubbed his mop of red hair and motioned to the driver to get going.

"I love you, babe," he said, forcing a smile.

"I love you, too," Sarah said as the taxi pulled away from the curb, sped down the block, and disappeared into the traffic on Fifth Avenue.

Ethan sighed heavily and looked for the Lincoln. It hadn't moved. Then he turned and slowly headed down Ninety-First Street, glancing over his shoulder every now and then, making sure the Navigator hadn't inched out onto the street behind him. When he reached the middle of the block, he broke for the corner, sprinting as fast as he could—legs churning, arms pumping, hair blowing in the wind.

At Fifth Avenue, he hailed a taxi, gave the driver the address for the Broadcast Center, and told him there was an extra fifty if he ran all the lights. The cabbie gunned the engine and peeled into traffic, weaving around slower-moving cars and trucks like a Formula One driver.

Ethan checked the back window.

The Navigator wasn't there.

When they reached the corner of Sixty-Sixth Street, he leaned forward and told the driver to take a quick right and head to the West Side through the transverse. The cabbie jerked the wheel and skidded through the intersection, nearly sideswiping a parked car. Hitting the accelerator, he raced across Central Park at sixty miles an hour, speeding past a group of pedestrians gawking from the sidewalk and making a quick left turn onto Columbus Avenue.

Ethan searched again for the black Lincoln.

Still no sign of it.

When they reached Fifty-Seventh Street, he paid the driver and hopped out of the taxi. *Where should I go? Where should I go?* he thought. *To the office? But what if they're watching there, too? Gotta think. Gotta think. Maybe it's better if I hide somewhere else till I figure things out.* Heading uptown, he looked for a coffee shop, then ducked into the Time Warner Building, losing himself in the crowd of people milling about the shopping arcade. Still paranoid, he pushed into a Starbucks and searched the room.

Nobody was following.

The coast was clear.

After ordering a Grande Mocha, he sat down at a table near the window and pulled out his iPhone. "Come on, come on, Mindy, pick up. We need to talk." He waited impatiently and dialed the number again.

"Ethan, you sound out of breath," she said, finally answering. "What's going on?"

"I just had some more fun with my friends in the black Lincoln," he said, alarmed. "They were outside my apartment building when I left for work."

"Did they come after you?"

"I lost them in a taxi. Are you at the office?"

"I'm stuck in traffic coming across Fifty-Seventh Street. I'm about two blocks from the Broadcast Center."

"Well, change of plans. Meet me at the Starbucks in the Time Warner Building instead."

"What are you doing there, Ethan?"

"Buying some time," he said, piqued. "How long will it take you to get here?"

"I'll get out and walk the rest of the way. I can be there in five minutes."

"Don't walk. They might see you. Stay in the taxi. I don't care how long it takes."

"But they don't know who I am," she said, sounding surprised by the fear in his voice.

"We don't know that," he said, wondering if everybody on his team was being followed. "Just get here, Mindy. And check the Broadcast Center when you go by. See if there's a black Lincoln parked out front. I wanna know if there's more than one team of goons watching me."

He hung up the phone and glanced out the window.

There was still no Navigator.

Maybe he'd really lost them.

. . . . .

Fifteen minutes later, Ethan spotted Mindy walking into the Starbucks. She bought a cup of coffee and sat down at the table. "Ethan, you look awful. They scared the shit out of you, didn't they?"

"Guess you could say that."

"Did you have a drink? I can smell alcohol on your breath."

"Just one," he said, ashamed, before changing the subject. "Have you reached David yet?"

"I talked to him a little while ago," she said, worried he was about to bolt to McGlades to tie on a bender. "He's placed calls to his sources in Washington. He should know about Kolkov and the black Lincolns sometime this morning."

"And what about Lloyd?"

"We can't find him."

"Well, David should keep trying."

"He will. He will, Ethan. But do you really think the Russian Mob is after you?" she said suspiciously.

"I'm pretty sure it's them," he said, peeking out at the street again. "Was there a Navigator parked outside the Broadcast Center?"

"A half block away. Two guys in the front seat, just like you said."

Ethan leaned back. "Shit, can't be the same two guys. I'm sure they didn't follow me."

"What are you gonna do, Ethan? Are you gonna tell the police?"

"And tell them what? I think I'm being watched by some really bad guys who may work for the Russian Mob? They'll laugh in my face."

"What about Paul?"

"I can't tell Paul either. I need proof before I go to him. He'll just get pissed at me again."

"You've got to tell somebody," she said.

"No. I need to think it through first," he said adamantly. "Sarah and Luke are safe. She's going to her sister's in Cleveland for a couple of days. I won't have to worry about them once they're out of the city."

"And what about you?"

"That's the sixty-four-thousand-dollar question, isn't it?" he said, checking the time. "It's almost eleven. Let's head to the office. I wanna talk to David and see if he's found out anything yet."

Then his cell phone suddenly beeped.

. . . . .

Sarah grabbed Luke's hand as the Minuteman Taxi pulled away from their apartment and turned onto Fifth Avenue.

"Mommy, where we going?" Luke said.

"I told you, sweetheart. We're going to visit your aunt Amanda and your cousin Jake in Cleveland. Won't that be fun?"

"I want Daddy to come."

"He can't, Lukey. He's gotta work. You know that. We'll come home in a couple of days, and you'll see him then."

"But I wanna see him now."

"Tell you what. We'll call him as soon as we get there. Then you won't miss him quite so much." She pulled him closer and hugged him, trying to console him.

The limo headed up Madison Avenue and across Ninety-Sixth Street, making its way through bumper-to-bumper traffic to the FDR Drive. Sarah kept looking out the window, searching to make sure they weren't being followed, apprehensive. When they stopped for a red light at First Avenue, she tapped the driver on the shoulder. "There isn't anybody suspicious behind us, is there?"

The driver looked at her through his rearview mirror. He was a Sikh and spoke with a heavy Indian accent. "There's a black Lincoln about a block back, mum. He pulled in behind us when we made the turn off Ninetieth onto Madison Avenue. He's been following us ever since."

"Is it the same car that was parked near my building?"

"No, mum, a different one. An older model."

Sarah checked again and spotted the Lincoln partially hidden by a cement truck, then fumbled in her pocketbook and called Ethan on her cell phone.

"Sarah, what's wrong?" he said frantically.

"Ethan, they're right behind us," she said, whispering into the telephone.

"That's impossible. I waited in front of our building until you were long gone before I left. The Lincoln never moved."

"The driver says it's a different car. What should I do?"

"Just stay calm, babe. Where are you?"

"Stopped at a red light. We're about to get onto the FDR Drive."

"Tell the driver to run the light," he said timorously. "And for heaven's sake, don't get off the phone."

"I heard your husband, mum," the driver said, still staring at her through his rearview mirror. "I'll do the best I can." He hit the accelerator, the tires spinning as the limo shot through the intersection and roared onto the highway. Within seconds, it was hauling along at seventy miles an hour, fishtailing as it swerved around cars jamming the thoroughfare, heading for the Robert F. Kennedy Bridge.

Sarah turned and looked out the window. "They're still behind us, Ethan. We're not getting away."

"You've got plenty of time to lose them, Sarah. How's Luke doing?"

"He's crying. He knows something's wrong."

"Tell the driver to go faster."

The cabbie pushed harder on the gas pedal, hauling up the ramp to the bridge at almost eighty miles an hour. Leaning on the horn, he continued accelerating, bursting around slower-moving vehicles, driving like a maniac.

"Are they still following you?" Ethan said.

"I can still see them," Sarah said, out of breath, "but they're not quite as close as they were before."

"Are you on the bridge yet?" he said, urgency in his voice.

"We just went through the tollbooth."

"And where's the Lincoln?"

"Stuck behind a line of cars."

The driver didn't slow as he merged into traffic, the engine roaring as he put more distance between his limousine and the Navigator. Sarah draped her arm around Luke, clutching him closer, hanging on for dear life. "Ethan, the Lincoln's boxed in between an eighteen-wheeler and a couple of cars. I think we're gonna lose it."

"You gotta get to the exit ramp at La Guardia Airport before it catches up to you," he said, now shouting into the phone. "If they don't see you pulling off, they may think you're headed to Kennedy. Then you'll be home free."

"Driver, keep going, faster," she said as she kissed Luke on top of his head, trying to mask her own fear. "Are you okay, Lukey?"

He wiped a tear from his eye. "Who's chasing us, Mommy? Is it the bad guys?"

"Yes, little man, but we're getting away." She looked out the window, hoping she was right. "How much longer, driver?"

"We're almost at the exit ramp, mum," he said.

"Hurry. Please hurry."

The limo screamed into the airport, shooting down the labyrinth of approach roads, until it reached the Delta Airlines Terminal. Sarah barely waited for the driver to stop before scribbling her signature on a voucher and racing with Luke and their luggage into the building.

"Sarah, where are you now?" Ethan said, sounding desperate.

"In the terminal, Ethan. We lost them," she said, panting. "I'm about to pick up our e-tickets. What the hell's going on? Those guys scared the shit out of me and Luke."

"I don't know, babe. I told you, I'm trying to figure it out."

"Well, figure it out soon. We're not coming home until you do. We can't," she said, bursting into tears.

"Pull yourself together, Sarah. For Luke's sake, and whatever you do, don't take your eyes off him."

"I'll watch him," she said, clutching his hand. "But I'm worried, Ethan. And I'm worried about you. Are you gonna be okay all by yourself?"

"I'll be fine. Really. Now go through security and call me when you're on the plane."

She wiped her eyes. "I love you, Ethan."

"I love you, too, babe."

"And please stay out of trouble. I want you in one piece when I get back." She hung up the phone. "Let's go, Luke. We gotta hurry."

Then she vanished into the throng of people as she passed through security and headed to the gate.

CHAPTER 21

ETHAN RUSHED OUT OF THE Starbucks, Mindy on his heels, still worrying about his family. The fog had burned off and the temperature had fallen into the upper sixties. But he was sweating profusely, his skin clammy, his clothes sticking to his body like an extra layer of skin. As he headed toward the Broadcast Center, his mind was a jumble of disconnected thoughts. "Come on, Ethan. Come on. Pull yourself together," he muttered under his breath. "Think, man, think. You gotta figure out what to do."

When he stopped for the light at Fifty-Seventh Street, Mindy put her hand on his shoulder. "Ethan, talk to me. You haven't uttered a word since you hung up with Sarah. Are they okay?"

"They're fine," he said, staring straight ahead, vacantly. "They're safe on the plane. Those guys can't get them anymore."

"Are you all right?"

"I'm fine, Mindy. Just rattled."

"Well, pull yourself together," she said, shaking him. "This is totally out of control. You gotta tell Paul. Those guys are gonna hurt you or Sarah or maybe even Luke. You gotta do something."

He turned and faced her. "Look, there's nothing we can do at the moment. Nothing. We need solid evidence before I tell Paul. All I have is a theory," he said, more determined than ever to find answers before going to his boss. "Show me where you saw the Lincoln before you got to the Starbucks. Let's start there."

Mindy peered down the block, trying to see around the waves of people jamming the sidewalk. "I don't see it," she said, pointing. "It was parked there on the north side of the street near Seventh Avenue. About a half block from the entrance to the Broadcast Center. It's not there anymore."

Ethan strained into the distance, trying to pick out a black Lincoln. Then he spotted a Navigator—now on the south side of the street—its engine idling, exhaust billowing out of its tailpipe. A big, burly man with greasy black hair was sitting in the driver's seat. Was it the same man he'd seen earlier in the day? The same man who'd stalked him back to his apartment? Or was it somebody else?

"What do you think, Mindy? Is that the car you saw earlier?"

"I don't know, Ethan. They all look the same to me. Maybe it's a different one? Lots of people drive Lincoln Navigators, right?" She looked around warily. "Where's the second guy? There were two of them when I drove by before."

"There's only one now. Let's get a closer look," Ethan said, taking off down the block, ignoring the new wave of fear rising in his gut.

"Are you crazy, Ethan? You can't go down there."

But Ethan was already approaching the Lincoln, glancing through the front window. The man staring back at him was grossly overweight with a bulbous red nose and crooked teeth. He was wearing a tight black T-shirt and wraparound sunglasses, gold chains hanging around his neck and dangling from his wrists.

"Is that the guy who's been following you?" Mindy whispered anxiously.

"No. It's a different guy," Ethan said, taking one last look before walking past the car and up to the front entrance of the Broadcast Center.

Then the Navigator pulled into traffic.

"Ethan, he's coming after us," Mindy said, trying to hurry him along.

"Hold up, he's not gonna do anything. There are too many people watching." He stopped next to a security guard, never taking his eyes off the Lincoln as it cruised by and disappeared around the side of the building.

Then he spotted the second guy.

"Mindy, that's him."

"Where?"

Ethan pointed to a surly looking man leaning up against a parked car about a hundred feet away. "Over there. In the blue sports coat and denim jeans. He's wearing a gray polo shirt and is smoking a cigarette. I think he's packing a gun in a shoulder holster. I can see the bulge under his arm."

"Where? I don't see him," Mindy said, moving a step closer to Ethan.

"He's on this side of the bus stop. See? He's staring at us," Ethan said, now positive that whoever had ordered the surveillance knew everything about him and his family.

"Are you sure that's the guy?"

"Positive. You don't forget somebody who looks like that."

"Should we tell the security guard?"

"No."

"Ethan, you have to," she said lividly. "The guy's here at the office threatening you. Just like he did this morning."

"I'm not telling anybody," he said, emphasizing each word. "If I blow the whistle now, I risk spooking whoever's watching me. Then I'll never find out who they are, and I'll never feel safe."

"Please, you've got to tell somebody," she said, begging.

"No. I need to know if it's the Russians and whether they're trying to stop me from doing my story. Come on; let's go into the building where it's safe."

. . . . .

Anatoly Gennadi continued watching until he was sure they wouldn't double back out of the building, then eased away from the car and strolled down to Eighth Avenue. Parked on the corner was the Lincoln Navigator. His partner, Mischa Polchak, was sitting in the driver's seat, an Uzi submachine gun resting on the floor by his feet. He opened the passenger door and climbed in. "Pull around block and head back to television station," Gennadi said. "Park close to front of building. I want to make sure Benson see me again when he leaves, even if we sit all day. Do you have clean burner?"

Mischa flipped open an old briefcase and handed him a cell phone. "This one's never been used."

Gennadi punched in Stanislov's telephone number. "Found him, Nikolai. He just goes to office."

"Did he see you?"

"*Da*. I was standing not too far away, down from front door of building, waiting on street. He still scared."

"Was he alone?"

"*Nyet*. He was with that girl—fat, dirty blonde. Same one always with."

"And his wife and kid?"

"Small problem. They get away on highway," Gennadi said, shrugging his shoulders as he smiled at Mischa.

"Shit, Anatoly, I told you not to lose them."

"Can't help. Viktor and Georgy say much traffic. Drive too fast."

"Where'd they go?"

"Maybe airport."

"Damn it. I want you to find them right away," Nikolai said, shouting angrily.

Gennadi covered the mouthpiece and leaned over to Mischa. "Stanislov big-time pissed off. Freaking out on telephone." Then he said to Nikolai, "I tell guys to look. Maybe find. Maybe not. We see."

"So where are you now?"

"Parked outside TV station. Not going anyplace." Anatoly lit another cigarette. "So what you think, Nikolai? Time to teach Benson big lesson?" He exhaled the smoke through his nose.

"Do it," Nikolai said. "I ran it by the *Pakhan* and he said okay. Let me know if anything changes."

Anatoly hung up the phone and tossed the burner into the backseat. He looked up at the Broadcast Center, his expression cold, his eyes dead. "So now time to have real fun with Ethan Benson," he said, grinning at Mischa. "And I know best way to make sorry he ever start television story."

. . . . .

Ethan unlocked his office door and dropped into the chair at his desk, running one plan through his head after another, trying to decide the best way to flush out the identity of the people chasing him. He turned to Mindy, who was standing quietly in the hallway, visibly upset. "Take five minutes and pull yourself together. They can't get by security and into the building. Then find David. Tell him I want to see him right away."

Without answering, she scurried away.

Ethan sighed.

He was confident Sarah and Luke were safe now that they were on a plane headed to Cleveland—unless the guys harassing him had a good network of connections and unlimited resources. Then, and only then, might they figure out where to find them. But was Mindy right? Was he in danger? Should he go to Paul? To the police? No. Not yet. That wasn't the right way to go. He had to figure out who they were first.

David and Mindy walked into his office and sat down on the couch.

"Mindy just told me what happened to Sarah and Luke," David said, concerned. "And that the same guy who tailed you earlier this morning is outside the building."

"Yeah, he's out there—big and muscular and scary as hell. Look, have you heard anything about the Lincoln Navigators?"

"One of my contacts at the DEA confirmed your suspicions. Alexey Kolkov has a whole fleet of them."

"And what did Howard say?"

"The same thing. Kolkov has some weird taste for high-end Lincolns. Black and only black."

Ethan rubbed his chin. "So it probably is the Russians. Now what? Did they tell you anything else?"

David stood and walked over to a swivel chair facing Ethan's desk. "My DEA source confirmed everything we were told by Howard and the junkies. The agency knows all about Pavel Feodor, his connection to Nikolai Stanislov, and about the heroin deal in the Meatpacking District."

"How do they know?" Ethan said.

"My source emailed me this." He leaned over and handed Ethan a document. "It's a list of informants the DEA relies on for information about the Russians. He told me he'd deny it was real if we put it on the air. So I promised I'd keep it confidential."

"What should I be looking for?" Ethan said, scanning the document.

"Read the second page."

Ethan ran his finger down a column of names, stopping in the middle and whistling. "Leonid Karloff is one of their informants?"

"Bingo," David said, grinning. "And my source confirmed Howard's take on him—the guy's intel is always dead on target. He may be a heroin addict, but he knows what he's talking about."

"So Karloff told the DEA the same story he told us? The same story he told Detective Jenkins and the cops? That the Russians were involved in Cynthia Jameson's murder?"

"Bingo again," David said.

"And the DEA believes him?" Ethan said.

"One hundred percent. They heard the same thing from many of their other informants."

Ethan shot Mindy a quick glance before turning back to David. "Did your source say whether they discussed this with anybody involved in Feodor's case?"

"It took me a little while to get him to answer that question, but he told me, off the record, that the DEA discussed the Russians and their role in the heroin deal not only with the cops investigating the murder—including Detective Jenkins—but also with the assistant district attorney herself."

"With Nancy McGregor?" Mindy said, stunned.

"Yup. At a meeting with McGregor and that other ADA, Nelson Brown."

"Why didn't McGregor pursue it?" Mindy said, grabbing the document from Ethan and scanning the list of names until she found Karloff. "If they'd followed up on the Russians, it might've changed the whole case."

"Good question," Ethan said, now wondering if Nancy McGregor was the mystery person in the crime scene video who wanted to review the police reports before they were placed in the case file. Could she be the mastermind tampering with the evidence? Was she giving the orders? It made sense, but why would she do that? "I've got another question, David. Why did the DEA sit on the Russian connection once they realized McGregor wasn't going to make it part of her case?"

"According to my source, their hands were tied. They had no jurisdiction over the murder and were pressured by some political bigwig here in New York to sit on it. So once they gave the information to McGregor, they backed off and left it to the ADA to use or ignore."

"And she obviously chose to ignore it," Ethan said, dumbfounded. "Look, we need more background on McGregor. Much more. We need to find out where she came from, who she's close to, and why she was given this case. I want both of you to work your contacts here and in Washington. I wanna know why Nancy McGregor buried the lead about the Russians and Feodor. I wanna know what she's hiding."

"Jeez, I know this shit about McGregor is important," Mindy said, climbing off the couch, "but before I hit the phones, tell me what you're planning to do about that guy downstairs."

Ethan hesitated, then looked up at Mindy looming over his desk. "I need to shoot some pictures of them," he said stonily.

"What? That's insane," Mindy said frostily. "How you gonna do that? You can't use a camera crew. That's like painting a target on your back."

"You're right, but I need pictures to show Lloyd. Maybe he can ID the guy downstairs and the other guys who are tailing me.

Then I can go to Paul and to the police." Ethan stood and paced around the room, then turned to David. "You're a good still photographer. Julie Piedmont showed me the press pictures you shot when she interviewed Paul McCartney. They were incredible. Spot on. Have you ever done any undercover shooting?"

"Lots of times," David said confidently. "It doesn't scare me. I have a Nikon digital camera and some high-powered lenses. I'm up for it. When do you wanna take the pictures, Ethan?"

"The sooner the better. How about tomorrow?"

"I can do that," David said excitedly. "And where do you wanna do it?"

Ethan wrote down his address on a piece of paper and handed it to David. "There's a black Lincoln Navigator staking out my apartment building. I'm a block from Fifth Avenue. You can get a clean shot with a telephoto lens from behind the big stone wall that runs around Central Park. You should be safe there."

"I know the spot. Should work."

"So we'll shoot tomorrow. In the evening. After dark," Ethan said reflectively. "But David, if you decide it's too risky, you can change your mind—at any time. I won't be upset. I'll find some other way to shoot the pictures."

"No, I'm good with it, Ethan."

"Well, I'm not," Mindy said crossly. "You're talking about messing around with the fucking Russian Mob. They're dangerous. They're killers. They're threatening you and your family. This is not a good idea."

"It's the only way," Ethan said emphatically. "If we're careful, they won't know we're spying on them—like they're spying on me." He paused a split second. "I just thought of something." He picked up the telephone. "Hey, Willy, it's Ethan Benson. I've got a question for you. Can you rig me a shoulder bag with a hidden camera for a shoot I wanna do tomorrow night?" Another short pause. "Great. I'll come by later today and pick it up. Thanks, pal." He hung up the phone. "What do you think, David?"

"Great idea. You can record a point-of-view shot as you walk by the Lincoln, while I snap away the still pictures from the park."

"And if it works," Ethan said, "we'll have images to show Lloyd and an extra undercover sequence to use in our story."

"Ethan, what's wrong with you? You're not listening to me," Mindy said, exasperated. "It's one thing exposing the Russian Mob's involvement in the murder. It's another going head-to-head with them on the street. You sure you want to do this?"

"I need the pictures, Mindy. I've weighed the risks and think we can pull it off without getting caught."

"It's a good plan," David said, adding his support.

"Well, I think it's absolute madness," she said, and without uttering another word, stormed out of his office.

"She gets this way whenever she doesn't agree with me," Ethan said, watching her disappear down the hall. "She'll come around once she thinks about it for a while. She always does." He checked the time. It was getting late. "I've got a bunch of loose ends to tie up and need to brief Sampson. Let's regroup before we head home."

"Sure thing, Ethan."

As David departed, Ethan picked up a portrait of Sarah and Luke sitting on his desk. They were smiling into the camera, arms wrapped around each other, beaming, without a care in the world. Suddenly, his heart sank. Was he making the right decision? Was he putting himself and his family in harm's way? Should he tell Paul? He looked out at Central Park, uncertain, then sighed deeply, grabbed his iPhone, and punched in Peter's number.

CHAPTER 22

JIMMY BENITO PULLED INTO THE employee parking lot out-side the North Infirmary Command Building. He was driving a broken-down Ford Mustang that had seen better days. The car was two decades old and had clocked over 250,000 hard New York City miles. The engine barely turned over and often stalled, always at the wrong time, like this morning on the highway when he was driving to work. Every day he prayed to the Virgin Mary before inserting the key, hoping the car wouldn't start so he could dump the junker into Flushing Bay and put it and himself out of misery.

After circling for ten minutes looking for a space near the building, he gave up and parked by the barbed-wire fence sur-rounding the complex. Opening the glove compartment, he pulled out the standard-issue handgun all corrections officers car-ried on duty, made sure it was loaded, and put it into the holster sitting on his hip. Then he looked at himself in the rearview mir-ror. It wasn't pretty. He'd been drinking heavily, one beer after another, and hadn't showered or shaved, his uniform wrinkled and dirty. There were deep circles under his eyes, blotches on his face, and his hair stuck out in every direction.

Reaching for a cigarette, he closed his eyes and tried to will away the pounding in his head. He wanted to call Nikolai Stanislov and tell him he hadn't come up with a plan to kill Feodor—that he couldn't go through with it—but the twenty-five thousand dollars was burning a hole in his pocket, and he could taste the second big payday once he took care of business and the little shit was dead.

He needed the money.

He could buy a new car.

So he avoided the call.

Checking the time, he realized he'd been daydreaming, that the windows were closed, and that he was perspiring heavily, beads of sweat dripping down his face and spreading under his arms. He wiped his brow, opened the car door, and staggered to his feet. After popping the trunk, he grabbed his rifle and nightstick and slowly made his way to the security entrance in the back of the building.

The ten-by-twelve-foot anteroom was packed with corrections officers. The warden had just finished a security check and added more personnel to make sure the interview would go off without a hitch. Jimmy Benito panicked. There was less time to make the hit than he thought—the odds of success diminishing each day like sand in an hourglass.

He walked up to an X-ray machine and emptied his pockets—unhooking his holster and handing his rifle and nightstick to a big African-American security guard. Then he walked through and set off the alarm. The guard put up his hands and stopped him. "Mr. Benito, sir, please turn out your pockets and spread your legs."

Benito looked at the officer's name tag and barked, "Jesus

Christ, Leo—that's your name, isn't it? Do you know who I am? I'm the commanding officer on H Block. Cut me some slack."

"Just doing my job, sir," the guard said apologetically. "Special orders from the warden on account of the interview." He ran his hands over Benito's back and sides and then down his legs. "Thank you, sir. You're all clear to go."

Benito picked up his weapons, snarled, and was buzzed through a steel door leading to a long hallway down to the cell-blocks. When he arrived at a second security checkpoint, he waited for a corrections officer to punch a code into a keypad, then walked through another steel door and onto H Block, where he was met by more firepower. *Shit, man, how am I gonna take out Feodor?* he thought. *There ain't this much security even when the building's on lockdown.*

Taking a deep breath, he opened the door to his office and sat down at his desk, the room spinning like a top. He reached for a bottle of aspirin, but it was empty. Cursing, he hurled the bottle against the wall and yelled at a guard named Miguel Johnson who was standing just outside the door. "I need aspirin. Get me some from the infirmary."

"Sure—sure—sure thing, Jimmy," Johnson said meekly. "Are you okay? You don't look so good. Are—are—are you sick?"

Benito wiped his nose with the back of his hand. "No, I'm not sick. I gotta a headache. Go the fuck and get the aspirin and stop your fucking stuttering. It's driving me crazy."

Miguel didn't answer. He stared at his CO and scooted down the hall.

Benito shook his head, trying to focus, then booted up his computer. Maybe he could find a way to take out Feodor some-where in the day's schedule. Was he due for a shower? Shit. Not until tomorrow. So he couldn't leave him alone in the bathroom with some half-crazy nigger who'd be more than happy to do the job for him. Maybe he was expecting a visitor? Maybe his attorney or his mother or somebody else? No luck there either. Pavel wasn't scheduled to see anybody. So there was no way to stage an accident.

How was he going to kill Feodor?

Think. Think. Think.

He opened the master intake log for the jail complex. A new inmate had been brought in early that morning. He'd been booked for beating an old woman to death and would soon be housed in a cell three doors down from Feodor. A vague plan took shape in his mind. Maybe he could make an unannounced visit to Feodor's cell when they brought the new inmate to H Block. He could say he was checking for contraband, then beat the living shit out of him and claim the little bastard was trying to escape. It was a long shot, but it might just work and give him a chance to put Feodor out of commission. That would buy him some more time to figure out the best way to kill him.

Miguel Johnson walked back into his office with Hector Ruiz, another prison guard who worked on the cellblock. "Here you go, Jimmy. I got some—some—some aspirin for you." He put the bottle down on the desk. "Can I get—get—get you anything else? You really don't look—look—look too good."

"Shut the fuck up," Benito said, exploding. "I'm fine. I told you I have a headache. And if you can't stop stuttering, don't open your mouth and say another word. I don't wanna listen to your bullshit."

"Take it easy, Jimmy," Ruiz said, holding out his hands, palms up. "Miguel's just trying to help. You look sick, man. Everybody can see it. Maybe we can tell the warden that's why you were late and missed the run-through for the interview. He's pissed you weren't there."

"I don't care about the warden. Fuck him. I had car trouble. That's why I was late." He started to get up, intending to push the two guards out of his office, but the room began spinning, round and round, and he fell back into his chair.

"Jimmy, what's wrong with you?" Ruiz said, raising an eyebrow. "Are you drunk? You smell like a brewery."

"I haven't had a drink since yesterday," Benito said nastily. "I must've spilled whiskey on my uniform. That's what you smell. There's nothing wrong with me but my head." He opened the bottle of aspirin, shook out a couple of pills, and popped them into his mouth. "Now get the fuck outta my office. I have work to do."

"Okay, Jimmy, but I don't think you should be here," Ruiz said acidly. "I don't think you can handle the pressure today. You should go home."

Benito stood up, screaming. Other officers turned and stared. "I don't care what you think. I'm the CO on duty today, and I say I'm fine, so get the fuck out of my office!"

"Sure thing, Jimmy. Take—take—take it easy," Johnson said as they slowly backed out of the room.

Benito closed his eyes. "Shit. The guys know I'm drunk," he whined to himself. "If they report me, the warden's gonna discipline me for sure. Maybe suspend me. I gotta take care of Feodor, and I gotta do it now. There ain't no time to wait for that goddamn new inmate to get here." He flipped off the safety on his handgun and made sure there was a bullet in the chamber. Then he picked up his nightstick and headed for the door, motioning to a security guard to buzz him onto the cellblock where he stumbled past a phalanx of corrections officers and made his way to Feodor's cell. "Well, well, well, if it ain't the most famous murderer on H Block. Lights, action, cameras. The man's gonna be a big TV star," he said, throwing his head back and howling like a wild man.

Feodor didn't move. "I know you think you're funny, Mr. Big Boss Man, but I'm not buggin' nobody. I'm just layin' here on my bed, smokin' a cigarette, mindin' my own business. So buzz off and leave me alone, motherfucker."

Benito tapped his nightstick on the bars—*rat-a-tat-tat*—hoping Feodor would lose his cool and give him an excuse, any excuse, to pull out his handgun and blow off his head. "So, Pavel, you little shit, what you gonna tell that television crew? You gonna make up some excuse for murdering that pretty little girl? You gonna tell them you fucked her after she was dead? You gonna tell them it was fun?"

Pavel stood and took two steps toward the bars, then stopped, put up his hands, and smiled. "I'm just gonna tell them the truth, what really happened that night, nothin' more. I bet you can't wait to hear what I say. I'm gonna be the talk of the town. Now go crawl under a rock and bother somebody else, you asshole." He turned and sat back down on his bed.

Benito had his opening. Feodor was disrespecting him in front of the other guards. He couldn't let that happen—not to him, the commanding officer on H Block. It was time to teach that motherfucker a lesson. He'd just go in there and push him around a bit, whack him a few times on the head with his nightstick, maybe mess up his face, put him in the hospital. The interview would get postponed. Maybe even canceled. It was as good a plan as any, and it might just work.

Benito whirled around and glared at the security guard standing behind him. "Open the fucking door, Jose. I want to check Feodor's cell. The guy's always hiding some kind of shit he's not supposed to have."

"We just checked his cell, sir. It's clean."

"I don't give a shit," Benito said. "I want to check it myself. Open the goddamn door."

As the guard unlocked the cell, Feodor climbed off his cot and backed into the corner, never taking his eyes off Benito and his nightstick. Then he slowly turned and put his hands behind his back. "Okay, Mr. Big Boss Man, you can cuff me whenever you want. I ain't gonna move, not even an inch."

"Fuck that. Look at me, asshole. I wanna see your face when I'm talking to you," Benito said sharply.

"Can't do that," Feodor said passively. "I can't face you until I'm cuffed. That there is the rule, and I'm goin' by the book today. I ain't gonna provoke you. That wouldn't be too smart, would it?"

Benito stopped short. *This isn't what's supposed to happen*, he thought. *He's supposed to turn and threaten me so I can give him a good beating. Why won't he play by the rules?* He began to feel lightheaded, wiping his brow with his sleeve, then took two steps toward Feodor and pushed him up against the wall, spinning him around, and violently shoving his nightstick into the pit of his stomach. Feodor doubled over in pain, trying to catch his breath, the wind knocked out of him. "What the fuck are you hiding in here? Tell me, you little fucker," Benito said, screaming. "I know you got somethin' you're not supposed to have." He raised his nightstick and clubbed Feodor's leg, sending him crashing to the floor. Then he brought up his nightstick again, and before he could bring it down on Feodor's head, he was grabbed from behind by Miguel Johnson, who had quietly slipped into the cell.

"Take—take—take it easy, Jimmy. You don't want to do that. You're—you're—you're going to kill the guy. Get—get—get a grip on yourself!"

Benito wrestled free and began beating Johnson, breaking a rib with his nightstick, a loud crunch echoing around the cellblock as the prison guard slumped to the floor, writhing in pain.

Then all hell broke loose.

Other guards rushed into the cell as Benito flailed away with his nightstick, striking anyone and everyone who came near. Two more officers went down, both bleeding from nasty head wounds, before Benito drew his revolver. Zeroing in on Feodor, now hiding under his bed, he aimed and fired, the bullet narrowly missing his face and embedding itself in the wall.

More chaos.

Corrections officers hurled themselves at Benito, grabbing his handgun and twisting his hands behind his back, struggling to subdue and cuff him. The warden and his chief press officer raced onto the cellblock, responding to sirens blasting around the jail complex, and pushed their way through the crowd of guards now blocking the entrance to Feodor's cell. "What the fuck happened?" Morales said in a rage. "Who fired the gunshot?"

"The CO, Jimmy—Jimmy—Jimmy Benito," Miguel Johnson said, clutching his chest and shouting above the din of inmates yelling and screaming and banging on the bars. "He marched—marched—marched down here and demanded to go into Feodor's cell, then—then—then he lost it—just like that. It happened real—real—real quick. We tried to stop—stop—stop him, but we couldn't get—get—get to him in time."

Morales spun around and leered at Benito. "What's wrong with you? You could have killed him."

Benito, now pinned to the ground by two officers, blood trickling down his cheek from a gash above his eye, looked up at the warden and started to speak, then stopped, deciding he was better off holding his tongue and not saying a word.

"Answer me," the warden said, shrieking. "Are you out of your mind?"

"He's not out of his mind, sir. He's drunk," said Hector Ruiz. "I tried sending him home when he first got here. Told him he was in no shape to work. But he refused to listen to me, sir."

"I can smell the alcohol on his breath," Morales said pitifully.

"Arrest his sorry ass and get him out of my sight." He peered over at Feodor. "You weren't shot, were you, Pavel?"

Feodor was now sitting on his bed, his hands clasped behind his head, a cigarette hanging from his mouth. "No. I wasn't shot, Mr. Warden, but my leg is all busted up. I need to go see a doctor." He blew a series of smoke rings. "That asshole's been after me for months. I want you to lock him up and throw away the key. Do you understand what I'm saying? I'm gonna sue you and him and the entire prison system. Now get the fuck out of my face." He flicked his cigarette across the cell and laid down as if nothing at all had happened.

The warden turned to Hector Ruiz. "You're in charge of H Block until I sort out this mess. Call the medics and get them down here to help the injured officers, then take Feodor to the infirmary. I want him patched up right away. Where the hell's Gloria?"

"Right here, Jose," the press officer said, inching her way through the crowd of guards.

"Put a lid on this," the warden said authoritatively. "Bury the incident in your daily press release. Explain there was a disturbance involving Feodor and a corrections officer. Don't mention the guard's name. Don't mention the shooting. Don't mention that anyone was hurt in the scuffle. I don't want the press—especially *The Weekly Reporter*—to find out about this before Pavel's interview. Can you do that for me, Gloria?" he said as he briskly walked down the hall to the security exit.

"Right away, Jose," Jimenez said, doing her best to keep up with him.

Jimmy Benito watched as they left the cellblock, stretched out on the floor surrounded by corrections officers, his eye swelling, his face a bloody mess. But Jimmy Benito wasn't feeling the pain. All he was feeling was the wrath of Nikolai Stanislov. *God, what's he gonna do now that I failed to take care of his problem?* he whined to himself. *Is he gonna get someone to draw and quarter me? Someone to beat the living shit out of me? Someone to kill me? God, I gotta find somewhere to hide. Maybe I can get them to throw me in solitary. He can't find me there. Can he?* He began to shake uncontrollably as the guards yanked him to his feet and dragged him like a ragdoll past one screaming inmate after another until he disappeared into the bowels of the prison.

CHAPTER 23

ETHAN WAS SITTING IN HIS study sipping a glass of scotch, missing Sarah and Luke, when Julie Piedmont, looking straight into the camera, began reading a report on the *GBS News of the Day* about an incident at Rikers Island. "The facts are sketchy," Piedmont said in her deep anchorwoman voice, "but the director of the press office just released a terse statement saying there was an altercation this morning between Pavel Feodor and an unnamed corrections officer. There were no serious injuries and the cellblock is back to normal." Ethan reached for a cigarette, then picked up his iPhone. "Mindy, it's me. Did you see Julie's evening news story about Rikers Island?"

"Just watched it," she said.

"What do you think?"

"I'm not sure," she said contemplatively.

"Think the guard was targeting Feodor?"

"Why would a corrections officer want to hurt Feodor?"

"I don't know," Ethan said, thinking the incident might be

somehow connected to their interview. "I want you to make a couple of calls. See if you can find out who the guard is and how Rikers could let something like this happen. Call me back if you hear anything."

He hung up the phone, finished his scotch, and searched the Internet for a verbatim of the press release. He found it almost immediately—headlining the latest news on the *Drudge Report*:

> At eleven o'clock this morning, there was a minor incident on H Block of the North Infirmary Command Building involving a corrections officer and an inmate named Pavel Feodor who is awaiting sentencing for the murder of Cynthia Jameson, the daughter of New York City's deputy mayor. The guard was carrying out a routine security search when the disturbance occurred. Other guards came to his assistance and quickly subdued Feodor. The corrections officer is now being questioned. There will be no further comments until the warden completes a full investigation. — Gloria Jimenez, Director of Press Information, Rikers Island Jail

Ethan reread the statement and noticed it hadn't been posted until shortly after six o'clock. That was strange. Why had the prison waited seven hours to issue a press release? Were officials hoping the story would disappear until the next news cycle? That was unlikely with all the instant reporting on the Internet. Ethan decided to call Mindy back and ask her what she thought when his cell phone rang. It was Lloyd Howard. "Hey, what's goin' on, Lloyd? Have you heard about the disturbance at Rikers?"

"Just read Jimenez's statement. It doesn't say much. So I checked a couple of police blogs, and you know, I think we're only getting half the truth."

Ethan scanned the verbatim one more time as Howard ticked off the random theories circulating on the Internet. "You're right, this press release is sketchy. Just a lot of spin. I've got Mindy checking with her sources. Maybe she'll come up with a little more detail."

"Don't hold your breath. The warden's gonna try to bury this as fast as he can. It's bad publicity for the jail, and Morales doesn't want to tarnish his reputation or bring any unwarranted attention to Feodor." Howard paused briefly. "But this isn't why I called, Ethan," urgency creeping into his voice. "I'm in my sur- veillance van just around the corner from Nikolai Stanislov's law office in Brighton Beach. I think you may wanna hustle out here right away."

"Why? What's goin' on?" Ethan said, pushing the Rikers inci- dent to the back of his mind. "I know I said I wanted to get a look at him, but I'm prepping for the Feodor interview and have tons of shit to do. Can't we do this another time?"

"No. I think you need to be here now," Howard said bluntly. "There's been a steady stream of Kolkov gang members going in and out of Stanislov's office all afternoon."

"Is that unusual?"

"I'll say. I've staked out this place dozens of times and have never seen anything like this."

"What do you think they're doing?" Ethan said cautiously.

"Something big. Alexey Kolkov just walked into the building, and he rarely leaves his booth at Sasha's Café—that shitty little restaurant where he conducts most of his syndicate business. I've never seen him go to Stanislov's. Never."

Ethan poured another finger of scotch. "Okay, I'm on my way.

Should I bring a video camera to shoot some pictures from the back of your van?"

"Don't bother. I've been rolling since I got here. I've got shots of everybody who's gone in and out of the building—including Kolkov. I'll make you a copy—free of charge. Get here as soon as you can. I want you to see this before the meeting breaks up."

"On my way, Lloyd." Ethan hung up the phone and downed his scotch, then headed to his bedroom, adrenaline pumping through his body. He glanced at his watch. Almost eight o'clock. "Shit. No time to check in with Sarah." He cursed under his breath. He'd promised to call. "I'll do it when I get back."

Rifling through his dresser, he grabbed a baseball cap, a windbreaker, and a pair of sunglasses, threw everything into a gym bag, then raced out the door. A black Lincoln Navigator was parked outside his building, two men sitting in the front seat. Ethan smiled and waved, then raced down the street toward Lexington Avenue.

He'd take the subway.

Maybe he'd lose them.

. . . . .

Alexey Kolkov paced around the office, holding a glass of Stolichnaya and smoking a Cuban Cohiba. The room was packed with other members of his crime syndicate, all smoking and drinking and sitting in silence. He sat down across from Nikolai Stanislov and inhaled a deep drag on his cigar, the smoke wafting to the ceiling, forming a puffy white cloud. "Is the van still parked out there on the street?" he said, scowling.

"Yuri, go take a look," Stanislov said tentatively.

The bodyguard walked over to the window and peered through the venetian blinds. "It hasn't moved, Mr. Kolkov."

"And you're sure it's Lloyd Howard?" the *Pakhan* said, glaring stonily at his underboss.

"I'm positive. Tell him, Yuri."

"That's his surveillance van, Mr. Kolkov. The asshole uses it whenever he's on a stakeout. I walked by and took a quick look inside when I saw it. Howard's sitting in the driver's seat watching the building."

"Did he see you, Yuri?" Kolkov said as he sucked away on his cigar.

"I don't think so, Mr. Kolkov. I was very careful."

The *Pakhan* finished his Stolichnaya and turned back to Stanislov, his eyes piercing. "Why is he parked outside your office, Nikolai? What's he doing here?"

"I have no idea, Alexey. I've never seen him out there before."

"Is he with anybody?"

"He's by himself," Yuri said. "I didn't see nobody else in the van."

"Could he be working for Benson tonight?" Kolkov said, pushing his underboss for an answer.

"There's no way to know," Stanislov said, a tinge of uncertainty in his voice.

"Well, I don't like it," Kolkov said. "I wanna know what he's doing and why he's watching us."

"Yuri," Stanislov said, "listen to the *Pakhan*. Take Petrov, go down to the street, and watch him from the front of the building. Make sure he sees you. I want him to know we're onto him."

The two men quietly slipped out the door.

Kolkov poured himself another vodka and ran his finger around the lip of his glass. "Nikolai, what the fuck happened today at Rikers Island? I thought you told me everything was under control. That the mole was going to call you with a plan before he tried to take out Feodor. But he didn't do that, did he?

He just went ahead on his own and screwed things up. Now we gotta worry about him as well as Feodor."

Stanislov lit a cigarette. "Don't worry about Jimmy. He's won't rat on us. I scared the living shit out of him at our meeting."

"But you obviously didn't scare him enough," Kolkov said, ominously pointing a finger at his underboss. "What went wrong, Nikolai?"

"I don't know," Stanislov said, cowering at the malevolence in the *Pakhan*'s tone. "I was just as surprised as you he fucked things up."

"So what do you propose we do now? Any more bright ideas, Nikolai?"

"I asked Pavel's attorney to swing by tonight. Maybe he can help us come up with another way to silence Pavel."

"Frankie O'Malley is coming here tonight with Lloyd Howard sitting out there watching us? That doesn't sound too smart, Nikolai. What if Howard spots him coming into the building?"

"I told O'Malley about Howard. He's gonna come in through the back door," Stanislov said reassuringly. "One of my guys is already standing there to let him in. We should be okay."

The *Pakhan* nodded, still not convinced it was a good idea. "Okay, Nikolai, we'll do this your way and wait for your friend, the public defender. Let's see what he has to say. Then I'll tell you what I want you to do."

The *Pakhan* drained his Stolichnaya and slammed the glass on the desk.

. . . . .

The doors opened at the Brighton Beach station, and Ethan hopped off the train. He'd already put on the clothes from his gym bag, hoping to disguise his appearance in case the goons in the black Lincoln had called ahead and their Russian colleagues were waiting on the street. Maybe they wouldn't recognize him. He pulled the baseball cap down over his eyes, adjusted his sunglasses, and hiked up the collar of his windbreaker, then peered around the platform. A handful of shopping bag–laden old women and a couple of teenagers waited for the next train. Nobody paid him much attention—even when he jumped as his cell phone buzzed to life in his pocket.

"Ethan, it's me, Lloyd. I got a heads-up for you. There are three guys guarding Stanislov's building—two in front and one out back. I'm sure they've made me."

"What should I do?" Ethan said, looking over his shoulder for anybody suspicious.

"Don't come down to my van. They'll see you for sure. Where are you now?"

"I'm on the subway platform."

"Good," Howard said, sounding relieved. "Go down to Brighton Fourth Street. It's on the far side of the platform opposite me. There's a bar on the corner called Dacha's Lounge. You can see the front of Stanislov's law office from the window. Buy yourself a drink and call me when you're settled in."

Ethan clicked off the phone, looked for the sign to Brighton Fourth, and headed for the exit. As he walked down the stairs and under the El, he carefully stared into the faces of everyone he passed—convinced he was about to be spotted—until he reached the entrance to the bar where he took a deep breath, adjusted his baseball cap, and eased through the door. An old man was slumped over a table nursing a cheap shot of whiskey, and a young couple was making out in the back, their hands hungrily exploring, caressing each other's bodies. Nobody paid him any attention as he crossed the room and walked up to the bartender.

"Give me a shot of Johnny Walker Black," he said nonchalantly.

He paid for the drink and sat down in a booth next to the window. Reaching for his iPhone, he called Lloyd Howard. "I'm in the bar."

"Were you spotted?"

"I don't think so."

"Can you see my van? It's a white Ford Econoline."

"I can see you plain as day. Which building is Stanislov's law office?"

"It's the two-story red-brick building between you and me on the far side of the street. Number 717. Can you see the three thugs? They're watching me very carefully."

"I can see them," Ethan said.

"Do you recognize any of them?"

Ethan took a long, hard look. "No. The guy who's been tailing me is much taller and more muscular than those guys. The fat guy in the back could've been sitting shotgun in the Lincoln the other morning, but I can't tell for sure. They're too far away."

"Don't worry about it," Howard said calmly. "We'll figure out who's been harassing you. Maybe I've already got him on tape. Hold on, Ethan. There's another Navigator coming toward us on Brighton Beach Avenue. Do you see it?"

"I see it," Ethan said. The Lincoln was crawling in heavy traffic as it passed Howard's van and pulled into the alley next to Stanislov's building. A well-dressed man in an expensive blue pinstripe suit, white shirt, and yellow tie hopped out of the passenger seat and was immediately surrounded by the three men as he disappeared around the back of the building.

"Who was that, Lloyd? Did you recognize him?"

"No. I didn't have a clean shot. Do you want me to stop and check the tape? I've got a playback machine in my van."

"I'll screen it later," Ethan said. "Think he's a big player?"

"Could've been a captain. Somebody I don't know. But most

of the heavy hitters are already inside—Kolkov, Stanislov, and their most trusted advisers."

"So the guy could be anybody," Ethan said, baffled. But he looked so familiar. Had he seen him before? "Keep rolling, Lloyd. Let's see what happens."

· · · · ·

Stanislov was waiting at the top of the stairs when Frankie O'Malley pushed through the back door and trudged up the steps to the second floor. Nikolai said hello and ushered him down the short hallway to his office. The *Pakhan* was smoking his Cohiba, the tip flaring red each time he inhaled, as they made their way over to the desk and sat down. Nikolai cleared his throat. "Alexey, Frankie here has some good news. He's pulled some strings at the courthouse and has been appointed the mole's public defender. Now he'll be able to keep an eye on Jimmy as well as Pavel."

"How much is that going to cost me?" Kolkov said.

"Not too much," Stanislov said. "We agreed on another twenty thousand."

Kolkov pulled out a wad of cash, licked his fingers, and dropped twenty one-thousand-dollar bills on the desk. He pushed the money across to O'Malley, who quickly scooped it up and stuffed it into his suit jacket.

"How do you want us to handle Benito?" Nikolai said, trying to diffuse the anger in the room.

The *Pakhan* poured another Stolichnaya. "I don't want him making bail," he said, sipping the vodka. "And I want you to get rid of him, Nikolai. Make it look like an accident. That shouldn't be too hard, should it? I'm sure there are lots of inmates in that fucking place who hate his guts enough to kill him."

"I'll take care of it," Nikolai said. "And what do you want us to do about Pavel?"

"It's a dilemma, isn't it," the *Pakhan* said, irritated. "The mole can't kill him anymore, can he? What do you propose we do?"

"I've been talking to Frankie," Nikolai said, trying to sound positive but failing miserably. "He's going to visit Pavel tomorrow and tell him we ordered the hit, see if he understands what that means."

"And how's that gonna help us?" Kolkov said, his eyes flashing like two daggers of light.

"Tell him, Frankie," Nikolai said, turning to O'Malley.

"Pavel called me this afternoon and told me what happened," O'Malley said. "He didn't really want to talk on the phone. Thought somebody might be listening. But he said he doesn't feel safe on H Block anymore and wants to be transferred to another cellblock. Of course, I told him I couldn't do that."

"What else?" Kolkov said expectantly as he tapped his fingers on the desk.

"I think if I tell him you're planning another hit with somebody else, I can get him to back off and keep his mouth shut."

"Can you get him to cancel the interview entirely?" Kolkov said. "That would be better, Frankie."

"I'm not sure about that, Mr. Kolkov, but I think I can scare him enough to keep your name out of whatever he tells *The Weekly Reporter*."

"How can I be sure of that?" Kolkov said, shooting a quick glance at Stanislov. "I don't want to hear, when all is said and done, that he compromised my business empire in any way. If you can get him to keep his mouth shut, there's another fifty thousand dollars in it for you."

O'Malley smiled. "I'll tell him he's as good as dead if he says anything about you or Nikolai or the syndicate. I'll make sure he doesn't connect any of you to the heroin deal or the murder."

"And how am I gonna know what he says to Sampson?"

"Because I'm gonna be sitting right next to him during the interview," O'Malley said triumphantly. "And I'll tell him I'm gonna report everything he says back to you. That should scare the living shit out of him, don't you think? There's no way he's gonna talk."

"You better hope not. I'm paying you a hell of a lot of money to control your client, and if you don't, well, things won't go too good for you, either, Mr. O'Malley."

Nikolai leaned forward in his chair, sensing the public defender's unease. "Come on, Alexey. Cut Frankie some slack. He's gonna take care of Pavel for us."

"Words are comforting, Nikolai, but I've heard all this before."

"Alexey, listen to me," Stanislov said, still trying to placate the *Pakhan*. "Pavel's gonna be too scared to talk."

"No, Nikolai, you listen to me. I don't care how you do it, just make sure Pavel keeps his mouth shut. Am I making myself clear?"

Stanislov swallowed and nodded his head yes.

"Good. I've heard enough bad news today."

Nikolai loosened his tie, sweat pouring down his face, as he watched the *Pakhan* finish his Stolichnaya and motion that the meeting was over.

· · · · ·

Ethan peered out the window, the minutes ticking away, then waved at the bartender and ordered another Black Label, hoping it would settle his nerves. Suddenly, his iPhone beeped—nearly scaring him out of his chair.

It was Lloyd.

"Ethan, they're leaving the building, some through the front and some through the back. Are you watching?"

"I see them."

"The big man dressed in black surrounded by all those body-guards is the *Pakhan*, Alexey Kolkov," Howard said, whispering into the phone.

Ethan strained forward to get a better look. "So that's him," he said, surprised. "He's not flashy like an Italian Mob boss."

"No, but he's just as sadistic. Maybe more. All those guys with him are butchers in their own right and are absolutely terrified of him."

Ethan shuddered as he thought about the man who'd been tailing him, then watched as Kolkov walked under the El, suddenly stopped, and shot Howard the finger before making his way down the street to Sasha's Café.

"Did you see that, Lloyd? He definitely knows you're watching him."

"Yeah, but he doesn't know you're watching too," Howard said. "He never once looked over in your direction."

"Well, that's comforting," Ethan said, feeling cold on the inside. "Who's the guy dressed in the fancy gray linen suit that just walked out the front door?"

"That, my friend, is Nikolai Stanislov in the flesh."

"So that's him. He's short. Not very imposing."

"But he's just as sadistic as the *Pakhan*. Nobody messes with him. Nobody. And don't you forget that, Ethan."

"Yeah. Yeah. I know," Ethan said, trying to burn a picture of Stanislov's face in his memory. "You still rolling, Lloyd?"

"Capturing everything in living color."

"And where's the mystery man who got to the meeting late? Do you see him?"

"He's standing in the back of the alley. But he's turned away from the camera, and I still can't see his face."

"I can't make him out either," Ethan said, craning his neck, hoping to catch the man turning around. "Are you sure it's the same guy?"

"Positive."

"Who the fuck is he?" Ethan muttered to himself. *I know I've seen him before. I just know it. But where? When?*

"Ethan, you still there?" Lloyd said, breaking the silence.

"I'm here, Lloyd."

"Let's wait until they're all gone, and then let's get the hell outta here."

"Where do you want to pick me up?" Ethan said, beginning to feel uneasy. "Can't come down here. Somebody may still be watching in Stanislov's building."

"There's a 7-Eleven about five blocks down Brighton Beach Avenue on Tenth Street," Lloyd said. "It's always busy. Lots of people going in and out. You should be safe waiting for me there."

"Meet you in a half hour," Ethan said, clicking off the phone.

He ordered another scotch, knowing he'd already had way too much, but at that moment, he didn't care. Somehow he'd just captured the brain trust of the Kolkov crime syndicate on tape. All he had to do now was find out if their meeting was related to his story. If he could answer that question, then maybe he could figure out what happened to Cynthia Jameson and get to the truth. He downed his scotch, slipped on his sunglasses, and left for the 7-Eleven.

CHAPTER 24

ETHAN SHUFFLED OUT OF THE kitchen with a pot of coffee and a half-eaten bagel, his eyes watering from a curl of smoke trickling off the end of a cigarette perched in the corner of his mouth. He walked into his study and opened the blinds, flooding the room with a stream of sunshine. After pouring a cup of black coffee, the aroma thick and pungent, he sat down and waited for his Final Cut Pro editing program to boot up in his computer. Reaching into his briefcase, he pulled out the DVD Lloyd Howard had copied the night before and inserted it into his laptop.

An image of a busy street with traffic in the foreground and people milling around in the background filled the screen. The roar of a train blotted out the sound as the camera panned back and forth under the elevated tracks and finally settled on a medium shot of Nikolai Stanislov's law office. Three beefy men were standing guard, all smoking cigarettes and eyeballing everyone who passed by.

Fast-forwarding, Ethan scanned the video, pausing to take notes on his iPad, then slowing down the image to real time when the camera swish-panned up Brighton Beach Avenue and settled on the Lincoln Navigator as it crept by Stanislov's building and turned up the alley.

The mystery man.

Ethan backed up the shot and ran it again—watching as the man got out of the car and hurried to the back of the building. He could almost make out his face. Almost. But not quite. So he played the image in slow motion, freezing the shot right before the mystery man was about to walk out of frame. Excited, he typed another command into his editing program and stared at the picture as it advanced frame by frame in the monitor.

Then he froze the image again.

This time a clean shot of the man's face filled the screen.

It was Frankie O'Malley.

What in God's name was he doing there?

He lit another cigarette, more confused than ever, then checked the time. It was almost eight thirty. Was it too early to call? He didn't think so. Grabbing his iPhone, he speed dialed O'Malley's number. "Frankie, it's me, Ethan Benson. I thought I'd give you a ring and see how Pavel's doing."

"He's just jim-dandy," O'Malley said cynically. "Just had another typical day at the office—stuck in his cell, bored out of his mind, whiling away his time."

"Doesn't sound like fun," Ethan said, deciding to wait a moment before asking about the Russians, not wanting to spook him. "Is he all set for our interview on Friday?"

There was strained silence.

"Well, he still wants to do it," O'Malley said tentatively, "but I'm sure you've heard about what happened yesterday. Pavel got pretty banged up during a scuffle with a corrections officer."

"All I know is what the warden released in his press release. It didn't say he was injured. Is he okay?"

"The guard cracked him pretty good with his nightstick. Didn't get his face. Just whacked his leg, so he's walking with a limp. But we've got a couple of days before the interview, so I don't think there'll be a problem."

"What brought on the altercation, Frankie?" Ethan said, trying to pump him for information. "Sounds like it was more than just a simple misunderstanding between an inmate and a prison guard."

"Pavel claims he wasn't doing anything wrong," O'Malley said bluntly. "That the guard jumped him for no reason."

"Do you know who the guard is?"

"He didn't tell me and neither did the warden. All I know is the guy was drunk and snapped when he walked into Pavel's cell to do a security check."

Ethan paused, suspecting O'Malley knew much more than he was saying. "So, Frankie, Pavel's still planning to tell us what really happened the night of the murder, isn't he?"

"Well, he's pretty scared after yesterday," O'Malley said disingenuously. "He says he's still eager to talk to Peter Sampson, but I just don't know how forthright he's gonna be."

Ethan rocked back in his chair and lit a cigarette. "Any chance he's gonna cancel on me?"

"I don't know. Maybe," O'Malley said. "I'm headed out to Rikers Island to see him this morning. If things change, you'll be the first to know."

Ethan hesitated. Maybe it wasn't a good idea to bring up the meeting in Brighton Beach. No reason to give O'Malley, or Pavel for that matter, another reason to back out. Maybe he'd spring Kolkov on them during the interview. "Frankie, you still planning to be there on Friday?"

"That's my plan," O'Malley said. "I wanna sit next to him in case he needs help answering any of Sampson's questions."

"Fair enough," Ethan said, more suspicious of O'Malley than ever. "Anything else we need to talk about?"

"Just one more thing. Can you send me a copy of the questions? Pavel wants to make sure he's fully prepared for the interview."

"I can't send you the questions, Frankie," Ethan said, positive O'Malley would shoot any document straight off to the Russians. "That's against company policy, but let me tell you what I can do. I'll email you an outline of the subjects we hope to cover in the interview. How does that sound?"

"That'll do."

"Anything else we need to talk about, Frankie?"

"No, I don't think so. We're good."

"So we'll see you Friday?" Ethan said guardedly.

"Let's hope so, Mr. Benson."

Ethan hung up the phone and stared at the image of Frankie O'Malley on his computer. Smiling, he pointed at the screen and muttered, "The plot thickens, but I'm gettin' closer to the truth. Thank you very much, Mr. O'Malley."

Then he headed down to his bedroom, and as he climbed into the shower, his cell phone rang. *Must be Sarah*, he thought, draping a towel around his waist and answering cheerfully, "Good morning, babe. I was gonna call before I left for the office."

But it wasn't Sarah.

It was Ms. Templeton.

"Sorry about that," he said, embarrassed. "I thought you were my wife." There was an awkward silence. "So why are you calling me, Ms. Templeton? You told me you didn't want to communicate on the telephone."

"I told you not to call me, but I didn't say I couldn't call you," she said in a hushed tone. "I've got more evidence that my boss, Nancy McGregor, has refused to send you, Mr. Benson."

Ethan sat down in a chair at the foot of his bed. "What evidence, Ms. Templeton?"

"Not on the phone."

"Do you want to meet somewhere and give it to me?"

There was a long pause—as if she was trying to make up her mind. "That might be a good idea, Mr. Benson."

"When, Ms. Templeton?"

"Right now, before I change my mind," she said, her voice trembling. "Where can we go?"

Ethan racked his brain, trying to come up with a place that was private. "There's a restaurant not too far from here on Madison Avenue and Ninety-Ninth Street. The Caribbean. It's small and out of the way and usually empty at this time of the day. We can meet there if you like."

"Will anybody recognize you?" she said dubiously.

"I rarely go there," Ethan said sincerely. "I'm sure nobody will know who I am."

"How fast can you get there?"

"It shouldn't take me long."

"Well, hurry. I wanna get this over with," she said, abruptly hanging up the phone.

. . . . .

Fifteen minutes later, Ethan climbed out of a taxi, checked to make sure he wasn't being followed, and slipped into the restaurant. Sitting at a table in the back was an older woman wearing a big floppy hat and sunglasses and clutching a satchel in her arms. She was the only woman in the restaurant. It had to be Ms. Templeton. Ethan hurried across the room, past a handful of construction workers eating breakfast at the counter, and sat down in a chair across from her. He called the waiter and ordered two cups of coffee.

"I was surprised to hear from you again, Ms. Templeton."

"And I'm more surprised I'm about to give you this package, Mr. Benson."

"What is it?"

The paralegal nervously glanced around the room as the waiter placed two mugs of hot coffee on the table. "More information about the case. Information nobody, and I mean nobody, has ever seen before. I've been wrestling for days with whether I should give it to you."

Ethan waited patiently, Ms. Templeton still struggling with her decision. "Can I ask you to be more specific?" he said delicately.

"Promise me you won't tell anybody where you got it."

"I won't, Ms. Templeton. I gave you my word the last time we talked, and I give you my word again this morning."

Ms. Templeton clutched the satchel closer to her chest. "This could get me into a lot of trouble with the assistant district attorney."

"Ms. McGregor will never know I got it from you," he said soothingly. "It'll be our secret. So tell me. What is it?"

"I made copies of the crime scene photos you wanted and have a copy of a police report that was purposely omitted from the court docket. I was told not to give this to anybody and especially to you."

"Who told you not to give it to me?"

"I can't tell you," she said.

"Ms. McGregor?"

"Please, Mr. Benson, don't ask me."

"Why not, Ms. Templeton?"

"Because it goes all the way to the top—well beyond Ms. McGregor," she said reluctantly, unzipping her satchel and pulling out a small box carefully wrapped in the same brown paper as her first package. "It's in here, Mr. Benson. And there's one more thing."

Ethan waited for her to continue.

"There's somebody you need to meet."

"Who, Ms. Templeton?" Ethan said curiously.

"The cop who wrote the police report. I wrote his name on a piece of paper. It's in the box—along with all the information you need to track him down."

Ethan took the package, then looked at Ms. Templeton. "Do you want to tell me where you got all this stuff?"

"From a locked file cabinet."

"Whose file cabinet?"

"Please don't ask me that question. I can't tell you, Mr. Benson," she said, paranoid.

"Why not?" he said, trying to keep his voice level. "I need to know, Ms. Templeton. It's very important."

"I can't tell you. I just can't," she said pleadingly.

Ethan thumbed the paper on the box and decided not to push any harder. "Why are you giving this to me?" he said.

"Because if I don't, you'll never know what really happened to that sweet girl, and that's all I'm gonna say, Mr. Benson." She pushed her chair away from the table and stood. "If there's anything else you need, call Nelson Brown. It always trickles down to my desk, and if he won't give it to you, I'll make sure you get it." She turned, pulled her hat over her eyes, and dashed out of the restaurant.

CHAPTER 25

ETHAN CLIMBED OFF THE ELEVATOR and hustled down the hallway, Ms. Templeton's package tucked in his briefcase. Mindy was standing in front of his office sliding a document under the door. "Mornin'. Where's David?" he said excitedly as he pulled out his key.

"He just went out for coffee. Should be back in a little while," she said questioningly. "What's goin' on, Ethan?"

"I just got another care package from my source," he said, picking up the document and quickly glancing at the latest production schedule for the Rikers Island shoot.

"The same source who gave you the crime scene video?" she said, following him into his office.

"Same one," Ethan said as he tore off the brown paper and pulled out a file folder containing half a dozen new police photos.

"What are they?" Mindy said as she watched Ethan spread the pictures side by side on his desk.

"Better shots of Cynthia Jameson's body."

"What do they show?"

"Come around and take a look."

She scooted around his desk and stared open-mouthed at the images. They were a series of tight shots taken from different angles—showing Cynthia's body sprawled on the sidewalk. "Well, this confirms what I suspected," Ethan said triumphantly as he pointed at the pictures. "There's no blood at either the entry or the exit wounds, and no blood pooling around her body."

"Jeez, Ethan. Detective Jenkins and the other cops all lied in their police reports. And that son of a bitch lied to us when we walked around the crime scene."

"The prosecutor and the public defender lied too. They both said she was swimming in blood."

"Why would they all do that?" Mindy said as she picked up a tight shot of the bullet wound just above Cynthia Jameson's left breast.

"To cover up the truth."

"What truth?" Mindy said uncertainly.

"I don't know for sure," Ethan said, hesitating. "But I don't think Pavel Feodor murdered Cynthia. I think she was already dead when he shot her. That would explain the absence of blood in all these pictures."

"Are you saying he's innocent?"

"Maybe."

"But you can't prove that, Ethan," she said skeptically.

"You're right. I can't. But it sure stands to reason. If she was alive when he shot her, there'd be lots of blood—like everybody's claiming."

"But he confessed and a jury convicted him. You're gonna need much more proof than these crime scene photos before the network brass buys into your theory. Did your source give you anything else?"

Ethan reached into the package and pulled out the police report. It was written by an Officer Colin Haggerty. "Just this," he said, holding up the document. "My source says this police report was never entered into evidence. That nobody has ever seen it before." He lined up the three pages and scanned the document. "Take a look at the last page, Mindy," he said, handing her the sheet of paper.

She sat and carefully read a section he'd circled with a red pencil:

```
The victim was found sprawled on the side-
walk—her left arm pinned under her body and
her right arm twisted at a funny angle. Her
head was bent awkwardly forward and tilting
unnaturally from her shoulder. CSI at the crime
scene who examined the body thought her arms
and neck were broken. There was a bullet wound
in her chest right above her heart, but no
blood on the front of her coat at the entry
wound or on her back at the exit wound. There
was no blood on the sidewalk. Confirmation of
the cause of death will be made by the coroner
after the autopsy.
```

Mindy handed the document back to Ethan. "This is more proof there was no blood and that maybe something happened to Cynthia before she was shot. This guy says her upper body was pretty mangled when they found her—like she'd been beaten by somebody and maybe dumped there. But why wasn't it included as evidence at the trial?"

"My guess," Ethan said, "is that whoever approved all the paperwork told Detective Jenkins to omit it from the case file.

This is part of the cover-up—just like the crime scene photos of her body and the police video."

"But who would do that?"

"Can't answer that yet."

"Think it was McGregor?"

"Could be. But my source hinted she was taking orders from somebody else."

"But who, Ethan?"

"Maybe somebody she works for?"

"We need to talk to Haggerty," Mindy said thoughtfully. "Maybe he knows. But how we gonna find him, Ethan? We don't have much time before our interview with Feodor."

"This is how," Ethan said, showing her the slip of paper Ms. Templeton had included in the packet. "Haggerty's a beat cop out of the Sixth Precinct in Lower Manhattan. My source says he works the noon to eight p.m. shift. What time is it now?" He checked his watch, his eyes flashing. "Almost eleven. If we hurry, maybe we can catch him before he goes out on patrol. Email David and tell him where we're going. Then find a picture of Haggerty on the Internet. I'll meet you in the lobby in fifteen minutes."

· · · · ·

An hour later, they were sitting under an umbrella at an outdoor café on the corner of Hudson and Tenth Street in Greenwich Village right across the street from the precinct. Ethan was clasping a photo of Haggerty in his left hand and watching a parade of cops as they walked in and out of the station house. Haggerty was a small man, maybe five foot six and a hundred and fifty pounds, with a neatly trimmed mustache and tufts of gray hair rimming an otherwise bald head. His face was long and thin and his ears stuck out—his thick tortoiseshell eyeglasses making him look more like an accountant than a police officer.

"Do we know anything else about this guy?" Ethan said, dropping the picture on the table.

"A little," Mindy said, passing him a newspaper clipping she'd found on the Internet when she was looking for his picture. "He's thirty-seven and should be wearing the same standard-issue NYPD uniform as those guys across the street. Oh yeah, almost forgot. He was shot two years ago during a bar fight. It left him with a slight limp in his right leg."

"That'll help us spot him," Ethan said. "Let's hope he's still in the precinct."

"How long you planning to wait here?"

"All day, if we have to. We'll keep moving around so the cops don't figure out we're watching them." He glanced down at the picture, then back up at the station house.

"Do you want anything from inside?" Mindy said, pushing back her chair. "I'm gonna use the ladies' room."

"No. I'm good."

"Okay. Back in a few minutes."

Ethan lit a cigarette. A dozen patrol cars were parked diagonally along the sidewalk, and small groups of cops were shooting the breeze in the sunshine, oblivious to everybody and everything going on around them. Ethan decided it was time to find a new location, and as he reached for his wallet to pay the bill, he spotted Haggerty pushing his way out the front door of the precinct and limping down the steps.

He studied the picture to make sure.

It was definitely him.

Haggerty stopped to joke with a couple of officers, then waved good-bye and took off by himself down the street. Ethan quickly searched for Mindy, and when he couldn't find her, got up and headed after him. Hanging back, he weaved in and out of the heavy foot traffic and ducked into doorways whenever Haggerty slowed down to chat with a shopkeeper. Then when he was sure he was far enough away from the precinct that he wouldn't be noticed by a random patrolman walking his beat, he picked up his pace, angled across the street, and stepped out in front of him.

"Officer Haggerty?"

"Yes."

"Can I have a few words?"

"Of course. How can I help you?"

"My name is Ethan Benson. I'm a producer for *The Weekly Reporter*. I'm doing a story on Pavel Feodor and the Cynthia Jameson murder."

Haggerty reared back, bug-eyed. "Sorry, I can't talk about that case."

"Why, Officer Haggerty? Who told you not to talk to me?"

"All I can say is I've been told to say nothing about the murder. Not to you or to anybody else," he said, shoving Ethan aside and limping away.

Ethan hurried after him—down the block and across Hudson Street. "Please, Officer Haggerty, I read your police report. I just wanna know what you saw that night."

"Don't ask me that question," he said, refusing to look Ethan in the eyes as he picked up his pace.

"Did you see blood on Cynthia Jameson's body?" Ethan said, not letting up. "Every other cop who was there said she was covered in blood. But I know that isn't true, and so do you. I've got crime scene photos of her body. There was no blood. None. Not a drop. What did you see, Officer Haggerty?"

Haggerty abruptly stopped and faced Ethan. "Okay, Mr. Benson, you're right. The pictures don't lie. I didn't see any blood, and that's what I put in my police report."

"So you're standing by what you wrote?" Ethan said hopefully.

"Yes. And that's all I'm gonna say. No more questions, Mr. Benson."

Haggerty started walking again.

Ethan followed.

"Why wasn't your police report included as part of the evidence?" he said, continuing to press the police officer.

Haggerty didn't answer.

"Why didn't you testify in court?"

Haggerty still didn't answer.

Ethan hurried around in front of him, forcing him to stop. "Talk to me. Tell me who told you to keep quiet. I already know from the crime scene video. I just want to hear it from you."

Haggerty's face turned white as a ghost. "The lead detective, Edward Jenkins," he said, sounding defeated. "I refused to rewrite my report. So he left it out of the case file and threatened to get me fired if I ever said anything to anybody."

"And who was he working for?" Ethan said, pushing for a response. "I know he passed everything up the chain of command. I need names, Officer Haggerty. Who told him to withhold your police report and change the evidence?"

Haggerty took a deep breath, then whispered, "Nancy McGregor and that sleazeball public defender, Frankie O'Malley. That's who, Mr. Benson. That's all I know."

"So all three of them were working together?" Ethan said, not surprised. "Were they working for somebody else?"

"I've already said too much, Mr. Benson. No more questions!" He pushed his way around Ethan and slowly limped down the block, never once looking back.

Ethan stood stone still until Haggerty disappeared around the corner, then turned and headed back to the restaurant. He now had an eyewitness corroborating what he already suspected—that

Cynthia Jameson was dead before she was shot, and that at least three people involved in the case—Edward Jenkins, Nancy McGregor, and Frankie O'Malley—were doctoring evidence to pin the murder on Pavel Feodor. The question was why? And who was pulling the strings? He was still trying to make sense out of everything he'd just learned when he got back to the café.

"Where'd you go, Ethan?" Mindy said frantically.

"After Haggerty."

"You found him?"

"He walked out of the precinct just after you left for the bathroom."

"Did you talk to him?"

"Indeed, I did," he said, smiling.

"What did he say?"

"He's sticking to what he wrote in his police report. He said there was no blood."

"Are you gonna go with it?"

"Yup. We have plenty of proof—Haggerty, his police report, and the pictures. The GBS attorneys will definitely let us report it in our story."

"Did Haggerty say anything else?" Mindy said soberly.

"Enough to blow the lid off the entire case." Ethan was about to tell her when he noticed a detective staring at them from across the street. "Time to go, Mindy," he said, dropping enough money on the table to cover the bill. "I don't want that cop to put two and two together and figure out I just talked to Colin Haggerty." Then they collected their belongings, hailed a taxi, and headed uptown to the Broadcast Center.

CHAPTER 26

MINDY HANDED ETHAN A Grande Mocha she'd purchased from the Starbucks across the street and plopped down on the old leather couch in his office. "Jeez, Ethan, how we gonna tie up all the loose ends before Sampson sits down with Feodor? We only have one more day."

"It ain't gonna be easy," he said, booting up his computer. "My biggest concern is nailing the ring leader who ordered the cover-up. It could be Alexey Kolkov. We know O'Malley's in bed with him, but I can't figure out why the prosecutor or the lead detective would be working for the Mob. It doesn't make sense, does it?"

"Not to me. None of this makes sense to me."

"Tap into your sources in the US attorney's office and see if they have any active investigations linking Kolkov to Nancy McGregor or Edward Jenkins. Call David and ask him to do the same thing with his sources in Washington."

"We'll get on it right away," Mindy said, sipping her coffee and moving to a swivel chair closer to his desk. "I know you've got a lot on your plate, Ethan, but we need to talk about the logistics at Rikers Island."

"Is there a problem?" he said, furrowing his brow.

"There's always a problem. You know that. Gloria Jimenez changed the ground rules on us this morning." Mindy handed him an email. "Everything's the same except for this." She pointed to a paragraph on the second page. "It says right here that she plans to open every case of equipment we bring into the complex. Each and every one of them. When I told her how much stuff we had, she said that it's all part of the special security for the interview. That there's no way around it."

"Shit," Ethan said, scanning the email. "It'll take hours to go through everything. We're bringing tons of camera and sound equipment. Call her back and get her to change her mind," Ethan said furiously.

"Already did that. She won't budge on the security. Says it's too risky."

Ethan rubbed his temples. He was getting another headache. "Even if we bust our humps and only unload what we think we'll need to build the set, there won't be enough time to get ready for Sampson. And you know how he gets. He won't want to wait for us."

"Neither will the jail. Jimenez is giving us one hour to shoot the interview beginning at eleven o'clock sharp. She's agreed to let us tape Feodor walking onto the set and leaving after we're done. We can follow him to the first security checkpoint and that's it. We can't go down to his cell."

Ethan wheeled around and gazed out his window, his mind spinning as he tried to figure out the best way to get everything done. "We'll have to use both crews to shoot the walking sequences," he said, "and to shoot Sampson and Feodor meeting and greeting before the interview starts. That'll give us the images we need at the prison." He grabbed the hard copy of the production schedule Mindy had slid under his door earlier that morning. "What time do we have to be wrapped and out of there?"

"Two p.m. No later. It's in the new itinerary."

"Let's move up the start time," he said, reading through the document. "We should meet here at six instead of seven. That should give us a cushion to drive out to Rikers, sort through the equipment with security, shoot the visuals, build the set, and do the interview. Can you change the schedule in the computer, call the crew, and make sure they know?"

"Right away, Ethan."

"And fax a copy to Sampson. He needs to be kept in the loop."

"Will do," she said, adding it to her checklist on a yellow pad. She finished her coffee and dropped the cup in a trash can, then looked up at Ethan sheepishly. "Are you and David still planning to shoot the still pictures tonight?"

"Come on, Mindy, we've been through this," he said, annoyed. "I haven't changed my mind."

"Don't you already have enough on the Russians?" she said, not backing down. "You've got them on tape in Brighton Beach."

"Yeah. But I don't have the guy who's been harassing me, and I need his picture to ID him. There's no way around it."

"Ethan, you're as stubborn as they come." She got up and started to leave, then turned and said urgently, "I hope you know what you're doing. I have a real bad feeling about tonight."

. . . . .

Ethan spent the rest of the day taking care of last-minute details for the interview before turning off the lights and heading out of the building. A specially designed backpack containing the hidden camera was slung over his shoulder as he began the three-block trek to Madison Avenue and the uptown bus to his apartment. He'd just gotten off the phone with David Livingston, who was hiding in Central Park snapping pictures of a black Lincoln Navigator as it cruised by his apartment, circled the block, and parked on the northwest corner of Madison and Ninety-First Street.

All the pieces were in place.

Soon he'd have all the proof he needed to go to Paul.

He hurried down Fifty-Seventh Street, stopping for a red light on the corner of Seventh Avenue, when Sarah called. "Hey, babe. Sorry we haven't talked today. Got caught up in a lot of unexpected shit on my story."

"Where are you?" she said pointedly. "You sound like you're on the street. Are you walking Holly?"

"No. I'm on my way home from the office," he said, searching for any sign of a black Lincoln. "Are you and Luke okay?"

"We're fine, Ethan. There's been nobody watching my sister's house since we got here. No bad guys with guns. Are they still following you?"

"I haven't seen them all day," he said, not mentioning that he and David were about to snap a series of still pictures of two men sitting in a Navigator parked up the street from their apartment.

"Are you sure you're okay?" Sarah said, worried.

"I'm fine, babe, really."

"When can we come home? Luke and I miss you. We're tired of hiding here."

"Maybe in a couple of days. As soon as I'm sure—"

Ethan stopped suddenly in his tracks. There was a black Lincoln parked about fifty feet up the block.

"Sarah, I'll call you back in a little while. I love you."

"Ethan, what's goin' on?"

"I can't talk anymore."

He clicked off the phone, then checked to make sure the hidden camera was rolling and approached the Navigator, straining to see who was inside. There were two men he'd never seen before. Adjusting the shoulder bag, he aimed the camera at their faces, and without warning, the man in the passenger seat flipped a burning cigarette out the window. Ethan winced in pain as it bounced off his cheek.

The two men smiled malevolently, and as they swung open the doors, Ethan took off running, overwhelmed with fear.

· · · · ·

The Russian in the driver's seat pulled out a burner and punched in a telephone number. It was answered immediately. "Hello, Anatoly, it's me, Grigori. He just left the office and walked by us. We scared the shit out of him. He hauled off down the street, freaking out."

"Where he go?" Anatoly said in his heavy Russian accent.

"He just crossed Fifth Avenue. I think he's headed to the bus stop on Madison. Do you want us to follow him?"

"*Da*. Make sure he gets on bus. I want to be ready when he gets here. What Benson do now?" Anatoly said, salivating into the telephone.

"Hang on a minute. Boris, can you still see him?"

"He just got to Madison Avenue and is pushing his way through a crowd of people," Boris said, watching him through a pair of binoculars. "He's definitely getting on the bus. Should be up at his apartment in fifteen minutes."

"Did you hear that, Anatoly?" Grigori said.

"I hear. Good. I wait. About to become worst nightmare. Go after him."

Grigori hung up the phone and threw the car into drive. "Hold on, Boris. I don't want to lose him." Then he screeched away from the curb, hung a U-turn, and began weaving in and out of traffic, trying to catch up to the bus.

. . . . .

Ethan was panting heavily as he made a mad dash down Fifty-Seventh Street, dodging a young couple holding hands and enjoying the warm summer night, his arms pumping up and down, his feet pounding the pavement. He ignored a red light at Sixth Avenue and was almost hit by a taxi as he sprinted through the intersection, bumping an old woman who was inching along in front of him. She waved her cane furiously, but he kept on running, never hearing the obscenities she was screaming. When he reached the corner of Fifth Avenue, he dropped his briefcase, spilling out his research. A circle of people gathered around him as he knelt down to pick up documents blowing across the sidewalk in the cool breeze. "Out of my way. Out of my way," he said, losing control. "They're comin' after me. I gotta get away." He glared at a young man who was laughing, fire in his eyes, then pushed through the crowd and sprinted to the corner. Approaching the bus stop, he turned and looked back for the black Lincoln as it pulled away from the curb and gunned down the street toward him.

This was it.

They were going to hurt him—real bad.

His imagination running wild, he cut the line of people waiting for the bus, shoved his way to the back, and sat down in the corner. Out of breath, he looked out the window, the black Lincoln now stuck in bumper-to-bumper traffic, and slowly began to calm down. Grabbing his iPhone, he punched in David's number. "It's me," he whispered, not wanting to be overheard. "I just had one of the worst experiences of my life."

"What happened? You sound terrible."

"Two guys were waiting for me outside the office. They threw a cigarette from their car. It burned my face."

"Are you all right?"

He rubbed his cheek. "It hurts, but I'll be fine."

"Where are you now?" David said, concerned.

"On the bus heading uptown."

"Are they following you?"

Ethan looked out the window again. "I don't see them," he said, his voice trembling. "They got stuck in traffic."

"Did you get them on the hidden camera?"

Ethan unzipped his backpack and checked the recorder. The red light was blinking. "It's running. Hopefully I got it all on tape." He closed the bag. "Are you still in the park, David?"

"I'm here, hiding behind the stone wall, just as we planned."

"Is the Lincoln still there?"

"It hasn't moved in the past hour."

"Can you see who's sitting in the car through the lens of your camera?"

"Yeah. It's parked under a street lamp. I've already made dozens of great pictures. I've got wide shots of the car and tight shots of two guys in the front seat. You can clearly make out their features."

"Is one of the guys real big?"

"The guy in the passenger seat is huge. His neck and shoulder muscles are bulging out of his shirt. He looks mean as hell."

"And you're sure the camera's picking up details of his face?"

"I keep checking the images. The pictures are exactly what we need."

"Look, David, it sounds like the big guy is the same asshole who's been following me. He's dangerous. Shit, all these guys are dangerous. Don't let him see you. He'll come after you."

"Do you want me to pack up and leave?"

Ethan paused and debated whether they had enough to make a positive ID. He wasn't sure without seeing the pictures. "Let's finish what we planned," he said reticently. "I'm just about there. Can you see the bus yet?"

"The front end just creeped into my shot. The Lincoln's in the foreground."

"Keep shooting. I'll be there in a couple of minutes."

"Don't worry, Ethan. I'll get the sequence."

Ethan waited for the bus to pull to a stop, pushed open the backdoor, and stepped onto the sidewalk. He quickly crossed the street and headed down Madison, the overhead street lamps casting macabre patterns up and down the deserted avenue. Steeling himself, he approached the black Lincoln, hoping David was snapping away a series of shots. Then he stopped and aimed the hidden camera through the front window. There was only one man behind the steering wheel, staring at him like a guard dog ready to pounce. *Shit, that's not the guy who's been tailing me*, he said to himself. *Where the hell is he?* Puzzled, he let the hidden camera roll a moment and then hustled down to the corner, where he stopped and turned back to the Navigator.

The man was still watching him.

Where was the second guy?

He was supposed to be sitting in the passenger seat.

Eager to get away, Ethan hurried down the block, and when he reached his apartment building, a big, muscled man dressed in black like a wraith leaped out of the shadows and clubbed him on the head with the butt end of his handgun, sending him crashing to the pavement. At first, Ethan didn't know what had happened. He was lying flat on his back, a searing pain coursing through his body, a large lump welling up at the base of his head. Then, after a moment, he saw the man standing over him—the same man who'd been harassing him for days.

Anatoly Gennadi leaned over and waved his handgun. "I watch you, Ethan Benson. Know where you live. Know where you work. Know all about story. My boss, he a very important person, very powerful, and he don't like one bit what you're doing. Do you understand, Ethan Benson?"

Ethan nodded, too frightened to speak.

Gennadi leaned closer and placed the nose of his Beretta in the middle of Ethan's forehead. "I want you listen carefully. I want you stop shooting story. I want you cancel interview with Pavel Feodor. And I want you go to boss and make project go away." The Russian grabbed Ethan by the chin. "This is little warning. So listen up real good. If you fuck up again, I find you and family." Gennadi paused, smiled, then said in a cold, steely voice, "And if we talk again, things get much worse for you. Don't force me to pull trigger and blow off head. Kill pretty wife. Kill little boy. Nothing give me more pleasure. But your choice. *Vy mena panim Ayete*? Am I clear, Mr. Ethan Benson?"

Ethan blinked but didn't move.

"Good. I think you understand," he said, sneering. Then he kicked Ethan in the stomach for good measure. "As much as I enjoy beating you," he continued, "I hope we don't meet again. That would be big shame. Don't you think? Now, have nice evening, and don't tell anybody about our little talk." Then he kicked Ethan one more time and slowly headed back to the Lincoln, turning and glaring every few steps before jumping into the passenger seat and speeding away.

Ethan held his breath, then climbed to his feet, dizzy and disoriented, his cell phone ringing in his pocket.

"Ethan, are you all right?"

He'd all but forgotten about David, still hiding in the park taking pictures. He rubbed the ache in his side and said, "I don't think anything's broken."

"You need to call the police," David said hysterically. "That guy almost killed you."

"I'm okay. Really. Were you shooting when he beat me?"

"I got the whole thing. It's terrifying. I don't suppose you wanna take a look, do you?"

"Not tonight. I need to go home and figure out what to do next," he said, fingering the lump on the back of his head.

"Maybe I should go with you to your apartment," David said. "We can call the police together."

"No," Ethan said snappishly. Then he lowered his voice. "Those two guys could still be in the neighborhood. I don't wanna risk them seeing us together. Pack up your camera and go home."

"But Ethan, you shouldn't be alone. It would be better if I spent the night with you."

"No, David. I'll be fine."

"All right. All right. But I don't feel good about this."

"Stop worrying. And David, don't leave the park until you get down to the Metropolitan Museum. You should be safe there. It's well lit, and there are plenty of taxis."

"Okay, Ethan, but for God's sake, be careful."

"Goodnight, David." He punched off the phone and walked into his building. The lobby was deserted, the doorman asleep in the package room. "What if the guy comes back?" he thought as another wave of fear rushed over him. "What if he jumps me right here in my building?" Panicking, he rushed pell-mell into an elevator, rode up to his floor, then sprinted down the empty hallway, fumbling for his keys when he got to his apartment. After pushing into the foyer, he bolted the door behind him and made his way down to his study, flipping on all the lights and checking all the rooms. Then he staggered over to his desk, dropped the hidden camera bag on the floor, and poured a stiff drink.

He downed the scotch and poured another.

He downed that one too.

Then, before he could call Sarah or Paul or the police, he put his head on his desk and passed out.

CHAPTER 27

•

THE TELEPHONE BEGAN RINGING, sounding like a fire alarm ripping through his head. He opened his eyes and groped for his iPhone, knocking it to the floor, picking it up, and finally managing to answer, "Hello."

"Ethan, it's me, Mindy. Where the hell are you? It's after ten o'clock. We've been calling you for hours."

He grabbed a pack of Marlboros and pulled out a cigarette, taking a long drag before exhaling the smoke through his nose. Thinking a scotch might help, he reached for the bottle, then put it down on his desk, rubbing his temple, willing away the familiar pounding in his head.

"Ethan, are you still there? I can hear you moving around. Talk to me."

"Give me a second, Mindy," he said, his voice raspy.

"Ethan, you sound really hungover. Pull yourself together. Paul wants to see you right away."

"What do you mean?" he said, surprised.

"David called me late last night and told me what happened. He emailed me some of the pictures. It was the same guy we saw the other day. He beat the shit out of you. Did you call the police? Did you call Paul?"

"No. I've been too out of it."

"Well, David and I knew you wouldn't. So we called Paul ourselves, just after midnight. We tried conferencing you in, but we couldn't reach you." Ethan listened quietly, Mindy talking a mile a minute. "We told Paul the whole story. He was pissed you hadn't said a word to him about it. First thing this morning, we went up to his office and showed him the pictures. Paul wants to meet with the whole team right away and decide what to do. He wants to make sure these guys don't get to you again, or to any of us for that matter. How fast can you get here?"

Ethan opened a bottle of Motrin and chewed three tablets, gagging at the sour taste as he swallowed. "Give me an hour."

"Paul's sending a car service. He's already hired a private security firm called AAA Protection. It's the same company GBS uses at the Broadcast Center. There'll be a guard waiting for you in the car."

"I don't need a babysitter."

"The hell you don't. Paul doesn't trust you. Those are his exact words. You don't go anywhere without security."

Ethan closed his eyes. "All right. Sounds like I don't have a choice. I'm gonna shave and shower and eat a little breakfast. Then I'll leave."

"Good," Mindy said. "And don't forget the tape from the hidden camera. Paul wants to screen it."

Ethan looked down at the backpack sitting on the floor. "I'll bring it with me."

"And Ethan, Paul talked to Sarah when we couldn't reach you. You better give her a ring. She's really upset."

Ethan stubbed out his cigarette, remembering that he hadn't called after hanging up on her as he was heading to the bus. God, what was he thinking? "I'll see you in a bit, Mindy." He punched off and immediately dialed Sarah's cell phone. "Babe, it's me."

"Ethan, I've been worried sick. Paul told me what happened." She whimpered into the phone. "What did they do to you?"

Ethan recounted every detail of his beating, not leaving out a single detail as he apologized over and over for not telling her right away.

"Are you hurt?"

Ethan got up and looked in a mirror. There was a burn mark on his cheek from the cigarette and blood matted in his hair where he'd been clubbed with the handgun. He hoped once he cleaned up, nobody would notice. Then he lifted his shirt and peered at his stomach. It had turned a nasty shade of blue from being stomped on by that madman. "I'm a little banged up," he said, minimizing the damage, "but I'm okay. Really."

"Do you need to see a doctor?" she said anxiously.

"No. It's nothing. I'll be fine in a few days."

"What are we gonna do now?" she said, sniffling.

"I don't know. I'm about to head to the office to see Paul. He's hired some security company to stand guard over me. I guess I'm gonna have protection wherever I go."

"He's sending two guys to watch us, too. I told him I wanna come home and take care of you, but he didn't think that was such a good idea. Said Luke and I were better off staying here at my sister's until everything got sorted out."

Ethan was speechless.

"Are you still there?"

"Yeah, babe," he said apologetically. "I'm sorry. I really misjudged how dangerous these guys are, and Paul's right, until we figure out what to do, you and Luke should stay as far away as possible." He thought about how the big man had threatened his family and his heart sank. "I guess I shouldn't have taken this on by myself. Maybe if I'd confided in Paul or the police, none of this would've happened."

"Should you give up the story?" she said imploringly. "Maybe it's just too dangerous?"

"I gotta finish it. You know that," he said, listening to Sarah sigh deeply. "I can't give it to somebody else. That wouldn't be right."

"Ethan, I want you to listen to me," she said pleadingly. "I love you and so does Luke. Please be careful, and don't take any more risks."

"I won't, Sarah. And I love you guys, too. More than anything."

"Call me. Every day. I want to make sure you're safe."

"I will, babe. I will." He blew her a kiss and said good-bye, then hung up the phone.

. . . . .

It was almost noon when he got to the eleventh floor of the Broadcast Center, accompanied by his personal security guard. He said hello to Jennifer the receptionist and was buzzed through the door. He slowly limped down the long hallway, past two secretaries poised like palace guards in front of Paul's wall of fame, then stopped when he reached Monica's desk. She looked up from her typing. "You look like shit, Ethan. I heard somebody worked you over real good last night."

Ethan grimaced. "Not funny, Monica. Paul's expecting me?"

"He's waiting in the conference room." She turned to the security guard. "You can take a seat over there." She pointed to a couch across from her desk and went back to her typing.

Ethan opened the door and walked into the room. Paul was sitting at the head of the table, Lenny Franklin to his right, and Jamie Summers, chief counsel for Global Broadcasting, to his left. Mindy and David were across from them, wearing somber expressions, like mourners at a funeral. Alone in the corner, studying the still pictures, was Lloyd Howard.

Paul motioned to Ethan to sit down.

He slipped into a chair and nodded hello. "I guess you all know what happened last night."

"We've been briefed and seen the pictures," Paul said, carefully examining Ethan's face. "I can see you're banged up. Are you all right?"

"Just a little sore," Ethan said, feeling Mindy's icy stare. Was she trying to decide if he was telling the truth?

"Why the hell didn't you tell me?" Paul said pointedly. "Mindy says these guys have been after you for days. Why'd you pull this harebrained stunt on your own? They could've killed you."

"I thought I could handle it," Ethan said, putting up a front.

"But you couldn't," Paul said. "Instead, you were secretive. Arrogant. And downright disrespectful to me—again. I put you on notice when you started this story for just this kind of behavior and warned you what I'd do if you failed to keep me in the loop. I should suspend you for going around my back."

"I gave this a lot of thought before taking the pictures," Ethan said, defending himself. "If I'd told you first, you would've shut me down, and we wouldn't have the photos or any way to figure out who these guys are or if they're connected to Feodor and the murder. They would've disappeared as soon as they found out we were onto them."

Paul started doodling. "So who the hell are they?"

"That's why Lloyd's here," Mindy said. "David and I took

the liberty of asking him to join us. That was your plan, right, Ethan? You wanted to show Lloyd the pictures and see if he recognizes them."

Mindy nodded to the PI.

Howard glanced around the table, then held up a picture of the man dressed in black kicking Ethan in the side. "His name is Anatoly Gennadi. He first surfaced about five years ago in a heroin deal that went bad for the Russians. He's their muscle, their enforcer, their hit man." Howard turned to Ethan. "The only reason you're still alive is because the *Pakhan* told him not to kill you."

"Well, that's just great, Ethan," Paul said bitingly. "You decided to take on a contract killer for the Russian Mob all by yourself. Real smart. Who's the other guy, Lloyd?"

"His partner—Mischa Polchak. Another hit man. They work as a team."

Paul turned to Ethan. "So what do you want to do now, Ethan? We can't just let them stalk you until you're dead."

"The last thing I want to do is go to the police," Ethan said, not backing down. "That'll scare them off and jeopardize our story. The private security guards should give me and my family all the protection we need."

"Are you crazy?" Paul said. "Those guys will keep coming after you. We gotta go to the police. Otherwise, I'm gonna dump the story."

"You can't do that, Paul. It's my story."

"No. It's the show's story, and I make all the programming decisions."

"Hey, slow down," Howard said, placing the pictures on the table. "What happened last night is way out of the norm for the Mob. The Russians rarely go after journalists, and they never kill them. It would bring down too much heat. If you want my opinion, I think they're trying to scare Ethan into canceling the interview. They don't want Feodor talking to the press. That's one of the reasons they're secretly meeting with his attorney."

"What does he mean they're secretly meeting with his attorney?" Paul said, snapping at Ethan. "Are you hiding something else from me?"

"No, Paul," Ethan said carefully, not wanting to pour oil on the fire and further inflame his relationship with his boss. "I just haven't updated you on everything I've been doing. Lloyd and I staked out a Mob law office in Brighton Beach the other night and shot some undercover footage from his surveillance van. We've got tape of Frankie O'Malley meeting with a guy named Alexey Kolkov. He's the *Pakhan*—the godfather of the Russian syndicate—and we think O'Malley's part of a conspiracy to frame Pavel Feodor for Cynthia Jameson's murder. That's the other reason I don't want to bring in the police. As soon as the cops find out we know about O'Malley, they'll go straight to the district attorney's office."

"So what's wrong with that?" Paul said, irritated. "Shouldn't Nancy McGregor know about O'Malley and the Russians?"

"I don't trust Nancy McGregor," Ethan said firmly. "She's been warned about the Russians and their involvement in the drug deal that night. David confirmed it with his DEA sources in Washington. I can't prove it—not yet—but I think McGregor is somehow tied up with Kolkov and O'Malley and part of a massive cover-up to hide the truth."

"You think she's working with the Russian Mob?" Paul said, stunned by the revelation.

"Maybe," Ethan said, pausing and shooting a quick glance at Mindy. "Any news from the US attorney's office?"

"Nothing on McGregor. But there's a RICO investigation in the works. The US attorney is gathering evidence against Kolkov and his syndicate," Mindy said, checking her notes. "Besides the usual stuff—drug trafficking, prostitution, extortion, and money laundering—the Feds are pretty sure Kolkov is paying off Edward Jenkins for inside information about the Feodor case."

"Fits right into everything we know about the lead detective," Ethan said sarcastically. "But they've got nothing on McGregor?"

"Nothing yet," Mindy said. "But they're watching her."

Ethan turned back to Paul. "The Russians are pulling the strings in this case. So it's way too risky to tell the police about my run-in with the hit man. If Jenkins finds out, he'll tell Kolkov, who'll tip off O'Malley and maybe McGregor, and that, Paul, will be the end of our story. Everybody will bail out of their interviews, and we'll have nothing left but Feodor and the Jamesons."

Paul gazed at the GBS attorney. "Jamie, does the show face any legal issues if Ethan doesn't report the incident to the police?"

"If I were Ethan's personal attorney," Summers said, "I'd tell him to file a police report. That guy should be arrested and put behind bars. But the show has no legal responsibility to go to the police. It's Ethan's decision, and if he doesn't want to press charges, he doesn't have to."

"And what about O'Malley? Won't we be concealing a crime if we don't go to the cops? I'm sure he threw Feodor's defense," Paul said.

"All we have is a theory—based on a clandestine meeting in Brighton Beach we know nothing about. So legally—the show and the network should be in the clear if we don't tell the authorities about the public defender. Morally—well, that's another question."

Paul thought a moment, doodling furiously. "Okay, so we won't go to the authorities, at least not at the moment. But you and your family, Ethan, aren't going anywhere without a private security detail. Anywhere. And if you don't agree to this, I won't only report your run-in with Gennadi to the police, I'll shut down the production."

"Don't you think that's overkill?" Ethan said angrily.

"No. I don't," Paul said sternly.

"I have a better idea," Howard said. "The Kolkov crime family knows I've been trying to bust them for years. Let me guard Ethan. I won't charge you any more than AAA Protection. Once they see me, I think they'll back off. They don't want me digging up any new information on them. They know I'll feed it to the Feds."

"I'll buy that plan," Ethan said.

"What do you think, Jamie?" Paul said.

"No objections on this end," Summers said. "But I want security assigned to each and every member of the team until we're sure the syndicate backs off."

"That's going to cost a fortune," Paul said.

"I don't care," Summers said. "I'll get the network to pay for it. It's either AAA Protection or the police."

"Done," Paul said, turning to Lenny Franklin. "Set up a security detail for everybody starting the moment this meeting breaks up. And tomorrow, I want extra manpower for the trip to Rikers Island. Ethan, are you all set for your interview with Feodor?"

"Everything's in place and ready to go."

"And Peter's briefed?"

"I updated him yesterday with a new set of questions and a final production schedule. I'll call him one more time to make sure he's okay. Did you happen to tell him about last night?"

"I filled him in as soon as I found out. He was genuinely concerned about your safety but wasn't happy when I informed him I was going to station a security guard outside his house as a precaution. He grumbled for a few minutes and then agreed it was probably necessary."

"Sounds like Peter," Ethan said knowingly. "Look, Paul, I've got some last-minute housekeeping to do before the shoot. Is there anything else we need to talk about?"

"No. We're done here," Paul said. "Make me a copy of the hidden camera footage from last night. I wanna screen it, and Ethan, don't hide anything else from me. I wanna know immediately if that guy harasses you again. I'm gonna bring in the cops if he so much as breathes on you. Am I clear?"

"Perfectly," Ethan said as he watched Paul and his management team leave the room.

"Well, I just dodged a bullet," he said, trying to lighten the mood. "The big boss didn't lock me in the brig and throw away the key. I live to work another day." Nobody smiled. "I guess there's really nothing to joke about, is there? So let's get out of here before Paul changes his mind and decides to formally court-martial me."

They all burst into laughter and headed to the tenth floor.

CHAPTER 28

LLOYD HOWARD WAS WAITING by the front door when Ethan walked out of his building. It was six a.m. and still dark, the neighborhood dappled in weird shadows cast by street lamps kitty-cornered every fifty or so feet up and down the block. Ethan cautiously peered toward Madison Avenue but couldn't tell if a black Lincoln was hiding, ready to pounce as he made the trip to Rikers Island and his interview with Pavel Feodor. A chill cascaded through his body as he lit a cigarette. "Any sign of them, Lloyd?"

"There's a Navigator parked on Fifth Avenue and a second one on Madison and Ninety-Second Street. They're here in force this morning. I'm sure they know today's the day."

Ethan dialed a number on his iPhone. "Mindy, it's me. Are you with the crew?"

"Everybody's here. The grip truck, the two camera vans, and the extra car David's driving to the prison."

"Is there a black Lincoln watching you?"

"It's parked about a block away. Been here since I arrived half an hour ago. There are two guys sitting in the front seat, but neither one has gotten out of the car. They're just staring at us. It's creepy."

"How many security guards are with you?"

"Four. One for each car. And they're in full uniform."

"Good. Let's get rolling. Meet me on the corner of Ninety-Sixth and Madison in fifteen minutes. We'll link there and head to Rikers Island as a group. And be careful. There are two carloads of Kolkov's goons staking out my neighborhood." He hung up the phone and turned to Howard. "What do you think? Are we safe?"

"There's only one way to find out," Lloyd said, reaching for the passenger door of their rental car. "Let's see what happens."

Slowly, they made their way around the block, Ethan checking his rearview mirror as they passed the first Lincoln on the corner of Ninety-First and Fifth. It slinked away from the curb and settled in behind them as Ethan turned left onto Ninetieth Street and headed to Madison Avenue. "What are they doing?"

"Trying to scare us."

"Do you think we can shake them?" Ethan said, a thin layer of sweat forming on his brow.

"Maybe."

"Should we link up with the crew somewhere else? Should I call off the shoot?"

Howard didn't respond, checking the handgun in his shoulder holster as Ethan crawled up Madison and stopped for a red light—the Lincoln still behind him—the two men in the front seat staring tenaciously, their eyes reflecting in the rearview mirror like laser beams.

"There's the second Lincoln," Howard said calmly, "on the left side of the street, about halfway up the block. Do you see it, Ethan?"

"Yeah. What should I do, Lloyd?"

"Pull up right behind it," Howard said, not wavering for an instant.

"Why do you want to do that? They'll have us boxed in," Ethan said, alarm dripping from his pores as he remembered the hit man kicking him in the stomach as he lay on the sidewalk.

"Just do what I say," Howard said.

Ethan waited for the light to turn green, then slowly made his way through the intersection, stopping ten feet behind the Lincoln. He could see two men sitting in the front seat, smoking cigarettes.

They didn't turn around.

"Don't get out of the car," Howard said as he opened the passenger door.

"What are you doing?" Ethan said, grabbing his arm.

"I'm gonna try to get rid of them."

"How?"

"Never you mind. Just keep the engine running in case we have to make a run for it." He reached for his Glock .45, lowered it to his side, and started walking toward the Navigator. When he got to the rear bumper, he stopped, raised the weapon, and locked eyes with the man sitting in the passenger seat. Anatoly Gennadi was smiling as he pointed his finger and pulled an imaginary trigger. Then the Navigator suddenly screeched away from the curb and roared up Madison Avenue—followed by the second Lincoln that had pulled up behind them. Lloyd holstered his Glock and grinned at Ethan as he walked back to the car. "That was easier than I thought," he said gloatingly.

Ethan's heart was pounding. "That was the same guy who jumped me—the hit man. He could've opened fire and killed you. He could've killed me, too."

"He could've, but he didn't," Howard said, lighting a cigarette. "I know these guys. How they operate. How they think. The syndicate would never risk being caught in a gun battle on the Upper East Side of Manhattan. Not their style. I took a calculated risk and it worked."

. . . . .

Hovering in the passenger seat of his Navigator, Anatoly Gennadi watched through his side-view mirror as Ethan's rental car pulled onto Madison Avenue and stopped for a red light. He was talking on a burner with Nikolai Stanislov and Alexey Kolkov who were sitting in Stanislov's law office surrounded by bodyguards. "Nikolai, they're a block away," Gennadi said impassively. "I've got second car tailing them and third car with production crew just leaving Broadcast Center."

"Do they have security?" Stanislov said, his voice terse.

"*Da*. Four men dressed like soldiers with crew trucks, and Lloyd Howard sitting in car with Benson. Motherfucker. Wait a minute. The light turns green. Benson pulling very slowly through intersection and heading our way." The hit man placed his Ruger on the dashboard and motioned for Mischa to pick up his Uzi.

"What's going on, Anatoly? Talk to me," Stanislov said as he glanced at the *Pakhan* who was twirling a gold cigarette lighter in his fingers.

"The car just pull up behind us, Nikolai. Do you want me to get out on street and make go away?"

"Not yet," Stanislov said, sounding indecisive. "Just sit tight and watch them and let us know what they do."

"*Da*. I watch." He released the safety on his handgun. "Got big problem, Nikolai. Passenger door just open and Howard gets out. He's holding gun. Chicken-shit Benson stays in car. What do you want me to do? Nobody around. Street empty. You want Anatoly to kill Howard? Kill Benson? Give word and I shoot. Nice and clean. Then make getaway."

"Hold on a second, Anatoly." The hit man listened as Nikolai said to the *Pakhan*, "There's no way to stop the interview, Alexey, unless we kill them. Now's the time to decide. Do you want Anatoly to take them out?"

"Need decision," Anatoly said urgently as he slipped his finger onto the trigger, motioned to Mischa to get ready, and then peered back at Howard through the side-view mirror. "PI here soon. No time to discuss. Kill or no kill. What you want Anatoly to do?"

"Don't kill them," the *Pakhan* said, his voice booming through the telephone. "We can't risk the cops fingering us for a bloody massacre—especially one with a journalist and a former under-cover narcotics agent. They'd come after us for sure—even with all that fucking money I'm greasing those assholes. We're better off hoping Frankie O'Malley can control his client. Call the other cars and come back to Brighton Beach. I don't want things getting out of control with that fucking PI."

"Do you understand the *Pakhan*?"

"*Da*, Nikolai. We back soon." The hit man dropped the burner, clicked the safety on his Ruger, and motioned to Mischa to hide the Uzi on the floor. "No killing today. Mr. Kolkov says back off. Sounds pissed." He turned and pointed his finger at Howard and whispered maliciously, "Bang. Bang. You're dead, motherfucker. Now let's get hell out of here, Mischa. *Pakhan* has new plan."

. . . . .

Ethan kept checking his rearview mirror as he made his way up to Ninety-Sixth Street, worried the Lincoln would resurface behind them, when Mindy called on his cell phone. "Are they still follow-ing you?" he said anxiously.

"They were right behind us a minute ago, then they inexplicably zoomed around us, turned down a side street, and vanished. Are they tailing you?"

"They're gone here, too," he said, knowing how close he'd just come to another nasty confrontation with the hit man. "It's a long story. I'll fill you in later."

"Think we're okay?"

"I hope so. Are you with the crew?"

"We're all together."

"Good. Change of plans. We'll meet up when we get to Rikers Island. Call me if the Russians show up again." He punched off his iPhone and lit a cigarette, finally beginning to calm down. "What do you think, Lloyd?" he said, inhaling the nicotine.

"I think we're cool. We may see them again later in the day, but who knows, maybe the *Pakhan* called off his dogs."

The rest of the trip was uneventful, Ethan using the time to get ready for the interview. When he got to the Francis R. Buono Memorial Bridge, he pulled off the road, linked with his crew, then told Lloyd to wait with the four AAA security guards in a coffee shop until they finished the shoot. Then he drove over the bridge and up to the main gate where an officious-looking corrections officer was standing in the middle of the road motioning for him to stop. Rolling down the window, he said, "Good morning. I'm Ethan Benson from *The Weekly Reporter*."

"Credentials, please," the guard said bluntly. Ethan handed over his driver's license and waited as the corrections officer studied his face. "There should be a total of ten people in your party in two cars, two Chevy vans, and a small truck. Is everybody here?"

"They're all right behind me," Ethan said.

"Give me a moment."

The guard looked suspiciously into the backseat, walked over to the row of vehicles, then ran through the same routine with the other members of his crew. Each time, he wrote a short note on a clipboard. Ethan sat impatiently, thinking it was taking forever.

After fifteen minutes, the guard ambled back to his car.

"Everything appears to be in order, Mr. Benson," he said, glancing at the clipboard one last time as he handed Ethan his license. Then he told him to pull through the checkpoint and over to a small, windowless building a quarter of a mile down the road where Gloria Jimenez was waiting. Ethan thanked the guard, then drove up to the press officer and climbed out of the car.

"It's good to see you again," he said cordially.

Jimenez didn't respond, her face stern, her body language confrontational. She was wearing a navy blue suit, a matching tie, a white shirt, and black athletic shoes. There was a nightstick in her hand and a revolver in a shoulder holster peeking out from her jacket. Ethan introduced Mindy and David and the rest of his crew who were all standing behind him, drinking cold coffee in paper cups.

"Where's Peter Sampson?" she said, snapping at Ethan. "I thought he was doing the interview."

"He won't be here until just before we roll cameras," Ethan said jokingly. "He's lucky. Got to sleep late. Not like the rest of us who crawled out of bed at the crack of dawn to make it on time."

Jimenez didn't react. She just stared at a computer printout. "You're right. It says right here he's not due until ten thirty. I've got a corrections officer meeting him at the front gate and bringing him to our shooting location. Guess I forgot." She looked at her watch. "We're running behind schedule," she said sharply, "and we need to go through all your equipment before you set up your cameras. I suggest we get started."

It took more than an hour for a team of security officers to painstakingly examine each camera, lens box, cable bundle, light stand, microphone, TV monitor, and sound mixer, Ethan pacing back and forth, watching time slip by. When the officers finally finished, they piled into a Rikers Island bus and were driven down a winding two-lane road until they reached the North Infirmary Command Building, where they were ushered down a long hallway and into an institutional-green conference room.

Gloria Jimenez flipped on a bank of fluorescent lights. "I know this isn't much, but we rarely allow cameras in the complex, so this is the best we could do. You've got two hours before we start the interview. Not a second more. I'll be down the hall in case you need me." She turned and walked briskly out of the room, leaving two guards standing by the door.

"Damn, that woman's been a real bitch all morning. What got into her?" Ethan whispered as he peered around the room. "This space is tiny for a four-camera shoot. Can't be more than fifteen by twenty feet."

"And it's all concrete. So we're gonna have a big problem with voices bouncing off the walls," said Anthony Petulla, the soundman. "There's no carpeting, no curtains, nothing at all to absorb the sound. And all that screaming. Can we get them to stop? I know I can't filter that out with my mixer."

"They're inmates, Anthony. They'll just make more noise if we ask them to keep quiet," Ethan said, trying to remain positive. "There must be something you can do to deaden the sound so we can hear the interview clearly."

The soundman rifled through his equipment and pulled out two large sound booms. "We can use directional microphones and shotgun the interview," he said. "That'll muffle the yelling. Shouldn't sound any worse than background noise. That's the best I can do."

"That'll work," Ethan said, turning to his two cameramen, Herb Glickstein and Bobby Raffalo. "How do we build the set, guys?"

"Let's make use of the available light from the windows on the back wall," Glickstein said, placing two chairs opposite each other. "It'll save us a lot of time setting up lights. Sampson's only interviewing one person, right?"

"That's the plan, but his attorney wants to sit next to him. So we'll need to add a third chair and light for him as well," Ethan said, chagrined. "I've met the guy and don't trust him. He's bound to interrupt and say something."

"Does screen direction matter?" Raffalo said, pacing around the room.

"This is the first interview," Ethan said. "Feodor can be looking either way—screen left or screen right."

"Okay, we'll set the shot screen right and have Feodor facing the windows."

"And where do we put the DV cam for the wide shot?" Ethan said, beginning to see the first signs of a plan.

"If we don't care about the equipment," Herb said, "I'll mount the DV cam in the far corner on top of a ladder. We've got a big wide-angle lens. It'll make the room look enormous."

"Do it," Ethan said, satisfied. "I think the audience likes to see the lights and cameras in the wide shot. Gives them a sense of how much work goes into an interview like this." He checked the time again. "It's nine thirty. We only have an hour and a half before Feodor gets here. Can we make it?"

"We have to," Glickstein said, already positioning light stands around the set.

"And it'll look like a prison, even in the tight shots?"

"Piece of cake, Ethan. There are bars on the door and windows.

I'll make sure we see them in each shot," Raffalo said as he began roughing out camera positions.

Ethan smiled and plopped down on a chair in the corner of the room, David crouching down in front of him as he pulled a copy of the questions from his briefcase. "I've got Sampson on the phone. We've got a problem."

"What do you mean we have a problem?"

"He's running late. And he's in a foul mood." He handed Ethan his cell phone.

"Hey, Peter, it's me. What's goin' on?"

"I'll tell you what's goin' on," Sampson said belligerently. "I'm not gonna make it. I've been in this goddamn car for two hours, and the traffic's terrible. You'll have to delay the interview."

"Until when?" Ethan said, dreading the thought of broaching the subject with Gloria Jimenez.

"How should I know? Let me ask the driver." Ethan could hear bits of the conversation but couldn't make out what they were saying. "The driver says we've got about an hour to go. That should get me to the prison about ten forty-five. Hopefully you have somebody meeting me."

"There'll be a security guard waiting at the main gate. He'll bring you straight to the interview location. You should make it just in time." Ethan covered the mouthpiece and turned to David, who was pacing in front of him. "There's no problem. He's not that far behind schedule. He's just being Peter Sampson."

"Are you still there?" Peter said, screaming into the phone.

"Still here, Peter."

"I've been studying the new questions you emailed me. You've done an excellent job, but do we have to ask all these questions about the Russian syndicate? How do we know all this stuff is true? Paul told me they're the guys who beat you," Sampson said, pausing a moment. "By the way, how are you feeling? Better than yesterday, I hope?"

"Almost good as new," Ethan said. "You can hardly tell I had a run-in with a Mack truck."

"Glad to hear it," Peter said honestly. "So reassure me about the Russians. How'd you find out they're involved in the murder?"

"From multiple sources," Ethan said, making sure nobody from the prison was listening. "And this morning, on our way here, we had another dust-up with the same guy who jumped me the other night."

"What happened?"

"I can't tell you now. Too many people around."

"Okay. Okay. I get it. But you're certain it's the same guy?"

"Positive. Lloyd Howard was with me and scared him off."

"And you're sure he works for the Russian Mob?"

"Yeah. Lloyd says the cops, the DEA, and the FBI know all about him. They just don't have enough evidence to bust him and put him away."

"Okay. I'm with you, Ethan. I'll ask the questions." There was a short pause. "Traffic's easing up. We're gonna try to make up a little time. So I'm gonna ring off and read through everything one more time. See you soon."

Ethan handed David his cell phone.

"We cool?" David said.

"Everything's fine," Ethan said, smiling. "He's calmed down and is comfortable with our sourcing of the Russian connection."

"Perfect," David said, relieved. "I was worried he'd balk at the new line of questioning." David turned as Herb Glickstein motioned for him to sit down in one of the chairs on the set. "The cameraman wants to block shots and tweak the lights. I'll be back in a few minutes."

"Go for it," Ethan said, checking the time. Almost ten o'clock. They were cutting it close, but there was nothing more he could do but wait for his production team to turn the conference room into a television studio. A month of hard work was finally coming together.

CHAPTER 29

PAVEL FEODOR WALKED ONTO the set through a maze of cameras and lighting equipment, accompanied by three husky corrections officers. He was wearing a clean orange jumpsuit with the words *H Block* emblazoned just above his right breast pocket and *Rikers Island Jail* in bold letters across his back. A cigarette was hanging from his mouth, smoke slithering out of his nose as he moved with a cranky limp, his leg still sore from the beating he'd received at the hands of one of the prison's finest gatekeepers.

Herb Glickstein was inching backward in front of him, holding a small, versatile Panasonic camera. He began rolling as soon as Feodor had emerged through the locked security door separating H Block from the long hallway leading to the conference room, making one continuous shot lasting over two minutes. Ethan watched as Feodor walked up to Sampson, his hands and feet manacled in chains, and listened as the anchorman introduced himself as if he were talking to a friend at a dinner party.

Ethan had just endured another dust-up with Gloria Jimenez, who'd refused to slide the start time even five minutes to allow his crew a little extra time to finish checking the lights and adjusting the cameras. Her itinerary said eleven o'clock sharp, and by God, there'd be no deviation from the plan. As he stared into a bank of monitors at his command station, Frankie O'Malley walked onto the set and over to Sampson. They shook hands vigorously and made small talk as Feodor stood in silence, his cigarette burning down to the filter. Ethan leaned over and whispered to his cameraman. "Herb, you getting this?"

"On all four cameras."

"Excellent. I'm gonna need all this back and forth when I get to the edit room." He patted Herb on the shoulder and walked onto the set. Sampson had just taken his seat and was checking his makeup in a monitor as Gloria Jimenez explained to the public defender in no uncertain terms that the warden would issue a short statement to handle the rush of press inquiries once word of the interview leaked out. Ethan cleared his throat, interrupting Jimenez in midsentence, and said he was ready to get started. Then he motioned to O'Malley to sit on the left facing Sampson and for Feodor to sit next to him on the right. Kneeling, he looked into Pavel's eyes and asked if he had any questions.

"No, Mr. Producer, let's get this over with," Feodor said defiantly, "before I change my mind and cancel the whole damn thing." Then he spit his cigarette on the floor and turned to his attorney, who was still talking a mile a minute to the press officer. "Enough, Frankie. I can't listen to you babble anymore. Mr. Benson here is ready to start my interview, and it's my moment, not yours. So shut your fucking mouth and let's get started."

O'Malley began to protest but stopped as Ethan, surprised by the sudden outburst, walked Jimenez to a chair in the back of the room where she could watch the interview, and waited for the three corrections officers, still clutching their nightsticks, to move to a small observation window outside the door. Then he sat down between David and Mindy in front of his monitors and carefully checked the framing of each shot. Giving his crew the thumbs-up, he put on his headset and said in a calm but firm voice, "Turn off your cell phones and roll the cameras."

There was a moment of profound silence before Sampson cleared his throat, stared into the lens of his camera, and said, "Hello, I'm Peter Sampson, anchorman of *The Weekly Reporter*. Thank you, Mr. Feodor, for sitting down and talking to us today."

The opening moment was captured in vivid detail, Bobby Raffalo sitting on a medium shot of the anchorman, Herb Glickstein zooming into a tight shot of Feodor, the lockdown camera poised on a two-shot of Pavel and his attorney, and the small DV cam making a sweeping wide shot of the entire set from the top of a ten-foot ladder.

Ethan was ecstatic. The images were crisp. The lighting perfect. And the sound coming through his headset had just a hint of the inmates screaming in the background. It looked and sounded like a prison.

He held his breath as Sampson asked his first question.

"Pavel, I want to start by talking a little about your childhood. You got into a lot of trouble growing up in Brighton Beach, didn't you?"

Pavel grinned. "I guess you could say that. I had a few rough patches as a kid."

"Sounds like they were more than just rough patches," Sampson said, cocking his head to the side. "Were you ever arrested?"

"Plenty of times."

"For what?"

"All kinds of shit—drugs, breaking and entering, stealing cars, armed robbery, assault and battery. Stuff like that."

"Anything else?" Sampson said, glancing down at his questions.

Feodor hesitated, then smiled. "I once got arrested for attempted murder. Stuck some asshole kid with a knife. Put him in the hospital. But I was found innocent of all charges."

"You sound proud of it," Sampson said, peering into Feodor's face.

"I was a big shot after that," Feodor said gloatingly. "Everybody, and I do mean everybody, was scared shitless of me. I was the toughest kid in my neighborhood."

"I bet you were," Sampson said deprecatingly.

For the next fifteen minutes, the anchorman ran through a series of questions about Feodor's family and what it was like spending so much time in juvenile detention. As Pavel got more and more comfortable, his answers got more and more animated. Tapping his watch, Ethan reminded Sampson they only had an hour, and that it was time to push the interview forward.

"Let's go back to the night of the murder," Sampson said, picking up his cue. "In the transcript of your confession, you told the police you were drinking at a bar and that you met a couple of guys you didn't know who asked you if you wanted to make some easy money helping them pull off a drug deal. Is that correct, Pavel?"

"Yup, that's what I told the cops."

"You also told them you couldn't remember the name of the bar."

"Yup again. I said I was drunk and forgot. That was my story."

"Were you telling the truth?"

Ethan held his breath and looked at Mindy, waiting on pins and needles as Feodor took his time answering.

"Hold on a minute," Pavel said. "Frankie, I need a cigarette." O'Malley placed a Camel in his mouth and ignited it, then stared into his client's eyes, shaking his head, warning him not to change his story. Feodor took a long drag and turned back to Sampson. "The answer to your question is no, I didn't tell the cops the truth. I was lying." His voice was steady and unwavering.

O'Malley slumped in his chair.

"What do you mean you were lying?" Sampson said dubiously.

Feodor smiled. A devious smile. "I wasn't drinking that night. Not even one single beer. And I certainly didn't meet anybody in a bar. I made up the whole thing."

"Mr. Sampson," O'Malley burst in, gesturing wildly, "my client's gone over this many times with the police and with me. He doesn't remember who he was with that night. He was drunk. That's his story. That's the truth."

"Please, Mr. O'Malley, I wasn't talking to you," Sampson said, cutting him off. "I was talking to Pavel." He turned back to Feodor. "I'm going to ask you that question one more time. I just want to make sure there's no misunderstanding here." He paused and peered at Feodor. "You just claimed you lied to the police. That you made up the entire story about hooking up with a group of guys you didn't know in a bar. Is that what you're telling me?"

"Yup, I made it up," Feodor said. "The whole story about the bar is a figment of my imagination."

"Hold your tongue, Pavel," O'Malley said, his tone desperate.

"Mr. O'Malley, I just warned you. I'm not interviewing you," Sampson said, raising his voice slightly. "Let him talk." He turned back to Feodor. "Pavel, why should I believe you?"

"You don't have to, but I didn't meet nobody in a bar."

"So who were you with that night in the Meatpacking District?"

Feodor took a long drag on his cigarette, lifted his head, and blew the smoke toward the ceiling. Ethan inched forward in his chair, Herb zooming into a tight shot of Feodor, Bobby locking his camera on a medium shot of Sampson who was waiting with baited breath. "I was part of the crew working with a guy named Nikolai Stanislov."

O'Malley turned ashen gray.

"And who is Nikolai Stanislov?" Sampson said, pressing the point.

"He's the underboss in the Kolkov crime family." Feodor turned and glared at his attorney. "But you already know that, don't you Frankie? Now everybody else is gonna know it too."

"Hold on, Pavel. We'll talk about what your attorney knows in a minute. But first I want to back up a second. Are you telling me you were in the Meatpacking District the night of the murder with the Russian Mafia?" Sampson said incredulously.

"That's exactly what I'm telling you."

Ethan looked at David and winked. All their hard work—finding Lloyd Howard, interviewing the junkies in the middle of the night, staking out Nikolai Stanislov's law office—had just paid off in spades. Pavel Feodor was pointing the finger at one of the most notorious Mob families in the city, placing them at the crime scene the night Cynthia Jameson was murdered.

"Shut up, Pavel. Don't say another word," O'Malley said hysterically.

"Please, Mr. O'Malley," Sampson said, "stop interrupting. Your client wants to tell me what really happened that night. You'll have plenty of time to tell me your side of the story when we sit down and do your interview."

Ethan whispered into Herb Glickstein's ear. "You're getting all this, right?"

The cameraman nodded. "Haven't missed a word."

"Go on, Pavel. Tell me about that night," Sampson said, turning the page of his questions.

"The plan was to buy a big shipment of heroin from a Mexican cartel. I can't remember which one. They're all the same to me.

We had a million dollars in cash in two duffel bags, and they were supposed to sell us two hundred pounds of pure, uncut heroin."

"Hold on, Mr. Feodor," Sampson said. "Let's be clear about this. You're telling me you were involved in a major heroin deal as a member of this Russian syndicate. Why didn't you tell the police or the prosecutor?"

Feodor laughed. "Would you snitch on the Mob if you were in my shoes? I don't think that would've been too smart, do you?"

"No, ah, probably not," Sampson said, flustered.

Ethan held his breath, hoping Peter wasn't losing control of the interview.

Sampson went on. "Okay, Pavel, so explain to me what went wrong that night. Why was there a shootout?"

"The Mexicans tried to cheat us, those motherfuckers. They wouldn't let us test a random packet of heroin. They were going to sell us a cheap, watered-down product." Feodor was getting angry on camera, his face contorted in a mask of hate. "One thing led to another, and we all started shooting. Just like that, there were bullets flying everywhere."

Sampson looked stunned. "Were you part of the gun battle?"

"Hell, of course I was. I got me at least one Mexican—right here." He tapped his shoulder, the chains binding his hands rattling through the microphone. "Ripped a big hole in him. Splattered his blood everywhere." Pavel started laughing as he described the gun battle and the people who were shot and killed.

Ethan shuddered. Feodor's physiognomy was frightening. The man was a sociopath and needed to be locked away forever.

"So you admit firing your weapon and shooting a lot of people," Sampson said.

"I never denied it. I told the police during my so-called confession that I shot that Mexican and probably some others."

"And how did Cynthia Jameson end up in the middle of the

gun battle?" Sampson said, steering the conversation to the murder. "What was she doing there?"

"I have no idea."

"But you never denied shooting her. Why'd you kill her?"

"I didn't kill her," Feodor said, scowling into the camera. "That's a lie. I was shot, fell down, hit my head on the ground, and passed out. I have no idea who shot her."

"But that's not what you told the police. That's not what the assistant district attorney, Nancy McGregor, told the jury."

"I just told you I didn't confess. The prosecutor made it up."

"I'm not sure I believe you, Pavel. Your confession was played in court. The jury heard you say you killed her. It was on television, on the Internet, and in all the newspapers. I watched the video myself. You said loud and clear that you murdered her, didn't you?"

"Not true," Feodor said emphatically. "They changed it somehow. I may have seen the girl standing on the corner, but I have no idea how she was murdered."

"Pavel, are you telling me you didn't kill Cynthia Jameson?"

"Yeah. That's what I'm telling you. I don't know who shot her. It wasn't me. It must've happened after I passed out."

"So you're saying you're innocent?"

"That's what I'm saying."

"And you're insinuating you were framed by the police and the prosecutor, that they somehow doctored your confession and misled the jury."

"That's exactly what I'm saying." Pavel leaned over to his attorney. "And Frankie here knows that and went right along with them. He never told the jury I didn't do it. He never told them I was innocent."

Sampson turned to the public defender. "Do you want to comment on that, Mr. O'Malley?" The public defender blinked a couple of times and opened his mouth, but then shook his head no. Sampson continued. "Pavel, why didn't you recant your confession during the trial? Why didn't you tell the jury what you just told me? They might've found you innocent."

Feodor smiled. "Because Alexey Kolkov paid me half a million dollars to keep my mouth shut."

Ethan leaned back, surprised. This was the first time he'd heard anything about a payoff to Feodor.

"Would you repeat that?" Sampson said, glancing into the camera.

"No sweat off my ass," Pavel said. "The Russians paid me big money not to mention they were behind the drug deal."

"But why would they do that?"

"Why do you think?" Feodor said, smirking. "They run heroin big time, and the last thing they wanted was to be linked to that girl's murder. Would've brought down too much heat from the Feds. Would've fucked up their lucrative business."

Ethan quickly scribbled a follow-up question on a piece of paper and handed it to Sampson. "My producer wants to know what good all that money is now that you've been convicted."

"None. But at the time, I didn't think the jury was gonna burn me," Feodor said, jerking his head toward O'Malley. "My big-shot attorney swore he'd get me off and that I'd be rich when I got out."

"And you believed him?"

"Yeah, I believed him. But I didn't know until it was too late that the Russians were also paying him a shitload of money to throw the case. Isn't that right, Frankie? You work for the Mob, don't you?"

Ethan tapped Glickstein on the shoulder, motioning for him to pan over and zoom into a tight shot of O'Malley's face.

"Is he telling the truth?" Sampson said, staring at the public defender. "Were you paid off by the Russian syndicate to get Pavel convicted?"

O'Malley sat motionless, refusing to answer the question, Ethan understanding for the first time why the Russians had been so desperate to stop the interview. Pavel Feodor was a loose end. He was blowing their cover, describing their heroin operation, and implicating the syndicate in Cynthia Jameson's murder.

Sampson pressed on. "So if you didn't kill her, Pavel, who did?"

"Well, that should be pretty obvious," Feodor said, the camera picking up a facial tick on his cheek. "If I didn't do it, it had to be either the Mexicans or somebody else in Stanislov's crew."

"Are you saying that somebody in the Kolkov crime family may have killed Cynthia Jameson?"

Feodor nodded. "That's what I'm saying. It could've been Nikolai Stanislov himself, that scumbag, who fired the gun that killed her. But as I told you, I didn't see it. I was out cold in the alley."

Frankie O'Malley had heard enough. He stood and jerked off his microphone, grim-faced, the cameramen panning after him as he dashed out the door without saying a word.

"Shall we continue?" Sampson said, glancing at Ethan. "I don't think Mr. O'Malley plans to return." He wheeled back to Feodor. "So you don't remember what happened after you passed out in the parking lot, do you?"

"No. And I don't remember pulling the trigger and murdering that girl," Feodor said, staring into the lens.

"Mr. Feodor, I must say, many people in the audience aren't going to believe you. They're going to say you're a convicted killer, that you're changing your story to save your skin. Why are you coming clean? Why now?"

"Isn't it obvious?" Feodor said, his face fixed and determined. "The governor is talking about lifting the moratorium on the death penalty for little old me. I'm probably a dead man. So what do I have to lose?"

"But if the governor doesn't make that decision and decides to send you to prison instead, aren't you worried about the Russians and what they'll do after we broadcast our story? You just told me the syndicate doesn't tolerate snitches."

"Sure I'm worried, but if I'm gonna die, I'd rather go down telling the truth. I didn't kill Cynthia Jameson. Somebody else did."

Sampson nodded, then quickly scanned through his list of questions. "I think I've covered everything, Ethan. Is there something else you want me to ask?"

"No. We're good," he said, putting his copy of the questions into his briefcase.

"And what about you, Mr. Feodor? Is there anything else you'd like to say while we're still rolling our cameras?"

"There is one more thing," Feodor said, shooting a quick glance at Ethan. "The syndicate already came damn close to rubbing me out. They ordered a hit on me just this week."

Ethan looked up from his bank of monitors, startled.

"What do you mean the syndicate ordered a hit on you?" Sampson said.

"I don't want him answering that question," Gloria Jimenez said, jumping out of her chair. "It's not relevant to your story. Stop the cameras."

Ethan motioned to his cameramen to keep rolling. "I think it's more than relevant," he said, pointing at the press officer. "Mr. Feodor just told us the Russian Mob tried to kill him. Is that what happened the other day with the prison guard?"

"I'm telling you it's not important," Jimenez said, waving her arms as she rushed onto the set. "Pavel, don't answer any more questions." She addressed Ethan, furious. "The incident is still under investigation. I have no further comments. This interview is over." Then she ordered the three corrections officers—who'd raced into the room—to escort Feodor back to his cell. They yanked him to his feet, kicking and screaming, and dragged him across the floor.

"Answer the question, Pavel," Ethan said desperately. "Who was the prison guard?"

"An asshole named Jimmy Benito. He went berserk and tried to shoot me, but he was so drunk, the bullet missed my head and hit the wall behind me. Otherwise I'd be dead, and you wouldn't be here interviewing me today."

The corrections officers kept pushing Feodor toward the door, but when they reached the hallway, he leaned back and screamed, "That cocksucker works for the Russians. Fucking O'Malley told me yesterday. He was trying to get me to cancel the interview. He said if I talked, they'd hire somebody else to kill me. So you gotta get me out of here, otherwise I'm a dead man."

Ethan stood speechless, watching as Feodor disappeared through the security checkpoint and back onto his cellblock. Then he spun around and looked for Sampson. "Did he just say what I think he did? That the Russians hired a prison guard to take him out and that O'Malley knew all about it?"

Sampson nodded.

"Shit," Ethan said. "Now I understand why Gloria Jimenez was such a bitch today. She was worried we'd find out how close the prison came to losing their most infamous inmate."

"And she was worried we'd find out one of her guards was working for Alexey Kolkov," Peter said caustically. "We know O'Malley's working for Kolkov. So it's not too big a stretch for this guy Benito to be working for him too."

Ethan turned to Mindy, who'd just joined them. "Let's see if any of our sources can confirm a link between the prison guard and the Russians. I want a full-court press by the entire team."

Then he moved to the middle of the set. "Everybody listen up. We still have a full day of shooting ahead of us—exteriors of the prison and all those New York City street scenes. Let's wrap and get the hell out of here as quickly as possible."

Reaching for a cigarette, he sat down on a camera case and began replaying the interview in his head, focusing on the fear in Pavel Feodor's eyes. *Shit, Alexey Kolkov is a ruthless bastard. Is he gonna try to kill Feodor again now that the interview is over? Is he gonna try to kill me? My family? How far will this guy go to stop my story?*

Sweating profusely, he grabbed his iPhone and called Sarah. He had to make sure she and Luke were okay.

CHAPTER 30

IT WAS A LITTLE AFTER EIGHT when the black Lincoln cruised down Beaumont Street in Manhattan Beach. The weather forecast was calling for rain, and a dense fog was hanging over the million-dollar homes like tendrils of thick smoke. Mischa cut the headlights and slowed down in front of a big Tudor house halfway down the block. The windows were dark and shuttered, except for a thin beam of light peeking out from a room on the first floor. The two hit men checked their handguns. Anatoly was carrying his Ruger .357 Magnum, and Mischa a Sig Sauer 911 Scorpion, both fully loaded and fitted with silencers. They climbed out of the car and walked up the steps, glancing to make sure nobody was watching, then pushed their way through the front door—the Rolling Stones screeching the lyrics of "Gimme Shelter" booming from a stereo.

Anatoly turned and whispered to Mischa, "You watch Yuri. Say nothing. I do all talking to Nikolai."

Mischa nodded impassively and followed Anatoly into the living room. The underboss was sitting on the couch, sipping a glass of vodka and stacking one-hundred-dollar bills on a coffee table. Yuri the bodyguard was leaning over a countertop, smoking a cigarette and cleaning a handgun. They both turned as the hit men entered the room.

"Nikolai," Anatoly said with a straight face, "sorry to barge in with no phone call. We need talk." He was feeling serene, almost dreamlike, the way he always felt when he was out on a job.

"About what?" Nikolai said, surprise on his face. "I wasn't expecting you tonight. Do you want a glass of vodka? A coffee? Something to eat?"

"*Nyet*, Nikolai, no time for food, drink," Anatoly said as he reached for a cigarette.

"Why aren't you at Benson's apartment? You should be watching him. I didn't knock down the surveillance."

"I've got guys at apartment and at office. We still on his ass. No you worry about that."

"So why are you here? I didn't call and tell you I wanted to meet," Nikolai said as he continued counting bills.

"I just talk to *Pakhan*. He talk to Frankie O'Malley. He big-time angry about interview."

Stanislov put down the money. "Why didn't Alexey call me?" he said, irritated.

Anatoly inhaled his cigarette before answering. He had a plan. He always had a plan. That's what made him so good. "He no tell Anatoly. I no ask. But Feodor a problem. Little prick said *Pakhan* behind heroin deal. Said he no kill girl. Tells big-time anchorman somebody else guilty. Gives names. Says maybe even you murder deputy mayor's daughter."

"That little fuck fingered me?" Stanislov said, his face contorting in a fit of rage as he stood and began pacing around the room.

"Mr. Kolkov wants to meet at Sasha's Café," Anatoly said, his face expressionless. "Tells Anatoly to pick you up and drive back to Brighton Beach."

"Now? I'm in the middle of counting the protection money. I've got more stops to make tonight. I told Alexey I'd have all the money for him first thing in the morning."

"We go now. Mr. Kolkov hates to wait. He wants talk right away. You give him what's on table. Pick up rest tomorrow. We hurry."

"Why the change in plans?" Nikolai said, the first signs of anxiety seeping into his face. "I still don't get it. Alexey didn't tell me he'd called a meeting." He reached for his cell phone. "Maybe I should give him a ring? Find out what he wants?"

"*Nyet*," Anatoly said, sitting down in a chair across from the underboss. "Mr. Kolkov very specific. Wants to make big talk with you about Feodor and the interview with TV show. Meet in person. Not on telephone. Pack up what you need. My car outside. We go."

Nikolai put down the telephone. "Okay, give me a minute to get ready."

Anatoly shot Mischa a quick glance and gestured at Yuri, who had stopped cleaning his handgun and was listening to the conversation. Then he watched as Nikolai turned off the stereo in the middle of Mick Jagger frantically wailing "Let It Bleed" and followed him down the hall and into his bedroom, never taking his eyes off the underboss as he flipped on the lights, put on a blue blazer, straightened his tie, and tucked his Beretta into a shoulder holster.

"That everything?" Anatoly said impatiently as he looked at his watch. "We much late."

"I'm ready," Nikolai said, confidence returning to his voice.

Anatoly trailed the underboss back into the living room, flipping the safety off his handgun as Stanislov scooped up the protection money, put it into his briefcase, and nodded to the door. "Let's go."

Anatoly smiled. "Time to rock and roll, just like Rolling Stones," he muttered to himself as they hiked single file down to the curb and climbed into the black Navigator.

．．．．．

Ten minutes later, they were driving west on Oriental Avenue, heading toward Brighton Beach. It was nearly nine o'clock and the roads were mostly empty, only a handful of cars and a few wayward stragglers trudging their way home. Yuri was sitting in the front passenger seat next to Mischa, his eyes fluttering open and closed, his head lolling against the side window, the motion of the car slowly lulling him to sleep. Nikolai was sitting right behind him next to Anatoly, smoking a cigarette, absentmindedly staring out the window. "I still don't get why the *Pakhan* called you and not me. I'm his number two. He should have told me about Pavel's interview, not you."

Anatoly just sat there, smiling to himself, feeling a rush of adrenaline. Then he said, "You wait, Nikolai. Soon enough you know what Mr. Kolkov wants. Soon become clear."

"Don't belittle me, Anatoly," Stanislov said, raising his voice. "Show me some respect. You work for me, and don't forget that."

Anatoly sat quietly, his eyes fixed on Stanislov, cold and distant.

When the Navigator reached Coney Island Avenue, the bright lights on the boardwalk shimmering through the dense fog, Mischa spun the wheel and gunned the engine, picking up speed as he climbed the entrance ramp to the Belt Parkway. Yuri was jolted awake as the car weaved in and out of traffic and glared at the hit man. "Where the hell are you going, Mischa? This isn't the way to Sasha's Café. You gotta get off the highway and head back to Brighton Beach."

There was a flash of movement as Mischa pulled the Sig Sauer out of his shoulder holster and smashed it down on the back of Yuri's head. Then Mischa hit him again, harder, this time across his face, the gun shattering his nose and crushing his jaw. Blood began pouring down his chin and spraying the dashboard as his eyes rolled into the back of his head. Pitching forward, he bounced off the windshield, his mouth open, his tongue limp, before slumping off his seat and onto the floor.

"What the fuck?" Nikolai screamed, pivoting to face Anatoly and reaching for his handgun. But before he could grab it, the hit man clubbed him with his Ruger, opening a deep gash under his right eye, matching the scar he so proudly wore on his left cheek. Then he struck him again, the Ruger working like a sledgehammer, splitting his upper lip and knocking out his front teeth.

Nikolai groaned as Anatoly calmly removed the Beretta from his shoulder holster. "Don't say another word, you piece of shit, or Anatoly beat you to fucking death right here in car, right now." He tossed him a towel. "Clean up. You bleeding like pig all over fucking place. You ruin nice new Lincoln." When Stanislov failed to move, Anatoly grabbed him by a shock of hair and shoved the towel into his face. "Now you listen to me, you motherfucker. The *Pakhan* is more than pissed. He furious. Says he has to shut down business and, how he put it? Oh, yes, 'leave city and go run and hide like animal,' until things cool off now that Pavel talk to television show. Then he make me your boss and order me to teach you lesson." Anatoly grinned and drove his handgun into Stanislov's chest. "So Nikolai, just sit. Enjoy ride. And keep mouth shut. Make my job more easy." He laughed—an insane, hysterical laugh—before punching Nikolai in the gut for good measure.

. . . . .

They drove for an hour until they reached the south shore of Long Island, crossing the Jones Beach Causeway and heading east onto Ocean Parkway, a two-lane road running along a narrow stretch of land between the Atlantic Ocean and a series of tidal inlets. As they passed through Gilgo Beach in Suffolk County, it began to rain. Anatoly sat quietly, twirling his handgun, never taking his eyes off Stanislov, who lay in a stupor, drifting in and out of consciousness, blood crusting his face and drying in big globs on his sports coat. *Soon, my friend, be patient*, he thought, glowering. *Maybe ten more minutes. Just wait. Then Anatoly finish and you feel nothing.*

They kept driving and entered a remote stretch of scrubland. "Mischa, pull off road. Kill lights. This spot perfect." Mischa checked his rearview mirror and eased the Lincoln off the road and down a sandy path into the dense forest. "Get out of car, Nikolai." Anatoly prodded him with the Ruger, grinning widely as the underboss winced in pain.

"You don't have to do this," Nikolai said. "You've been part of my crew for a long time. You know I've got money. Lots of money. Take the fifty thousand in my briefcase as a down payment. I'll pay you more. Anything you want. Then I'll disappear, and the *Pakhan* will never know."

Desperation filled his voice.

"Shut up, Nikolai. Keep walking," Anatoly said, violently kicking Stanislov, knocking him to his knees. "Not there yet, ass-hole. Get up. Move." He heaved him off the ground and shoved him through the underbrush, the steady crashing of the waves on the beach muffling the sound of their movement. Then he turned to Mischa. "Wake up Yuri and get him into thicket."

Mischa had hoisted the bodyguard onto his broad shoulders and was hauling him through the tightly packed trees like a sack of potatoes. "Too late for that, Anatoly. He's already dead. I killed him when I bashed him over the head with my gun. Guess I hit him too hard," he said, laughing like a hyena. "I'll go dig a grave where we can toss the two of them once you're finished with Nikolai." He continued walking deeper into the forest until he all but disappeared into the dense fog.

"Let's go, Nikolai. Follow Mischa's tracks."

Nikolai started to weep. "Please, Anatoly, don't do this. There's got to be another way."

"Shut up. You man, not baby. Take medicine."

"Please, let me go," Nikolai said pleadingly. "I've always treated you fairly, like family, like my own brother."

"You pitiful," Anatoly said smirkingly as he placed the nose of the Ruger against the back of Nikolai's head and pulled the trigger, the gun making a soft pop as the bullet ripped through his brain and blew off his face. The underboss pitched forward in a heap, dead before he hit the ground. "I never like you, Nikolai, with rich clothes and big mouth. You no tough guy. You little fuck face. Mr. Kolkov right. Time for Nikolai to go." Then Anatoly grabbed his ankles and dragged him through the woods, his head thumping over rocks and tree roots, until he found Mischa putting the finishing touches on a shallow grave near the beach. "Bury the two of them. I call the *Pakhan*." Mischa rolled Yuri and then Nikolai into the six-foot-long pit, blood oozing from their corpses, soaking the ground.

"Mr. Kolkov, it's me, Anatoly. You no more worry. I take care of problem. I shoot Nikolai and bury in place nobody find."

"And his bodyguard."

"Yuri dead too. Just like you tell Anatoly."

"And you were careful?" the *Pakhan* said, whispering into the phone.

"Very careful. Nobody around. We gone in few minutes."

"And you'll cover your tracks?"

Anatoly looked back at the trail of blood left when he dragged Nikolai to his grave, the dark red stain slowly fading, washing away in the rain. "No problem, Mr. Kolkov. Mother Nature make evidence disappear. And what about reporter? Time to get rid of Ethan Benson too?" the hit man said, relishing the thought of killing somebody else that night.

There was a long pause, Anatoly waiting for the *Pakhan* as he weighed his options. "Too late to stop that asshole now," he said, hatred in his voice. "Pull your men and knock down the surveillance. There's nothing we can do about his story. But there is one more problem where I need your special skills. Somehow that little weasel, Jimmy Benito, made bail. He gets out tomorrow, and I want you and Mischa to pick him up at the jail and make him disappear. I don't care how you do it or where you dump the body. Just make him suffer."

"And what about public defender? He fuck up like Nikolai. Let prison guard walk. Feodor talk. You want me make go away too?"

"Not yet. I need that Irish prick for the sentencing," Kolkov said icily. "And Anatoly, until this blows over, you need to disappear for a little while. Figure out where you and Mischa want to go. Maybe Moscow or St. Petersburg. The Feds won't find you there. We'll talk more after you snuff out Benito. And Anatoly, get rid of the burner."

The phone went dead.

The hit man picked up a large rock and smashed the telephone, sweeping the broken pieces under the sand. Now there was no way to trace the call. No way to link the two executions to the *Pakhan*.

Then he hiked over to his partner who was spreading pine needles and tree branches over the grave. "Let's go, Mischa."

"Does Mr. Kolkov want us to kill Benson?"

"No. He wants us kill prison guard. Then he wants us to disappear."

"And what about our friends here? Should we say a little prayer before we leave?" Mischa said, grinning from ear to ear. "It's the right thing to do now that we've sent them off to a better place, don't you think?"

Anatoly lit a cigarette, shading the match from the rain with the palm of his hand. "*Nyet*, Mischa. Assholes got what they deserve. We take orders. Do job. Their time go to hell." Then he smiled at his partner. "But sure was fun. There's nothing I like more than killing. It's better than sex."

CHAPTER 31

IT WAS NINE SUNDAY MORNING, and Ethan was sitting in a yellow taxi attached at the hip to Lloyd Howard. New York City had that shadowy feel of a ghost town—the stores closed, the streets clear of bumper-to-bumper traffic, the weekend warriors shacked up in bed enjoying their one-night stands. Ethan was lost in thought, his mind on a treadmill, convinced the Russian Mob was watching from every corner—even though he hadn't seen any sign of a black Lincoln Navigator since the morning of Pavel Feodor's interview.

. . . . .

Ethan slipped off the elevator on the tenth floor and heard the sound of videotape being shuttled back and forth in a playback machine. It was a high-pitched whine that stopped and started as specific images were slowed down, cued up, and screened at real time. David Livingston was sitting in front of a large monitor, logging the footage they'd shot in the Meatpacking District after finishing Feodor's interview. Ethan walked into the makeshift editing room and stared over his shoulder. "How'd the pictures come out?"

"Unbelievable," he said, looking up at Ethan. "I just logged everything you shot on Little West Twelfth Street. Herb did an amazing job. How'd he get it to look so spooky?"

"He used the same Panasonic camera that captured Feodor's walking sequence before the interview. It picks up a sharp image even in the dark, see?" They watched as Ethan hit play and the camera panned by a row of meatpacking companies, settling on an exterior of Fernelli's Beef and Poultry. "Every time the camera passes a light source, like this one from the street lamp in front of the building, there's a quick flare that fills the screen." He pointed at the shot. "The wide-angle lens also distorts the picture, making it look like we're shooting through a fishbowl." A low-angle tracking shot of the alley leading into the parking lot where the shootout took place filled the screen. "Pretty cool, isn't it?"

"Definitely," David said. "I can't believe how cinematic it feels. It's as good as any feature film. The audience is going to think they're watching the shootout through the eyes of the gunmen."

"That's the idea," Ethan said. "Does the interview look as good?"

"It couldn't have been shot any better. Do you want to screen it?" He reached for a stack of disks sitting on the corner of his desk.

"No. I don't have time. I spoke to Paul a little while ago. He's coming into the office with Lenny for a quick update. They should be here soon."

"Today?"

"He said it couldn't wait until tomorrow. So stop what you're doing, go find Mindy, then come to my office. Paul wants to meet with all of us—not just me." After saying good-bye, Ethan walked down the long hallway, past dozens of closed doors, halting abruptly when he reached his office.

His door was wide open.

For an instant, he thought it was the hit man, Anatoly Gennadi. How had he gotten past the security guards? How had he found him in the building? Should he run, try to get away? Then he heard Peter Sampson's voice booming like a bellow.

Nerves.

Just nerves.

"Peter, what are you doing here?" he said, waving hello to Paul and Lenny who were sitting on the couch, their feet up on his coffee table.

"We're waiting for you," Peter said, sounding annoyed. "I made the mistake of calling Paul yesterday to tell him about our interview. Didn't realize it would bring things to a boil. He asked me—no, he told me—to come back into the city for this meeting at this ungodly hour on a Sunday morning. That's why I'm here and not in East Hampton playing golf."

Ethan sat at his desk and looked at Paul. "What's so important that Peter had to trek all the way into the city?"

"Where's everybody else?" Paul said, ignoring his question. "I only want to go through this once," he continued as Mindy and David hauled into the room. "Ah, we're all here. Finally. Now we can get started." He turned back to Ethan. "I did some hard thinking after Peter told me about the bizarre scene at the end of Feodor's interview. By the way, did you capture the guards dragging him off the set? Peter didn't know."

"I logged it this morning," David said. "We got it on all four cameras, and you're right, it's pretty damn unbelievable."

"Good," Paul said, pleased. "I wanna use it for the on-air promotion. Should help boost the ratings. But that's not the reason we're here. Brief me on where you are with the story."

Ethan thought a moment, then reached for his iPad and opened a page with his production notes. "We've finished shooting most of the outdoor scenes—the exteriors of the prison, the courthouse, the police station, the district attorney's office, the deputy mayor's condo on Fifth Avenue, Brighton Beach, and around the Meatpacking District. I'm sure we'll have some pickup shots, but we won't know until we write the script."

"And what about the rest of the interviews?" Paul said impatiently.

"Nancy McGregor and the Jamesons are scheduled for Thursday. Peter's agreed to come back from vacation and do both interviews," Ethan said, nodding a thank you to his anchorman.

"Who else?" Paul said, shooting a quick glance at Sampson.

Ethan caught the subtle exchange and wondered what was going on. "We've booked the lead detective, the public defender, and Lloyd Howard as well. And I'm trying to find Colin Haggerty—the cop I told you about who says there was no blood on Cynthia's body. But so far we can't get him to pick up his phone."

"That's it?"

"No. We're also trying to line up a couple of Cynthia's friends and maybe her boyfriend—Jacob Lutz. I'm hoping they'll give us some insight into her personal life that her family might not know." Ethan waited for a reaction. "Okay, that's your update. So what gives, Paul?"

"You've got to speed up your production," Paul said testily. "Your story's not gonna hold. I've gotten dozens of calls since you interviewed Feodor. Everybody and his brother wants to know what he said, and the senior management is worried about the other networks. I've been fighting with them all weekend and don't want to be forced to give any of the interview to hard news so GBS can stay competitive if pieces of the story start to leak.

It's ours, and I want to break all of it on *The Weekly Reporter*. I've given this a lot of thought and discussed it with Peter, and he agrees with me." Paul took a deep breath. "I want to get your story on the air right after you finish shooting."

"What does that mean?" Ethan said, already knowing where the conversation was headed.

"I want you to complete the fieldwork this week. You've got the documents, the hard news footage of the police investigation and the trial, the undercover footage you shot in Brighton Beach, the junkies, and a bunch of other stuff we've been talking about. Speed up the scripting and postproduction, because I'm planning to run your story in ten days—on September 1. That's the Thursday before Labor Day," Paul said, his voice determined. "Can you make it?"

"Impossible," Ethan said irritably. "I'll have to shoot around the clock, then screen the footage, write the script, edit, and fine cut in a little over a week. It'll kill me and everybody else in this room. There's no way we can do it."

"You don't have a choice. This story is important not only for the show but for Global Broadcasting." He looked Ethan squarely in the eyes. "We're running on the first. That's my decision." There was a brief pause as Paul rolled up his sleeves. "And there's one more thing, Ethan."

"I'm listening," Ethan said, staring skeptically.

"I'm making your hour a special edition of *The Weekly Reporter* and calling it 'The Killer Talks: Confessions of a Madman.' I can just see the headlines. We're gonna make lots of news."

"That title is outrageous," Ethan said, appalled. "Pavel Feodor is probably innocent—the target of a monumental cover-up by the people who arrested, convicted, and represented him." He glanced at Mindy and David, trying to control his temper. "Don't get me wrong, Paul, I love the idea of running the story as a special. I told

Feodor we were giving him the hour, but I'm still working on the facts and may not be able to nail down everything in the next ten days. We'll make a mistake."

"We'll go with whatever you can prove," Paul said, dismissing him. "This is what we're doing."

"And you're on board with this idea, Peter? You've been fighting me tooth and nail every time I ask you to work on the story. Are you ready to cancel the rest of your vacation, just like that?" he said, snapping his fingers.

"Watch your mouth, Ethan," Paul interrupted. "Peter's already agreed to work the next ten days to make this happen. He understands the importance of crashing your story to air."

"Well then, I guess I don't have a choice, do I?" Ethan said, resigned to the decision. "So let me make this perfectly clear. It's going to take a Herculean effort, and I'm gonna need a lot of help."

"Done," Paul said. "What do you need?"

"I want Mindy to take over the rest of the shooting. She's got plenty of experience directing cameras. The only day I want to spend on location is Thursday, when we interview Nancy McGregor and the Jamesons. There's a lot riding on those two interviews, and I wanna be there. Are you comfortable with that, Peter?"

"I'd rather have you in the field for all the shooting, but I know I can't split you in two. So Mindy and I will make it work," Sampson said reluctantly.

"What else?" Paul said.

"There are five full acts in the special, right, Paul?"

"That's the format."

"So I'll need five editors—one for each act—and I want to meet them this afternoon to get them up to speed. Who's gonna put together the research materials for everybody?"

"I'll do it, Ethan," David said.

"And what about the transcript of Feodor's interview?" Ethan said, his mind firing away like a machine gun.

"Already in a notebook," Mindy said. "I'll give you a copy as soon as we're done here."

"Good. I'll spend the rest of the day reading the transcript and organizing the sound bites. That's how I'll block out the hour." He turned to Mindy and Peter. "As soon as you finish shooting the interviews, I want you to tell me what's important. Then I'll add those sound bites to the structure." Ethan paused, looking at his desk calendar. "Then we'll write narrations on Saturday and track on Sunday. You'll have to work next weekend, Peter."

"I hate working weekends, but I told Paul I'd do it. Let's write in my office where I'll be comfortable. I'll get Consuela to come in and help. She won't be happy, but if I'm gonna be here, so is she." He checked his watch. "Are we almost done? I'd like to go to lunch."

"Almost," Paul said, addressing Lenny Franklin for the first time. "I want you to drop everything on your plate—and I mean everything. Give your other stories to Joyce and spend all your time helping Ethan. Find him five good editors and make sure they're here and ready to go in two hours."

"That's gonna cost a fortune in overtime," Lenny said.

"I don't care. This is what Ethan says he needs. Make it happen." Paul stood and started to leave, then stopped. "Where the hell is Lloyd Howard? He's supposed to be guarding you, Ethan."

"He's doing a background check on Nancy McGregor."

"You still trying to connect her to the Russians?"

"Still trying, but nothing yet."

"And how are Sarah and Luke?"

"They're fine, Paul. They want to come home."

"No," Paul said succinctly. "Still way too dangerous. Not till we're sure the Russians are gone. And Ethan, don't leave the building without security. I don't care if it's Howard or one of the guys from AAA Protection. Understood?"

"Understood, Paul."

"Now let's all get to work. We don't have a lot of time."

CHAPTER 32

IT WAS WELL AFTER DARK WHEN Ethan and Mindy walked into the lobby, leaving their AAA security guard standing in front of his building. There was still no sign of a black Lincoln, Ethan more convinced than ever the Russians had pulled up stakes and disappeared for good. He waved hello to the doorman, who reached under his desk and handed him a package. There were no markings on the now-familiar brown wrapping paper except his name and apartment number.

"Any idea who left this, Winston?"

"No, Mr. Benson," the doorman said, shaking his head. "It was already here when I came in for my shift."

"Think it's from your source?" Mindy said.

"Could be another care package," Ethan said, tucking it under his arm. "Thanks, Winston. See you tomorrow."

He handed the doorman a five-dollar tip and headed to the elevators.

After opening the front door and turning on the lights, he led Mindy down the hall to his study. The room was an ungodly mess—dirty dishes stacked on tables, cigarette butts spilling out of ashtrays, and garbage piled to the brim in the trash cans.

"Jeez, Ethan, this place is a pigsty. You don't do well as a bachelor."

He sighed. "I miss Sarah and Luke. I need to bring them home and get my life back on track. I hope Paul gives me the okay soon." He sat at his desk and booted up his laptop. "Can I get you something to drink?"

Mindy picked up an empty bottle of Black Label wedged between two seat cushions. "No. But get rid of this." She handed him the bottle. "Let's finish up the new research book for Peter and make sure the questions are okay for all his interviews. I gotta start early tomorrow. I'm linking with the crew at seven for our first sit-down with Detective Jenkins."

"Nothing like a short deadline," Ethan said, staring at the mess. He poured a short glass of scotch from a fresh bottle of Black Label, lifted it to his lips, then put it down. Better wait until later. He needed to stay sober. "Should we see what's in the package before we go over the notebook for Sampson?"

"Sure. Let's see if it's a missive from your mysterious source," Mindy said, sitting down on the couch.

Ethan carefully removed the paper and opened the cardboard box, revealing two legal-sized manila envelopes and an unmarked DVD. "There's no note," he said as he opened the first envelope. "This is another copy of the autopsy report."

"We've already seen that," Mindy said, examining the document.

Ethan searched through a pile of papers on the floor until he found the copy he'd received in the court docket. Then he stacked them next to each other and gazed back and forth between the two documents.

"Is it the same?" Mindy said, baffled.

"I think so," Ethan said, taking a closer look. "They're both written on the medical examiner's official letterhead and signed by the same guy, Leonard Toakling."

Mindy walked around behind Ethan and leaned over his shoulder. "The evidence numbers are the same, and each one is stamped and signed by Nancy McGregor. I don't see any difference, do you?"

"Not on the first page," Ethan said, beginning to read the two documents. Everything matched until he got to the third page. "This is different," he said, pointing to the last paragraph:

```
The victim had deep bruises on her body and
face. In measuring the size and shape of the
abrasions, they're consistent with a human fist,
suggesting the victim was beaten. There were
numerous cuts and lacerations above her eyes
and on her cheeks, her jaw was broken, and
her left eye socket was shattered. The vic-
tim's head was twisted to the left at an awk-
ward angle, and her C5 cervical vertebra was
cracked, severing her spinal cord and paralyz-
ing her from the neck down.
```

Ethan looked up, bewildered. "This says Cynthia Jameson was savagely beaten the night she was murdered. There's no mention of this in the original autopsy report, is there?" He carefully double-checked the document—the one entered into evidence and shown to the jury. There was no description of a beating.

"Any notation of a bullet wound in the new copy?" Mindy said, squinting her eyes as she scanned the document.

Ethan read the next couple of paragraphs. "Here." He pointed to the middle of the fourth page. "But it, too, is different from the original. It doesn't say there was any blood oozing out of the wounds or collecting around the body. And get this, Mindy":

```
Preliminary lab reports show traces of sperm
in the victim's vagina and panties, indicating
she had sex shortly before the murder. The lack
of bruising around her genitalia suggests the
sex was consensual. Preliminary lab reports
also reveal she had intercourse with more than
one partner.
```

He looked up from the document, perplexed. "What do you make of this? Did Cynthia have a wild reputation? Did she sleep around a lot? This isn't how she's been portrayed by the press or by her family. Have you or David talked to any of her friends about this kind of stuff?"

"Of course. I preinterviewed three of her college friends today when I scheduled their interviews. They all told me she was a focused, down-to-earth young woman. They said she was a straight-A student, a political science major who wanted to get involved in politics, just like her mother and father told us when we met them. They said she liked to party, drink a little, and occasionally do some recreational drugs. But nothing to excess."

"Remind me how we found these three friends," Ethan said suspiciously.

"We got their names and telephone numbers from Nancy McGregor. They all testified in court."

"That makes sense. These kids were handpicked by the prosecution to paint a sympathetic picture of Cynthia Jameson.

McGregor's hiding something. What about the boyfriend, Jacob Lutz? Did he testify in court?"

"No," Mindy said. "He was deposed by both sides and his transcript entered into evidence. He basically said the same stuff as her three friends."

"But why wasn't he called as a witness?"

"Good question," Mindy said. "I can't answer that."

Ethan stared at the tumbler of scotch sitting on his desk. Something wasn't adding up. Lutz was one of the last people to see Cynthia alive. Why didn't the prosecution put him on the stand? Why didn't the defense? Wouldn't his testimony have shed some light on the final hours of her life? "Look, Mindy, there's a side of Cynthia Jameson that somebody went to great lengths to hide from the jury. I know you've left messages for this guy, Lutz, but we need to find him before we go on the air."

"I'll do the best I can, Ethan, but he's not answering his telephone. I'll get David to reach out to some of Cynthia's other friends. Maybe they know where he is, but no promises," she said, jotting a note to make it a priority. "Anything else important in the new autopsy report?"

Ethan looked at the document, then lit a cigarette and highlighted the bottom of the last page before handing it to Mindy:

```
A bullet entered the victim's chest just above
her heart and exited through her lower back.
No bullet or bullet fragments were found in her
body. Due to the absence of significant amounts
of blood at the entry or exit wounds or on the
pavement around her, my preliminary findings
show that the victim was dead before she was
shot and that the cause of death was blunt-
```

force trauma to the head, neck, and body. The
time of death was approximately 2:00 to 2:30
a.m. on Monday, March 24, and the type of death
was a homicide.

"Well, this contradicts almost everything that was entered
into evidence and presented to the jury," Ethan said, waving the
new autopsy report. "Pavel Feodor didn't kill Cynthia Jameson,
just like he told us in the interview. He may be a sociopath with a
long rap sheet, but he's not guilty of her murder."

"But how do we know the new autopsy report is real and the
one from the court docket is a fake?" Mindy said, still skeptical.

"I don't know," Ethan said. "But we have to be certain before
we report the findings in our story."

"Can you ask your source?" Mindy said.

"I don't know. I gave her my word I wouldn't call."

Then—as if God in heaven were listening—his iPhone rang.
Ethan held his breath as he looked at the screen. The call was
blocked. "Don't say a word, Mindy. This may be my source." Then
he took a deep drag on his cigarette and answered, "Hello?"

"It's me, Ms. Templeton. Did you get my package?"

"I've got it. The doorman handed it to me when I walked in."

"Well?"

"I just read the autopsy report. It's different from the one we
got in the court docket. Why are there two versions?"

"Come on, Ethan, you're smarter than that."

"Because one's a fake, right?"

"See? You've answered your own question."

"How do you know?"

"Because I know, Ethan. You should trust me by now."

"Which is the real one?" Ethan said, shifting to the edge of
his seat.

"Not the one the DA's office entered into evidence. That one's a lie."

Mindy whispered, "What's she saying?"

Ethan held up a finger, motioning for her to keep quiet, then continued, "So the document you just gave me is the real autopsy report? I can bank on that as fact?"

"Absolutely. I was in the office when the coroner sent it over, and I can tell you there were a lot of long faces."

"Where did you get it?" he said, hoping to get a name.

"All I can say is somebody removed it from the trial boxes and deleted it from the computer. But I found the original hidden in a safe and made a copy for you late last night after everybody went home."

"Whose safe was it in?"

"Do I have to spell out everything for you, Ethan? Who's the boss here? Who's in charge of the case? Use your imagination. I won't say anymore."

Ethan turned to Mindy, muting his mouthpiece. "She's fingering Nancy McGregor."

"Have you screened the DVD yet?" Ms. Templeton said, sounding calm.

He clicked off mute. "I was just about to," he said. "What is it?"

"It's the confession. The entire two hours. I think you'll find it enlightening." She paused a moment. "And if you open the second manila envelope I gave you, you'll find a clean version of the transcript."

Ethan reached for the document and thumbed through the pages. There were no redactions, and the missing page—page 71—was sitting right where it belonged.

"And this matches up to the DVD you just sent me?"

"Word for word."

"Why wouldn't Nancy McGregor give it to me?"

"You'll know as soon as you go through it and screen the disk," she said, breathing a long, deep sigh. "What a relief to get this off my chest. I'm not hiding anything anymore. Maybe now I can get some sleep. I've gotta go, Ethan. We've been talking too long."

"Hang on. Please. I've just got one more question. I need a copy of the ballistics report. Do you have it?"

Ms. Templeton laughed into the telephone. "No. I don't."

Ethan paused. "Why not?"

"Because it doesn't exist. The police never found the bullet."

"But Detective Jenkins showed me a bullet hole in the building across the street from where Cynthia was murdered. He said they dug out a fragment that tied the bullet to Feodor's Beretta."

"Well, I guess he must've been pretty persuasive if you believed him."

"So there's no bullet and no way to link Pavel's handgun to the wound in Cynthia's body?"

"Nope. The ballistics report entered into evidence—the one conveniently left out of the court docket we sent you—is a fake. I could give you a copy, but I hardly see how it matters anymore."

"You're sure it's not real."

"I'm more than sure. I'm positive."

"Send it to me anyway. I need it for my records," Ethan said. "But I still don't understand why somebody would go to all this trouble to frame Pavel Feodor. What did Nancy McGregor gain from it? Was she working for Alexey Kolkov and the Russian Mob?" Ethan waited, but Ms. Templeton didn't answer. "Was it somebody else?"

"No more questions, Mr. Benson. You'll have to figure out the rest of the truth on your own. I can't help you anymore."

"But I need to know," he said pleadingly. Then the phone went dead. "Shit. She just hung up on me."

"What did she say?"

"You heard my end of the conversation. The entire case is smoke and mirrors. Nancy McGregor fabricated the evidence to get the conviction—the autopsy report, the ballistics report, the police reports, everything. They're all fake. We have to figure out who told her to do it."

"Did your source say anything else?"

"Just to screen the DVD. It's Feodor's confession."

"Unedited?"

"That's what she said." Ethan pulled the DVD out of its plastic sleeve and popped it into his computer. "We should screen this before we finish Sampson's research book. It may change some of the interview questions. Let's see what else Nancy McGregor is hiding."

"Well, I'm not goin' anywhere," Mindy said, pulling a chair in front of the computer.

Ethan reached for his scotch and swirled the liquid around the glass. *What would Sarah think?* he thought. *She'd say I was crazy to start drinking at this hour, and you know, she'd be right.* Then he put down the glass, hit enter on his laptop, and began watching the confession—following along in the new transcript.

The content was shocking.

Another piece of the puzzle.

Another smoking gun.

CHAPTER 33

LLOYD HOWARD WAS LEANING against the steering wheel in his surveillance van, staring through a pair of high-powered binoculars. Propped on the dashboard was a Canon Rebel T5i digital camera with a 250mm telephoto lens that he'd been using all day to snap pictures of Nancy McGregor as she tooled around the city. So far he had little to show and even less to report to Ethan. She was in the office by nine, had lunch with Nelson Brown at one, and then met with a group of button-down executives at the Harvard Club he assumed were corporate attorneys.

He lit a cigarette and focused the binoculars on two uniformed cops standing on either side of the front entrance to the district attorney's office as a horde of people, looking tired and haggard, streamed out of the building. He checked his watch. It was almost six. If McGregor stuck to her schedule, she'd be leaving soon. He put down the binoculars and peered through the viewfinder of his camera. Sure enough, like clockwork, she exited the building, hustled down the steps, and into a Charge & Ride Limousine.

Howard zoomed into the window and clicked another half dozen shots as McGregor made herself comfortable and began reading her iPad. Then he threw the van into drive and slipped into traffic. For the next hour, he tailed her around the city. First back to her apartment on Fifth Avenue and Tenth Street, where she stopped to change clothes, and then up the West Side Highway to Eighty-Third Street, where she signed a voucher for the limousine and climbed out in front of the Barnes & Noble. Easing behind a taxi double-parked on the corner, he started snapping more pictures—*click, click, click*—as McGregor carefully checked her surroundings and started walking down Broadway.

"Where's she going?" he wondered as he eased the van into drive and followed, hovering a safe distance behind as she window-shopped the ten-block walk down to Seventy-Second Street, stopped at a newsstand to buy a magazine, peered up and down the block one last time, and then ducked into a luxury high-rise. Howard continued snapping away, one shot after another, as McGregor said hello to the doorman, walked through the lobby, and climbed onto an elevator. Then he lowered the camera, parked, and made his way to an outdoor café with a clean line of sight to the front of the building.

After ordering a cup of coffee, he pulled out his cell phone and called Ethan. "Hey, it's me, Lloyd."

"Are you still following McGregor?" he said, the sound of editing equipment whizzing away in the background.

"Yeah, I'm on her like a glove."

"Any sign of the Russians?"

"No. And I'm pretty sure of that." Howard sipped his coffee and frowned. "You know, I'm beginning to think we've hit a dead end."

"I'm thinking the same thing," Ethan said, pausing a moment

to tell Joel Zimmerman to cut a line from a Pavel Feodor sound bite. "Where was I? Oh yeah, McGregor and the syndicate. Mindy's source at the US attorney's office has nothing linking McGregor to Alexey Kolkov, at least that's what he's telling us. If McGregor and Kolkov have been plotting together, they've been going through an intermediary—maybe Frankie O'Malley. But we can't prove that either, and we're running out of time."

Howard finished his coffee as a stretch limousine pulled up to the front of the building. "Hold on a second. Some guy is getting out of the biggest fucking car I've ever seen." He picked up his camera and started shooting as a tall, well-dressed man climbed out of the backseat and made his way into the lobby, flanked by two bodyguards. "Some big shot just arrived and walked into the building."

"Do you recognize him?" Ethan said pensively. "Is it Kolkov?"

"I can't see him. His back's to the camera. But it's not a Navigator. So it probably isn't him."

"Think he's there to meet McGregor?"

"Who the hell knows," Howard said, still taking pictures. "I've got the limo's license plate number. I'll run it through one of my contacts at the DMV and see if I can come up with a name. Look, do you have time to hustle up here and watch the building with me? I'm at Seventy-Second and Broadway—only a few blocks from the Broadcast Center. I've got a feeling something's about to happen."

"Can't leave," Ethan said distractedly. "I'm bouncing from one Avid room to another working on the special. I'm stuck here most of the night. But I want updates. Call me back when McGregor's on the move again."

"Shall do, Ethan." Howard punched off the phone and ordered another coffee, then dialed his contact at the DMV. *It's probably nobody important,* he thought as he waited for his source to answer. *But better be safe than sorry.*

. . . . .

Nancy McGregor got off the elevator on the top floor. There was thick wool carpeting on the floor and designer wallpaper on the walls. Expensive light fixtures hung from an elaborate inlaid ceiling, casting a patchwork of shadows as she hurried down the hallway past a series of custom-made wooden doors. When she reached the end of the hall, she checked to make sure she was alone, then put the key into the door and slipped into the apartment.

Making her way to the living room, she draped her suit jacket over the back of a chair, unfastened the top button of her blouse, kicked off her shoes, and dropped her briefcase on the floor next to a rolltop desk. After shutting the curtains and turning on the lights, she poured two glasses of Evan Williams 23 Kentucky bourbon, placed one on a coffee table, and sat down on a red velvet couch. She slowly sipped her drink and waited. Fifteen minutes later, another key was inserted in the door, and a handsome man with silver-gray hair, wearing a perfectly pressed gray charcoal suit, white shirt, and lime-green silk tie walked into the apartment.

It was the man from the limousine.

The deputy mayor.

Bernard Jameson.

McGregor put down her drink and smiled. "Hello, Bernard, I'm glad you could make it." She kissed him on both cheeks.

"Does anybody know we're here?"

"No. I was careful. I'm sure I wasn't followed."

"What about your brother?" he said adamantly. "Did you tell him you were using his apartment?"

"Of course not. He's in LA making a movie and has no idea I'm here. Besides, he wouldn't care."

"Well, I almost didn't make it," he said, picking up his bourbon and draining the glass all at once. "I just left a meeting with my advisers. They're all pushing me to go public with my candidacy for mayor. I think it's too soon, but they don't. I need to make a decision, and so do you if you want to join my campaign." He poured another bourbon. "So what's so important it couldn't wait?"

The first sign of fear spread across Nancy McGregor's face.

Bernard Jameson was not the kind of man to cross. He was a political animal with a public image as a loving husband and father who'd been crushed by the murder of his daughter. But on the inside, there was a darker side he kept well hidden, like Mr. Hyde lurking within Dr. Jekyll.

Nancy McGregor knew that darker side.

Maybe a little too well.

She'd met Jameson right after starting the Feodor case and was instantly attracted to his charm and grace—soon finding herself swept off her feet and sleeping in his bed. As their relationship grew, he made promises, lots of promises—to make her his campaign manager, to give her a prominent role in his administration once he became mayor, and to leave his wife and marry her. In exchange, all he seemed to want was to be by her side as she built her case. Deep down, she knew she should remain objective and keep her distance, but she was ambitious and believed his sincerity, and the sex, oh, the sex, it was just so wonderful. She bought his pitch hook, line, and sinker, and before she knew it, was embroiled in the conspiracy that now threatened her career—with no way to get out.

Smiling warily, she said, "Sit, Bernard, we have a lot to talk about. The interview with Feodor didn't go well. Gloria Jimenez at Rikers Island said Pavel told *The Weekly Reporter* everything—that he never confessed, that he didn't kill your daughter, and that I framed him in court."

"You said you had this under control," the deputy mayor said, raising his voice. "Sounds like you have a problem, and if you have a problem, I have a problem. So what are you going to do about it?"

McGregor sipped her bourbon, scrambling to find the right words. "There's nothing we can do about it now, Bernard. O'Malley couldn't control him. We have to do damage control and make sure Feodor doesn't hurt us."

"How do you plan to do that, Nancy?"

"Maybe I should just cancel my interview with Sampson."

"You can't bail out now," he said bleakly. "It'll make you look guilty."

"Yes. You're right," she said timidly. "I was just thinking out loud."

"Are you ready for him?" he said forcefully. "You can bet Peter Sampson is gonna come after you with one tough question after another. He's an anchorman. That's what he does."

"That's what I'm worried about, and that's why I needed to see you. Peter Sampson and Ethan Benson know much more about me than I first thought. Some of the other interviews they've shot this week are even more disturbing than Feodor's. Sampson absolutely took Detective Jenkins apart yesterday."

"Was Benson there?" Jameson said, pouring himself another bourbon.

"No. Sampson was with that associate producer, Mindy Herman—the girl you and Sandy met at your apartment."

"She seemed harmless to me," Jameson said dismissively. "Where was Benson?"

"He's working on the script," she said, avoiding the deputy mayor's icy stare. "Herman told Jenkins the network has moved up the airdate and given them the entire hour. It may actually run next week."

"That's not good. They wouldn't rush the story unless they think they have something nobody else knows. What else did the detective tell you?"

"Sampson pushed him very hard, and that's what scares me. At one point, he read a line from Feodor's confession where he claimed he had no memory of shooting your daughter."

"And how did Jenkins react?"

"He said he laughed and told Sampson all murderers deny killing their victims. That he hears that kind of thing all the time. But Sampson wouldn't buy his answer and wouldn't let up," she said, disheartened. "He wanted to know why I didn't play that portion of the confession in court. And whether the jury might have seen his denial as reasonable doubt."

"Did Jenkins hold to our story and insist he got a clean confession from Feodor?"

"Of course. But Sampson kept after him, kept calling him a liar all through the interview." Her posture deflated as she leaned back on the couch. "Jenkins said he didn't react well to the pressuring. That the audience isn't going to believe him because he looks like a fool on camera."

Jameson wiped a bead of sweat from his brow. "You know, Sampson's gonna ask you the same questions. But that shouldn't be a problem for you, should it? You're a prosecutor and a damn good one. You should be able to punch holes through his line of reasoning. If all he's got is the transcript of the confession—the one you sent him with the redactions and the page pulled out—you can obfuscate and say Feodor admitted to the murder loud and clear. There's no way they can prove he didn't. They'd need the unedited videotape to prove we changed what Feodor said. And all they have is the clip you played in court, right? They don't have the full two hours, do they?"

"No," she said, regaining some of her composure. "I destroyed every copy except one that's locked away in a safe where I put it. Nobody knows I still have it."

"So there should be nothing to worry about," he said smugly.

Nancy hesitated, biting her lip. "But we have another problem, Bernard."

"Christ, Nancy, what now?" he said, raising his voice again.

"Jenkins says Sampson has the crime scene video."

Jameson exploded. "How in God's name did he get that? Nobody was supposed to see that video. Nobody. I told you to get rid of it."

"I thought I did, but I must've missed a copy."

"Who gave it to him?"

"I don't know, Bernard. Somebody in my office must've found it and slipped it to Benson," she said, avoiding his eyes.

"Shit, Nancy, if you have a Deep Throat who gave Benson the crime scene video," he said, his face contorting in rage, "he knows the evidence has been doctored. And if he's managed to get his hands on the other evidence I told you to change—the autopsy report or the ballistics report or those crime scene photos I told you to hide—he's gonna know there was no blood and that my Cynthia wasn't murdered during the gun battle." The deputy mayor stood and began pacing around the room. "Where the fuck is the deputy coroner—that guy, Leonard Toakling? Benson can't get to him, can he?"

"He's trying. His people are hounding the medical examiner's office, but I put Toakling on paid leave. He's not coming back until I tell him to."

"Do we need to give him more money to keep him quiet?" Jameson said, looking more like Mr. Hyde than Dr. Jekyll.

McGregor sipped her bourbon, trying to build up her courage. "I think we need to pay him one more time. I think we need to pay everybody who's been helping us one more time."

"Who else?"

"Jenkins, his partner, Randy Tempko, some of the other cops from the crime scene, maybe Colin Haggerty, and Nelson Brown in my office. They all know too much, and they're all worried about Benson and his story."

"How much?"

"Twenty-five thousand apiece," she said without taking a breath. "That should guarantee their silence."

"I'll get you the cash," he said, beginning to calm down, money always the answer to his problems. "I've got plenty stashed in a safe at home with no way to trace it. Look, I can't stay much longer. I told Sandy and the kids I wouldn't be late."

"We're not quite finished, Bernard."

"What now?" he said, rolling his eyes.

"It's Frankie. He also called me after his interview with Sampson. They know about Kolkov."

"How's that possible? I gave that sleazeball attorney a hundred thousand dollars to keep his mouth shut—the same amount the *Pakhan* gave him."

"And he denied everything about the Russians just like we told him to," McGregor said coldly. "But he was there when Sampson interviewed Feodor, and that's where we have our problem. O'Malley said Pavel told *The Weekly Reporter* everything he knows about the Mob and their role in the drug deal the night Cynthia was murdered, and that they paid him to take the fall and O'Malley to throw the case. He even blurted out that the Russians hired the prison guard, Jimmy Benito, to kill him so he wouldn't talk."

"And Sampson believed that little asshole?"

"That's what O'Malley told me. And I know for a fact that Benson's people have been snooping around with the Feds trying to confirm all of it."

"Christ," Jameson said tersely. "Do they know about our connection to Kolkov?"

"They're trying to find a link, but so far, they know nothing. It hasn't come up once during the interviews," Nancy said meekly. "But if *The Weekly Reporter* ever finds out we knew about the Mob's involvement in the heroin deal, and that I ignored the Feds' warning, then we're screwed, Bernard, just screwed."

"Well, your job is to make sure Benson doesn't find out, and if it comes up during your interview—deny, deny, deny at all costs," the deputy mayor said urgently. "The last thing we want is for Ethan Benson to learn that I told you to ignore the DEA and leave organized crime out of the murder to make it easier for us to convict that little shit. If this gets out, the judge'll call a mistrial in a heartbeat, you'll be the laughingstock of the legal world, and my run for mayor will be dead in the water before it ever gets started. I don't want that TV show figuring out what really happened that night or uncovering the truth about my daughter. That's my secret. It'll ruin me and my family."

"So what should we do about Sampson?" Nancy said, trying to get the deputy mayor to agree on a strategy before they left. "If we can just get through our interviews and hold on until the sentencing, then the press will lose interest like it always does, and this case will fade into history."

"We shouldn't change a thing. We should hammer away that Pavel Feodor is a monster. You brilliantly painted a picture of him in court as a cold-blooded killer. You need to do the same thing tomorrow with Sampson."

"I will, Bernard. I'll protect you and your daughter," she said faithfully. "You know that."

"You better, Nancy. Otherwise, we'll both take the fall."

. . . . .

Lloyd Howard was still waiting when Nancy McGregor strode past the doorman and onto the street. Ducking behind a group of teenagers eating dinner at a table in front of him, he aimed his camera and started snapping away. Within seconds, the man in the gray charcoal suit walked into the frame, ran his hand down the ADA's lower back, blew her a kiss good-bye, then climbed into the limo and drove away. "Goddamn," he whispered under his breath, "that was the fucking deputy mayor."

He grabbed his cell phone and dialed Ethan. "Well, you should've joined me," he said as soon as Ethan answered the phone.

"Why?"

"The same guy I told you about just walked out with McGregor, and they were mighty friendly—maybe too friendly."

"Who was it?" Ethan said, shouting at Joel to turn down the sound in the edit room.

"Bernard Jameson."

There was a long silence. "What the hell was he doing there?"

"Beats me. But he blew her a fucking kiss and put his hand on her ass before he left."

"Do you think they're having an affair?" Ethan said, astounded.

"I don't know. Maybe."

"And you got it on camera?"

"The whole thing."

"Shit, Lloyd. Did McGregor go with him?" Ethan said.

"No. She's still standing in front of the building, trying to hail a taxi."

"I need to figure out what's going on between the two of them before Peter does their interviews," Ethan said keenly. "Email me the pictures. I'll get Mindy and David to do some digging. Call me back with updates."

Howard hung up the phone, then grabbed his camera and hurried back to his van, watching as Nancy McGregor found a taxi and headed downtown in bumper-to-bumper traffic. Easing away from the curb, he pushed in behind a Chevy Trailblazer and began to follow. Then his contact at the DMV called. "Hey, thanks for getting back to me, Benny," he said, "but I already know who owns that fucking limo. It belongs to the deputy mayor, and he's been a very bad boy." Chuckling, he clicked off his cell, fell back two car lengths behind the taxi, and tailed the ADA as she slowly made her way back to her apartment.

CHAPTER 34

ETHAN WAS STILL HALF ASLEEP when his phone rang, buzzing away like an alarm clock. He fumbled for his cigarettes and grabbed his iPhone. "God, what time is it?"

"Well, good morning to you too," Mindy said buoyantly. "It's seven o'clock and you sound wiped out. Another rough night?"

"I didn't leave the edit rooms until four. And didn't get into bed until five. It's taking much longer to cut together the interviews than I thought. Hold on a second." He sat up, lit a cigarette, and took a deep drag. "That's better. Now I can think straight. Are you at the district attorney's office?"

"I've been here an hour. The crew's setting up in the law library."

"And you'll be ready at ten o'clock?"

"Shouldn't be a problem. We're running ahead of schedule."

"Good," Ethan said, relieved that Mindy was prepping the set like clockwork. "Did you get the JPEGs I emailed you of McGregor and Jameson?"

"Jeez, Ethan, I got them," Mindy said, sounding shocked. "What the hell were they doing together?"

"That's a damn good question," Ethan said, taking another long pull on his cigarette.

"Do you think Jameson is tied up in all the bullshit swirling around the murder of his daughter?"

"I don't know," Ethan said, pausing a moment. "Sure would be nice to find out before Peter does the interviews. Have you filled in David?"

"Already forwarded him copies of the pictures," Mindy said pointedly. "He's gonna call his sources at City Hall as soon he gets to the office."

"We don't have a lot of time. Our first interview with McGregor starts in three hours."

"He'll do the best job he can, Ethan. You know that."

"Yeah, yeah, yeah. I know. I know," Ethan said, worried the pictures were somehow the key to unlocking the truth and that he wouldn't have an answer until it was too late. "Has Sampson seen them?"

"He's got them."

"How'd he react?"

"Appalled."

"Did you tell him to show them to McGregor during the interview?" Ethan said, now fully awake. "Maybe he can get her to tell us on camera what they were doing together last night."

"He said he would," Mindy said levelly. "But he's not happy about it. Thinks we're blindly chasing a lead we know nothing about. But I prodded him, and in the end, he said he'd hand her the pictures and see how she reacts."

"Good. Make sure he understands how important this is," Ethan said, hopping out of bed and heading to the bathroom. "One last thing before I go. Tell Herb to shoot the B-roll we discussed—McGregor walking around her office, sitting and working at her desk, and talking on the telephone. Then get her looking at all those documents we saw in the war room. I want to make it appear as if she's working on the case."

"You want me to shoot the visuals before the interview?"

"Yes. As soon as she gets there. I'm not sure she'll stick around after the interview is over. Sampson's gonna ask her a lot of tough questions, and she's not gonna be happy when we're done."

. . . . .

An hour later, Ethan walked through the front door and picked his way down the long hallway and into the law library. Sampson had already arrived and was sitting on the set in full makeup. Ethan grabbed a copy of the latest set of questions from Mindy, quickly scanned through them, then faced his anchorman. "Good morning, Peter. Are you ready for the interview?"

"As ready as I'll ever be," he said, grumbling.

"Do you have the documents and the photos we wanna show McGregor?"

"Right here in this folder," Sampson said, waving it in front of him. "Does she have any idea we've got all those nasty pictures of her with the deputy mayor that your Mr. Howard shot last night?"

"She doesn't know about the pictures, and may not know we've got the documents. But I'm sure she's talked to Jenkins and O'Malley and has heard about the Feodor interview. So she probably knows we've figured out she doctored the evidence and framed Feodor."

"I'll show her the documents and see how she reacts, but Ethan, are you sure you want me to hand her those damn pictures of Jameson?"

"Positive," Ethan said unflinchingly.

"But we know nothing about them. They could be perfectly harmless."

"I know. But we gotta do it."

"Has David talked to his sources? Mindy said he's trying to find out what they were doing together in that apartment building."

"There's nothing yet. He'll call if he hears anything."

"Okay. Okay. I'll show McGregor, but I don't like the idea. It seems downright lurid to me," Sampson said, peering into a monitor. "Why's my face so shiny?"

Ethan smiled. *Always the same Peter*, he thought, amused. *Beauty before substance.* Then he waved to hair and makeup to attend to his anchorman and looked around the set. The crew was still blocking camera shots, moving light stands, adjusting sound equipment, and dressing the background with props. "Are we almost finished?"

"Almost there," Herb Glickstein said. "We just need to white-balance the cameras, and we'll be ready to go."

Then, as if cued by the stage manager, Nancy McGregor strode into the conference room, followed by Nelson Brown and a bevy of assistants. She made a beeline over to Sampson and graciously introduced herself—her chin jutting forward, her head held high, her voice strong and confident. "It's a pleasure to meet you, Peter. I've been looking forward to this for weeks. Ms. Herman just finished my B-roll, and I'm ready for the interview. But I gotta warn you that I'm scheduled to depose a witness on another case later today and don't have a lot of time. So shall we get started?"

"I believe we're ready," Sampson said reassuringly as he walked her onto the set where Anthony Petulla, the soundman, clipped a microphone on her blouse, and the cameramen did their final light-check. Ethan carefully examined each shot in his monitors—the two close-ups of McGregor and Sampson and the big, wide shot with all the equipment in the background. "The set looks fabulous," he said, nodding to Mindy who was sitting next to him. Then he stood and shouted, "Turn off your cell phones and let me know when you have speed."

Herb Glickstein glanced about the room, made sure all the cameras were running in sync, then said, "We're rolling."

Ethan put on his headset and nodded to his anchorman. "We're good to go, Peter."

Sampson took one last look at his questions, puffed up his chest like a peacock, and said, "Ms. McGregor, thank you for sitting down with us today and for agreeing to talk about your brilliant handling of the case and the trial." The ADA instantly relaxed, Sampson playing right into her sense of vanity. "Let's begin with the murder. Tell us what happened that night."

For the next fifteen minutes, McGregor discussed the facts of the case—the bloody scene in the parking lot, Cynthia's lifeless body sprawled on the sidewalk, and Pavel Feodor lying unconscious in the alley holding the murder weapon. Step by step, she walked him through the police investigation, the decision to charge Feodor, and the ins and outs of the trial.

The questions were straightforward.

The answers deliberate.

Then Sampson zeroed in on the evidence.

"Ms. McGregor, one of the turning points in the trial came when you introduced a transcript and showed a video clip of Pavel Feodor confessing to the murder of Cynthia Jameson. How would you characterize what he said?"

McGregor didn't hesitate, her answer strong and straight to the point. "Mr. Sampson, I'm sure you've read the transcript and watched the video, and I'm sure you know Mr. Feodor admitted several times during the police interrogation that he pulled the trigger and gunned down Cynthia Jameson. It was as clear as day in the document and in the clip I showed the jury. Pavel Feodor is the murderer."

Sampson paused a moment to allow the cameras to capture the look of confidence on the assistant district attorney's face. "Are you sure that's what he said? Are you sure he confessed to murdering Cynthia Jameson?"

"Yes. I'm positive. So was the jury. They convicted him. Pavel Feodor is the killer. No doubt about it."

Sampson pulled two documents out of the folder he was holding on his lap. "Ms. McGregor, I want you to take a look at these documents. They're both stamped with your name and the seal of the district attorney's office." He handed the first one to the ADA. "As you can see, I've given you pages 69 through 73 of the confession. They're part of Exhibit 16 that you submitted into evidence and showed the jury. You also gave this to my producer as part of the public record of the trial."

McGregor carefully scanned the pages. She looked up and smiled at the anchorman. "Yes, this is one of the sections of the transcript where Mr. Feodor clearly confesses to the murder. It's one of the many times he did so."

"Would you read me the first four lines on page 72?"

The ADA put on her reading glasses. Ethan sat behind his deck of monitors looking at each shot and listening on his headset as McGregor cleared her throat and started to read. "'I was firing my weapon at anything that moved. Bullets were flying everywhere. I hit the main guy who was trying to cheat us out of the heroin. I know I got him because he was covered in blood.'" She pointed to the document and looked into the camera. "It says here, right in the transcript, that Mr. Feodor laughed at this point."

"Yes, it does, Ms. McGregor. Please keep reading. Just the next few lines will do."

"Okay. 'I think I saw a girl under the High Line at the end of the block. I think she was standing near the corner. I was firing my weapon in her direction. One of my bullets hit her. I killed her when she got caught in the crossfire.'" She finished reading and took off her glasses. "That's what it says here at the bottom of page 72, Mr. Sampson. It sounds like a confession to me." She handed the document back to the anchorman and waited for the next question.

Sampson looked at the document and then looked at the ADA. "Ms. McGregor, your office crossed out a lot of words in this section of the transcript. You see all of the black marks?" He pointed at the redactions. The ADA leaned over to take a look, the cameras capturing the moment from all three angles. "Ms. McGregor, what didn't you want us to see?"

The prosecutor stared at the sheet of paper. She looked back at Sampson, the camera zooming into her face. Her left eye was twitching. "Well, if I remember correctly, there was a lot of noise in the background on the videotape. You couldn't understand what anyone was saying. So to make it easier for the jury, we blacked out all the extraneous gibberish in the transcript."

Sampson stared at the ADA. There was a long pause before he asked his follow-up question. "Are you sure that's why you blacked out all these sections? There's quite a bit missing."

"Yes, I'm sure."

"You're positive?"

"Yes. I'm positive." There was irritation in her voice.

"Ms. McGregor, my producer has gotten his hands on a second copy of the transcript. It was given to him by a source. It, too, is marked with a stamp from your office." He pointed to the top of each page. "There are no sections blacked out in this document. I'm going to read you the same section you just read us." He paused and stared at the ADA. She was visibly shaking. She knew what was coming. "According to this version of the transcript,

Pavel Feodor never confessed to the murder. Let me read you the passage." He paused again to let the weight of his words sink in. "'I think I saw a girl under the High Line at the end of the block. I think she was standing near the corner. And I may have fired my weapon in her direction, but I really don't remember. Everything happened so fast.' And here, Ms. McGregor, is where there's a big discrepancy in the two documents. It says right here, 'I can't imagine how one of my bullets hit her when she got caught in the crossfire. I emptied my gun into the back of the fucking Mexican drug dealer's getaway car. I'm a good shot. I know I didn't shoot her.'" He handed the document to the ADA. "Now, that doesn't sound like a confession to me."

McGregor took the document, beads of sweat forming on her upper lip. She began stuttering as the camera zoomed in for an extreme close-up. Then Sampson cut her off before she could answer. "Hold on just a moment, Ms. McGregor. I'll give you plenty of time to respond, but I want to read you one more section from this second version of the transcript, the one my producer got from a source in your office. It's from page 71, and to refresh your memory in case you've forgotten, you didn't give us page 71. It was missing from the document we received from you," Sampson said, his tone tough and accusing. "It says right here, and I quote, 'I didn't do anything wrong. I didn't kill that girl. You've got the wrong guy.'" Sampson handed her the document. "That seems more like a denial than a confession to me, Ms. McGregor."

Ethan watched, holding his breath, as the ADA carefully read the missing page and then handed the document back to the anchorman. "I don't know where Mr. Benson got this, but I've never seen it before. It's a fake."

"Are you sure it's a fake?"

Ethan couldn't have scripted Sampson's line of questioning

any better. He'd totally underestimated the anchorman. Peter was a much better interviewer than he'd thought.

"I'm positive," McGregor said. "This is not real. Somebody's trying to mislead you. Pavel Feodor never once denied killing Cynthia Jameson during the police investigation. He confessed to the murder many times. I just read you one of his admissions of guilt." The ADA had regained her composure, the camera picking up every nuance of incredulity on her face.

"Well, Ms. McGregor, I don't think I believe you. I think you're hiding something you don't want to tell us, and so does my producer. I've screened the videotape, not the forty-second video clip you entered into evidence, but the one you hid during the trial—the full two hours and four minutes of the interrogation you refused to give to my producer."

"What are you talking about? The police interrogation didn't run nearly that long. We didn't hide anything from you or the jury."

"I beg to differ. I have a copy, and I've screened it many times. Pavel Feodor never confessed to murdering Cynthia Jameson, not once during the entire videotape. I think you're lying to us, and I think you lied to the jury."

"That's preposterous."

Sampson cut her off. "Ms. McGregor, why did you hide the videotape? Why did you conceal the parts of the confession where Pavel Feodor denies killing Cynthia Jameson?"

"I—I—I—," she paused, unable to speak, beads of sweat dripping down her forehead, as Sampson calmly pointed to a monitor the crew had set up on a table between the two of them.

"Ms. McGregor, one of my producers, Mindy Herman—I think you know her—has loaded the videotape into this playback machine. The portion I'm going to show you corresponds to the missing page 71. I want you to watch it with me and then tell me what happens when your two detectives, Edward Jenkins and Randy Tempko, can't get Mr. Feodor to admit to killing Cynthia Jameson. This will just take a moment." He hit enter and rolled the video.

McGregor peered into the monitor and watched in stunned silence as Randy Tempko stood up and screamed at Feodor, "I don't believe you. You're guilty and a fucking liar, and I'm going to beat the truth out of you." Then Tempko shoved Feodor to the floor, punched him in the stomach, and viciously kicked him, opening the bullet wound in his leg. As Jenkins tried to pull him off, shouting over and over for somebody to turn off the camera, blood splattered the floor and smeared the walls.

Sampson stared at the assistant district attorney. "Do you care to comment on what we just saw, Ms. McGregor?"

She glared back at the anchorman—at a loss for words.

"You have nothing to say, Ms. McGregor? You must have some comment?"

She continued to sit quietly, now looking at the monitor.

Sampson calmly pushed on. "Your detectives, Ms. McGregor, beat Pavel Feodor into a bloody mess, all captured right there on that videotape. Is that why you decided to hide it from the jury?"

"No, no, no! That's not it at all!"

"Is it because you wanted to get a conviction at any cost?"

"Of course not!"

"So why did you doctor the tape and make it seem like he was confessing? It's easy to do. We duplicated the clip you showed the jury in one of our edit rooms. The interrogation was recorded with an old camera. The video is fuzzy, so you can't see Mr. Feodor's mouth moving, but you can certainly see the police beating him. Why didn't you show that to the jury, Ms. McGregor?"

"I don't know what you're talking about. I'm sure you've got it all wrong, Mr. Sampson."

Ethan glanced at Mindy, stunned the ADA was stonewalling as the cameras captured her in one lie after another—her case and career going down in flames.

"Were you withholding evidence to frame Pavel Feodor?" Sampson said, drilling away.

"No! No! I would never do that."

"But I think you did, Ms. McGregor. Your entire case is built on lies, and I don't understand why." He pulled two more documents out of his folder—Officer Colin Haggerty's police report and the real autopsy report. He handed them to the ADA. "Recognize these? They, too, are signed by you and stamped by your office in the upper right-hand corner—like all the other documents in the court record."

Ethan tapped Herb on his shoulder and whispered in his ear. "Zoom in real tight on her face. She's about to unravel on camera."

"I see the stamp," she said stammering. "It's from my office, but I don't know how it got there." She wiped her brow and licked her lips.

"And what do these two documents say about the murder, Ms. McGregor?"

She looked from the documents to Sampson then back to the documents, her eyes blinking uncontrollably.

"I'll tell you what they say," Sampson said. "They say there was no blood on Cynthia Jameson's body. That she was brutally beaten that night. And that she was dead long before she was shot. So Pavel Feodor couldn't possibly have killed her. Somebody else murdered Cynthia Jameson." Sampson paused to let his line of reasoning sink in. "So let me ask you one more time. Why did you frame Pavel Feodor? He's innocent, isn't he?"

That was it. The ADA couldn't take any more. She exploded in a fit of rage, screaming into the camera. "You're twisting the facts, Mr. Sampson. I don't like your questions. And I don't like you. I have nothing more to say!"

"But we're not finished yet," Ethan said, removing his headset as she stood and tore off her microphone. "Keep going, Peter. Ask your next question."

"Ms. McGregor, don't leave," Sampson said sternly as chaos broke out on the set. "I wanna know why you hid Officer Haggerty's police report. Why you hid the real autopsy report? Why you changed the evidence and rigged the trial?"

"No more questions!" she said, still screaming.

Ethan rushed onto the set, hoping to placate the ADA, hoping to get her to sit down, but McGregor kept moving, more furious than ever.

"And what about Feodor's connection to the Russian Mob?" the anchorman said, not giving an inch. "Wasn't he part of the Kolkov crime syndicate? The cops knew—and our sources at the DEA say you knew about it too—that they told you in a meeting that the Russians were behind the heroin deal the night Cynthia Jameson was murdered. Why didn't you pursue that lead? Why did you hide it from the jury?"

"No comment! No comment," McGregor said as she stumbled over a cable and knocked over a light stand.

"What other games did you play, Ms. McGregor?" Sampson shouted, standing and joining Ethan who was motioning to his cameramen to keep rolling. "Did you conspire with Detective Jenkins? Did you tell him to alter the evidence? And what about Frankie O'Malley? Were you working with him? We have undercover footage tying him to the Russians. Were you working with the Mob? Did you know they hired a prison guard named Jimmy

Bento to kill Pavel? Or was somebody else pulling the strings? Who are you protecting, Ms. McGregor?"

"No comment! No comment! No comment," she shrieked, finally making her escape, slamming the door behind her as she stormed out of the law library, followed by Nelson Brown and her team of shell-shocked assistants.

Ethan was almost too stunned to react, then turned to his crew. "Stop rolling and not a word about what just happened until we're out of the building. I don't want to be accused of coming in here with an agenda and ambushing the ADA. If that gets back to Paul, it'll haunt us for the rest of the production. Let's wrap and get the hell out of here as fast as we can."

As the crew began breaking down the set, Sampson calmly put his hand on Ethan's shoulder. "Nice job, Ethan. Your research was flawless. Your questions superb. We caught the ADA in one lie after another."

"Yeah, but we didn't show her the pictures," he said, disappointed. "And we didn't ask her what she was doing with the deputy mayor last night."

"We'll show them to Jameson and see how he reacts," Sampson said, smiling. "I'm gonna head back to my apartment and put on a clean suit. Gotta look my best for the next interview. Call me on my cell if you need anything. Otherwise, I'll see you at the deputy mayor's at three o'clock sharp."

"No you won't," Mindy said as she bounced onto the set. "I just got a call from David. The deputy mayor canceled."

"What do you mean?" Ethan said, crestfallen. "He can't pull out now. What happened, Mindy?"

"He thinks we're on a witch hunt, that we're doing a smear job, and he doesn't want any part of it."

"Do you think he knows about the pictures?"

"How's that possible?" Mindy said. "Besides, his press secretary didn't mention anything about the pictures when she called David."

"Can we get him to reconsider?" Ethan said.

"Probably not. Rosenberg said his decision is final. The deputy mayor's not gonna change his mind, Ethan."

"So what do we do now?" Sampson said questioningly.

"We do the hour without him," Ethan said, already rethinking the special. "You just did a blockbuster interview with Nancy McGregor. You already have most of the other principal characters on camera. And your exclusive with Pavel Feodor is the kind of television everybody and his brother wants to see. We don't need Jameson or his wife. Give me a couple of hours to add the ADA to the sound bite structure, then we'll start writing the script. I'll make it work."

CHAPTER 35

ETHAN WAS SITTING IN JOEL'S editing room holding a cup of cold coffee, flipping through his script. He'd just finished screening the first act with Peter and Mindy and was worrying about the interview with Cynthia's three friends. Susan Knoxville, Annabel Taylor, and Sebastian Robbins were emotional and articulate and described in vivid detail all-night study marathons, fraternity parties, and clubbing at the trendiest nightspots, but none of them seemed to know anything about Cynthia's parents or her two younger siblings or her privileged upbringing as an heiress to one of the richest and most powerful dynasties in the city. The images of Cynthia smiling in the home movies and family photos certainly helped—bringing her to life on the screen—but Ethan knew he was missing something, the stories behind the pictures, the memories only a mother and father could share.

But that was never going to happen.

The deputy mayor and his wife refused to budge.

They wouldn't sit down for an interview.

No matter how many times he called.

Frustrated, he turned to Peter. "What do you think?"

"The act is flat," Peter said dispassionately. "The whole special is flat. And if the deputy mayor decides to pull the images, then we're really in trouble."

"Well, so far we still have permission to use them," Ethan said hopefully. "So we don't have to worry about that—not yet. Is there anything better in your interview with Cynthia's friends?"

"Nope. That's the best of it," Sampson said disappointedly. "It was almost as if they were coached not to say anything about Cynthia's private life." Sampson chewed on the end of a pencil, reflectively. "Maybe we should describe the pictures with a little more oomph in my narrations. Maybe if you find out a little more about what she's doing, we can compensate for not having the deputy mayor or his wife on camera. That's a failure on your part, Ethan. A big failure."

Ethan ignored the personal dig and turned to Mindy. "What do you think? Any rabbits in your hat? Maybe a high school friend? A cousin? An aunt or uncle who can talk to us about Cynthia? Peter's right. We need somebody to bring the special to life. Paul's gonna want more details about her relationship with her family."

"I've reached out to my contacts, and so has David," Mindy said contemplatively. "Nobody's willing to tell us anything beyond what we already know. We're at a dead end, Ethan. A complete dead end."

"So what are we gonna do?" Ethan said, craving a cigarette.

"Maybe we should just tell Paul we can't give him the hour," Peter said. "Maybe we should shoot for two or three acts and kill the idea of a special."

"It's a little late in the game for that," Ethan said soberly. "The network's been promoting us around the clock. We've got to deliver the full hour." Then his iPhone pinged and an email landed in his mailbox from David. Ignoring Sampson, who was still ranting to himself, he opened the message:

> Hey, Ethan. I have news—some good and some bad. First the bad news. I've run out of options on my search for Leonard Toakling and Colin Haggerty. The coroner is nowhere to be found, and the cop was really pissed he'd talked to you in the first place. He told me in no uncertain terms to leave him alone. So it's a no-go with those guys for interviews. Now the good news. I found Jacob Lutz and am sitting in his living room. Can you get your ass over here right away? He lives at 2900 Broadway in Morningside Heights. He says he'll do an on-camera interview, but only with you. So I brought a camcorder and a tripod. I'll be ready as soon as you get here. Hurry before he changes his mind.

Ethan typed a quick response, then grabbed his briefcase. "That was David. No interviews with Toakling or Haggerty. We'll use the documents—the autopsy and crime report—and say we couldn't get them to go on camera. Will you add that to the script, Peter?"

"Of course. Right away. But where are you going?"

"David just found Jacob Lutz," he said hurriedly. "I'm sure he has insights about Cynthia and her family that'll help us flesh out Act I and the rest of the special. I'm headed out to interview him."

"Do you want me to come with you?" Mindy said.

"No. We need to split up the workload if we wanna make the

deadline. You work with the editors while Peter does the rewrites. Then we'll all regroup when I get back."

. . . . .

A half hour later, Ethan stood at the front door of Jacob Lutz's apartment. Finding Cynthia's boyfriend had been a top priority—not only because he knew about her family—but because he was the last person to see her alive, and Ethan wanted to know what she was doing all alone in the Meatpacking District in the wee hours of the morning on the night she was murdered.

He rang the doorbell, and Lutz invited him in.

A small man, no more than five foot six and a hundred and fifty pounds, Jacob was handsome with neatly combed black hair and bright hazel eyes that shined like the stars. He was wearing tailored gray slacks, an open-collared blue oxford shirt, and brand-new Italian loafers. "Mr. Benson," he said, thrusting out his hand.

"Pleasure to meet you," Ethan said cordially. "I'm glad we finally found you."

Lutz's lips curled in a forced smile. "Sorry about that. I've been out of the country and just found out you're doing a story about Cynthia." He motioned for Ethan to follow and led him into a large, well-appointed living room. David was standing at a tripod adjusting the electronics on a Panasonic DV cam.

"Hey, Ethan. We're almost ready to go," he said, pointing to the camera. "It's only a one-chip, but it's the best I could do on short notice. I had to grab whatever was available before I came over to meet Jacob."

"That'll do just fine," Ethan said as he looked around the room. Jacob was certainly wealthy—super wealthy, in fact—just as the deputy mayor had told him when they met. Original art-work hung on the walls, oriental rugs covered the floors, Venetian lamps sat on the tables, and expensive designer furniture was perfectly placed to take advantage of the natural light streaming through the floor-to-ceiling windows. *A trust fund baby*, Ethan thought. *No wonder Jameson was impressed. He was the perfect match for his daughter.*

"Shall we sit and chat a few minutes before we do the interview?" Lutz said uneasily. "There are a couple of things I need to tell you." He pointed to a couch with a beautiful view of the Columbia University campus. "I was in love with Cynthia. Madly in love with her. She was bright, outgoing, and absolutely beautiful. Everything a guy could ever want in a woman." He sighed wearily. "But there was something else about her that I didn't see at first. Something sad, fragile, almost imperceptible, that took me a long time to figure out." He paused and looked off out the window.

Ethan waited a second, then said softly, "Where did you meet Cynthia, Jacob?"

Lutz took a deep breath. "In constitutional law. She was studying to become a lawyer and so was I, but I'm sure her father must've told you just how proud he was of his little girl," he said sarcastically.

Ethan was taken aback by the harsh tone in his voice. "As a matter of fact, he told me his daughter was planning to follow in his footsteps and enter public service."

"That's what he tells everybody," Lutz said bitterly. "And I'm sure he seemed quite sincere. But I bet he won't talk about his daughter on camera." He raised an eyebrow. "Am I right?"

Ethan stared at the young man cryptically. "How'd you know that?"

"Because the deputy mayor never talks to anybody about Cynthia in front of cameras," Lutz said, grabbing a cigarette from a silver case. "Mind if I smoke?"

"Go ahead," Ethan said, lighting his own Marlboro. "Why won't he consent to an on-camera interview, Jacob?"

Lutz laughed nervously. "Because he worries he might slip up and that some reporter might learn the truth."

"What truth?" Ethan said, puzzled.

Jacob's face turned harsh. "That they hated each other."

"What do you mean they hated each other? I've never heard anybody say that."

"Of course not," Jacob said, laughing. "Bernard Jameson is a son of a bitch, a control freak, and very good at hiding their secret. I know because I saw them fighting many times." He took a long pull on his cigarette. "He berated her. Humiliated her. And threatened—at least once that I can remember—to cut off her money if she ever went public."

Ethan shot David a quick glance. "I don't understand, Jacob," he said cautiously. "If she ever went public with what?"

"That he physically abused her. How's that for a shocker? The big-time politician is really a big-time child beater." He took a long pull and snuffed out his cigarette. "In fact, she told him shortly before she was murdered—and I was there, watching as the confrontation unfolded—that she was going to tell the whole world what he did to her."

"Did Cynthia's mother know about this?"

"She knew, but she looked the other way," Jacob said, his shoulders sagging. "Tragic, isn't it? Cynthia was alone with nowhere to go and nowhere to hide from her father."

"Maybe we should roll the camera?" David said, interrupting a long pause. "Then you won't have to go through this twice, Jacob. Would that be easier for you?"

Lutz didn't respond. He just lit another cigarette, tormented.

"Let's hold off a moment, David," Ethan said, leaning over and placing his hand on Lutz's shoulder. "I know this is difficult, but I still don't understand what any of this has to do with Cynthia's murder."

"It has everything to do with what happened to Cynthia. Everything," he said, his eyes now ablaze with anger. "I've got something to show you, Mr. Benson." Lutz stood and walked over to a vanity in the corner of the room, unlocked a drawer, and removed a thick envelope. "Cynthia gave this to me for safekeeping, but I can't keep it a secret any longer." He handed Ethan the envelope. "This will explain everything. Why we were at the Standard Grill that night. Why I had to leave her alone at the restaurant. And why her father needs to be punished."

Ethan opened the envelope and pulled out a stack of documents. He quickly thumbed through each one, his expression changing from shock to astonishment to fury. Now he understood what had happened to Cynthia. Now he understood what she had been doing in the Meatpacking District. Now he understood the truth. He carefully slid the documents back into the envelope and tucked them into his briefcase. "Are you ready to tell us the rest of your story, Jacob?"

Lutz nodded.

"Good. Let's roll the cameras."

. . . . .

Ethan pushed into the edit room and handed Joel the disk. "This is the Jacob Lutz interview, and it's fucking explosive. We're gonna use it in every act of the hour. Where's Peter? Where's Mindy? I want to show them right away."

"Well, you're just gonna have to wait," Joel said as he continued fine cutting a sequence of pictures. "They're upstairs with Paul dealing with some crisis that came up right after you left."

"Shit, what now?" Ethan said, dismayed. "Lemme see what's

goin' on. I'll be back in a few minutes. Then we'll screen the interview."

Ethan rode the elevator up to the eleventh floor and headed straight to Paul's office. "Glad you could make it," Monica said in a condescending voice. "They're duking it out in the conference room. Paul's waiting for you."

Ethan ignored her comment and slipped into the room. Paul was sitting at the head of the table across from Peter and Mindy. To his right was Jamie Summers, and to his left, Douglas Fitzgerald—the president of the news division. They were poring over the script, circling words and writing notes in the margins.

Sampson looked up and smiled. "Sorry, Ethan. We couldn't wait for you to get back. Paul wanted to meet right away. So Mindy made copies of the script, and we're all going through it line by line."

"But this is a rough version," Ethan said as he sat in a chair next to Mindy. "It's too early to show it to management. I just finished the Jacob Lutz interview and haven't cut it into the story. Everything's gonna change."

"We can talk about Lutz later," Paul said acrimoniously. "We've got a much bigger problem. The deputy mayor has seen our promos and had a heart attack. Fill him in, Doug. He doesn't know what's going on upstairs."

Fitzgerald sipped a cup of coffee. "I'm not going to pull any punches, Ethan. George Pierce, the chairman of the board, isn't happy."

"Why?" Ethan said, beginning to worry.

"He had dinner with the deputy mayor last night. They're close friends. They golf together, vacation together, and hobnob in the same social circles." Fitzgerald paused and finished his coffee. "Jameson accused you of twisting the facts, of manipulating the truth, and demanded that we cancel the special. He called George again this morning after seeing today's promo—the one that implies the Russian Mob was connected to the murder and conspired with the assistant district attorney to throw the case. Jameson said, and I quote, 'It's all pure poppycock.' Then he threatened to sue Global Broadcasting and you for libel and slander and defamation of character."

Ethan listened, appalled.

"I know your work and reputation as an investigative journalist," Fitzgerald said placatingly, "but you make some serious allegations in your special that are going to turn this city upside down and destroy a lot of lives. I need to be certain that every fact is accurate. We can't afford to make a mistake."

"I can guarantee you there are no mistakes," Ethan said unbendingly.

"And I'll second that," Sampson said, for good measure. "Ethan's a pain in the ass, but he's thorough. He doesn't leave a stone unturned."

"I expect nothing less," Fitzgerald said, eyeing the two of them. "But George has asked me and Jamie to take a look at your documentation, and then he wants to sit down and talk to us before he makes his decision to run or cancel your special."

"I've put together a notebook of documents for the lawyers," Ethan said with confidence. "I just need to insert some new evidence from Jacob Lutz before I give it to you."

"Fine, fine, Ethan, but the sooner we get it the better," Summers said, speaking for the first time. "I've been on the phone with George since late last night fighting to save your hour, but I gotta tell you it's been an uphill battle. Without the deputy mayor's interview, I'm not sure even the documents will convince him to air your show."

"But Jamie, we can't kill the special," Ethan said, pleadingly. "Pavel Feodor is innocent. He didn't murder Cynthia Jameson. The documents don't lie."

"Ethan's right," Paul said, chiming in. "This is the biggest story we've produced in years. The whole nation's gonna watch. It's a little late to be questioning its veracity or the ethics of my producer. I've been grilling Ethan for weeks. He's done his homework. He knows the facts. We can't pull the hour just because the deputy mayor doesn't like what we're saying."

"I don't disagree," Summers said forthrightly. "But we still have to convince the man who runs this company. He's gonna make the decision. Not us."

There was a knock on the door, and Monica poked her head into the room. "Ethan, the deputy mayor is holding on line one. He wants to talk to you and only you. He says it's urgent."

A hush fell over the room as Ethan picked up the phone. "Mr. Deputy Mayor, this is Ethan Benson."

"I've been looking all over for you," the deputy mayor said, seething. "My press secretary finally found your researcher, David Livingston, and he told her you were in a meeting with your senior staff, or I never would have found you." There was a short pause. Ethan held his breath. "Is your offer still on the table?" Jameson said lividly. "My wife and I have changed our minds. We want an opportunity to respond to your litigious allegations and salacious innuendos."

Ethan cupped the mouthpiece and smiled. "I think we just hooked our big fish." He removed his hand. "The offer still stands, Mr. Deputy Mayor. There's plenty of time to sit down and do the interview."

"Good. Here's what I propose."

Ethan listened as Jameson laid out his ground rules. "Okay, okay. We can do that." There was another pause. "We'll shoot the interview to time, so there'll be no editing." Ethan continued listening. "Yes, sir, I understand. I give you my word. Thank you, Deputy Mayor."

He hung up the phone.

"What did he say?" Summers said eagerly. "Do we have the interview?"

"He and his wife will do it," Ethan said triumphantly. "He wants a chance to defend himself against what he calls my 'baseless lies and blatant inaccuracies.' But he wants to do the interview live to air on Thursday night, and he wants to do it from his apartment. Those are his conditions. And I agreed to them."

"That doesn't give us much time," Paul said. "Can you finish the editing and get the shoot set up in two days?"

"I won't sleep much, but yes, I'll get it done," Ethan said.

"And how do you plan to make room in the special?" Paul said, still worrying. "Mindy says you're already running three minutes too long, and you still have to cut in this new character, Jacob Lutz."

"I'll squeeze out the time," Ethan said, quickly skimming through the script. "The bigger question is how we structure the show to make room for a live segment."

"Any suggestions?"

"Can we add a commercial pod and create a sixth act?"

"Sure. I'll call the network and get them to change the format."

"So that's what we'll do," Ethan said with conviction. "I'll shave a minute and a half out of each act, and if we lose the promos and bumpers, that'll give us nine minutes for the deputy mayor and his wife." He looked at Paul. "That should be enough time, don't you think?"

"Plenty," Paul said, waving his hand. "But Ethan, I still don't get what happened. Why did the deputy mayor change his mind?"

"Because he's got a big ego and is worried about his political future," Ethan said smoothly. "He wants the airtime to convince our viewers that Feodor is guilty and that there's been no cover-up and no conspiracy to get the conviction. He's adamant we're wrong, and he wants the face time to appeal to his constituents." He turned to the chief counsel. "Jamie, this should help us with Mr. Pierce, don't you think?"

"It should ease his biggest concern," Summers said, turning to Douglas Fitzgerald. "Let's go tell George about the interview. And Ethan, get me the documents so I can show George the proof if he has any questions."

"Right away, Jamie."

Paul waited a moment for them to leave, then smiled conspiratorially. "We just dodged a bullet, Ethan. When Doug first called this morning, he said outright that Pierce was pulling your special and replacing it with a rerun of some crime show called *The Investigators*. I thought we were toast." He picked up his script. "Is there anything I should know about this guy, Jacob Lutz? Anything important?"

"Let me show Peter and Mindy the interview first, then I'll come up and tell you."

"Okay. Surprise me."

"That's my plan, and I think you'll be more than just blown away once you know what he has to say about the deputy mayor."

CHAPTER 36

BERNARD JAMESON PACED AROUND the formal library on the top floor of his penthouse, torn with self-doubt. Why had he listened to Sandy and agreed to the interview? Why had he changed his mind? He'd spent all that time working on George, telling him the promos were a pack of lies, threatening to sue if the special made air. So why in God's name was he about to sit down and talk to Peter Sampson? He was the deputy mayor of New York. He owned one of the biggest corporations in the world. He was rich and powerful and didn't have to answer to anybody. Not anybody. Especially *The Weekly Reporter*.

Grabbing his cell phone, he dialed Nancy McGregor's private line, but the call went directly to voice mail. He cursed and left a short message. "Goddamn it, where the hell are you? What did you tell Sampson? What does he have on me?" He slammed down the phone and sent her an email, no longer worried about covering his back. Had she betrayed him? Had she implicated him in the cover-up? Had she told Sampson about his daughter? Well, he'd bury her if she did. If she'd uttered one word about Cynthia. One word about his secret.

He closed his eyes and rubbed his temples.

The GBS production crew had been setting up in his apartment all evening with that pushy producer, Ethan Benson, putting up their lights and cameras and turning his home into a television studio. What was he going to say if they knew? How would he defend himself? How would he break the news to Sandy? He needed to come up with answers, and he needed to do it fast.

Wendell, the butler, knocked on the door. "Mr. Jameson, your wife asked me to inform you that Mr. Benson needs you downstairs. He's ready to start the interview."

"Thank you, Wendell. Tell Mrs. Jameson I'll be down in a few minutes. Please shut the door on your way out."

The butler nodded and left.

He dialed Nancy one last time, but there was no answer. Shit. He was on his own. Standing, he stared at his face in the mirror. His eyes were puffy and bloodshot, his visage drawn and slack. Somehow he had to pull himself together for the cameras and look powerful—like the deputy mayor of New York. After straightening his tie, combing his hair, and putting on a blue blazer, he took a deep breath, stood up straight, and made his way out the door.

. . . . .

Ethan looked at his watch. It was just after ten. The show had just hit the airwaves, and he wasn't close to being finished—the crew still setting up lights, the grips still running cables down to the remote truck, the cameramen still tweaking the electronics in the four Sony HD cams Ethan was using to broadcast the interview. He peered into his bank of monitors. There were no pictures, only dark empty screens. He turned to his lead cameraman. "Herb, are we going to make it?" he said, trying to hide his anxiety. "We have less than forty-five minutes until we go live to the network."

"I'm working as fast as I can," Herb said as he checked the color settings on his camera. "I usually get a full day to build a set like this. Not just a couple of hours. But I guarantee you it's gonna look great once we're done."

"Okay, that's all I need to hear." He sat down at his command station, put on his headset, and checked his communications, flipping the talk switch on his control panel. "Mindy, are you there?" There was no response. "Mindy, answer me."

"I'm here, Ethan. Hold on a second," she said, chaos in the background.

"Is the feed up yet?" he said, yelling into his headset. "Can they see us at the Broadcast Center? Talk to me, Mindy."

There was another long pause. "We just linked in, Ethan. They have bars and tone. We're good to go."

Mindy was sitting in a mobile control room next to Stanley Kramer, the show's director, who was switching the cameras and feeding the interview back to the network from a remote truck parked outside the Jamesons' building on Fifth Avenue. "Hey, Ethan," Stanley said in a soothing voice, "I'm talking to Paul at the Broadcast Center. We're headed into the first commercial break, and he says the switchboard is lighting up like fireworks. People are calling in from all over the country, outraged by your story. Just about everybody thinks Pavel Feodor was framed and that Nancy McGregor should be fired. Your story's blowing the lid off corruption in our legal system."

Paul chimed into the conversation. "Let's hold off on the self-congratulations. We have a long way to go before the show's off the air. And I don't want to risk fucking up your live insert. Has Peter arrived yet?"

Ethan searched the room. "He's here, Paul. Lemme go talk to him." He pulled off his headset and rushed over to his anchorman. "Peter, I was starting to get worried you weren't gonna make it. Have you gone over the new questions?"

"Of course. Ten times since we screened the Lutz interview. I'm ready for the Jamesons." Sampson gazed into his monitor. "I look pretty good, don't you think?" He turned back to Ethan. "Reassure me one more time. We can prove all this stuff, right?" He waved his questions. "I gave George Pierce a heads-up on the telephone this afternoon, and he wasn't happy we were going to ask Jameson all these personal questions about his daughter. You don't have any doubts, do you, Ethan?"

"None," he said adamantly.

"And Lutz is for real?"

"David did a thorough background check on the guy. There are no skeletons in his closet."

"Let me see Jacob's proof one more time."

Ethan handed him a folder.

Sampson quickly read through the documents. "Well, I guess there's enough here, and since you're positive it's the truth, so am I." He put the documents back into the folder and handed them to Ethan, who nodded, then slowly made his way back to his monitors. "Herb, we've got fifteen minutes. We ready to roll?"

"What do you think, guys?" Glickstein said, peering at his crew.

Everybody gave him the thumbs-up.

Ethan smiled, then leaned over to David. "Time to get the Jamesons," he said succinctly. "Herb, take the extra HD cam and go with him. Paul wants a walking shot as they come onto the set. He's gonna use it as a live tease going into the commercial break just before we start the interview."

"And you'll cue me when you want them to start walking?" Herb said, grabbing the camera.

"I'll wave you in," Ethan said as he checked the time. "Listen up, everybody. We've got less than five minutes. Turn off your cell phones and take your places." He put on his headset and listened as Paul and Stanley screamed at each other.

Everything was moving along.

They were ready to go.

. . . . .

Bernard Jameson made his way past a gallery of Renaissance art and down a formal staircase to a marble foyer on the main floor. Sandy was already standing there with Sylvia Rosenberg, surrounded by members of the production crew. "You still wanna go through with this?" he said, peering deeply into her eyes. "We still have time to pull out."

"Oh, I wish we could, Bernard," she said fretfully. "All these lights and cameras make me nervous. But we have to do the interview with Mr. Sampson for Cynthia. We owe it to her memory."

Jameson sighed deeply. "Don't you worry, dear. It'll all be over in a little while, and then we can get on with our lives." But the deputy mayor wasn't so sure. Not on the inside. He had a sinking feeling they were about to walk into a buzz saw. After introducing himself, he turned to David, who was standing next to Herb Glickstein. "Will we start soon?" he said pleasantly.

"Yes, sir. We just need to wire you up for sound." Anthony Petulla clipped a microphone to Jameson's sports coat and snaked a cable through his shirt and down to a portable transmitter attached to his belt. Then they made their way through the apartment and to the door of the great room. "We'll wait here until we get the go-ahead from my producer," David said, pointing to Ethan. "Then I want you to walk into the room, introduce yourselves to Mr. Sampson, and sit down in the seats opposite him. Herb here is gonna follow you with his camera, and we're going to broadcast the entire sequence live to the network as we go into the commercial break. Then you'll have a couple of minutes to get comfortable before we start the interview."

"Seems simple enough," the deputy mayor said, turning to his wife. "Do you understand what they want us to do, Sandy?"

"Perfectly, dear," she said stoically.

He squeezed her hand and stared straight ahead, focused and confident. All he had to do was maintain the web of lies he'd so carefully constructed, and if the audience didn't believe him, well then, it was just too bad for them.

. . . . .

A moment later, Ethan heard Stanley yell into his headset. "Three, two, one—cue the deputy mayor. You're on the air." Ethan frantically waved to his cameraman, and the Jamesons slowly walked onto the set, the deputy mayor somber, his wife downcast. They approached Sampson and shook hands, Herb slowly circling, making a sweeping pan shot as they said their hellos and sat down—Sylvia Rosenberg slipping off to watch the interview from the corner of the room.

Ethan waited for his next cue, then stood and said, "We're in the commercial break and have three minutes before they come back to us live." There was a frenzy of activity—the lighting director eliminating a hot spot on Sandy's forehead, the soundman balancing audio levels, and the cameramen adjusting the framing of each shot. "One minute," Ethan said, his voice now booming. Grabbing his questions, he stared at Peter, hoping his anchorman was on his game, ready to work his magic and get to the truth. "Five seconds. Four seconds. Three. Two. One. Go, Peter. We're back on the air."

Sampson peered into his camera. "I know losing a daughter who was so young and full of life must be devastating, but thank you, Deputy Mayor and Mrs. Jameson, for putting aside your grief and sharing your thoughts with us tonight." He paused as Sandy grabbed a tissue to wipe away a tear. "Mrs. Jameson, I'd like to begin with you. May I call you Sandy?"

"That would be fine," she said, heaving a deep sigh.

"Sandy, what's it been like to wake each morning knowing your beautiful daughter, Cynthia, isn't asleep in her bedroom? Isn't coming down for breakfast? Isn't part of your life anymore?"

Ethan looked down and checked off the first question on his list.

"I'm not quite sure words can express my feelings," she said, the camera zooming into a tight shot as she struggled to control her emotions. "Cynthia was my oldest child, and I loved her with all my heart. And she loved me and her little brother and sister, Ned and Susan. We did everything together. We talked and laughed and shared secrets. I miss her terribly—every moment of every day."

Sampson turned to the deputy mayor. "I want to ask you the same question, Mr. Jameson. What's it like for you? Knowing you'll never see your daughter again?"

"Cynthia was my princess, the light of my life," he said, struggling to find the right words. "I rocked her when she was a baby, took care of her when she was sick, and watched her grow into a happy and responsible young woman with a great future ahead of her. Now she's gone, just a memory, and I'm never going to get over the loss."

For the next two minutes, Sampson asked about Cynthia's

childhood—the Jamesons responding with a series of poignant anecdotes about their favorite memories, about her friends and boyfriends, about her hopes and dreams—their answers heartfelt and filled with melancholy. *Peter's sticking to the game plan*, Ethan thought as he drew a line through each question.

Then Sampson asked about the murder.

"Sandy, describe that night to me. What were your first thoughts when you found out Cynthia was dead?"

Mrs. Jameson's lip began to quiver, the camera slowly zooming into a tight shot of her face. Ethan studied the image in his monitor and whispered to Herb to move even tighter. "I remember the phone ringing next to the bed as if it was yesterday, and I remember thinking something was wrong. It was four o'clock in the morning, and it's always bad news when the phone rings at that hour. I remember Bernard waking up and asking me to answer it."

The deputy mayor interrupted. "Yes, I looked at her and wondered why she was letting it ring on and on and on like that."

"I was afraid to pick it up, Bernard," she said, glowering at him. "I knew something bad had happened." She grabbed a tissue and blew her nose. "Then I remember this very nice policeman asking if he could speak to the deputy mayor. And I said, 'Why? What's wrong?' And he paused a moment, then said, 'It's your daughter, Mrs. Jameson. We just found her.' And I remember screaming, 'Is she all right? Is she all right?' And he wouldn't answer me. He just kept asking for my husband. But I wouldn't put Bernard on the phone until he told me." Tears were now flowing down her cheeks, the moment captured on all four cameras as the deputy mayor leaned over and touched her hand.

"I know this is difficult, but tell me, what happened next?" Sampson said soothingly.

"I remember screaming into the phone," Sandy said. "'Please

tell me. Is Cynthia hurt? Is she okay?' And the policeman wouldn't answer me—"

"—It was actually the police commissioner, darling. He was the person who called us—"

"—Oh, you're right, Bernard. It was the police commissioner." She wiped her eyes, her emotions overflowing. "He told me they'd found our darling Cynthia and that somebody had shot her, and that she was dead." Her voice trailed off as she began shaking hysterically.

"Would you like a moment to compose yourself?" Sampson said, waiting for Sandy to stop sobbing before asking his next question. "I'm sorry to be dredging up all these difficult memories, Mrs. Jameson, but this is very important. Can you tell me what Cynthia was doing that night before she was murdered?"

Sandy wiped her eyes with another tissue. "She was out celebrating the end of midterm exams with friends, and you know how kids are, they went down to the Meatpacking District and were going from one bar to the next having a good time." She paused, gasping for breath. "Then she met her boyfriend, Jacob Lutz, and had dinner at that high-end steakhouse, the Standard Grill. But he went home about one o'clock, and she stayed behind for some reason. When she finally decided to leave, she walked straight into that dreadful gun battle. That's when she was shot and murdered by that horrible man. Now she's gone forever, and I'll never see her again," she said, covering her face with her hands.

Paul yelled into the headset. "This is great television, Ethan, but you've only got four minutes. Give Peter a cue. Let him know we're running out of time and that he has to pick up the pace."

Ethan held up four fingers, and Sampson nodded as he turned to the deputy mayor, his face hard and challenging. "Mr. Jameson, what was your daughter really doing in the Meatpacking District that night? I know it's trendy, but parts of that neighborhood like Little West Twelfth Street are downright scary at three o'clock in the morning."

"Well, well, well, I know it can be dangerous," Jameson said, stuttering. "But I really don't know why she didn't go home with Jacob and remained there all alone in the middle of the night. Like Sandy said, she was just trying to have a good time with her friends."

"But wasn't she a bit young to be hitting the club scene?" Sampson said, pushing the deputy mayor a little harder. "All those places serve alcohol, and Cynthia was underage, wasn't she?" Ethan leaned forward, watching the change on Jameson's face as fear began creeping into his eyes.

"Yes," he said bitingly. "She was underage, and my wife and I talked to her many times about why she shouldn't go out drinking at all those fancy nightspots. But she had a mind of her own, and like many young adults, she refused to listen to us."

Ethan ran through his questions, than caught Sampson's attention and mouthed, "Number twenty-five." The anchorman shook his head, then turned to Sandy. "Mrs. Jameson, do you know who Cynthia was really partying with that night?"

"I told you she was with friends and then Jacob," she said, puzzled.

"Yes. But I want to make sure she didn't see anybody else that night. Think hard, Mrs. Jameson."

"There was nobody else," the deputy mayor said, interrupting. "What are you insinuating, Mr. Sampson? Everything we've told you is in the public record. We're not making it up."

"I know it's in the public record, Mr. Jameson. I've read it and so has my producer. But I'm not sure you're telling the truth. Is there any possibility that your daughter may have spent at least part of the night with somebody else?"

"No," the deputy mayor said indignantly.

Ethan smiled to himself. Peter had just caught the deputy mayor in a blatant lie. His scheme to pin his daughter's murder on Pavel Feodor was about to unravel live on national television.

Sampson asked his next question, his expression skeptical. "Well, that's not what we've heard, Mr. Jameson. My producer just interviewed Jacob Lutz, and he told us a far different story about the night Cynthia was murdered. He also told us that you ordered him not to talk to us."

"That's not true. He's lying."

Ethan turned to David and whispered, "Here we go."

Sampson pressed on. "Mr. Lutz says you bribed him with a lot of money to keep his mouth shut. A half million dollars to be precise. We have his allegation on camera and just aired it to millions of Americans watching our special."

"That's preposterous. I never gave him a single penny," the deputy mayor said dismissively. "And I'm gonna sue you and your television network if you dared to report that on the air."

"I'll ignore your last comment," Peter said, looking into the deputy mayor's eyes. "But let me tell you what Jacob Lutz insists is the truth. He said that your daughter only spent a short time partying with her friends and only a few minutes with him the night she was murdered. That her friends lied to the police and to the jury and to us when we interviewed them. Did you also bribe Cynthia's college friends?"

"I won't answer that question. You have no proof," Jameson said, beads of sweat soaking his brow.

"But I do have proof, Mr. Jameson," Sampson said confidently. "All three of Cynthia's friends signed legal affidavits admitting to us that you paid them quite handsomely to say they were with your daughter most of that night."

"Bernard, what's he talking about?" Sandy said, gaping at her husband.

The deputy mayor smiled tentatively. "It's nothing, dear. Jacob is the one who's lying. I didn't pay anybody any money to make up a story about our Cynthia. You know I wouldn't do that."

"But that's exactly what you did, Mr. Jameson. You fabricated most of what Cynthia did that night. Jacob told us that your daughter was working the night she was murdered."

"What are you implying?" Sandy said, shocked.

"I'm not implying anything. Cynthia's boyfriend, Jacob Lutz, told us on camera that your daughter was a high-priced call girl."

Sandy Jameson gasped. "Bernard, why is he saying these awful things about Cynthia?" Her voice cracked as she fought off another round of tears.

"Don't believe him, dear," the deputy mayor said pleadingly as he turned and faced the anchorman. "Mr. Sampson, these allegations are outrageous. Jacob Lutz is trying to smear my daughter's good name, and you're trying to destroy my family's good reputation on national television." He looked directly into the camera. "My daughter was not a call girl. She was an outstanding young woman." He pounded his fist on his knee for emphasis, then wheeled on Sampson. "This is why I didn't want to do your interview. This is why I told your boss, George Pierce, not to run your special. You're doing exactly what I said you'd do. Lying. Lying. Lying. And you have no proof. None whatsoever."

Ethan leaned over and handed Sampson the folder with the Jacob Lutz documents. "Thank you, Ethan." He pulled out the evidence. "Mr. Jameson, I wasn't planning to show you this, but you're leaving me no choice. I'm going to ask you one last time. Was your daughter, Cynthia, a high-priced call girl who worked for an escort service called the Sophisticated Lady?"

"No," Jameson said scornfully. "My daughter was not a prostitute."

"Well, these telephone records beg to differ." He passed Jameson a printout showing a dozen phone calls from the Sophisticated Lady to Cynthia's cell phone made the night of the murder. "I've also got copies of your daughter's email records and credit card receipts, and they're all real. I can assure you of that. My office checked out everything." He handed the documents to the deputy mayor. "How do you explain all this? It seems pretty clear to me that Cynthia was working for an escort service."

Stanley boomed over the headset, "Ethan, Paul's killing the credits. You've got another two minutes before we go off the air." Ethan held up two fingers, motioning to Sampson to keep going, hoping they had enough time to get to the end of the interview and the truth.

"Well, Mr. Jameson, doesn't that look like proof to you?" Sampson said.

The deputy mayor scanned the documents, shot a quick glance at his wife, then turned back to Peter. "These are all fake. I don't know where Jacob Lutz says he got them, but they're not real." He tossed the documents on the floor.

"I'm confident they're real, Mr. Jameson, and I'm confident you've known about Cynthia's secret life for quite some time." There was a momentary pause as Herb Glickstein locked his camera on the deputy mayor's face, and Bobby Raffalo tightened on his wife. "Is that why you sweet-talked Nancy McGregor, took her to your bed, and promised her a place in your election campaign so she'd frame Pavel Feodor and protect your daughter's reputation?"

The deputy mayor sat motionless, his face contorted in a mask of hatred as he glared at Sampson.

"Come on, Peter," Ethan whispered. "You've got him. Don't let him off the hook."

Sampson shifted and faced Sandy. "Mrs. Jameson, your husband had an affair with the prosecutor so he could manipulate the evidence in the court case. We have pictures of them together, and my team worked very hard checking it out with sources in his office. I'm afraid it's all true. Would you like to see the pictures?"

"No. No. Please. I don't need to see proof. I know he's been cheating on me. He's cheated on me all through our marriage." She lowered her eyes, ashamed.

"And there's something else, Mrs. Jameson, something else your husband has been hiding from you and the public for a very long time. Something I think you may have known about but were too afraid to confront." He turned to the deputy mayor, his eyes boring into him. "Cynthia hated you and everything about you, didn't she? And that's why she turned to a life of prostitution. To get even with you. Isn't that right, Mr. Jameson?"

"That's ridiculous," the deputy mayor shrieked, spittle flying out of his mouth. "My daughter loved me, and I loved her." He spun around to his wife—Herb's camera capturing the panic on his face. "Don't believe a word of this, Sandy. Not a word. None of it is true."

Sampson grabbed another set of documents from the folder, and this time handed them to Sandy. "My producer was skeptical, too, when Jacob told him about your husband's relationship with your daughter—until he gave us the evidence you're now holding—police reports you won't find anywhere at the NYPD. Your husband made sure of that. He threw around lots of money to get them deleted from their computer system. Didn't you, Mr. Jameson?"

"Where'd you get them?" Jameson said, stunned.

"Cynthia kept copies and gave them to Jacob in case something happened to her," Sampson said fiercely. "And we know they're real because we're working with a private investigator, a former NYPD narcotics agent, who authenticated them with his contacts in the police department."

Jameson turned ashen gray on camera.

Ethan knew they had him.

Sampson went on. "Mrs. Jameson, those police reports are legal proof that your husband beat your daughter, and on at least one occasion, even tried to rape her."

"You tried to rape Cynthia? You beat her? Why, Bernard? Why?" Sandy said, devastated, the documents slipping through her hands and floating to the floor. "I knew you didn't get along. I knew you fought like cats and dogs. But you physically abused our Cynthia? You sexually molested her? Why didn't she tell me?"

"She tried, Mrs. Jameson. She tried. But she told Jacob you never listened to her," Sampson said. "And that's why she became a prostitute, isn't it, Mr. Jameson? She was so desperate—so emotionally destroyed by you—that she spiraled into this dark world to get even." Sampson paused, waiting for Herb Glickstein to pan from the deputy mayor to his wife and then back to the deputy mayor. "Your daughter knew if she ever went to the press with her secret life—the secret life you pushed her into—she could bury you forever. And according to Jacob Lutz, you discovered right before the murder that she was planning to go public with everything. Isn't that what really happened, Mr. Jameson?"

The deputy mayor began to laugh, a high-pitched, maniacal laugh. "You think you have it all figured out, don't you, Mr. Sampson?"

"Not all of it, Deputy Mayor. Care to enlighten me?"

Jameson just smiled.

Ethan checked the time.

They were down to their last forty-five seconds. There wasn't enough time to get to the end of the interview. Whispering into his headset, he said, "Paul, you gotta go to the network and tell them to bump the top of local news. Something big's about to happen. I can feel it."

"Ethan, it's me, Stanley. Paul's already on the phone with George Pierce and network operations. Hold on a second."

Ethan waited breathlessly, time ticking away.

"Got it," Paul said, his voice booming over the headset. "Pierce says we can go five more minutes, but that's it."

"I owe you, Paul," Ethan said, turning to Sampson and flashing five fingers.

The anchorman glanced down at his questions, then back up at the deputy mayor. "Okay, Mr. Jameson, here's your chance to come clean. Tell us what really happened to your daughter the night she was murdered."

The deputy mayor was silent, his expression grim as Herb zoomed back to a two-shot revealing Sandy—her body trembling—as she suddenly slapped him across the face, the sound exploding through the microphones like a thunderclap. "Bernard, how could you do this to our Cynthia? How could you make her into something so terrible and hide it from me? Why? Why? Why?" she said, stumbling over each word.

Jameson rubbed his cheek, his mouth hanging open, unable to speak.

"You're an animal. An animal. An animal," she shrieked, bursting into tears.

Ethan stood, worried the deputy mayor was about to storm off the set, and motioned wildly for Sampson to ask the last question again.

Peter leaned forward, his face inches from the deputy mayor. "What happened to Cynthia that night, Mr. Jameson? We can prove beyond any reasonable doubt that your daughter wasn't killed by a bullet, that she was dead before she was shot, that Pavel Feodor didn't murder her, and that Nancy McGregor rigged the entire case to get him convicted with the help of the public defender and the Russian Mob. We suspect that you were the mastermind behind the conspiracy. Is that the truth, Deputy Mayor?"

There was a long pause, Jameson's eyes darting back and forth spasmodically. He took a deep breath. "Yes. It was me," he whispered. "I pinned the murder on that lowlife."

"Why, Mr. Jameson? Why did you frame Pavel Feodor?"

Jameson didn't answer. He just stared into the camera.

"Well, if Feodor didn't do it, then who did?" Sampson pressed on.

Herb zoomed into an extreme close-up, the deputy mayor's face riddled with anguish.

"Who, Mr. Jameson?"

There was another long pause, Ethan staring into his monitors, mesmerized, before the deputy mayor finally spoke. "It was my fault," he said, defeated. "I did it. I murdered my daughter, but it wasn't supposed to happen. I hired a pimp to teach her a lesson. He was just supposed to push her around, rough her up a bit, but she laughed in his face, thought it was some kind of joke. So he beat her, pummeled her over and over again, until she collapsed and died right there on the sidewalk in front of the restaurant." He turned to his wife. "I didn't mean to kill her. I didn't. I didn't," he wailed. "But I couldn't let her go public. It would've been the end of me, the end of my political career, and the end of our family."

Sandy sat perfectly still, staring at her husband, color draining from her face as Ethan stood and slowly walked onto the set—not caring about the cameras. He leaned over and said to Peter, "We know what happened to Cynthia. Take us off the air. We've got the truth." He sat back down and clicked on his headset. "Paul, call the police. They need to arrest the deputy mayor."

"They're on their way, Ethan," Paul said. "The police commissioner was watching and just called the control room. There's an army of cops about to take him into custody."

"How long before they get here? We're not gonna be able to detain him for very long. Hold on a second," Ethan said as the door swung open and the police stormed the room.

"What's happening?"

"The cops are cuffing Jameson. There's gotta be twenty of them. Now they're reading him his rights and escorting him out of the room," he said breathlessly, the last bit of energy draining from his body. "Look, Paul, Sandy Jameson is just sitting there all by herself, crying uncontrollably. She's a wreck. I gotta go see if I can find some way to comfort her."

"Go then. And Ethan?"

"Yes, Paul?"

"Damn nice job tonight."

"Thanks. That means a lot coming from you." He yanked off his headset and made his way over to Sandy. "Is there anything I can say or do to make this any easier for you, Mrs. Jameson?" Sandy looked up, inconsolable, her expression blank, tears cascading down her cheeks. He handed her a tissue and sat down beside her. She didn't say a word. And neither did he. Closing his eyes, he reached for a cigarette and thought about Sarah and Luke.

It was time to be with his wife and son.

Time to bring them home.

EPILOGUE

THE WEATHER HAD TURNED unseasonably cold, the temperature dropping into the lower forties, making it feel more like the beginning of winter than the end of the summer. Ethan shivered as he climbed off the elevator holding a dozen red roses, hoping the flowers with their dazzling color and scent of sunshine would make Sarah happy. He unlocked the front door and walked into his apartment, placing his briefcase on the floor and draping his trench coat over the back of a chair.

Then he began searching for his family.

He found Luke in his bedroom watching television, half asleep on the couch, Holly lying on the floor beside him, wagging her tail. Ethan smiled and quietly closed the door, tucking the roses under his arm as he headed off to look for Sarah. His family had returned the day after the broadcast, Ethan arguing with Paul, insisting it was safe for them to come home. There'd been no sign of a black Lincoln Navigator, no sign of the hit man, the Russians vanishing from his life almost as suddenly as they'd appeared.

He stopped at his study, flipped on the lights, and poured a tumbler of scotch.

Sitting in the middle of his desk was a front-page story in *The New York Times* lauding his special. He picked up the newspaper and began to read, marveling like a cub reporter at the power of the press. Nancy McGregor, Frankie O'Malley, and Edward Jenkins had all been suspended and indicted—accused of evidence tampering, conspiracy, and falsely convicting an innocent man. Alexey Kolkov, Anatoly Gennadi, and Nikolai Stanislov, long dead and buried, were the subject of a nationwide manhunt—charged with drug dealing, racketeering, and bribery. And political leaders across the country were clamoring for justice, demanding that Pavel Feodor be released and set free. The man once loathed as a vicious sociopath was now being hailed as an innocent victim—even with his long criminal past and his role in the gun battle the night of the murder.

Ethan lit a cigarette and inhaled the sweet smell of the scotch. Closing his eyes, he thought about the deputy mayor and wondered how a man with so much power and wealth could turn out so cruel and heartless. Bernard Jameson was locked away on H Block—just a few cells down from Pavel Feodor—awaiting trial for the sexual abuse and murder of his daughter. His family had been all but shattered—his wife hospitalized in a psych ward, his two children placed in the care of her family. Lost in the firestorm of public outrage was Cynthia herself, and the search for the pimp who had killed her. The tabloids had fixated on the details of her secret life—the sex and the prostitution—forgetting a fugitive was still out there, hiding in the belly of the beast, waiting to strike again.

Ethan put down the newspaper and stared at the scotch, wanting a drink in the worst way, then rummaged through a stack of papers on his desk until he found the business card Sarah had given him all those weeks before. Reaching for his iPhone, he punched in the number and waited until an answering machine picked up the call. Pausing briefly, he whispered, "Dr. Schwartz, my name is Ethan Benson. I've got a drinking problem I can't control. Can I come in and see you? I need help. Please call me back."

He sighed and hung up.

Then he peered at the scotch one last time.

And pushed it to the corner of his desk.

He'd taken the first step.

As he reached for another cigarette, Sarah walked into his study. She was barefoot and wearing a sheer satin nightgown, her long blonde hair flowing down her back, her face pure and angelic, her eyes sparkling in the fading sunlight streaming through the window. She made her way over to Ethan and kissed him on the top of his head. "Who were you talking to, Ethan?"

"I was leaving a message for Dr. Schwartz. I want to go see him."

"Are you serious?"

"Yeah. I want to stop drinking."

"I was wondering if you'd ever get around to making that call," she said, tenderly running her fingers down his back. "I'm proud of you, Ethan."

He smiled warmly and handed her the roses. "These are for you," he said, kissing her forehead.

She inhaled the bouquet, then looked into his eyes. "I just checked on Luke. He's down for the night. Shall we go climb into bed for a little mommy and daddy time?"

"I'd like that very much," he said softly. "And you know what, babe? You're about to cuddle up close to a new senior producer."

Sarah backed away and smiled. "What do you mean?"

"Paul was so happy with my special, he wants me to produce all of Peter's programming. So from now on, I'm management and forever attached to the hip to Mr. Anchorman himself."

"Well, that should make life interesting," she said, playfully kissing the tip of his nose.

Then he took her by the hand and led her down to the bedroom, slowly pulling off her nightgown and carrying her to bed. Soon they were lost in their lovemaking, the roses scattered on the sheets about them, a symbol of hope and happiness and their life together as a family.

AUTHOR Q & A

Q: When did you first know you wanted to write a novel?

A: I've been writing my entire life, hundreds of scripts for television newsmagazine and documentary productions. I've also been a voracious reader of all kinds of fiction. About ten years ago, I began wondering whether I could write a novel about my experiences as a producer and a reporter—which is very different from crafting a television script—and when I retired from ABC News a couple of years ago and had all this time to fill, I decided to give it a whirl. That's when the inspiration really hit, and I sat down and began to write *Live to Air*.

Q: Do you follow any particular practices when you're writing?

A: I definitely follow a very set routine. I'm an early riser and like to begin work first thing each day. I'm usually sitting at my desk by eight o'clock and spend four to five hours writing before my brain goes to mush, rarely getting out of my chair except to fetch a cup of coffee or to stretch my legs. My office looks out over a thick forest and majestic rolling hills, so it's the perfect place to dream up new storylines and plot twists. But, unlike Ethan, who, at times, is scattered and disorganized, I'm a neat freak. Everything in my office is ordered and has its place— except for my golden retriever, Bailey, who's incorrigible and makes herself comfortable wherever she wants.

Q: Did you have the plot developed to the end, or did the novel unfold in terms of plot as you wrote it?

A: This is a great question. I think all writers approach their stories in different ways. I thought about the plotline for *Live to Air* for quite some time before I sat down and started writing, but I never outlined the book and didn't have a game plan for the story. What I did have was a beginning and an ending. They were fixed in my mind right from the start, even though the last chapter where Peter Sampson interviews the deputy mayor changed several times before I got it just right. The rest of the book evolved as I was writing, flowing out of my head, changing over and over as I polished the prose and moved around clues to add drama and suspense to the narrative.

Q: Which scenes did you find the most difficult to write?

A: I found the Rikers Island prison scenes the most difficult to write, even though I spent a lot of time in and out of lockups during my career. I never visited Rikers Island for any of my stories, so it took a lot of reading and telephone work to come up with a mental picture of the location to use in my book. Most of what I wrote was based on this research, and when I couldn't answer a question about the physical layout of the prison, I borrowed from what I'd seen at other penal institutions and used my imagination for the rest. I think writers call this "creative license."

Q: From early on in the book, it seems that your knowledge of the TV production business is extensive. Is this a business you know well?

A: I spent almost forty years working for ABC News, NBC News, FOX News, and Martha Stewart Living Television. I was a writer and producer and experienced many of the big changes that revolutionized TV production during my long career. It's been my life's work, and I love every aspect of the business.

Q: Did you base any of the characters in Live to Air *on your real-life experiences?*

A: Everybody who's read *Live to Air* asks me this question, and let's just say that during my career, I produced dozens of high-profile crime stories, where I met gang members, rapists, killers, and serial murderers, and I worked with some of the most famous prosecutors, defense lawyers, detectives, and private investigators in law enforcement. I've also collaborated extensively with news correspondents and anchors, production teams, and TV news executives. Yes, all my characters are based on real-life experiences and are a product of the many people who helped me report and produce my stories.

Q: Can you tell us more about the character of Ethan and why he is so unhappy with the general state of journalism?

A: Ethan's unhappiness is something I certainly felt during the last few years of my career. As audiences grew smaller and ratings collapsed, television news began looking for ways to streamline production and save money. For Ethan, serious reporting was the bread and butter of his career, but in his new reality at *The Weekly Reporter*, with its shorter deadlines, fewer shooting days, and tighter budgets, there was no room for in-depth reporting. Now, don't get me wrong—I believe strongly that there's a place in television news for crime stories. I produced many and hope to build a new career based on my experiences, but for Ethan, who sees himself as a hard-nosed journalist, the transition from investigative reporting to crime reporting was difficult to swallow and is an underlying storyline throughout the book.

Q: Ethan does not want to do crime stories and makes it clear in the novel. Is there a particular reason for this aversion?

A: Ethan's sentiments mirror those of many producers who work in television today—especially those who remember an era when newsmagazines like *The Weekly Reporter* concentrated on hard news and investigative reporting. I found it quite difficult making this transition myself but gradually realized that crime stories serve a unique purpose in the programming of a news broadcast.

Q: Does GBS reflect any place you have previously worked?

A: GBS is definitely a synthesis of all the news divisions where I worked. There are scenes in the novel drawn from ABC News, NBC News, Fox News, and many television shows—such as *20/20, Dateline NBC, World News Tonight*, and even *Martha Stewart Living*. In writing *Live to Air*, I tried to craft the television scenes as authentically as possible—from the types of cameras used in the field to the staffing required to build a set for an interview—and in order to accomplish this and make it seem real, I needed to draw on a treasure trove of experiences from all the networks where I was lucky enough to hang my hat.

Q: When Ethan's people build the set for the deputy mayor's interview, they say they're doing in a couple of hours what usually takes a day. Can you explain what goes into building a set?

A: Building a set is a complex process, especially when an anchor is involved in the interview. It usually requires a huge production crew—cameramen, soundmen, lighting directors, electricians, and grips, to name just a few. For a live interview like the deputy mayor's, cables were run from the set in the deputy mayor's apartment down to a remote truck on the street, which Ethan used to feed the interview back to the GBS Broadcast Center, where it was switched live to the network. That too had to be built from scratch and staffed by a team of people. The scope of this kind of production is enormous and takes a high level of coordination from every member of the team. My personal experience in constructing a set like the one in *Live to Air* comes from producing dozens of interviews with Barbara Walters at *20/20*. Each and every one required a staff of at least fifteen people and a full production day before we were ready to roll cameras.

Q: Ethan's instinct seems to be a great and powerful driver in this story. Can you comment on this and how it relates to your own life or career?

A: Well, this is difficult to answer. As a producer, my stories were always grounded in the research and based on the sources who fed me information. And like Ethan's, my stories were built around the facts. But there were always moments during production when I knew I was missing something important and knew that if I just did a little more digging, I'd learn a critical piece of information that would affect my storyline. That's why I made instinct such a big part of what drives Ethan as a producer. It's what makes him special and gives him an edge.

Q: Do you identify with Ethan? Who was your favorite character to write?

A: This is another great question. Many fictional characters are based on an author's life experiences. How else can a novelist create a living, breathing hero like Ethan Benson? There are definitely elements of my personality in this character, but having said that, I'll leave it to the reader's imagination to figure out which ones they are.

Ms. Templeton has a special place in my heart. At the beginning of my career, I produced dozens of investigative stories on consumer products, military spending, and medical malpractice. And yes, on almost every one of these projects, I had a source like Ms. Templeton who slipped me information under the table. She represents the essence of journalism, the whistleblower who helps Ethan unlock the hidden secrets essential to unraveling his story.

Q: This book seems a bit like a love letter to New York City, and you seem to know the city well. Why did you pick NYC as the setting for your story?

A: I picked New York City for a plethora of reasons. I spent forty years living in Manhattan and know all the neighborhoods in *Live to Air* like the back of my hand. I also spent days on location visiting each community I wrote about, mastering the subtleties and nuances that make them unique. Of course, the television news business is based in the city, and that's probably the main reason I chose Manhattan as the center of Ethan Benson's universe.

Q: And why did you decide to set the key shoot-out scene in the Meatpacking District?

A: I struggled to find just the right spot to set the shoot-out scene for quite some time and surveyed numerous locations in Brooklyn and Queens. I finally picked the Meatpacking District, in Manhattan, because of its notorious nightlife.

When you stroll the neighborhood, there are dozens of expensive restaurants and ritzy nightclubs. It seemed like the kind of place where the wealthy daughter of the deputy mayor of New York might want to party with her friends. But there are also pockets in the community that depict the underbelly of New York. Little West 12th Street—which I chose for the location of the shootout—is a case in point. It's a throwback to fifty years ago, with boarded-up buildings, sleazy old-man bars, and the last remaining meatpacking distributors still located in the city. It felt perfect for the book from the moment I saw it.

Q: The scene with Nikolai Stanislov and his prostitute was particularly graphic. How did you come up with this scene?

A: Explosive violence is endemic in the world of organized crime. That's a given. All of us have read about it in newspapers and magazines and seen it on television in shows like *The Sopranos*. Nikolai Stanislov is an underboss in my fictional Russian crime family. He represents the essence of cruelty and ruthlessness. Short-tempered and explosive on the outside, he is also insecure and vulnerable on the inside. The scene with the prostitute was written to illustrate these personality traits so common in many real-life mobsters and to set up Stanislov's downfall at the end of the book.

Q: Will there be a sequel?

A: Yes. The second Ethan Benson thriller is already finished, and the third book is sitting in the back of my mind, ready to be written in the not-too-distant future.

READING GROUP GUIDE

1. What was your overall impression of the book? Did you find it exciting, disturbing, frightening, or informative?

2. Did you identify with any particular character or characters?

3. Do you feel as if you know Ethan and what motivates him? Which one of the characters do you feel you know best? Why? What did you think about Pavel Feodor's character? Was he someone you felt you understood?

4. How did it make you feel each time Ethan neglected his family or lied to his wife? Did you understand his motivation?

5. Was the setting of New York City interesting to you? Did you find it at all disturbing that in a city like New York that is known for Broadway plays and culture, there could be active networks of criminals operating on almost any street at any time of day?

6. What motivates Ethan? What do you think about his feeling that the networks only wanted to produce low-quality, sensational stories?

7. Is the story of police and justice system corruption shocking? Disappointing? Do you believe that the justice system is generally fair or not?

8. Are Ethan's difficulties with Paul Lang something you are familiar with? Have you ever been threatened with termination at your workplace like Ethan was?

9. Have you been in a work situation that caused you to miss out on being with your family? Can you identify with Ethan in that regard? Are you a family member who is not receiving the attention you need from an overworked spouse or parent?

10. Who makes you most uncomfortable? Will you think differently when you see a group of burly men on a random city street or at a beach? Will you think of Anatoly, Mischa, and Yuri?

11. Did you find it interesting that the television network was paying Lloyd Howard (the private investigator) for information? Did this give you an insight into television practices that you weren't familiar with?

12. When the criminals talk of bodies being dumped, was that surprising? Do you think this type of activity is happening in New York City today?

13. Does *Live to Air* have the feel of a film noir in the sense that the main characters are male and that the female characters play supporting roles?

14. Was it shocking to hear Alexey Kolkov refer to the police detectives and cops being on the syndicate's payroll?

15. When at the end of the book, Ethan marvels at the power of the press, how does it make you feel about him? About the press in general?

16. Do you think that now that he has recovered his standing at work, Ethan will be a different person in terms of drinking and attending to his family?

17. How do you feel about Ethan risking his life in the pursuit of the truth?

18. Can you imagine this novel as a film? Who would play Ethan?

ABOUT THE AUTHOR

Jeffrey L. Diamond is an award-winning journalist with forty years of experience in television news who has produced stories for ABC News's weekly newsmagazine *20/20* and ran *Dateline NBC, Martha Stewart Living* Television, and Judith Regan Television.

At *20/20*, his responsibilities spanned every aspect of storytelling—research, budgeting, interviewing, directing, writing, editing, and postproduction. He's been nominated for dozens of awards and has won six national Emmy Awards, two duPont-Columbia Awards, one Peabody Award, one National Press Club Consumer Journalism Award, two CINE Golden Eagle Awards, and countless others.

Mr. Diamond lives in the Berkshire Mountains of Massachusetts, where he is now embarking on a new career as a mystery writer. He's an active member of the Board of Trustees at the Austen Riggs Center and at the Berkshire Film and Media Collaborative. A graduate of Lehigh University, he's married, has two sons, a daughter-in-law, two grandchildren, and a golden retriever named Bailey.

CPSIA information can be obtained
at www.ICGtesting.com
Printed in the USA
FSOW01n0144150715
8776FS